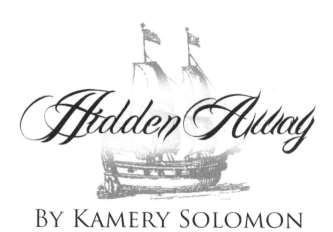

Hidden Away

By Kamery Solomon

Praise for *The Swept Away Saga*

"Amazing! The best way I can think to describe it is **Pirates of the Caribbean meets Outlander!** There is action, adventure, romance and so much more! You will not be disappointed!"
~Heather Garrison, *Amazon Customer*

"Kamery Solomon never disappoints a reader in her ability to tell a great story. She has proven she's not a one trick pony and capable of writing across genres. **Highly recommend reading** any and all of her books."
~Lisa Markson, *The Paranormal Bookworm*

"This book has so many twists and turns that **will keep you reading all night long**. I love the characters and the mystery. The author does a fantastic job weaving every part in this story that will leave you wanting more. I highly recommend!"
~Laura Collins, *Amazon Customer*

"I was pulled in right away and **I did not want to put the book down**, nor did I want the story to end . . . a must read!"
~Holly Copper, *Amazon Customer*

"This is the book you **MUST** be reading **NOW!**"
~Julie Engle, *Amazon Customer*

"This is a story I will read time and time again."
~Angie Angelich, *Book Banshee*

"What else could you want?!"
~Vonnie Hudson, *Amazon Customer*

Other Books by Kamery Solomon

Forever
Hell Hall (A Halloween Novella)

The God Chronicles
Zeus
Poseidon
Hades
Adrastia
Exoria

Dreams Novels
Taking Chances
Watching Over Me

The Swept Away Saga
Swept Away
Carried Away
Hidden Away
Taken Away (A Swept Away Saga Origins Story)

By Kamery Solomon

For my fellow privateers and our mermaids

Scott Williams
2016

The aching feeling in my knees was always worse when it rained. It wasn't all that bothersome, to be honest, but with each little water drop that fell from above, it felt as if the muscles and ligaments tightened the tiniest bit, until I would consider maybe taking some pain medicine for it. In the past year or so, my elbows had joined in the fun, giving me a pinching, tingling feeling as the humidity wrapped around my body. My mind would wander at points, wondering what would be next. My feet? Hands? Perhaps my back would hurt and I would stoop over like the old man I was. Whatever was going to happen, one thing was very clear to me.

I was too old for this.

Rain pounded against the tin roof, practically screaming all around me, the lightning flashing brightly through the large sliding glass doors that led out to the deck attached to my tiny home. Watching the storm from my queen-sized bed, I sucked in a deep breath, feeling my eyes widen at the monstrous display of elemental power outside. It was hard not to feel insignificant under the scrutiny of the skies, or to wonder what my part was in this blip of life I had to make my own. At the same time, it was almost impossible to ignore the electricity in the air and the driving force it filled me with.

Suddenly, the magic of the squall was broken by a loud pounding at the door. Jumping slightly, I turned toward the sound in the dark, reaching to pull back my covers. With the power out, I couldn't see what time it was on my digital clock, but I knew it was at least past ten. Who would be coming over so late?

The hammering increased as the icy touch of the ground seeped into my bare feet, my form flitting down the hall to the living room, the lightning and my memory the only guides I had through the space. Cool, hardwood floors sent a chill through me, my fingers lightly dragging down the cream-colored walls. If there'd been enough light, perhaps I would have stopped to look at the pictures hanging up, to appreciate the things I'd gathered around myself. Now wasn't the time, though, even if there had been power, and I hurried into the large living room, frowning at my uninvited company. Narrowly avoiding the couch on the right hand side of the room, I grabbed the handle and wrenched the door open, shivering slightly as the cold air rushed through the thin layer of my striped, button up pajamas.

"Yes?" I asked the burly man on the other side. He was hunched down in his black rain jacket, looking thoroughly soaked through and somewhat annoyed, though apologetic. A cap covered most of his head and face, but I wouldn't have recognized him without it; I had no idea who he was.

"Are you Scott Williams?" He shook his shoulders slightly, water droplets cascading off him as he waited in what appeared to be anxiousness.

Compassion shot through me and I nodded, instantly wanting to help this poor, wet stranger. "I am. Here, come in out of the storm." Moving to the side, I watched him pass, curious as to who he was and what he wanted.

"Thanks. That's some rain, eh? I was hoping I'd make it here before it hit, but no such luck. Of course, all the power is out, so I couldn't just call around." His voice was low, warm, and friendly enough. However, there was the slightest distinction to it that made me feel like he was worried about something. The small talk also suggested he didn't know how to say whatever it was he needed to share with me.

Realizing he might need a little prompting, I decided to be blunt. "I'm sorry. Who did you say you were?" Smiling tightly in the darkness, I kept my hand on the door knob, ready to show him out if need be.

"Oh, right! Joe—Mark's friend." He straightened some, extending a hand toward me.

Relief flooded through me at that and I sighed, releasing the handle to shake. "Of course. It's your dive and salvage company he's working for. You must be keeping him pretty busy. I haven't heard from him in over a month."

Even in the shadows, I saw Joe's face fall, his bushy moustache seeming to droop even more after its rain bath. "You haven't?"

"No?"

Nodding, he pulled the cap off, revealing his bald head. A great sigh slid from him as he fiddled with the

13

sopping hat, his eyes focused on my face. "I haven't either. He left to do some research for our project and basically disappeared. The last I knew, he was in New York City."

Eyes widening some, I felt my own peaceful mood dip. The last time I'd seen Mark he'd been in New York. I knew all too well how easy it was to fall into isolation while doing research, but a month was a long time for him to have not contacted anyone. The fact that his employer was here suggested that Mark had been unreachable through all his normal routes of communication, as well. Clearing my throat, I nodded, adding what little I knew to Joe's narrative. "I met up with him in the city and asked him a favor. Well, it was more like I convinced him to run an errand for me." Seeing that the information I'd offered didn't really help, I bit back the story of what I'd needed assistance with and continued. "He told me he was leaving to Arizona and then returning to Texas to work. He never came back?"

"Nope. Didn't even leave a message for where he was going and why. I didn't even know he was heading out west."

An uneasiness spread between us, silence blanketing the room as my mind searched over the last time I'd seen Mark Bell, looking for any clues as to what could have happened.

He was in New York City, doing research for a work project, just as Joe had said. There had been something about the way he was acting that worried me, though. It was as if he were constantly looking over his shoulder for something, a nervous motion always present in his eyes. He'd never been like that before. The ambitious, self-sufficient, and determined young man had seemed a shell of his former self, his smile rarely appearing as we spoke together.

Thinking back even further, I thought of the Mark I knew when he lived here, in Maine. He'd been a history professor at the university and a part of the team working on Oak Isle. I could easily recall his laughter as he worked on the island, continually slaving away to find what he was sure was pirate treasure. The sound of his voice, as he suggested new paths and ideas for getting to the bottom of the mysterious Treasure Pit, was instantly played over in my mind.

At the same time, I could recall exactly how his face had looked when the Treasure Pit collapsed and killed Michael, our leader and friend. The sound of his ragged, disbelieving breath filled my mind as I remembered a moment only a few weeks later, when our group was told that Samantha, Michael's daughter, had drown in the Pit and the efforts to recover her body had failed. I could feel the tension in the air as he announced to me some time later that he was leaving. The image of him as he walked away would forever be burned in my mind's eye.

We had each handled the deaths in our own way. Mark's was to leave, mine was to keep working toward an answer from Oak Isle. After more than two hundred years of people trying to get to the bottom of the mysterious, booby trapped pit, I wasn't having much luck finding my resolution. That was why I'd met up with Mark in New York City; I wanted him to help me get more information about a vase that had been found in Samantha's bag. It was the only thing they were ever able to find when she was claimed by the Pit.

He'd seemed unwilling at first, but Mark had agreed to take the vase to his professor friend in Arizona for me, to have tests run. The container was very old and I believed it came from the treasure vault in the bottom of the Pit. If I could prove that, the state would have to lift the ban they'd put on the island after Sam and Michael were killed and let me excavate the other artifacts down there. To some, it appeared that I was hungry for riches, but all I really wanted was to discover the answers my dearly departed friends had sought. Maybe, once the Treasure Pit was solved, their souls would rest, their business finished.

Thinking of spirits brought another recollection of my time with Mark to the surface. It had taken him a while to admit, but he believed Samantha had been haunting him. It was part of the reason he'd been so nervous and unhinged, I realized now. At the time, I'd dismissed the notion as the troubled dreams of a mourning friend. Now that he was missing, though, I suddenly found myself wondering if his specter had anything to do with his sudden and extended departure.

What if he'd done something to himself in his grief? Why hadn't I realized how badly he needed help at the time?

Frustrated with myself, I tried to think of anything else he'd said to me that would lend any clues to where he'd gone after we'd met. If it wasn't Arizona, I didn't have any idea where to even start looking.

The storm outside seemed to be slowing down some, and there was a surge to the air, suddenly. Lights flickered on around us, the power finally coming back on and throwing Joe into full focus. He appeared upset, his brow furrowed and lips pursed tightly as he clasped his hands around his hat, water dripping off his jacket and splattering lightly against the floor. It was clear that he didn't know who else to turn to in his search.

Thinking quickly, I raised a finger, nodding once more. "Let me get you the name of the professor in Arizona," I said, moving away from the door and toward the end table on the other side of the couch. "It's not much, but it's another avenue you can follow to try and find some answers. He might have an email or office phone you can try. I'll call the university office and see if Mark ever made it there in the morning."

"Thank you." The relief was palpable in his tone. "I don't know where he could have gone. It's not just that we miss him at work. He's my friend, you know? I'm worried that something's happened to him."

More alarm bells rang in my head. What cause did Joe have to worry about Mark's safety? Did he know about the supposed ghost, too? "I agree," I responded tightly. "He is my friend, as well, after all." Smiling slightly, I sat and opened the drawer on the small stand, pulling out a pen and paper. Scribbling down the information, I tore the parchment from its pad and handed it over, trying to ignore the mounting worry that was growing within me.

Taking the note, Joe stared at it, pursing his lips once more. It was clear that he'd hoped I would be able to give him more information, but he would have to settle for what I'd offered. Breathing deeply, his expression changed from that of worry to curiosity as he looked up, glancing around the living room, his eyes lingering on the antique coins, salvaged anchor, and other artifacts I'd gathered over the years. "That's some collection." Motioning to the coins, he stepped forward as he tucked the paper into his pocket, as if asking permission to study at the bookcase housing them.

Caught off guard by the change in conversation, I nodded for him to have a closer look. "I'm somewhat of a coin aficionado." Watching as he went to the shelves and stared at the beaten pieces of metal, I imagined that he was ready for some type of break from his search. It was too late to call the professor now, so there was no sense in hurrying him out. He seemed more than willing to gawk at my findings, his face as close to the glass barrier as it could be without smudging it up.

"You ever work for a dive company before?" His voice had a calculating tone to it now, like he was trying to think of where and when each of the coins came from.

"When I was younger," I offered. "Before I really knew anything about Oak Isle."

Regarding me over his shoulder, Joe grinned. "I hear it's easy to get sucked into it here. What's that all about?"

Laughing, I shook my head, slowly walking over to join him, my worries about Mark slightly capsized by the conversation in front of me. "If I told you, you would only want to know more. That's how it starts, believe it or not. You're curious about what's going on, so you ask someone, but the information is never enough. You find yourself reading about it at the library, researching online, asking those who've been working there what they think. Your own opinions start to form and you suddenly realize that you want to get out there and try your own hand at it. And who knows? Maybe you'll be the one who solves the Treasure Pit. There's no way to ever know. You could be out there for a week or a decade. The island is like a capsule; she holds everyone who comes ashore suspended in time for as long as they'll allow her."

Turning from the cabinet, Joe watched me with curious and cautious eyes, seeming to think over what I'd said. "How long have you been in the time capsule?" The question hung in the air, not insulting but directly to the point he wanted answered.

"Several decades." Smiling tightly, I stared hard at the coins, one of which was the very piece Mark had found in the swamp. It was the first real proof we had that something of value was waiting to be discovered on the island.

"You're still out there, aren't you? Even though the state won't let you set foot on Oak Isle, that's where you are, mentally."

Realizing that Joe had been examining me for the length of our meeting, as I had him, I felt a tiny prick of amusement at his assessment of me. The probing felt a little odd, coming from a stranger, but I agreed all the same. "I see it every time I close my eyes."

Blowing air out, he half laughed, shaking his head. "I would have given up a long time ago, especially with everything that happened." The tone of his voice brought Mark back into clear focus in my mind, and I was certain that he was thinking of our mutual friend in worry again. Mark had given up on Oak Isle, after all, but her mysteries continued to follow him.

Pursing my lips, a non-committed noise gurgling

in the back of my throat, I stared hard at the coin once more. Mark had run, yes, but that didn't mean he'd escaped the repercussions of what happened on the island. "That's the problem with being stuck in a time capsule," I replied, suddenly wishing I could understand the ghosts that plagued our friend. "It doesn't want to give you up."

"Hand me that notebook, would you, Eric?" Motioning to the table behind me, I continued to study the photocopy of the old letter in my hands. It had been written sometime in the seventeen hundreds, just after the Treasure Pit was first discovered. So much had changed in the centuries since people had been searching on the island, I felt it was important to glean as much information from the original find as possible. God only knew what had accidentally—or purposefully—been destroyed in the hunt.

"Here you are, Scott." Giving me the book I'd asked for, Eric smiled tightly, glancing through the door, toward the sound of his twin brother's voice.

"The restaurant is busy today," I noted, returning his uncomfortable grin. "That's good."

"It's picking up with all the summer tourists coming through, yeah."

Inhaling, I savored the smell of baking pepperoni and crust, catching a hint of the hot, yellow peppers in the air as well. It always smelled delicious to me in here, like the parlor my own father had taken me to when I was a boy. It was familiar—safe, even. Just like that tiny shop in my childhood, things got a little more crowded when summer rolled around here, what with people wanting to come relax, spend time at the beach, and maybe ask some questions about the mysterious Oak Isle. Something felt different this year, though, and I had a sinking feeling that I knew just what it was.

Eric Ray, and his brother Kevin, had been part of The Oak Isle Treasure Trove Company for a few years, taking a direct part in the efforts out on the island eagerly. Their parents even bought stock in the company. When Samantha came to stay with Michael, we'd moved our weekly meetings to the back room of the Ray's restaurant, where they continued to occur to this day. However, change had been in the air since the day Michael died, and it seemed that everything was about to come crashing down around my head.

"Sorry that took so long," Kevin said as he appeared in the doorway, flour in his short, brown hair. "There's a huge family here for a reunion or something and they've ordered ten pizzas! Could you come help me get them put together really quick, Er?"

"No problem." Pushing away from the table, Eric grabbed a white apron off the hook by the door and pulled it over his green shirt, hiding the eatery's logo on his chest.

"I apologize for coming during business hours today, boys. I have the closing shift at the bank today."

"It's no prob, Scott!" Kevin replied as they both disappeared in the direction of the kitchen. "We're happy to help. The team is family, too."

Guilt pricked at me as I sat down, Kevin's words ringing in my head. I'd decided once more to keep the news of Mark's disappearance from them, even if it was just for one more night. I *would* be working the closing shift, but the reason I couldn't spend time with them later was because I had scheduled a phone call with the professor in Arizona. The university secretary had given me his office number and hours, stating that video calls were his normal route of communication over long distances. It was my hope that our "face to face" conversation would bring to light Mark's whereabouts, as well as news about the vase I'd sent, and I wouldn't have to tell the twins another member of their family had disappeared without a trace.

Sighing, I put all the issues I needed answers for out of my mind and returned to the letter, opening the notebook I'd asked for and picking up a pen. I didn't know how many times I'd read this particular clue, but it still felt like I was missing something, as if there were a hidden message somewhere in the letters that would instantly lead me to where I needed to be.

The clock on the wall seemed to tick loudly as I perused my notes, sounds of laughter reaching my ears from the kitchen and dining room. The air felt hot from the heat of the ovens, the smell of mushrooms now joining the pepperoni. As I stared at the words on the page before me, I felt everything around me slip away, though, my mind taking the place of the young man whose words I now studied:

An impression in the ground first alerted us to the Pit's existence, the letter read. *Beside it was a tree, with a long branch hanging over the indentation. Some old rope had remained in the canopy—it appeared whoever had dug here had used the oak to help hoist earth away. Naturally, we returned home to retrieve shovels and pails of our own, but it quickly became clear that we had stumbled onto something much more complex than a regular hole in the ground. Whatever was hidden here—they didn't want anyone to get to it.*

The young man continued, explaining the first effort to get to the bottom of the Treasure Pit. I already knew that they would give up after a year and digging to fifty feet. The group that came after them would only make it to ninety, where they would trigger the flood trap that would keep every company until ours from getting to the bottom of the mystery. Two hundred plus years of searching and this boy with a shovel had been the start of it all.

Well, he had been the start of the search part, anyway. It was anyone's guess what was at the bottom of the Pit and who had put it there. Personally, I had spent many years believing that it had to be riches from South America, hidden by Spanish conquistadors who were worried about pirates overcoming them on their journey home. It seemed the most logical to me; who else would be so concerned about their resources that they would hide them away with such care and secrecy? Buccaneers wouldn't have put in so much effort, and Michael's idea that it was the lost haul of the Knights Templar felt downright laughable.

However, the vase that was found in Samantha's bag had looked distinctly Greek to me, which didn't fit in with my concept at all. In fact, it didn't really seem to measure up with any of the theories—except for Michael's, by a long stretch. The Knights Templar could have had Greek objects in their vaults, but their treasure was a myth itself. No, it was best to stick to things that could be surely laced together, not just a bunch of guesses tied into one scheme that sort of panned out. Michael had done loads of research and made a convincing argument, but I had never been sold on the knights of old.

"Any luck with the letter, Scott?"

Turning, I saw Kevin leaning against the doorframe, wiping his hands off with a clean, wet rag. He was smiling, but I could still see the hint of his underlying emotions on his face. It was a gift I'd always had; reading people was easy once you discovered what it was that basically kept them going. The twins were driven forward by a desire for growth and adventure, as most young people were. Unfortunately, the Treasure Pit was no longer fulfilling either need in them now.

"It says the same things it always has, if that's what you mean." Laughing slightly, I put the correspondence away and leaned back in the metal, folding chair, readying myself for what was about to come.

"I hear you on that," Kevin replied, chuckling as well. "Everything has to be difficult on the island, doesn't it?"

He was trying to lead up to it, maybe even waiting for Eric to come and help him some. They weren't afraid of me, or what my reaction would be to their news, but I could clearly see that they both felt bad. It was no matter to me, though. At this point, all I wanted to do was reassure them in their choices.

"So." Sighing, I regarded him, smiling tightly. "When will you boys be bowing out, fully? Is today the day?"

Surprised, he opened his mouth to reply, then shut it, shaking his head as he laughed again. "How do you do that? How do you always know what someone is going to say?"

"I don't," I replied easily. "But I've spent enough time on Oak Isle to recognize the look of someone who's ready to throw in the towel."

"I'm sorry, Scott." His voice was true and sincere, his eyes almost pleading as he pushed away from the doorway and joined me at the table. Sitting in the chair across from me, he sighed, a defeated sound, and stared down at the notes spread in front of him.

"We've worked so hard," he started, his tone broken up. "I thought for sure that we would figure it all out. When we lost Michael, Er and I both knew that Sam needed us to stay on and help. It wasn't even a question of if we would do it or not. When she . . . died . . . it felt like everything we had done was coming full circle, you know? Like all the good stuff we'd accomplished was being balanced out with horrible things. Then Mark left, and we felt like you needed us to stick around, but—"

"It's time for you to step away, now." Nodding, I grinned reassuringly. I'd been expecting this for some weeks, whether the boys realized it or not. "I understand, Kevin. You're young, with a whole life ahead of you. No one expects you to stay here and search for a prize that might not even exist."

"We were so close, though!" Frustration shot through him and he tapped his fingers on the table quickly, frowning. "It feels like everything is just one more step away. If we kept going, if we did one more thing, it would all open up and make sense at last."

"But now it feels like we'll always be one more step away, no matter how many things we do." Eric's soft voice drew our attention to the doorway, his form

26

standing in the space with folded arms and an apologetic expression.

"You two have done so much for the company and myself," I offered, feeling a little weight lift off my chest as I did my best to show them I accepted their resignations. "But there is a time and place for everything. You still have so much to experience and learn. Life has great things in store for the both of you. What are your plans now, if you don't mind my asking?"

The direction of the conversation seemed to help ease their feelings and I saw them physically relax at my words. Relief was present in both of their expressions, too, and I felt my own sense of acceptance set in fully.

"I applied at New York University," Kevin stated, smiling again. "I start in the fall."

"That's wonderful!" Pride burned in my chest, happiness at his success filling any space I had for disappointment at his departure. "Are you going as well, Eric?"

"Actually, no." He laughed, his face flushing some as he rubbed the back of his neck. "I'm going to stay here and, uh, inherit the restaurant."

"Mom and Dad announced it at dinner last night," Kevin butted in, grinning like a fool.

"I figure, I could do worse. What man doesn't want his very own business to run? Maybe I'll find a wife to go with it in the future, too." Eric shrugged, chuckling once, his face still bright red.

"Congratulations! Really, that's wonderful news, for the both of you!" Rising from my seat, I crossed the space and gave him a hug, feeling elated for both.

Breaking away, I moved so I could see them, grinning like a fool. "Look at you two . . . all grown up and leaving the nest. I couldn't be happier for either of you."

"You're not upset then?" Kevin asked, unsure.

"Why would I be upset? You're both young and ready to get on with your lives. I say that's exactly what you should be doing now."

"But what about you?" Eric frowned as he watched me, concern washing over his features. "Will you keep trying to get out on the island?"

"Yes." There was no mistaking the surety in my voice. "But I'll be just fine on my own. You forget, I've been doing this much longer than anyone else on the team."

At the mention of our friends, the mood in the room deflated some, the memory of the departed hanging over us like a cloud.

"I hope Mark is doing good," Eric suddenly said, turning away as his feelings got the better of him. "We haven't heard anything about him since he left."

Guilt shot through me again, but I held firm to my earlier decision to not say anything. They didn't need to hear that another one of our group might have been taken from us. We all knew it wasn't like Mark to disappear without saying anything. The news would only bring them down further, when they should be celebrating their recent successes.

"I'm sure he's fine." The statement felt more like a reassurance to myself than to them. Anxious, I looked at my wristwatch, wishing it was already time for my meeting. If the professor could tell me anything about Mark's whereabouts, I would let the twins know how he was doing tomorrow.

Our combined grief at the loss of our departed friends hung in the air for a moment, before I finally sighed and turned to the table. "Would you mind helping me pack up all these notes, then? I have space at my house to keep them. You don't need to have all this stuff here, anyway."

"Are you sure? It feels like we're kicking you out, Scott." Eric frowned as he stared back at the space that had been our center of command for the past while. His gaze traveled over the stacks of papers, memories that I could easily recall myself traveling across his face. This was the space our little treasure family had met. This was where we found out the coin from the swamp was genuine. This was where Michael had told our rival, Duke McCreary, exactly where he stood in the scheme of things on the island. Sam had helped make pizzas here. Mark had sat in the corner chair, snacking on things, more times than I could count. There were many late nights, several good conversations, and the feeling of friendships that stood the test of time residing in this room.

"I'm sure," I stated softly. "It's time."

There was a pause as we all absorbed that, a collective sigh seeming to hang in the air, and then the moment broke.

"Of course." Kevin reached out and pulled a pile toward himself, organizing it into a nice stack and looking around for an empty box to put them in.

"Thank you." Joining him at the table, I began going through the items and sorting them a little better.

I'm truly all alone now, I thought, surprised that I could be so happy for my friends and still so sad to see them all go.

"You're the second person to have called me about Mark Bell today," Professor Stevens stated, his nose twitching as he stared at me through his computer screen. "The first video call, but still. I told your friend, Joe, that I haven't heard from him in about a month or so."

He looked like an overstuffed teddy bear, with reading glasses perched on top of his nose like an old spinster, though he couldn't have been more than thirty-five. The camera angle made him look like he had ten chins and shot straight up his nostrils, his hairline practically vanishing at the top of his head, but he didn't seem to care. All around Stevens, papers and photographs crowded the shot, marking his as the type of person who can exist in chaotic control. Under different circumstances, I would have loved to examine the photos of what appeared to be Egyptian archeological sites and pick his brain about his work, but there was something about him that made me feel like my call wasn't a welcome one.

"I apologize. I didn't realize Joe was calling today, as well. We are more plain acquaintances than friends, and I haven't spoken with him in a few days. However, once he alerted me to Mark's disappearance, I felt I should look around for him myself. Naturally, I called you."

Smiling in the friendliest manner I could muster, I folded my hands together, watching the screen with interest. Stevens face seemed to darken and then lighten all at once, as if he had been getting angry and then decided to be happy instead.

"Ah. Scott Williams, you said? That would make you Mark's friend with the vase. From the supposed Treasure Pit, yes?" There was a flicker of something across his face that was off putting, but I agreed all the same.

"It was my understanding that you were going to meet with him to examine the piece? Did that ever occur, or did he simply not show up?"

"We had dinner at the Compass Arizona Grill in Phoenix. I'd just finished a convention and he caught me before I headed home to Tucson." He paused, clearing his throat, and pushed his glasses up the bridge of his nose again. "He had the vase with him. It's quite the remarkable specimen. A beauty to behold, actually."

"So, you have it, then?" I pressed, anxious for the answer. At least that would be one part of the mystery solved.

"No."

The answer was sharp and short, almost a scolding, surprising me into silence. Stevens's tone was somewhat defensive as he shook his head, leaning back in his chair and folding his arms over his gray sweater vest.

"Mark was staying at a hotel down the street and

was going to drop it off with me the next morning, so I could study it some more here, at the University. He was a no show, though. I thought he'd decided to take it somewhere else."

"You didn't get to look at it at all?" I asked, baffled. Why would Mark go all the way to Arizona, just to stand up his friend and run off with the vase?

"Only at the restaurant. It's a shame, really. I think he could have had something."

Thinking quickly, I tried to come up with some reason for Mark to disappear with the vase and not contact anyone for over a month. Nothing came up.

"That was the last time I saw Mark," Stevens continued, fiddling with the ring on his finger. "Haven't spoken with him since, either."

Staring blankly into the camera, I continued to rack my brain for whatever reasons Mark would have had for running off. Soon, I found myself staring at the gold band Stevens continued to spin around, a cross etched into the metal with a black dot at its center. Shaking my head, I refocused, deciding on my next steps.

"What hotel was he staying at?" I finally asked. "Do you know? Perhaps someone there can tell me when he left and if he said where he was going."

"You a part time detective now? What about your Treasure Pit?" Stevens raised an eyebrow, giving off the impression that he didn't think an old man such as myself should be going around, asking questions and sticking my nose in other people's business.

It was a strange vibe to get from him. He had attended school with Mark, after all. Shouldn't he be worried about what happened to his academic friend, even if they were only casual in their relationship? I knew it would worry me if someone I knew was missing—I *was* worried. This was Mark we were talking about, our mutual friend, and, as far as I was concerned, part of my family. Stevens, on the other hand, only seemed to be upset that he hadn't gotten the chance to examine the vase, though, not alarmed that a man he knew was missing, possibly hurt and in need of assistance.

"I am capable of thinking about things other than treasure," I replied rather sharply, frowning. "One of my closest friends is missing, and not long after the death of another close friend and his daughter. I am sorry that you didn't get to look at the vase in depth, but I think we can both agree that a missing man is more important than a missing jar."

This seemed to shake him a little and he sighed, nodding. "Yes, I agree. I apologize. It's been somewhat of a strenuous day." He paused, as if considering his next words, biting his lower lip in thought. "No, I don't know what hotel he was staying at exactly. I wish I could be a better help to you, but I'm afraid I simply haven't heard from or seen a single thing involving Mark Bell since he left our dinner appointment."

Deflated, I felt another of the threads I'd been desperately trying to hold on to unravel and fall away. Mark was gone and every lead I'd pursued had led to a dead end. My only options left now were shots in the dark, half-hearted attempts to locate a man who had vanished from a place where virtually no one would remember who he was or where he'd gone.

"Well, thank you anyway," I finally said, grinning

tightly as I studied the professor's eyes once more. "If anything, you've at least given me some more clues as to where I might look for him again."

"Sorry I wasn't able to help more." He shook his head once, leaning forward in his chair, reaching for what I assumed was the touch screen computer.

"Have a nice day."

"You too."

The call cut off abruptly, the screen on my own computer filling with my own image as the connection was severed. Disappointment, worry, and exhaustion washed over my face as I leaned back, slouching in my wooden chair, a hand on my balding head. The discussion had left me with more questions than answers and the uneasy feeling that I'd been lied to. What would Professor Stevens gain from lying to me, though?

Then, of course, there was Mark. Why would he go all the way to Arizona, meet up with his friend, and then run? Why would he take the vase with him? Had he discovered something about it that he thought no one else should know? Had he decided to keep it for himself after the Professor told him it was genuine, or perhaps even sold it to someone on the black market?

No, Mark wouldn't do something like that, not to me. The man studied pirates, but he wasn't a villain himself. Something was very, very wrong. Every single nerve in my gut was screaming that he had been compromised somehow, that I needed to find him, to help him. The vase was important, yes, but Mark was more so. Any leads I had, however small, would have to be followed until I'd found him and made sure he was safe.

I'd lost enough family members because of the Treasure Pit. There was no way in hell I was about to let it claim another.

Rubbing a hand over my face roughly, I took a deep breath and closed the video chat app I'd been using. Opening a plain Internet search, I typed in the name of the restaurant Mark and Professor Stevens had eaten at. It was inside a hotel, on a street near the airport. There were several other places to stay around that area, as was to be expected with an international travel hub nearby.

"Time to work," I mumbled quietly, pulling my cell phone out of my pocket. Picking a phone number at random, I jotted down the name of the hotel on my computer notepad as the phone rang.

"Hotel San Carlos, this is Kim speaking. How can I help you today?"

The cheery, female voice was rushed, but polite, her tone that of a low soprano.

"Yes, my name is Scott. I was wondering if you had any record of a Mark Bell staying at your establishment about a month ago."

"Oh." The question had caught her off guard and she fumbled, whatever stock answers she'd prepared in advance clearly not any help now. "Uh, I don't think I'm allowed to release that kind of information, Mister . . . ?"

"Williams," I offered, having assumed as much before I called. "I didn't know if you would be. He's gone missing, though—my friend, Mark. All I know is that he was last staying in a hotel somewhere around you." Keeping my own voice as even and professional as possible, I tried to be assertive but kind at the same

36

time. "I'm trying to find someone who might know where he went next."

"Have you filed a missing person report with the police?"

"I haven't. I've only just realized that he might be truly missing, not off on some adventure of his own creation." That much was true. It hadn't even occurred to me that I should call the police. Mark was a grown man, more than capable of taking care of himself. Calling the police seemed like a last ditch effort, once I'd decided that he really was truly, missing and unable to be found.

"Well, if you file a report with them, we should be able to help answer any questions in their investigation. I'm sorry, I can't do more to help."

"It's fine," I assured her. "Thank you for your time. Have a wonderful day."

"You as well."

Hanging up, I typed a large "X" next to the name of the establishment and moved on to the next place on the list.

Ringing, ringing, ringing. It seemed like that was all I heard lately. Sighing, I looked at the list of places I'd called over the past three days. Some of them had told me the same thing as the first, that they weren't allowed to share information about guests staying in their rooms. Others, upon hearing that I was merely trying to find a missing person, obliged easily enough. Some of them connected me with managers, or put me on hold while they asked for permission to fulfill my request. Then, surprisingly, a few places told me right away, without any convincing at all, that Mark had never been there. The last hotel had been one such place and I marked a big "NO" next to it on the list, to remind myself never to book a room there.

Finally, the automated phone system of the hotel I was now calling picked up, directing me to either enter a room number or request a different service. Pressing the option for the front desk, I waited a moment more before a low, male voice came over the line.

"Wyndham Garden, how may I help you?" There were keys clicking in the background, like the man was typing away at something, and I stifled my reaction at having to deal with someone who was already preoccupied. In my experience, they always managed to be the rudest, even if they didn't mean to.

"Yes, I'm looking for a missing person who may have stayed at your hotel about a month ago. Are you able to help me with that at all?"

"Unfortunately, sir, we are unable to share personal information, such as the names and room numbers of our guests, how long they stayed, and so on. If you're part of an ongoing police investigation, I can connect you to our corporate legal office and see if they can help you at all."

"No, that won't be necessary." Shaking my head, I laughed despondently, feeling like I was running in circles. "You'd think it would be easy to find your friend if they went missing. I mean, I know where and when he went, where he had dinner, who he saw, and where he was supposed to be going after. But I don't know any of the important stuff, like where he stayed, or why he didn't go where he was supposed to. For all I know, Mark was abducted by aliens and all of his things, including the vase he was supposed to have checked out, are floating somewhere between here and Mars."

"Hang on, did you say vase?" The man's tone had changed entirely, the clicking of keys halting in an instant. "Like, an old vase with Greek stuff on it?"

"Yes!" Excitedly, I jumped from my chair, my heart practically stopping at his words.

"I don't know anything about a man named Mark," he continued. "But I was just promoted from housekeeping about a month ago. We had someone leave all their stuff in the room, including an old vase. The room keys were there, too, so we just assumed whoever it was had checked out. That happens now and then. I mean, people forget stuff more often than not, but everything? I've only seen that once or twice. It all goes in the lost and found. After a month, the employees are allowed to buy it, if no one else has claimed it."

"Do you still have the vase?" I pressed, suddenly imagining some random individual taking the priceless piece of history and accidentally destroying it.

"No," he said, surprised. "We were robbed not long after that. Everything in the lost and found was taken."

"What did you say your name was?" Instantly feeling that whoever had broken in had done so to steal the vase specifically, I started forming a plan in my mind.

"Marcus."

"Can I book a room through you, Marcus? I think

I need to come see all of this for myself."

The dry heat of the Arizona desert washed over me in a wave of perspiration, the clear blue sky doing nothing to shield the people below from the merciless rays of an unforgiving sun. Wyndham Garden had a free airport shuttle that came through every thirty minutes and I found myself waiting for it in a group of shorts and flip flop clad people, chatting happily about their waterpark vacation they had embarked on. When the van arrived, a valet helped pile all our belongings into the back and we packed ourselves into the seats, like sardines. Visiting happily, the driver and valet asked everyone what had brought them to The Valley of the Sun—a very spot-on nickname, in my opinion— and how long they would be staying.

After a short drive, in which I did mostly listening, we arrived at the hotel and were ushered inside to the waiting and welcoming air conditioner, free coffee and cookies, and a pair of front desk hosts who stood ready to check us all in.

"Mister Williams," the male host called, motioning me over to him from across the gray tiled and high ceiling space. He looked as if he belonged on a beach somewhere, his skin dark and tanned, black hair styled in a nice wave, and the company polo shirt he was wearing ironed to perfection. "I'm Marcus, Marcus Garcia," he explained, shaking my hand over the counter as soon as I was close enough. "We spoke on the phone?"

"Yes, I remember," I replied, pleasantly surprised. "Nice to meet you in person."

"I asked to work front desk today, so I could be here when you arrived. I have some news for you, regarding your friend, Mark Bell."

"Oh?" That caught me off guard. Apparently, Marcus had been doing a little digging in the week since we'd spoken; I'd never shared Mark's last name with him.

"Here." Laying a yellow file folder on the counter between us, he shrugged. "It's not much, but I asked the manager about him after you called. She said the hotel had tried calling him to see if he wanted his belongings, but they could never get hold of him. Another man came in a few days later, asking for everything, but it wasn't Mark, so they refused to hand it over to him. I put his picture from the security camera in the file, in case you recognize him. The manager also called the police because of the vase. She was worried that it was stolen or perhaps being passed off as an ancient artifact and didn't want to be involved with it."

"Let me guess, it was stolen before the police arrived to collect it, wasn't it?" Opening the file, I glanced over the first page. It had the details of Mark's stay, which of his credit cards he'd used to pay for the room, a copy of his driver's license, things like that. It was all typical information that a hotel collected when you checked in.

"It was," Marcus confirmed, watching as I looked everything over. "That's all I could find. Like I said, it's not much, but I thought it might be of some help to you. Maybe you can call the credit card company and see if he's used the one he paid with anywhere else."

"Maybe." Flipping the page, I froze, staring at the picture Marcus had printed off for me. It was grainy and obviously from a security camera somewhere behind the desk, but I recognized that teddy bear figure anywhere.

Professor Stevens was wearing a brown sport coat and sweater vest, looking every bit the scholarly man he was. His face was scrunched up in anger, though, and he appeared to be having stern words with whomever he was speaking with. One finger was pointing menacingly toward the unknown host, his eyes giving a piercing glare.

Fury coursed through me, a sharp breath getting caught in my chest as I stared down at the lying brute of a man. Fingers trembling, I forced them to lay flat on top of the photograph, somewhat surprised at how upset the revelation that Mark's friend was not to be trusted had affected me.

Hadn't I felt that he was hiding something when we spoke? My gut had been telling me that something was wrong with the man from the start, but I had ignored it. Now, the proof of my suspicions was laid out before me. All I could think was how stupid I had been to trust the statement of a man I barely knew. I'd cast Professor Stevens to the side as no longer useful in my search. It was clear now that he was right at the center of it, though.

He might even know where Mark was right at this very second.

The thought of Mark flushed my face with guilt for a moment. I had given him the vase that brought him here. It was my fault that he'd been dragged into this mess. Was he alive? Dead? Only God knew at this point.

God, and possibly Professor Stevens.

Clearing my throat, I tapped my finger on the picture, regaining some of my composure.

"Do you know him?" Marcus asked, seemingly just as curious as I was to find out what had happened.

"I do," I stated slowly, closing the folder and peering up at him. The expression on my face must have alerted him to the fact that I was not happy with what I saw because he frowned apologetically and shrugged.

"I'll get you checked in so you can do what you need to. Sorry I couldn't help more." Turning to his computer, he started typing in various codes and getting keys ready.

"You've done more than you know." Still slightly fuming, I provided him with my identification and signed the papers he printed for me. Thanking him for his help, I turned to the elevator, ready to go to my room and think things through. My mind was spinning, anger at being lied to boiling inside me, and all I wanted to do was sit down and sort things out for a moment.

Entering the lift, I squeezed myself into a corner, making room for the other guests joining me, and pressed the button for floor number three. When the doors opened, it was to an open walkway, the entrances to the different rooms facing me. Behind me, a court yard housed the pool and hot tub, as well as palm trees and other greenery.

Leaving the empty elevator behind, I slowly walked down the corridor to the right, finding my room on the very end, next to a staircase leading down to the ground. The room was simple and somewhat small, but it had its own sitting room apart from the bedroom. There was a tiny refrigerator tucked away under the counter in the right-hand corner, a microwave displaying the time from just overhead. A standard coffee maker and plastic wrapped mugs sat next to the silver sink. On the left-hand side of the room, a fold out couch and small dining table sat, a large, flat screen television across the room from them. I found the bathroom in the short hall in the middle of the space, the bedroom beyond housing a large bed, dresser, and television of its own.

Sighing, I set my bag on the bed and rubbed my face. I hadn't known exactly what I was going to do once I got here, but knowing that Stevens was still involved made it seem all the more complicated.

Was he the one that broke in and stole the vase? Most likely not. The staff would have recognized him on the security footage, if not the police. No, he must have been working with someone else. One of his students, perhaps? Another professor? Had they immediately recognized the value of what Mark had and decided they had to do whatever possible to get it?

"That doesn't make sense," I grumbled, walking back into the sitting room and resting at the table.

Mark was going to give Stevens the vase. There would have been no need for them to kidnap him or steal it. Why act maliciously when you already have what you want?

Mark had disappeared. Why? Was it something Stevens said to him at dinner? Had he been kidnapped, or did he run? If he had left of his own accord, why leave his belongings and the vase behind?

None of it made sense to me. There was something I was missing, something huge, and I didn't know how to figure it out.

The phone, sitting on the other side of the couch, let out a shrill ring and I jumped, torn from my frustrated musings. Rising, I picked the handset up.

"Hello?"

"Sorry to bother you, Mister Williams," Marcus apologized. "There's an officer down here to see you. His name is Detective Guster—he's been assigned to our robbery case."

"And he wants to talk to me?" I asked, surprised.

"I told him you knew the man who brought the vase here in the first place."

My gut was telling me something was wrong again, an uncomfortable feeling settling around my shoulders. "I'll come down there," I stated firmly. "If he doesn't mind waiting a moment."

"I'll let him know."

Putting the phone down, I looked around the room again. It seemed suspicious that a police officer had arrived so soon after myself. He was a member of law enforcement, though. Shouldn't I be relieved that he was here to help? He might have more information that I needed, more leads that I could help pursue.

Heading downstairs, I decided to save my judgments and suspicions for the detective until after

I'd met and spoken with him. Stevens betrayal had put me on edge, but I didn't need to broadcast that onto anyone else.

Upon entering the lobby, I immediately saw the officer, standing in a gray suit, his badge proudly displayed on a chain around his neck. He wore aviator sunglasses, his brown, buzzcut hair making him look like a member of the army more than a local police force.

"Mister Williams," he said, stepping forward and holding his hand out. "I'm detective Guster, Phoenix Robbery Unit."

"Pleased to meet you." Shaking his offered hand, I smiled, feeling the presence of authority that the man exuded.

"I understand you have a missing person you're trying to find?"

"Yes. Mark Bell. His items were among those stolen from the hotel here."

"Including this vase I keep hearing about?"

Grimacing slightly—everyone seemed more interested in the vase than Mark—I laughed and nodded. "Unfortunately."

"Well, I can certainly help get you set up with our missing persons unit, but I'm actually here to talk about the vase. I hope that won't seem too harsh to you." He smiled, his eyes still hidden behind his glasses, and I felt another pang of doubt, instantly thinking I shouldn't trust this man for all the money in the world.

"I'll do what I can to help."

"Good."

Tilting his head toward the front desk, he waved

at Marcus, apparently either thanking him or dismissing him. He motioned for me to follow him outside. It was then I realized a car had been sitting outside the doors this whole time, a black Sudan with windows tinted so darkly I couldn't even see anything inside.

"Are we going somewhere?" I asked, surprised.

"Just to the station. I have a couple mug shots there to show you, plus that's where we can get your report filed for your friend. You don't mind, do you?"

"No." It sounded more like a question than a statement, my intuition telling me not to set one toe in the car. What could I do, though? He was a police officer. There was no need for me to be afraid of going to the station.

Hesitantly following, I allowed him to open a door for me, thanking him as I sat down. As the door shut, I was plunged into almost complete darkness, the driver's seat blocked from view by a glass partition, which was tinted just as darkly as the rest of the back of the car.

The entry across from me opened and Detective Guster slid in beside me, popping a piece of gum into his mouth. "Nice, isn't it?" he asked, motioning around us. "The drug team seized it from a dealer. It works well as an undercover car, plus, it provides comfort from the sun outside."

"I suppose." Nervous, I tried to relax as we pulled away from the curb, heading out onto the street. It was hard to see where we were going through the tint, but the detective kept trying to draw my attention away from the window anyway.

"We've had an outbreak of robberies involving

ancient artifacts," he said, watching me intently. "We think there might be a black-market ring starting up here. You wouldn't know anything about that, would you?"

"Why would I?"

He didn't seem to like that answer. "What about your friend, Mark? Would he know anything about it?"

Suddenly, I realized I was being interrogated. I wasn't just going to the station to have a look around and file a report. Detective Guster's eyes seemed to burn as he looked at me, his mouth set in a displeased line.

"Mark would never disrespect the history he loves by selling it to criminals in a black market," I replied strongly, frowning. "And neither would I. If you're hoping you've caught part of your theft ring, I'm afraid I'm going to have to burst your bubble—you're looking in the wrong place."

He frowned, leaning back against the seat and folding his arms. "We'll see about that, Scott Williams, age sixty-four, home state Maine, current owner of the Oak Isle Treasure Trove Company, and known artifact hound."

"What?" I asked incredulously. "I am not a hound!"

"You've spent several decades searching for artifacts on the east coast. You worked for a dive company that was later tried and found guilty for stealing artifacts from some of the wrecks they worked on. Some of the members of your team have died, conveniently leaving you the sole heir to the company and any fortune you might find on Oak Isle. And now, suddenly, you've sent your friend here with an old vase, with no explanation on where it came from or how you got it. That all seems very suspicious to me, don't you agree?"

My mouth hung open in surprise, my eyes bulging as I looked at him. He had painted me as a thief and villain, just by putting a spin on my entire life. Even worse, he didn't seem like he was about to be dissuaded by any retort I could make.

"Am I under arrest?" I asked weakly.

"That depends."

"On?"

"On what you have to say to me."

The car rolled to a stop and I peered out the window, suddenly feeling like I was in a cage. It looked like we were in some type of parking garage, cement and darkness all I could see.

"We're here," Detective Guster stated. "Get out."

The station looked like every police drama I'd ever seen. Gray walls, long, bright lights, cubicles, and general business was everywhere. Officers were in uniforms, others in suits like the detective, and there were several people who looked like secretaries. The phones were constantly ringing. Here and there, a person rushed by with paperwork, and every now and then, someone wearing handcuffs and a scowl would be escorted past the room I'd been put in.

Thankfully, since I wasn't technically under arrest, I hadn't been shackled and led around like a common criminal. The thought of it made me rub my wrists gently, grimacing as I imagined the cold metal around them.

"I promise, I don't know anything about your theft ring or black market," I stated again, turning away from the window to watch Detective Guster once more. "And Mark didn't, either."

"Then why is he missing? Where did he run off to, if he wasn't trying to escape the law?"

"I don't know," I replied, frustrated. "But I know Mark. He would never do anything like that."

Shaking his head, the detective glared at me from

his seated position behind the table. "I think you and your friend picked that hotel as a drop space. He left the vase and took off. Whoever you two sold it to broke in and took it. The whole thing was a set up."

"If that was the case, why on God's Green Earth would Mark use his real name? And why would I come to the scene of the crime?"

"Maybe you're just stupid." He shrugged, standing. "Criminals aren't always the best at thinking things through."

"You are being very demeaning," I said sourly. "I can't help you. I can't tell you what I don't know."

"I can arrest you for obstructing justice, you know that, right? I don't have to prove you're a thief to lock you up right now."

"And I can request a lawyer at any time," I shot back. "But I'm trying to comply with your interrogation and not give you any more reason to think I'm guilty."

"You want a lawyer?" He sounded like he was bullying a small child, striding over and getting in my face, trying to intimidate me.

The action only made me angrier, though, and I smiled tightly, finished with trying to work with him. "If you insist on acting like this, then, yes. I would like a lawyer."

"Fine," he snapped. "Wait here a while. I'll be back with your precious lawyer."

Storming out of the room, he slammed the door behind him, drawing the attention of several peoples, and headed down the hall to the right, disappearing from my view.

I knew my rights. I didn't have to be treated this

way, locked in a room, accused and threatened. Never in my life had I felt that law enforcement was a mess of horrible individuals. It was always my stance that there were a few bad apples, but after watching everyone here let Detective Guster scream at me like a child and berate me, I was starting to think that maybe there was no such thing as good cops.

Sitting down, I sighed, resigned to the fact that I would now most likely be stuck in this room for the next several hours, waiting for a lawyer. Then I would be questioned again. Hopefully I would be allowed to leave after that. There were no legitimate charges that could be brought against me.

The time passed slowly, with nothing to entertain myself with. After sitting for longer than I would have liked, I rose and went to the window again, staring at the hub of activity outside. It occurred to me that there were no windows filled with sunlight, only the harsh, bright light of incandescent rods overhead.

Suddenly, one of the lights exploded with a magnificent pop. The woman beneath it screamed, cowering to the floor, the papers she'd been holding scattering around her.

Another pop sounded as the room erupted into chaos, people diving under desks and running from the space. Others pulled guns out of holsters, pointing them away from me.

Slowly, I realized that the office was under attack. Men in riot gear swarmed through the door that led to the parking garage, guns blazing as they fired at the officers, mowing down anyone who got in their way. One of the detectives jerked back, falling over a desk and becoming still.

Gunfire sprayed around the entire space, shattering the window in front of me. Coming to my senses, I flung myself onto the floor, crawling to the back corner. Glass shards stuck in my skin, stinging and burning, bullets still flying into the room and embedding themselves in the wall. Desperate, I knocked the metal table over on its side, dragging it toward myself and using it as a shield. Throwing my arms up over my head, terror ripped through me.

What was happening?

Praying I wouldn't get shot, I squeezed my eyes shut, trying to ignore the screams and shouts outside. It sounded like a world war had erupted in a matter of seconds, explosions and smoke filling the air. Coughing, I pulled my shirt over my face, feeling like I was in some type of terrible nightmare.

"Get up!" A voice yelled in my ear and I jumped, staring up at one of the men in riot gear.

No, not a man. A *woman*.

"Move, now!" she screamed, grabbing me by the arm and hauling me to my feet.

Kicking the table out of the way, she pushed me to the side, peering through the kicked open door. Not even looking back, she moved into the fray, firing her gun at the left side of the room. "Let's go!"

Her command couldn't have been for anyone but me, and was so forceful that I found myself obeying without even thinking, running out behind her. Instantly, four more people in riot gear swarmed around me, creating a human shield on all sides. As one, they moved through the room, shepherding me along like some lost lamb. We were running, guns still firing, shouts echoing, sparks and bits of cement raining down on the group. Smoke made it hard to see what was happening, but it seemed like the entire police department was holed up on the other side of the room, using the desks as shields.

The group around me surged forward, bursting through the door they'd entered from and into the garage. There was fighting here, too, both shooting and fists flying in hand-to-hand combat. There must have been at least double the number of riot geared individuals here, fighting one on one with the members of the police department. It was as if the law enforcement had doubled in size as well, people that I hadn't seen before joining the skirmish in a bloodthirsty frenzy.

Detective Guster appeared out of the haze, blood dripping down his forehead, shouting as he shot at the woman who had grabbed me.

"Clear a path!" She was clearly the leader of the group, everyone doing exactly as she said in the small mob around me as she led them to a car waiting on the other side of the garage.

Guster was having none of it, though, firing again and again, taking down one of the attackers as they rushed him. This caused the woman to growl and hold up a hand, halting the circle.

Breaking away from the rest of us, she swung her rifle around her back and met Guster head on, dodging another shot and punching him right in the face. Grabbing his gun, she wrestled it from his grasp, grunting as he kneed her in the stomach, her armor taking the brunt of the hit.

"You'll never find it!" he snarled in her face, grabbing her arm and twisting it the second he'd had the upper hand. "So long as there's air on this earth, I swear, a Dog will never set sight on it!"

Huffing, the woman stamped on his foot, throwing her head into his face. Pained, Guster released her, reeling backward, hands not hiding the blood now pouring from his nose, as well.

"I've never met a Black Knight who was able to keep a promise," she said smoothly. Raising the gun she'd stolen from him, she fired once, right between his eyes.

It occurred to me that the shouting I was hearing was my own voice, my hands desperately beating the shoulders and backs of my new captors as I watched the detective crumple to the ground. It was to no avail, though.

Rushing onward, the group escorted me and the woman to the waiting car, all but shoving me inside and shutting the door in my face. There was no handle to open it or a way to roll the window down, but I clawed at the exit all the same, still shouting and screaming for help.

Something sharp stabbed into my neck—a needle. Shocked, I felt whatever substance they'd pushed into my system take over, the world going dark around me as I slipped into a still slumber.

My arms were burning, as well as my head. It felt like I'd been clobbered with a large baseball bat. Groaning, I tried to lick my lips, the inside of my mouth feeling like cotton.

"Would you like some water?"

Starting, my eyes popped open and I sucked in a breath. I knew that voice. Where had I heard it? It was much calmer now, not as . . . commanding.

Above me, a low ceiling displayed a recreation of the Sistine Chapel, the walls covered in paintings and framed documents. It was as if every inch of the space had been covered, the paint behind it all not even visible.

Glancing over, I saw a woman in a business suit staring at me. She was seated at a round table, a man and another woman with her. They all faced me, apparently waiting for me to join them in the empty chair beside them.

It all came back as I watched them, slowly. This was the woman who'd dragged me out of the police station—who'd shot the detective in the face. I recognized another of the group as one of the soldiers who had ushered me into the car.

These people had kidnapped me.

Blinking, I looked down. I was resting on a lounge chair, unbound, my glass wounds bandaged nicely.

"Where am I?" I asked, my voice raspy.

"Washington, D.C." Her voice was crisp and businesslike now, not terrifying and murderous. "You've been asleep for about twelve hours. We wanted to give you time to relax and ourselves time to tend to your wounds."

The words confused me. "Why?"

"You don't want to keep glass shards in your arms, surely." Smiling lightly, she leaned back in her chair, raising an eyebrow.

"No, I mean, why did you kidnap me? Who are

you?" Struggling, I sat up, pausing as my head spun lightly for a second.

"I think you mean why did we save ya, mate," the man said, in a thick Australian accent. "We coulda left ya there, if we wanted."

"Peter." It was a warning from the woman leader, her eyes turning cold as she stared down the man in the black suit.

Frowning, he glanced away, huffing slightly.

"Mister Williams—do you mind if I call you Scott? There are a lot of things we need to explain to you. If you'd like to join us all at the table, we can get introductions out of the way and move on to the business at hand." She smiled again, her eyes sharp and focused as she stared at me.

Swallowing hard, I tried to ignore the warning bells going off in my head. These were not people who should be messed with, that much was clear. As I glanced around the room, there was no door that I could see and no windows. All that met my gaze was the overwhelming amount of decoration around me. Gingerly, I left the lounge and occupied the empty chair, resisting the urge to laugh nervously.

"Very good." Sitting up straight once more, the woman cleared her throat. "My name is Lucy. Lucy Cavanaugh. You may or may not have noticed my military training during your extraction." Her eyes twinkled as she smiled slightly. "Extractions can sometimes be a messy business. I apologize for any alarm we may have caused you. As for my role here, I am the Grand Master of The Order of The Knights Templar."

Unable to help myself, I laughed outright, looking

around the room, as if waiting for someone to jump out and yell "surprise! We got you!"

No one did.

"You can't be serious," I asked, staring at her with disbelieving eyes.

"Why not?" She appeared thoroughly amused by my reaction, as if she'd expected no less from me. "Because I'm a girl?"

"No, because The Order of The Knights Templar was destroyed back in the thirteen hundreds. I know you don't mean The First Order of The Knights Templar, either. They are a strictly male society." Studying at each of them in turn, I felt my stomach drop as they all continued to stare at me with somewhat amused expressions.

"You're right on both accounts," she agreed. "However, I am still the Grand Master."

"Only half the Knights were destroyed back in the day, mate." Peter, the Australian, rose from his seat and nodded toward me. "Peter Smith. Second in Command. Served my time in Her Majesty's Navy before joining the ranks here. Lucy and I don't always get along." He shot her a look then, followed by a friendly smile. "She's the best GM this Order has ever had, though. I'd follow her anywhere. Which, coincidentally, is why I agreed to the asinine plan to get you outta the Black Knights' hole in the ground."

"Black Knights?" Confusion rattled me. I must have been part of some horribly elaborate ruse. Maybe Mark would be the one to pop out and say the whole thing was a joke.

"Allow me," the other woman stated, nodding toward Lucy and Peter. "My name is Rebecca

O'Rourke. I'm the secretary around here, in charge of making sure everything we do is recorded. I'm also in charge of the care and protection of all the records our Order has ever kept. Unlike the others, my family has been part of this secret society since it was first founded, during the Crusades. I was trained from a very young age in the art of war and secrecy. However, that is not the reason we have brought you here today."

Carefully, she brought a box up from under the table that she'd been holding on her lap. It was old and worn, the brown wood seeming like it was barely held together. At first glance, I thought it might be more than three hundred years old.

As if guessing what I was thinking, Rebecca smiled and nodded. "It's around three hundred and eighteen years old, if I've done my research right." Turning the case to face me, she tilted it upward, so I could see the top. There, unmistakably carved into the cap, was the name Scott Williams.

Gaping in surprise, I gawked at the three of them, not knowing what to do or expect. They didn't seem to mean me any harm, but what exactly did they want? "That's . . . a coincidence," I finally managed to say, staring at the container in a mixture of awe and confusion.

"Not really." Lucy stared at me pointedly.

"You can't be serious," I half laughed. "Of course it's not for me! That doesn't even make any sense."

Clearing her throat, Rebecca slid on some gloves and pulled another object off her lap. This time, it was an old piece of paper in a plastic sleeve. Donning a pair of reading glasses, she spoke loud and clearly.

"One box. One foot by six inches. Wooden. To be delivered, late in the year two thousand and sixteen, to one Scott Williams, whose name is etched in the wood. None else shall see the contents or die. Signed, WM, GM." Turning the letter toward me, she pointed to the bottom, left-hand corner, where someone had written additional information. "That's your address, is it not?"

The laugh I emitted was nervous this time. "Anyone could fake that," I said unconvincingly.

"Here, have a look at it yourself." Pulling a pair of gloves from her jacket pocket, she offered them to me, along with the paper. "Take it out of the sleeve. You know ancient artifacts. If anyone can spot a fake, it's you."

Hesitantly, I took the gloves and slid them on, handling the plastic covered paper with care. After a moment, I reached through the opening and gently removed the letter. It was so brittle, I worried it might crumble under my touch. As I glanced over it, I felt my heart sink. If this was a recreation, it was a very good one. The paper was of the right thickness and material, the ink old and cracked. It appeared that, at one point, the parchment had been rolled and stored with others, some residual ink from other items dotting the backside.

"It's not a fake," Peter said roughly. "You're taking damn forever to accept what's right in front of you."

"What would you expect me to do," I snapped, suddenly feeling very ostracized and alone, not to mention scared of what was being presented to me. "Accept it without question? Did you? Or do you blindly believe whatever is said to you?"

"Watch your mouth old man," he growled.

"He has a point, Peter," Lucy offered, casually. "You know that outsiders typically have a hard time accepting what we know."

"But this outsider has a three hundred year old box with his name on it. He knows something." Peter glowered at me, crossing his arms again.

"What's in the box?" I asked him. "What could I possibly know that you don't?"

"We don't know what's inside." Lucy sounded miffed. "No one has opened it since it was added to our treasury."

"Why not?" I asked, surprised.

"It's cursed," Rebecca said simply. "If anyone but you opens it, they'll die. That's what the letter means when it says 'or die.' You're the only one."

"Cursed," I scoffed. "Knights Templar. This is ridiculous." Handing the letter back to her, I shook my head. "What's really going on? Why did you break into a police station and kidnap me? I want the truth, not this fairytale crap you're trying to sell me."

"It is not fairytale crap," Lucy replied sternly. "It is real. Your extraction was not from a police station, it was from a Black Knight base. Black Knights are the reverse of our order, determined to destroy the world as we know it. They are evil, evil people. Trust me when I say, if we hadn't pulled you out, you never would have left that bunker except in a body bag."

"We've been trying to locate the base for years. We knew it was somewhere in Phoenix, but every undercover agent we sent it was discovered before they could relay the location to us. When we saw that you were on the move, it looked like the perfect opportunity to finally find out the truth." Peter smiled, as if this revelation brought him great joy.

"What do you mean? You've been watching me?" Staring at the three of them, I felt my face flush. Kidnappers *and* spies? Just what had they been watching me do? What had they learned about me without my knowledge?

"Of course we were watching you," Rebecca said. "We have a three hundred year old box with your name on it and instructions to give it to you."

"Why not sooner, then? Why wait until I was in Phoenix?"

"There was some . . . argument, about whether we should alert you to our presence." Lucy shared a glance with Peter. "By the time we deemed it late enough in the year to give it the go ahead, you were in Arizona."

"We saw a known Black Knight talking with you and decided to see where he took you." Peter sighed, tapping his fingers on the table. "There were more of them there than we anticipated."

"Hold on," I butted in. "Are you saying you used me as *bait* to find where the base was?" Anger pricked at me through the haze of confusion, disbelief, terror, and curiosity.

"It's not like we were going to leave ya there for dead," Peter replied defensively. "We got you out. Patched you up."

My mouth was gaping again, this time in outrage. Turning to Rebecca, I motioned for the box. "Give it to me," I said roughly.

"Just like that?" She was surprised.

"You want me to open an old cursed box? Fine, I'll do it. Maybe then the lot of you will get the hell out of my life and I can forget this ever happened."

Taking the item from her, I set it gently on the table and slid my finger under the lid. It opened easily, with almost no effort. Ignoring the flinches of those around me as the lid popped up, I took in the contents of the box with even more surprise.

"It's a letter," Rebecca said, watching over my shoulder.

"Two," I corrected her.

The pair were set on top of a silk bed, the fabric old and worn as the box it had been kept in. The folded papers seemed ancient as well, yellow with age and the edges showing signs of deterioration.

Carefully, I picked up the first, observing the wax seal holding it shut.

"That's my family crest," Rebecca said quietly.

Gently breaking the wax, I unfolded the sheets, feeling my heart stop as I stared at the writing inside.

"I recognize this penmanship," I said softly. "But it's not possible." Thumbing through to the back page, I inspected the signature, one I had seen many times on the paperwork for the Oak Isle Treasure Trove Company.

"Samantha Greene O'Rourke," Rebecca read, leaning in close to scrutinize it. "That's my however many times great grandmother.

"The wife of Tristan O'Rourke?" Lucy asked sharply.

"Yes." Rebecca gave her a look of complete astonishment. "The rumors were true! I mean, I didn't ever not believe them, but still. They were true!"

"Who is the second letter from?" Peter demanded, standing to better see what was inside the case.

Putting the unimaginable letter down, I picked up the second, broke the seal, and gazed at the signature on the last page. "Mark Bell," I stated thickly.

Falling back into my chair, I surveyed the papers in my hand and the one in the box. There was no way— none at all. This was some kind of cruel joke, played by a harsh group of people who had no heart.

"This isn't funny," I said quietly, glaring at them all together. "Do you hear me? This is not funny.

Samantha died not long ago. This kind of practical joke dishonors her memory. Mark is missing. He could be dead, too, for all I know. I don't appreciate being brought here, under these circumstances no less, to be made fun of. I don't know who you work for, or why they would go to such lengths as this, but I demand you take me home this instant. I never want to see any of you ever again." Hating that my eyes had teared up, I looked down, hands shaking.

"It's not a joke, Scott." Lucy's voice was suddenly very consoling and understanding. "We are as surprised as you. We've heard rumors of the O'Rourke's and where they came from, but I never imagined that they were true. This box has been the only thing that made me think they might be, and you've just proven our suspicions by opening it."

"Rumors of what?" I demanded, glaring at her once more.

"Read the letters. I imagine they will share the whole story with you."

"I will not," I replied vehemently.

"Please, Scott," Rebecca said, her voice catching for some reason. "Read them. Tristan and Samantha were some of the most influential people in our Order. Mark, too. The fact that you've been given this is highly important and a changing point for us."

"Then you read them." Tossing "Mark's" letter back in the box with the other, I closed the lid and shoved it toward her. "I don't want anything to do with your Order."

"Are you sure, Scott?" Lucy asked.

"Let the bloke go home," Peter piped up, nodding once. "He doesn't want anything to do with it? Fine.

Whatever is in those letters obviously isn't going to be any help to him if he refuses to believe they're real."

"If you truly want nothing to do with it, Mister Williams, I am more than happy to arrange a flight home for you. We can get you a room here for you to rest in until your transportation is ready." Lucy sounded like she was back to business as usual, her eyes scanning my face thoughtfully.

"Nothing would make me happier."

"Fine. Peter, show him the door, will you? All you need do Mister Williams is go to the front desk and tell them that Cavanaugh is calling. You'll have a room before you can blink."

Grumpily, Peter stood and went to the wall, tilting one picture to the side. It was apparently hiding a trap door mechanism, because the door opened right up, swinging over to reveal a long hall, filled with more artwork, statues, and curious objects.

"Thank you." Giving the box on the table one last shaky look, I stood and left the room, jumping as the entrance shut tight behind me. Even though I'd just passed through it, the door was shut tight, hiding its existence from even the most determined of sleuths.

Breathing a great sigh of relief, I glanced around, surprised by the sheer number of artifacts here. Some of them looked old, others new. They ranged from the magnificent to the strange, a few of the items recognizable as reproductions. Others appeared to be the real things, like a small Greek statue that couldn't have been less than a thousand years old. It was in a glass case, a price tag attached to the outside of the glass. Upon further inspection, it appeared that everything here was for sale.

Slowly, I made my way through the space, examining everything. Eventually, I came to a cross with another hall. Not sure which way to go, I picked blindly and continued on with my perusal, interested in practically every single thing I saw.

It seemed like at least an hour had passed before I finally stumbled on the front desk. True to Lucy's word, as soon as I'd uttered the phrase she said, I had a small room down three halls and around two corners, decorated in the same fashion as the rest of the place. Looking at the key in my hand, I read the name of the establishment.

"The Mansion on O Street," I mumbled, feeling like I'd heard the name somewhere. Maybe on the Travel Channel? That was it. I remembered because they claimed that secret societies met in their hidden rooms.

Apparently, that part hadn't been a bit for the Travel Channel special.

Sighing, I flopped onto the bed. The letters couldn't be real, could they? It was impossible! But so was The Order of The Knights Templar, here in D.C. So was a group of people walking into a police station and destroying it. So was the fact that I was here, under these circumstances.

Restless, I left my room, hoping to distract myself with more of the artifacts. Moving slowly, I checked the price of each item, mentally deciding if it was something I would buy or pass on. Eventually, I came to a case full of jewelry. One of the rings caught my attention, causing my stomach to drop again.

It was gold, with a cross etched into it, a black dot in the middle. Just like Professor Stevens' ring.

"What happened to you Mark?" I asked quietly.

"It's an interesting ring, isn't it?" Rebecca stopped beside me, a large, manila envelope in her hands. "Pretty, even. Too bad it has such a horrible history."

"What do you mean?" I sighed, not knowing what to think of this whole ordeal.

"That symbol is the mark of The Black Knights of The Order of the Templars. Even today, they still use it to help identify each other with. Of course, three hundred years ago, they used to brand the mark on their actual bodies. Then they realized that was a good way to get caught by the Templars and the went with the rings instead." She laughed, looking at me with sparkling eyes. "Easier to get rid of in a pinch."

"This is the symbol of the bad guys?" I asked, hesitantly remembering my negative feelings for the professor.

"It is. You probably didn't see it when you were in their base, if they were masquerading as law enforcement."

Silence stretched between us, myself staring hard at the ring and wondering if Mark had fallen to these so called Black Knights. If he had, it would be my fault. All because I wanted to know how old the vase was and was too cheap to send it off myself.

"Do you know where the vase is?" I asked suddenly. "The one I gave to Mark? Was it your group that stole it?"

Surprised, she shook her head. "No. It's disappeared out of thin air, it would seem. We were worried the Black Knights had seized it, but they appear to be searching for it just as desperately as we are."

Nodding, I fell silent once more, thinking over the revelation. I still knew nothing about what had happened to my friend.

Clearing her throat, as if she'd sensed I was thinking of my friends once more, Rebecca offered the envelope to me. "I know you don't want to read them, but you might. Someday. It didn't seem right to keep them from you. Samantha and Mark wanted you specifically to have them. I've already made copies—these are the originals. Don't tell Lucy or Peter, though. They'd have me court marshalled." She laughed lightly then, shaking her head. "These are yours, though. They can't argue with that."

Peering down at the offering, I swallowed hard. "Thank you." The reply was soft and quiet, but she heard it, passing the file to me with ease.

"Stay safe," she cautioned. "If you ever need any help, my number is in there. Don't hesitate to call."

The house seemed strangely empty when I finally arrived at home, late that night. It was as if all the joy had been sucked out of my life.

The envelope, still unopened, rested on the dining room table, like a siren calling me to it. I didn't want to read the letters, though. What if they were a cruel prank? Or worse.

What if they were real?

Sighing, I slumped down in the kitchen chair, running my hand over the container, trying to decide what to do.

"This is ridiculous," I laughed to myself. "Of course they aren't real!"

The package seemed huge as I stared at it, like it contained some life altering secrets I would never be able to unlearn once I'd seen them.

What could be the worst that would happen, though? I could read the letters and discover that they were a joke. Then the issue would be over.

My gut was telling me I had something important here, though. Why go through all the trouble if it was just a joke? I'd seen Lucy kill someone. That wasn't fake. The Mansion on O Street wasn't fake. The two letters sitting here, now, could very well be real as well.

Seized upon by a moment of decision, I opened the flap and pulled out the top letter, which had been carefully slid inside several plastic sheets, now tied together in the corner, through a hole punched through the protective covering. The second letter had also been prepared in the same fashion and I removed it from the folder as well, setting the two items on the table before me.

Taking a deep breath, I pulled the one written in Samantha's handwriting toward myself and began to read.

Dear Scott,

I don't even know how or where to begin. I've started this letter at least one hundred times, but it never seems to come out right. The odds that you'll even receive it are not very good. On top of that, I'd never assumed that I would have to tell someone from my own time what happened to me. Mark changed all of that, though. He had more understanding of what I'd gone through, since he did it as well. For some reason, it feels harder, telling someone who has no idea. Even more so, telling someone who won't hear what I have to say until I've been dead for three hundred years.

Look, this is going to be confusing. I feel as though I'm simply spewing my thoughts out on the paper, with no rhyme or reason. I hope you'll forgive my nervousness and uncertainty.

I've traveled back in time. Really and truly. I've been here for a few years now, in fact. When I first arrived, it was sixteen ninety-five. That was just over two years ago. So much has happened between now and then. A lot of it was great and a good portion of it was . . . bad.

I know you've seen the video of me climbing into the Treasure Pit. Mark told me you all thought I had died. However, once I got inside the treasure vault at the bottom, I opened a vase—the one you gave to Mark—that transported me through time. I hate to tell you, but Dad was right about what's down there. It's the treasure of The Knights Templar, and it holds terrifyingly powerful things. I've seen it in both times now. If I'd known what was actually down there, what those things could do, I don't think I ever would have agreed to help Dad with it at all.

Either way, the Pit flooded, and I thought I'd drowned. Instead, I woke up on the beach, surrounded by pirates, and soon found myself carried off by one of them. Ironically, that man would become my husband, Tristan. He's not just a pirate, by the way. He's a member of The Knights Templar. He oversaw hiding the treasure on Oak Isle before everything happened.

And not that I must defend my decisions to anyone—or that you would ask me to— but, Tristan O'Rourke is everything I could have wanted in a husband, despite the fact that he has no idea what The Declaration of Independence, Germany, or a movie is. But, he knows how to be a husband. How to take care of matters of politics, secrecy, strength, and compassion. Matters of the heart. He has known hardships and stared his trials in the eye, never backing down from a fight. I love him so very much and have caused him so much pain and frustration. It's a wonder he doesn't declare he's tired of me and run away. I think he needs a little saving himself now and then, though, and I'm proud to say that I can do that for him.

This last year was so awful. What I would give to go back and do it all over. To avoid all the horrors that befell my family. To save Tristan and myself the heartache that we feel now. To erase the horrible, awful, heartbreaking things that I was forced to suffer through alone.

Thank heavens for Mark. I know he's had a horrible time of it, too, stuck here for the past ten years, with no idea of how he'd made it to this time or that I'd traveled as well. It was shocking, when we found each other. Without him, though, I don't think I would have survived the things that happened to me.

I think maybe I saved him some, too.

The vase, though. It's Pandora's Box, Scott. You <u>must</u> find it and protect it. Give it to The Order. They will take care of it and assure that it doesn't fall into the wrong hands. Whatever you do, though <u>do not</u> open it. I'll not go into the whole story of how I found out what it was, but it is quite literally a life and death situation. Do not, do not, do not open it! Don't let anyone else do it, either. If the vase doesn't find them worthy, it will suck the life out of them right there. I've seen it happen. That's not a risk I think you're willing to take.

That's the real purpose of this letter. Not to tell you I'm alive and happy, or that I'm on some strange adventure. I need you to get that vase. Whatever it takes. There are people in this world who would try to abuse it, or unknowingly put themselves in harm's way. Give it to the The Order and wash your hands of it. Wash your hands of the whole thing. Oak Isle is not something you should get wrapped up in any longer. My wish for you is that this letter will bring you some closure on that part of life as well.

Thank you for being my friend. I'm sorry that I disappeared without a trace. I'm sorry that you thought I was dead. I guess, technically, I am.

That's all I have to say, I think. Anything more would result in an entire novel's worth of story and explanation. I wish it were as simple as picking up the phone and filling you in, but it's not. I know you're a good man, one who can help with this important issue, though. Not to sound cliché, but the fate of the world is practically resting on your shoulders. Get the vase to The Order.

Please do this for me. Please.
Love,
Samantha

Scott~
You're probably worried sick about me by now. Sorry about that. Honestly, if I could have done it any different, I would have at least gotten that damn vase to Stevens for you. But, who knows. Maybe he would have been the one to end up here, alone.

I don't know if you've already read Sammy's letter

or not. I bet you're freaked out that some random people brought you an old box of letters, claiming they were over three hundred years old. It seems like a joke, maybe pulled by McCreary or some other sap trying to mess with you.

It's not.

Do you remember December 2013? You and I were at the university library together, reading up on local history and searching for any clues about the island. You told me that you'd been diagnosed with cancer, but that it was only a small mole on your hand. The doctor had already removed it and you'd told everyone that you'd cut it chopping firewood. I was the only one who knew the truth.

Now you know *that it's really me, not some jerk face trying to string you along.*

I traveled through time. It was an accident, of course. I opened that stupid vase to see if there was anything inside. There was a sand storm then, and I got caught outside. When it cleared, I was in the desert, with no idea of how I'd gotten there. It took me a while, but I eventually realized I was in a different century.

I lived with the Apache for a few years, then, in Mexico City. Eventually, I made my way to the coast and got a job on one of the merchant ships. We were taken over by a crew of Black Knights—I trust The Order has already told you about them—and I was pressed into their service.

That's where I found Sammy. The captain of my ship, Thomas Randall, has a history with her and her husband, Tristan. It was so awful when we ran into each other, Scott. Randall and his men had kidnapped and beaten her so much that I almost didn't even recognize her.

So much more has happened since then. It was almost all bad. But, you should know, Tristan came for her. I was almost killed in the process because he thought I was a Black Knight, but I survived the gunshot.

It feels like I'm telling you some magnificent story I came up with. It's almost funny, trying to write this for you. It's been ten years since I last saw you, can you believe that? Ten years. It's probably only been a month or two for you. I couldn't remember the exact date from when I traveled, so I had to guess. We didn't want these letters getting to you while I was still there. It would confuse the timelines too much, maybe even stopping me from coming. As horrible and lonely that the past decade has been, I wouldn't wish that I never came here.

Samantha needed me. I would choose this path every single time if it meant that I could help ease her suffering.

The main reason we both decided to write you is because of the vase. Sammy says it's Pandora's Box—apparently, she had some opium with a Greek priestess and they were visited by Zeus (yeah, I hardly believe it, too. I'd think she was crazy if I hadn't traveled myself)—and it's very dangerous. There's literally a fifty/fifty chance that you could die if you open it.

I don't know what happened to the vase, though. I imagine it's in the hotel's lost and found. I was staying at the something Garden in Phoenix. Maybe it started with a "w" or an "h?" I can't remember exactly, sorry. They should, hopefully, still have it. Stevens was going to come pick it up in the morning, I don't know if they would have given it to him. Wherever it is, though, you need to find it. Don't let anyone open it, for any reason. The Order will be able to protect it, if they are anything like they are now in our time. Get it to them and then stay far away.

I know you're dedicated to getting to the bottom of the Treasure Pit. Having seen what I've seen, I can't even imagine how glorious it would be to find what is hidden down there. You would be a household name. The Knights Templar are dangerous people at times, though. I don't know if they would even allow you to get down there. Here's my honest advice and you can take it or leave it: stay away from Oak Isle. You don't want or need to draw these warring factions into your life. God willing, there won't be an active group of Black Knights while you're living. If there is, though, you don't want to be anywhere near either side.

I have so much more I want to say to you, but I don't know how to fit it all into one letter. I've missed you. Often, I feel guilty for disappearing. You're one of my best friends in the world, my colleague, my go-to man for advice and compassion. You are such a kind soul, Scott. I know you've been trying to find out where I am and if I'm okay. Now that you know, I hope you will rest easy. Don't be sad that I am gone, or that I will have been dead for centuries by the time you get this. In this world, you haven't even been born yet, but you are still alive to me. I hope you can think the same of me.

Take care of yourself. Above all, I just want you to be happy. I hope this revelation can help some in that. My only wish would be that Michael had somehow managed to travel as well, instead of being buried alive. Then we would all be alive and together here and you wouldn't have anyone to mourn.

Live a good, long life, my friend.
Mark

The knock at the door pulled me from my thoughts and I turned away from my research covered table, glancing at the clock on the wall. It was just past ten in the evening and rather late for company. The last time someone had come over at this hour, I'd found out Mark was missing.

Swallowing a bit uncomfortably, I rose and went to the door, thinking over and over that a visitor after ten didn't automatically mean bad news.

"Hey Scott!" Eric beamed at me from the other side, holding a tiny package in his hand, his restaurant shirt sporting some flour residue and a tiny spot of pizza sauce. "Long time, no see!"

"Eric, what a surprise!" Reaching through the doorway, I pulled him into a hug, feeling genuinely happy to see him. I'd missed the twins very much since they'd set out on their own, though I did enjoy seeing their updates on their lives online.

"I'm sorry I haven't been over sooner, but actually owning and running a restaurant by yourself has turned out to be more work than I thought it would be." Laughing, he came into the living room, peering around at the artifacts with a smile.

"I could have told you that," I joked, shutting the door and turning to face him. "How are you, though? It's all going well?"

"Of course." He waved a hand in dismissal. "A lot of it just has to do with Kevin taking off a few weeks ago. We haven't ever really been apart. I miss him like crazy." He seemed embarrassed at that and cleared his throat, holding up the box he'd brought along.

"I actually came over because you had something delivered to the restaurant. It looks like it came from that carbon dating company. You must have forgotten to change your address with them when you moved everything over here." He shrugged, holding it out to me.

"Oh, I'm so sorry! I must have." Taking the small container from him, I felt a few butterflies in my stomach. It wouldn't matter if he had opened it or not, but I didn't want him to ask questions about what I was having dated. "Thank you for bringing it over."

"Sorry it's so late. I had to wait until the shop was closed up."

"No, no, I completely understand."

In the kitchen, the kettle on the stove began to whistle. I'd forgotten I was making tea and looked down the hall, frowning.

"I'll get it," Eric stated, laughing. "You open your box and find out how old whatever's inside is." He turned and strolled down the hall, putting his hands in his pockets.

As soon as he disappeared around the corner, I pried open the box, pulling out the sheet of information inside. One month ago, after reading the letters given to me, I'd carefully cut a small portion of each, including ink samples, and sent them off to be dated. Given the circumstances in which I'd received the correspondence and the information they contained, I'd decided to treat them as I would any other artifact and run them through some tests.

Once the samples had been sent, I went to the library, checking out naval histories, family genealogies, and subscribing to many sites that would help me look back through time. Learning about The Knights Templar had been a must. I'd also studied Free Masonry and any other links that I could get my hands on.

I'd first discovered the name Tristan O'Rourke in an old ship's log, through the online catalog at the New York Library. Thomas Randall had appeared as well. It wasn't until a few days later that I found Samantha's name, in connection with her husband.

Mark was much harder to locate. Finally, after what felt like years' worth of searching, I found his name listed among the crew of a French privateer vessel, captained by a man named William MacDonald.

Tristan O'Rourke was also listed among the crew.

Still, it could have all been simple coincidence, couldn't it? Someone else could have done this research and tied it together as a prank. However, I was willing to admit that it was a large amount of work to do for a plain, practical joke.

Glancing over the findings of the carbon dating, I felt a strange, excited flip in my stomach, as well as dread.

The letters were real.

According to these results, the paper had dated to

around the end of the seventeenth century. The ink was tagged at almost seventeen hundred exactly.

Mark and Samantha were alive, three hundred years in the past.

Sitting down on the couch in shock, I stared at the floor, feeling a million thoughts race through my mind. How? If what they'd stated in their letters was true, the vase had taken them there. Why? I had no idea. What was I supposed to do with this information? Everything I knew about the world was wrong. Magic was real, so were gods, it would appear. The Knights Templar had a treasure.

A person could travel through time.

Dazed, I suddenly remembered Eric in the kitchen and froze. All of my research was laid out for anyone to see, including the letters. If he read them . . .

Rising quickly, I hurried to the kitchen, feeling my heart stop as I caught sight of him, standing at the table, one of the letters in his hand. Eyes wide, he looked like a statue, his mouth open in a small "o" shape as he read. The research on the table had been moved around, books not where I'd left them. Several of the notecards I'd filled with information were laying scattered over the top of my computer, obviously having been looked at as well.

"I can explain," I said softly, coming to stand beside him.

"Scott . . . what is all of this?" He sounded like he might be worried I was crazy, or that he was crazy for having even seen everything laid out here.

"It's a long story." I sighed. "But I promise, there is an explanation. For all of this."

"The letters are cut." His voice was slow and filled

with wonder, his eyes moving to look at me. "You had them dated?"

"I did."

Swallowing hard, he looked back down at the paper in his hand. It was part of Mark's letter, the page that had stated Samantha was kidnapped and beaten. "What did the test say?"

Hesitating, I glanced over everything on the table. It was obvious that I was legitimately pursuing the idea that the letters were real and that Samantha and Mark had traveled through time.

"They're as old as they claim to be."

The statement made us both take a deep breath, an uncomfortable air brushing through the room.

"And all this? You found proof elsewhere?" He sounded scared now, perhaps intrigued. Whatever he was feeling, he was doing a good job of keeping the emotion off his face.

"Yes."

Silence stretched between us as he read the letter again, and then again. "How?" he finally whispered, looking at me with concern in his eyes. "How did you get these?"

"I was . . . ah . . . kidnapped. So to speak."

The whole story came out then. I told him of Mark's disappearance and my decision to keep it from him and his brother. I explained my video call with the professor and my subsequent trip to Arizona, leading up to the ambush at the Black Knight base and subsequent meeting with The Knights Templar in Washington D.C.

"It seemed crazy," I confessed. "More than crazy. But once I'd read the letters, I knew I had to find out if they were real or not. And they are!"

"What are you going to do?" Eric had taken a seat at the table, a glass of tea in his hands that I'd poured while sharing the story.

"I don't know. I suppose I'll have to try and find the vase. If it was so important that the two of them felt they needed to reach through time to get to me, I can't ignore it."

"Will you give it to The Order?"

"No," I replied sharply. "I know that's what Samantha and Mark asked me to do, but I don't trust them. They used me as bait. I could have been killed! Mark warned that they were dangerous, as well. I'm going to have to come up with another plan on my own to keep it safe and away from those who would abuse it."

"You can't do it alone," he said suddenly, standing. "No way. You need my help."

"That won't be necessary." Instantly interrupting him, I held up a hand. "You just got out of this mess. If you try and help me, you'll be putting yourself right back in the middle of the problem. You read the letters; they don't want us to mess around with any of this more than we have to."

"I don't care," he insisted. "I know all of this, too, now. You can't deny me the chance to help my friends. This is important, Scott. I can feel it in my bones. Besides, you ended up kidnapped last time. You need someone with a little more muscle to come along and make sure you're okay."

"What about the restaurant?" I inquired. "You're the owner now. Kevin is away at school. Your parents have moved away to enjoy their early retirement. You can't just leave it behind."

Thinking, he shook his head. "I don't know what I'll do. But I do know you're not doing this without me."

"Eric, I—"

There was another knock at the door and I turned toward it in surprise. "Who on earth could that be?"

The pounding occurred again, this time accompanied by shouting.

"It's Rebecca O'Rourke, Mister Williams! I need you to open the door. Right now!"

Eyebrows rising in surprise, I shared a look with Eric and then moved to let the Templar Knight inside. No sooner had I opened the door, did she shove herself inside and lock it, leaning against it, breathing heavily.

"We need to leave," she stated crisply. "Gather everything you deem necessary."

"What's going on?" Eric asked in confusion, gawking at her like a deer in headlights.

She regarded him for half a second, smiling in a friendly manner, and then pushed past us, opening the coat closet in the hall and removing my jacket.

"The Black Knights are on their way. Someone let it leak that you had been given letters of importance."

Tossing the coat to me, she turned and went into the kitchen. "Eric is going to have to come, too," she called over her shoulder. "They know he was involved with your search for the treasure and has seen the vase. He won't be safe here anymore."

"What?" Eric croaked, eyes somehow getting even wider.

Rebecca appeared in the hallway again, her arms full of the research and letters we'd laid out on the table. "You are both under the protection of The Order of The Knights Templar now. If you value your lives, you will do as I say and come with me right this instant."

Mark Bell
1698

Staring at myself in the long mirror, I tried to fix the lacy piece of cloth tied around my neck once more, frowning at the scratchiness of the uncomfortable garment. The rest of my outfit was no better. A heavy, forest green jacket, adorned with gold buttons that flashed gaudily every time the sun hit them, covered the pale shirt underneath. It was stuffy, making me feel as if I were suffocating. Then there were the tight, black breeches, covering a pair of white stockings that led down into black, buckle shoes. Sitting on the dresser to my left, a powdered wig waited, looking just as ridiculous as it always had.

Grunting in annoyance, I gave the neck piece one last tug, surrendering to the fashion devil. I'd never needed to follow the latest trends before. When I was with the Apache, I wore Apache things. In Mexico City, I'd worn a mix of my Native clothing and general clothing from the city. At sea, all I'd needed were some pants, a good belt and boots, and a shirt that would stay out of my way. Now, in Paris, though, it seemed The Knights Templar were determined to make me appear like a well-to-do member of society, not some street rat, begging for coins.

"Why, don't you fix up nice!"

Startled, I turned to the side, peering past the large bed, toward the doorway. There, in the entrance, stood the housekeeper, Madame Bordeu. Recently widowed, and about twice my age, the woman had taken to mothering me in a strange way. Half the time, I felt like she was hitting on me. The other, it was as if I'd committed some great wrong and she had come to scold me.

Hunched over some, she smiled her gap-toothed grin, patting her chest over her kerchief as if she were suddenly having a fit. "I knew you would, Monsieur Bell. Knew it when I first put my eyes on you. I told Monsieur Dubois 'that young man needs a good bath and a haircut and he'll be as handsome as the king Himself.' *Oui, Monsieur.* I was right."

Blushing slightly, I cleared my throat, nodding in her direction as thanks. When I'd first arrived at the home The Order had prepared for me, I'd been a little worse for wear. In my defense, I'd also spent the last four months trekking through the desert and crossing the Atlantic. It hadn't really been a priority for me, making sure that I shaved and kept my hair under control. The moment I'd set foot on French soil, though, I apparently looked like a wild caveman to everyone else. My hair reached past my shoulder blades by then, my beard long, scraggly, and patchy at best. Even Samantha suggested I find myself a barber and a bathtub as soon as possible, a small smile on her face.

Samantha.

My heart hurt, just thinking of her. She had made the crossing fine, so far as I knew, but we were all plagued by the memory of what had happened in Arizona. Images of the battle inside the mountain were burned in my mind. Skeletons, brought to life by old magic, fighting to protect the enormous treasure they had been buried with. The hammer of Thor, alive and crackling in my hand. A Viking ship, flying away into the thunderstorm, disappearing. Thomas Randall, shouting at me to kill Tristan or watch Samantha die.

Sam had fought well and hard in the battle, despite the fact she was both injured and mentally abused from her abduction. The skin on her wrists had been so red and cut open, she would probably have scars for the rest of her life. Worst of all, her captor had escaped once more, failing to stand trial for his actions.

That wasn't what pained me, though.

She was with her Tristan now. Her husband, the man she loved more than anything in the world. There was no need for me to stand beside her and protect her, to be a part of her everyday life, or even to speak with her about more than trivial items. I loved her more than any words I could put together, and now I was practically gone from her life. Alone in the world. Again.

It was so repulsive to me, my feelings for her, because of all the issues that love brought into my life. At the same time, all I wanted was to fall into those emotions and let them rule me completely. I'd never meant to love her. She was my friend, young enough to be my own daughter, and not available. I'd known all these things from the start. And yet, it hadn't mattered. It had proven impossible, not giving myself to her completely. How could I not? She was the only person who understood what it meant to fall through time. She knew what my life had been like from every angle. We had been the hostages of Thomas Randall together, forced to fight for our lives as one. She was my heart, the one thing that kept me driving forward, the star in my sky of darkness.

It was devastating, knowing that she would never feel the same. There was an eternal knife stabbing me in the heart, along with a painful twist, causing a stitch in my side. It felt as if I couldn't breathe fully when I was with her, everything around me seeming to shout that she could not be mine. I knew there was no chance to find happiness down this road. And yet, I couldn't pull myself off the path, turn back, or even step off to the side and accept I was going nowhere.

Whenever I closed my eyes, though, all I could see was the image of Sammy's face. It was thin and tan, her eyes fierce and full of energy. Lips that I had kissed only once before seemed to shine in the bright light of open water, her long, brown hair blowing gently around her face. Her expression was strong and commanding, like it had been when I'd known her in the future. She was a woman worth fighting for. A woman I had risked everything to save. A woman whom I had dared to love, even when I knew I had no chance of ever being with her.

Anger coursed me for a moment. Why would God, or whatever higher power existed, put me through this if I wasn't meant to stay with her? Why put her on that ship with me? Why make me care for her, nurse her back to health, coach her through the loss of her child? Why did I join the Black Knights to spy for her, allow them to brand me with their mark, fight in a war I wanted no part in? Why was I destined to travel through time, if not to find her and care for her? Samantha had needed me in her darkest moments, when she'd had no husband to cling to. Who was to say those moments wouldn't return?

"Are you feeling well, Monsieur?" Madame Bordeu took a hesitant step in the doorway, her mothering side instantly manifesting itself in a worried look on her face.

"Fine," I replied huskily, locking the dangerous, painful thoughts back in their box. Giving her a tight smile, I straightened my jacket, standing tall. "It looks right?" Turning to the side some, I allowed her to examine me, suddenly wishing I had declined the invitation to visit the O'Rourkes and could stay in bed all day.

"Like a proper gentleman." Grinning again, she pointed to the wig on the dresser. "You're not going to wear it?"

"No." The reply was firm, matched in my pointed glare toward the object in discussion. "I will not. My natural hair will do just fine."

Glancing in the mirror again, I examined my newly cut hair. It was a style that was more becoming of the twenty-first century, with the sides cut as close as I could get them to my scalp and the top left long enough to be styled in a messy manner, but I didn't care. Ten years had passed since I'd had a haircut that I liked and I wasn't about to let a man in tights tell me how to present myself.

Well, not completely, anyway.

Frowning at my own tights, I sighed, running a

hand over my head. The lace cuffs of my shirt brushed over my face and I suddenly fought the urge to laugh. I felt like I was about to walk onto the set of a period drama. This wasn't pretend, though, I reminded myself. This was winter in France and I was about to step outside into the real world.

"I'll get your coat, shall I?" Madame Bordeu smiled, the skin around her eyes so wrinkly that they almost disappeared in the folds. "It's been raining all morning, as I'm sure you saw. Catching the winter fever now will do you no good—best to stay warm and dry as possible. But, surely you know that, what with working at sea and all."

"It is hard to stay warm and dry at sea." Chuckling, I watched as she waddled into the room, opening the wardrobe behind me and pulling out a long, black, trench coat and matching hat. "I saw many men who became sick because of it when I was working as a doctor on board."

"You know the art of the physician?" She sounded surprised, shrugging as she came over, holding up the cover for me to put on. "That's good information to have. I'll wager you could make a fine amount of money here, in the city, should you wish to employ yourself in such a manner. I, myself, would be willing to pay you, should any of my humors ever fail me."

Having never considered working as a medical guru, I raised my eyebrows, pondering the option. It would give me something to do, at least.

"I'll have to think about it more," I finally said, sliding my arms into the sleeves and pulling the heavy jacket over my shoulders. "But, if you ever are unwell, Madame, you don't need to worry about paying me for help. You work in this house—my house, I suppose. I'll take care of you."

"What a fine young man." Patting me on the back, she turned, hobbling toward the hall. "I'll make sure the coach is ready for you, Monsieur. Do you require anything else before you set off?"

"That will be all, Madame. Thank you for your help and your company." Smiling, I watched as she made her way toward the stairs, visible at the end of the hallway.

Rain pattered on the window, a cool draft wafting in from somewhere. Not wanting to return to a cold room, I moved to close the curtains, plunging myself into firelight. The hearth was blazing, putting out more heat than I'd ever thought possible, and the closed off space suddenly felt ten times more comforting. Once again, I found myself wishing I had refused the invitation sent me. The chance to see Sammy had been too much for me to turn down, though.

Placing the hat on my head, I strode out of the bedroom, down the hall, and took the steps quickly, finding myself on the landing of the bottom floor just as the coachman entered the front door.

"Monsieur." Tipping his hat, water dripping off him onto the wood below, he motioned to the door, apparently not able to speak English.

"*Oui*." Leading the way, I stepped outside, hesitating on the doorstep. The storm was continuing in earnest now, the cold drops falling from the sky much quicker than a moment before.

Dancing around me, the coachman leapt from under the overhang and into the wetness, opening the door to the small, black carriage. He pulled his coat around him tighter, waiting for me to get in, shivering through his almost toothless smile. Even the horse seemed to be freezing, its head shaking impatiently.

Not wanting them to be pelted for longer than was needed, I quickly slid into my seat, jumping slightly as the door snapped shut behind me. In a matter of seconds, we were moving away from the house, headed toward the other side of town.

The streets were still somewhat clogged, despite the storm, people bundled up and selling wares everywhere I looked. Several store fronts were crowded by individuals trying to avoid the rain, but the wheels of carriages cackling over the cobblestone streets and splashing through puddles made the bystanders wet anyway.

Once more, I found myself thinking of Samantha. Was she okay? She had been through so much in the past year . . . I didn't know if I would be doing alright if I'd had two face to face battles with a man who wanted me dead. Then there was the fact she'd been kidnapped, beaten, and suffered through the death of her child. She'd been separated from her husband for almost half a year, after spending almost two years straight with him.

The journey back from Arizona had been hard on her, just because her wounds were still so fresh. She appeared more and more distraught every time I'd seen her. We'd been in Paris for a week now and I'd not been able to check on her. Perhaps, being at her home in the city had helped her heal some.

It hadn't really helped me that much.

Pushing the thoughts of my own, self-imposed exile of sorts away, I focused on the fact that I'd finally found someone who understood my life completely. I'd been unable to be myself before finding Sam again, because no one would understand. They would think me a witch, or crazy, maybe even both. It had been a hard life, isolating myself from everyone in this time. I didn't want to go back to that now, not when I knew I could be with people who would accept me and treat me normally.

The carriage lurched to the side and came to a halt, drawing my attention to the outside world. We were on a street full of beautiful homes, much nicer than the tiny place I'd been given. Smoke curled from the chimneys, candles illuminating the windows, and delicious smells wafting to me through the curtains of my ride.

Suddenly, the door to the home directly in front of us opened, a stout woman with a slight frown on her features waving to the driver. She said something in French, waving him down the road, and we were moving again. After a brief ride down a side alleyway, we found ourselves in a stable yard, horse stalls down one side and the back of the house we'd just been in front of on the other.

"Mark?" Tristan O'Rourke appeared in the window, a strained smile on his handsome face. "Get out, why don't ye? We're having a bit of a situation."

His black, chin length hair was soaked through and sticking to his face in places. Green eyes watched me with an unwilling plea for help, his lips pressed together tightly as he stepped away, allowing me out of the carriage. Even his clothes—a white shirt and black breeches—were thoroughly saturated, sticking to him like they were skin tight. His boots were caked in mud, a sword held in one hand.

"What's going on?" I asked, alarmed by his appearance. "Where's Sam?"

Jerking his head to the other side of the muddy courtyard, he sighed, suddenly looking exhausted.

Following the motion, I finally saw her, standing in the far corner, hacking away at a crudely put together dummy. The sword in her hand was flying every which way as she stabbed and swung, spinning her body a different direction each time. Even more waterlogged than her husband, she didn't seem to notice the storm pelting her, all her attention focused on the mannequin in front of her.

"She's still practicing?" I asked, surprised.

"She insists," Tristan muttered. "I can't even get her to come in out of the storm. She's been like this for the past three hours."

Samantha had often asked members of the crew, including Tristan and myself, to help her practice her sword play on the return journey. Her maid, a French girl named Abella, had taken part as well. I'd assumed once she had returned home, she would relax, though, feeling the safety and comfort her home brought her.

"How often does she do this?" Speaking in an undertone, I glanced over Tristan again, noting that he seemed very agitated.

"Every damn day. All day. I can't hardly speak to her without having a sword shoved in my face." The Irishman sighed, his concern finally showing through his current frustrations. "I'm worried, Mark. I've never seen the lass act like this before."

"Ready!"

Abella's voice sounded from inside one of the horse stalls and she appeared soon after, wiping her long hair from her eyes. She, too, was soaked to the bone, her shirt and pants sticking to her like honey on bread. Reddened fingers grasped the hilt of a sword, mud smeared across her face and one arm.

Turning quickly, Sam abandoned her dummy, sinking into a defensive pose as she watched Abella approach her tiredly. "You sure you're up for it?" she called, noticing the slowness of her movements.

"*Oui*. I'm not going inside until you do." Finding her own pose, the two girls began to circle around each other, watching carefully for the first sign of attack.

Suddenly, Sam leapt forward, stabbing her blade in the same direction. Thinking that Abella was about to be skewered, I sucked in a deep breath, but the shout never reached my lips.

Abella deflected the attack with ease, parrying and delivering her own backhanded blow as quickly as a snake attacks its prey.

Samantha, dodging the blow with mere millimeters to spare, sidestepped the maid, swiping at her legs. She hit her opponent with the flat side of her sword, slapping the metal hard against the poor girl's boots.

Hissing, Abella doubled over, drawing her leg in close for protection, but Samantha already had the upper hand.

Reaching out, she shoved Abella, hard, knocking her into the mud. Raising her sword high, she moved to strike at the poor woman again, a crazy fire in her eyes I'd never seen before.

"Enough!" Tristan's voice rang through the space as he strode forward, grabbing Sam by the wrist and yanking her away. "Can't you see you've hurt her? Again? You've done enough today!"

"Let go of me," Sam hissed, pulling her arm away. "And I'm not finished! I'll be done when I say I'm done, not when you decide I've had enough. I can think for myself and I intend to be able to fight for myself, so either help me or get out of the way!" She shoved him, another action I'd never seen from her, and made to go back to Abella, sword in hand.

Growling, Tristan raised his blade, moving forward with purpose. Before I even knew what was happening, he had engaged Sam in another fight, not pulling back on any of his attacks.

Abella, scrambling to get out of the way, seemed terrified as she watched them, her eyes wide and tear filled. Hurrying to her side, I grabbed her icy hand and pulled her away from the fray, backing up against the wall of the house. Removing my coat, I wrapped it around her shaking shoulders, rubbing her arms to try and warm her up. As I held her, cradling her against my chest, we both watched in growing horror as the couple continued to fight in front of us.

Sam had gotten good. *Really* good. It occurred to me that she hadn't learned all of this in a week and must have been practicing her fighting whenever she was alone on the ship as well. She had a rage in her that was to be expected after what she'd been through, but I never would have thought she would direct it at Tristan like this.

The pair moved through the space like a machine, swiping and dodging, stabbing and jumping around. The rain made the ground slick and dangerous, both of them slipping every now and then, only to quickly regain their footing. Whenever it appeared that Sam might gain the upper hand and win, Tristan somehow thwarted her, causing her to shout in frustration. Finally, he drew up short in front of her, shoving her to the ground as she had Abella. Throwing the point of his sword into the ground by his feet, breathing heavily, he put a foot on her chest, keeping her from getting up.

"I said that was enough," he breathed, glaring at her. "Ye have hurt Abella more than once today. Ye're going to catch yer death in this storm. Sparring practice is done."

"Get off me!" Grabbing his foot, she squirmed beneath him, trying to wiggle her way free. The action only buried her deeper in the mud, though, making her even more frustrated than she had been. "Let me go, damn it!" she screamed, now slapping any part of him that she could reach.

"Stop it, Sam!" he yelled. "Can't ye see ye're frightening everyone?" Removing his foot, he reached down and pulled her up, shaking her hard. "They're afraid!"

Suddenly, I realized what he was saying was true. The coachman who'd brought me was cowering in his seat, Abella hidden in my arms. I could feel the look of horror on my own face and saw it reflected on another maid who was peering through one of the windows in the house.

"They're afraid?" Sam asked incredulously, shoving away from him. "What about me?" She was yelling, standing her ground in front of him, not even caring about everyone watching.

"I'm afraid! I don't feel safe in this house!"

Surprised, Tristan took a step back. "What do ye have to fear here? No one could even think to get to ye while I'm here."

"What about when you're not?" she asked, fuming. "Because you weren't here. You weren't here when Randall broke in and killed all the servants. You weren't here when they broke down the door to our room. You weren't here when they shot Abella. You weren't here when they carried me away, beating me and your unborn daughter inside me. You weren't here!" Her voice cracked, tears streaming down her face in the rain. "You weren't here to protect me. You weren't there, on Randall's ship, or in Nassau, or in the desert, when he caught me again."

Her voice softened then, as if the expression of pain and regret that was spreading across Tristan's face had made her realize how cruel she was acting.

"I don't blame you. Not at all. But I must do this, Tristan. I need to learn how to defend myself and the people around me. If I'd known how to do it before, maybe . . ."

She stopped, staring at the ground, all the fight seeming to seep out of her in one instant.

"Maybe Rachel would be alive." Tristan's voice caught as he said it, a surge of emotion coming from him as a tear of his own rolled over his cheek. "Aye, lass. Maybe the bairn would be. Ye cannot blame yerself for her death, though." He paused, clearing his throat. "I thought we had shared our feelings on this before."

"We have," she responded roughly, sniffing heavily and drawing a sleeve across her face. "But I'm done talking. It's not just Rachel. Abella was shot—Mark, too—and all those men went in to battle and lost their lives because I'm not bloody good enough with a sword. I'm tired of having to be rescued. So, you can either help me, or you can get out of my way."

Reaching down, she picked up her sword and moved toward the dummy again, chest heaving. Before she had taken three steps, though, Tristan gathered her into his arms, picking her clean up, and started toward the house.

"Put me down!" she shouted, kicking and hitting him.

"Ye'll not catch yer death today, lass. Whether ye like it or not, ye're goin' inside."

Striding past the two of us, he carried his upset wife in through the door as if we weren't even there, his features drawn and tired. Even after the door had closed, I could still hear her shouting at him, calling him all sorts of names before she finally broke down crying and the house fell somewhat silent.

"*M-m-merci, M-monsieur*," Abella squeaked, still trembling against me. "I couldn't quite get my feet underneath me in time."

Turning my attention back to the girl in my arms, I felt a sudden pang of realization to her condition. "Let's get you inside," I said, quickly. "Hopefully you aren't sick already."

Keeping my arm around her shoulder, I gently guided her to the back door, opening it and revealing a long hallway. At the other end, I could see the front door and a set of stairs. To the right was a storage room, the kitchen directly to the left. Guiding her that way, we settled in front of the large fire, and I asked the maid standing nearby to fetch some towels.

"*Merci*," Abella said again as I removed her boots, followed by thick, wet socks. Bright red, clammy toes rested in my hands and I felt a sense of alarm shoot through me.

"Here." Scooting the chair closer to the hearth, I placed her feet as close to the flames as I dared.

She sighed, leaning forward to warm her freezing hands as well, her hair continuing to drip on the floor and into her lap. My coat was the only semi-dry thing on her, but I was sure the inside had long become wet after wrapping her in it.

Rising, I went to the table, picking up a clean glass. A teapot sat beside it, still full of warm liquid, and I poured a cupful, hoping the drink would help warm her insides as well.

"You are too kind." Laughing slightly, she took a

long sip, leaning back in the chair and closing her eyes. There were dark circles under them, a feature that had been absent when she was on board the ship just a week earlier.

"How bad is it?" I asked quietly, glancing to see if anyone was in the doorway.

"This was a worse day. There are many nightmares that she suffers with. The whole house can hear the screaming, the neighbors most likely, as well. Tristan is the only one who can help calm her during those. She fights with him quite often, though. I confess; I'd hoped your arrival would help soothe her some. That was why I invited you over today. It didn't make any difference in the end, did it?" She smiled lightly, staring at me.

"You were the one who sent the invitation?" Surprised, it suddenly occurred to me that the reason I'd shown up at such a bad time was because Tristan and Sam hadn't been expecting me. The revelation also stung my heart some, knowing that Sam hadn't sent for me after all. She hadn't missed me or wanted to see me. I'd simply been summoned because the maid thought I might be able to help calm her.

"Samantha misses you." It was as if Abella could read my thoughts. "She would never ask for you to come. For Tristan's sake."

Of course. They both knew I was in love with her. Sammy loved Tristan, though, despite her earlier tantrum. She wouldn't do anything to hurt him, not on purpose. Tristan probably didn't want another man with feelings for his wife around, either. I was being ignored for the sake of their marriage.

"I've missed you, too. You were the only one

besides those two who would talk to me on the ship." Sitting up, she took another sip of her tea. "I thought the house might be a little happier if you were to come call. I should have picked a better day, it seems." Sighing again, she wiggled her toes, as if she were just now getting the feeling returned in them.

"Here are your towels, Monsieur." The maid from before came through the doorway, carrying the folded fabric in her arms.

"I'll leave you to change," I said to Abella, turning toward the exit.

"Don't forget your coat," she said, struggling to detangle herself from it.

Holding up my hands as a sign for her not to worry, I continued to inch toward the door.

"Will you not see Samantha, then?" Her expression fell, her attempt to remove the coat falling short.

"Do you think she wants to see anyone right now?" I asked, skeptical. "I don't think she even realized it was me out there just now."

"I did."

Turning toward the sound, I felt a sigh of relief leave me as I examined her. Leaning against the wall, just inside the kitchen, she looked like she had just gone an entire year without sleep. She'd changed, her form now clad in a dressing gown and overcoat instead of her mud covered clothes. Red eyes stared at me, her face tear streaked, hair braided and resting over her shoulder.

"Sammy." My voice was quiet and filled with worry, everything inside me wanting to take her in my arms and comfort her.

105

She heard as much, smiling tightly as she peered at the floor. After a moment, she finally met my gaze again, lips trembling. "I'm sorry." Her voice broke and she cleared her throat, shaking her head. "I'm fine, really." Smoothing her hands down her dress, she blinked a few times, trying to steady herself.

Tristan appeared in the doorway behind her, his clothes changed as well, and put a hand on her shoulder. Leaning in close, he nuzzled her hair muttering something in her ear. Whatever it was, she visibly relaxed, a slow breath escaping her as she took his hand.

Turning his attention from his wife, Tristan smiled at the rest of us in the room. "Are ye well, Abella?" he asked, looking past me.

"As well as ever, Monsieur." She sounded tired, but was otherwise friendly, beaming at the pair like they were royalty.

Sammy bit her lip, obviously still upset, her eyes watering once more. "Abella, I—"

"I was thinking Monsieur Bell could stay for dinner. There is a chess set in the sitting room that is practically growing dust. I, for one, would like to see him try his hand against Monsieur O'Rourke. We already know he would lose in a game of cards." Abella smiled slyly, refusing to let Sam finish her apology to her.

"Hey now," I retorted, trying to help ease the mood as well. "I'm not half bad at cards." Folding my arms uncomfortably, I tried to ignore the awkward air that was practically suffocating the room.

"I'm not bad at any cards," Tristan added, earning a feeble laugh from Sam. The sound lightened everyone considerably and he nodded toward me, still grasping her hand tightly. "What say ye, Mark? Do ye fancy a match?"

I knew I should've said no. There were issues here, things they needed to sort out as a family. However, staring at the pair of them like that, Sam with tears in her eyes and Tristan with mild pleading in his, I knew I couldn't say no.

"If only to learn your strategies for next time." Grinning, I gave Sam my most encouraging expression, acting like nothing had happened.

She hesitated, looking as if she might burst into a heaping mess again, and then nodded. "I'll let Madame Fairfax know you'll be joining us, then."

The air in the room seemed to relax after that and I felt my heart sputter at the thought of getting to spend the rest of the day with her. Maybe Abella was right. Maybe it was better for me to be here, to help distract her from the horrors she was facing. If that were the case, I would be here every day, no matter the cost or hardship on myself.

Tristan, seeming to be thinking along the same lines, gave me a cautious stare and then nodded, moving to go down the hall. "Let's see if you're any good at chess, Bell."

"Ye look fine."

Tristan, having mistaken my uncomfortable fidgeting as concern for my appearance, continued to move around the tiny shop, stopping to appreciate any and everything that caught his fancy. Paintings, knickknacks, fabrics, seashells, and every other possible item that could be sold here was on display. Rugs hung down from ropes overhead that had been stretched across the courtyard of the large building we were now visiting. They boxed us in, making it impossible not to talk to the owner of the establishment. It was rather good marketing on his behalf, seeing as how there must have been at least one hundred other merchants crammed in the space. At the moment, though, I was more preoccupied with loathing my clothes than admiring the wares.

"How do you not feel like you're suffocating in these things?" I asked under my breath, still tugging at my necktie. It seemed that there were somehow more ruffles on my outfit today, as if the number of frills directly correlated to how important one was in society. By that standard, though, I should have appeared less like a decoration and been dressed more like Tristan.

He somehow managed to still look commanding and handsome in his formal wear. He wore no wig—which was the only way in which we matched—his hair swept back in an artful swoop, as if the sea breeze had just then ruffled the locks into the perfect style. A brown coat covered a matching vest and white shirt, the collar buttoning high around his neck, keeping his plain necktie in place with ease. The closest thing to resembling a ruffle there was the knot he'd tied to hold it together. Also, infuriatingly, he somehow managed to pull of the stockings, his lower half seeming like he'd never missed a leg day at the gym in his life.

I, on the other hand, was basically a blue cream puff. There were frills around my neck, sticking out of the sleeves of my jacket, running around the cuff of my pants, hell, there was even a small flower design sewn into my socks. If I'd somehow managed to jump into the sky, everyone would think I was simply a funny shaped cloud, floating along without a care.

Glancing around, I could see other men dressed in the same fashion. This was the style of this time, when France was increasingly becoming the center for beauty and fine apparel. I should've been grateful that The Order had gone so far out of their way to make me fit in with the high society. The more I looked at Tristan and his simple elegance, though, the more I wished they wouldn't have bothered.

"How much for these?" Tristan held up a pair of brass bookends shaped like spheres, staring at the seller happily.

The man told the price and Tristan shook his head, thanking him anyway.

"We shouldn't be here," I muttered, the heat getting to me for a moment. "We should be searching for Randall."

"You sound like my wife," he replied, grinning ruefully as he set the objects down. There was an underlying harshness to his tone, though, and I saw his gaze dart outside the shop for a moment, worry in his eyes.

Looking out myself, I watched Samantha and Abella shopping at the table across the lane. It was covered in shining jewelry and fabrics, but none of the products held a candle to the women in front of them.

Feeling my breath catch, I watched as Sam turned, the green and black skirts of her dress rustling over the dirt, the edges browned from dragging across the ground. She hated wearing anything remotely like a corset, we all knew that, but she was so tall and regal wearing one now, the stays decorated to match the rest of the outfit, gold threading creating an intricate pattern across the bodice. Lace gathered around her elbows and across the top of her breasts, the whiteness of it making her appear even more tan than normal. The way she'd curled and piled her hair under her wide, black hat made her neck seem to go on forever, a simple, black ribbon tied gently tied at the base. She'd taken to wearing black cuffs around her wrists, I'd noticed, to hide the scarring there. They should have drawn attention to the place, but instead, somehow, made her entire ensemble come together.

Seeing me staring, she smiled softly, nodding her head in my direction. Her gaze moved past me then, to her husband, and her face flushed some, much like the many other women who had been admiring him all day.

Embarrassed and somewhat perturbed, I quickly looked away, my gaze falling on Abella. Surprised to feel my breath catching again, I examined the young woman in awe, wondering how I'd never noticed her impeccable ability to dress not only Sam, but herself as well.

She didn't hold herself in a manner that called attention, nor did she dress to impress, it seemed, but there was something about the way her light yellow bodice clung to her form, belling out into the matching skirt, her brown shoes barely visible from under white petticoats. It was a simple gown, with a stomacher piece being the only form of decoration I could see, and somehow seemed to have been made for only her. On Sam, the dress would have been plain and unimaginative, something to do chores in. On Abella, it was like staring at a princess who knew she didn't need jewels to attract attention. Also tan from being at sea, she seemed more like a Mediterranean goddess than the small, pale thing she'd been when I'd taken her inside my coat for warmth and safety. Long, black curls were pinned loosely around her head, a small pin placed above her ear. It was the only jewelry she wore, but it shone like a diamond.

Glancing up, she, too, saw me staring and flushed, looking back down at the ground as she smiled. Suddenly, I realized I was blushing as well and cleared my throat, turning around to study the inside of the store again.

Abella and I had a curious relationship. I'd never seen her before the way I did just now, but she held a special place in my heart. She was the one who had initially patched me up after being shot, her small hands making quick work of the wound in my chest. It had been her who asked for a real doctor to see me and stood by my side as I was told the bullet had stuck into my rib. It was a miracle I had survived at all.

We had sailed for The Mission in what would become Texas, and she had been my friend, visiting with me and continually checking to make sure I was healing well. Somehow, she'd known I was having a hard time, watching Sam with Tristan for the first time, and she'd been there in the only way she knew how.

When we were ambushed by Black Knights in the cove in Texas, Abella had been there again, loading my guns and passing them off. I'd almost had a heart attack when she followed me onto the opponents' vessel, sword in hand. We'd had an unspoken bond during the fight, though; we protected each other.

I could easily recall when she'd slipped, falling to the deck as a Black Knight came at her with his sword. Without even thinking, I'd defended her, helping her to her feet. When I went overboard in the explosion that sank the ship, she had pulled me up, out of the water, saving me from drowning.

After that, I left her to go after Randall and Sam. We didn't see each other until the battle inside the mountain was over. Something was different then, like she blamed me for leaving her behind.

It had never been the same.

Glancing over my shoulder at her again, I felt the embers of that friendship warm some. We'd spoken together on the journey home, yes, but only about superficial things. Now that the excitement of war was settling, perhaps we would find our balance as friends again. Heaven knew I needed a friend right now.

Upon seeing me watching again, Abella grinned outright, checking both ways before hurrying across the lane to meet me. "You look like a pastry," she said in a matter of fact tone as soon as she was close enough for me to hear.

Snorting, I smiled, offering her my arm. She took it easily, a slight redness to her cheeks, and we moved toward the next stall, silent for a moment.

"Are you excited to be visiting the Temple?" Her tone was curious and innocent, the smile she gave me sweet and teasing at the same time.

Glancing around at the old fortress, I shrugged. This place had been one of the great strongholds of The Order before they were very publicly demonized and executed in the thirteen hundreds. I'd since learned it was only the Black Knights who were executed and kept imprisoned here, but the knowledge made me view the place in a more negative light. So many bad things had happened here. Who knew how many secrets were still hidden in these walls?

"It's not exactly what I expected," I confessed, stopping to stare at a collection of quills and ink. "I thought it would be more . . . empty."

Laughing, her eyes sparkled as she peered around. "It was at one point, I'm sure. Over time, it filled with people who loved the arts and finer things of life. Many of the souls you see now probably live inside the abandoned Temple itself. I know for a fact that the musicians who play at the gate live inside the old chapel with many others who are otherwise homeless. Despite its grim history, I would say the Temple still has a legacy to uphold, *oui*?"

"You know the musicians personally?" Grabbing onto the one new piece of information she'd given me, I nudged her on to the next stand, guiding her through the crowd of people around us.

"*Oui.* I stayed here a few nights after leaving my father. Not as a beggar—I sang for my bread."

Stopping in surprise, I looked at her fully once more. "You stayed here? I thought Father Torres put you up in Notre Dame."

"He did. I was only here for three nights."

"But . . ." Confused, I looked at her hand resting on my arm. The scars from when her own father had tried to cut her hand off were still visible.

Flexing her fingers, she cleared her throat, causing me to glance up at her face again. "I was . . . proud. The people here helped bandage me up the best they could. After the three days, though, I knew I would die if I didn't get help, but I was a wanted thief. I knew if I went to Hospital that they would turn me over to the law. So, I went to the cathedral and claimed sanctuary. The priests paid the baker I'd robbed and the charge against me was dropped. After that, the Father introduced me to Samantha. You know the rest."

Placing my hand over hers, I stared at her intently. "I'm sorry," I said softly. "Truly. To be so young and to have suffered so much doesn't seem fair."

Clearing her throat, she shrugged, looking down at our touching fingers. "What is life, if not one trial after another? It's not the suffering that matters in the end. It's the person you were during the hardship. A test from God cannot be failed if you rely on him in all things and trust that they have happened for a reason." Lifting her head, she met my gaze, a sad smile playing on her lips. "Even now, we must each suffer. If we are lucky, we will get our reward before we are in Heaven."

Surprised by the maturity of her statement, I simply stared at her with wide eyes. When I finally found my voice, it was quiet and hoarse, as if I were afraid of hurting her feelings. "You were a good person before your trials, Abella, and you're still a good person after. Whether or not it was a test from God, you didn't deserve the things that happened to you. If you ask me, you should get whatever reward you desire right now."

Laughing lightly, she blushed again, flexing her fingers under mine. "You are too kind, *Monsieur*. I'm afraid that if you say too much more, it will all go to my head."

Grinning, I opened my mouth to reply, but stopped short, having caught sight of Samantha once more. She was with Tristan, holding his hand, pointing to something at one of the stands, her face lit up like the morning sun as she spoke with him.

The all too familiar stabbing of my heart seized me and I felt my features fall, a sadness filling me as I watched them.

Abella, confused, turned and saw them as well, her shoulders slumping some. Removing her hand from my arm, she smoothed the front of her dress, turning to face me again. "Samantha is as beautiful as ever today."

"She is," I agreed.

Abella straightened, as if squaring herself for battle and I suddenly realized I'd hurt her feelings. Scrambling to find some way to make up for it, I gaped for a second, looking around as if I were hoping someone would feed me a line to say.

"You do a wonderful job of dressing her," I rushed to say. "I bet she'd be lost without you."

"The woman would wear a pair of breeks and a loose shirt every day if I didn't insist she at least clothe herself like a proper lady." The hasty compliment seemed to smooth her ruffled edges some and she sighed. Then, everything about her seemed to deflate and her voice caught in her throat, her gaze turned toward the ground. "She would still be beautiful, even without my help. Excuse me, *Monsieur*." Turning sharply, she walked away, her hands held tightly together in front of her. I didn't know if I'd been imagining it or not, but it had looked like there were tears gathering in her eyes as she dashed away, her lip trembling as she held her head high.

"Abella!" I called out, feeling like I'd majorly goofed up our friendship, yet again. Guilt coursed through me, creating a pain in my heart, and I jogged a few steps in the direction she'd gone.

"Abella!"

The group of shoppers closest to me all stared in my direction, watching as I gaped after her. A few of them whispered, some even giggling, before I gave them all a glare that would silence even the chattiest of women. Scattering, they finally cleared, but Abella was still nowhere to be seen.

"Is everything alright?" Coming up beside me, Samantha watched as Abella disappeared into the crowd, curiosity written on her face. "What did you say to her?"

"Honestly? I have no idea. We were talking and then she left." Raising my hands in surrender, I continued to look around, hoping to catch sight of her so I could properly apologize for whatever it was I'd done to upset her.

Sam raised an eyebrow, clearly not believing me, and folded her arms. "What were you talking about?"

Flustered, I glared at her, huffing. Normally, I

loved talking with Sam. Right now, though, I didn't much feel like telling her how I'd been ogling her in her dress. "We were talking about you and what a good dresser she is, if you must know."

"What's amiss?" Tristan stepped beside Sam, putting his hand on the small of her back and pulling her into the crook of his arm. "The lass acted as if she were ready to break down right in the aisle."

"What? No! I have no idea what I did." What were they talking about? We were just talking! Abella had been fine one moment and then she was upset the next.

A flash of thoughtfulness and then understanding passed over Sam's face and she nodded, picking her skirts up out of the way. "I should go get her. We'll meet you at the door." Popping onto her toes, she kissed Tristan quickly on the lips, grinning as she pulled away. "Don't you go in without us!"

"I wouldn't dream of it, love." Laughing, he grabbed her hand and kissed it as she moved away, smiling like a man who had found a gold mine. Watching her leave, he muttered something in a language I didn't understand, placing a hand over his heart.

"I didn't quite catch that." It sounded colder than I'd intended, but Tristan still treated me as a friend all the same.

"*Grá mo chroí*—love of my life. I've not seen this side of her in some time. Did ye know, she only insisted on one hour's worth of sword practice this morning before she agreed to get ready?" He continued to grin, basking in the moment as she wandered away. "She seems to do much better when she knows she will be out and about. It helps when ye come to visit her as

118

well." He sighed then, some of his happiness diminishing. Pausing, he glanced over at me, as if trying to decide a difficult decision, and then nodded.

"Ye know I can not let pass the feelings ye have for my wife, Bell. I will be the first man to admit that it's difficult to see her struggles lighten so when ye are around. But, ye were there for her when I couldn't be. I think ye remind her that she can be strong—of who she was before . . . Rachel." He swallowed hard, frowning as he looked in the direction the women had gone. "She's still broken, *mo shíorghrá*. So much so that I can't seem to find all her pieces on my own."

Staring after her as well, I felt the overwhelming sense of guilt build inside me once more. I had some of those missing pieces. He knew it, I knew it. There was no use in denying it. I'd been picking up the pieces of her soul as it shattered all around me since the day Randall dropped her in front of me, bloodied and beaten. The only problem was that I didn't know how to give them back, or even if I could.

She was holding me together just as much as I was her.

Motioning for me to join him off to the side, he stepped over to a section of wall, peering around to see if anyone was listening. When he was satisfied that he could speak freely, he hedged again, muttering to himself in Gaelic.

"Will ye allow me to petition for ye to join my crew?" Tristan asked suddenly. "I know it's hard for ye, being around her, but it's good for her. Wherever my ship sales my wife is sure to go; ye'd not have to part from her until ye were ready."

Shocked yet again, I gaped at him. "I'm not a

member of The Order. If anything, they'll see the brand on my arm and hang me right on sight."

"Ye would be safe, so long as I was captain. I'm sure Bevard would agree to induct ye to The Order, should ye wish, as well."

He watched me expectantly, eyes searching my face for any hint of answer. "This isn't an easy thing for myself that I'm asking, Bell. But, it's not for me. It's for Samantha. I'm not so blind and proud as to not see that ye do her good. I can put my own insecurities aside for her. Can ye?"

Giving him a hard stare, I folded my arms. He was really laying it on thick, trying to get me to agree. Why? Was Sam worse off than I thought? The fact he was even asking for help was a huge sign that she might be. What kind of friend would I be if I didn't stay to help her? Could I put my own fears and pains aside to help her again?

Finally, I sighed and nodded. "I'll think about it. I don't have much else to do here, though, do I?"

"*A dhuine choir*!" Sounding thoroughly pleased, he clapped me on the shoulder, motioning for me to move ahead. "We'd best get inside, now. It's not wise to keep the Grand Master waiting when it comes to a meeting like this."

Leading the way, he wove through the crowds of people, stopping here and there among the vendors, sharing a friendly word, before stopping at a store where the merchandise overflowed into one of the actual rooms of the old Temple.

Tapping his finger on the table, he waited for someone to come assist him.

"May I help you, *Monsieur*?" It was a small

Englishman, with eyes so wide he might have been an owl in a past life.

"I inquired about a paining last week and was told it has been finished?"

"It would be inside then, *Monsieur*." Stepping to the side, he allowed Tristan to pass.

Motioning for me to come, Tristan strode inside, weaving through the tall aisles of products. When we reached the wall at the back of the room, Samantha and Abella were already there, waiting. They had been whispering together but stopped as soon as we appeared.

Abella, glancing at me quickly, turned away from us, wiping her face for some reason. Sam, putting her hand on her shoulder, smiled at Tristan, nodding.

"We're here," he said to me.

"This is the door?" I asked incredulously, looking at the solid stone barrier.

Reaching out, Tristan tapped the same pattern he'd been doing on the table, the rhythm sounding as if it were second nature to him. Suddenly, the wall cracked, a rectangular opening appearing. As the stones slid across the floor, I saw a long passageway behind the secret entrance, leading down into the earth. A guard stood duty, apparently having opened the door when the correct password was tapped onto the rocks.

"*Oh mon*," Abella whispered, her eyes going round.

"Wait till you see the rest of it," Sam said under her breath.

Passing through the secret entrance, Tristan led us farther and farther down the hall, each step taking us to a new point underground, until I thought we must be at least a full two stories beneath the surface. Finally, we turned down another hallway and doors began to appear on each side. They had names and symbols carved into them, like a conference center in a big hotel would use to identify where a group would be gathered. The floor, plain stone before, was now of a higher quality, the walls decorated in many fine paintings and tapestries. At the end of this hall, a large, double-doored room sat waiting, the oak entrance thrown open in welcome. Inside, I could see several of the crew from our adventure in Arizona gathered around a table. The buzz from their chatting felt warm and welcoming and I found myself smiling, happy to be among people I knew again.

"Capítan O'Rourke."

Captain Lomas, the man who had helped lead the Templars into the desert and fight in the mountain, held out his hand to Tristan, shaking it firmly. "It is good to see you again, friend. I did not think I would miss your company, but I find myself sorely lacking in good jokes this past week."

Laughing, Tristan clapped him on the shoulder, appearing genuinely happy to see him as well.

"Señoras," Lomas added stiffly, bowing to Samantha and Abella. It was clear that he was much less pleased to see the two women again.

"Señor Bell." Shaking my hand as well, he smiled tightly, the scar on the side of his face making him look like a monster you would find hiding under your bed.

A banging on the table caught everyone's attention then and we all turned, watching the ancient man who had slammed the cup down repeatedly. He seemed as if he would topple over at any minute, his hand shaking slightly as he placed his cup on the table top. Balding, with white hair patches, he could have used the wig I refused to wear. Still, he was dressed in his finest, his voice strong and steady as he addressed the group.

"Thank you all for being on time," he said smoothly, smiling. "*S'il vous plaît*, have a seat."

The room rustled as those who were still standing found a place at the table. Sam and Tristan ended up just beside the old man, while Abella and I claimed seats a few places down.

"For those of you who I have not yet had the honor of becoming acquainted with, please allow me to introduce myself. I am Bevard, the Grand Master of The Order." Pausing to cough into his handkerchief, he cleared his throat and continued. "You've been called here today to help make an account of the past several months and your mission in the Americas. While I was briefed on most of what occurred while I was at the King's Court this past week, I would ask that you leave nothing out. These are trying times among our Brotherhood and I would wish that we are able to find the roots of corruption on this day and cast them into the fire."

"Here, here!" One of the men called, raising his flask and drinking from it.

The room shared a chuckle, the seriousness of the situation lifting some, and Bevard smiled. Then, his attention turning to me, he pursed his lips. "Mark Bell, *oui*?"

"Yes, sir."

He nodded, settling into his chair and folding his hands together over his stomach. "Would you tell us how you came to be on Thomas Randall's ship? From the beginning."

I told them everything. The words flowed out of me like water, at times seeming impossible to stop. Samantha had been the only other person I'd told the story to in full, and even then, I hadn't shared each detail the way I did now. Wide eyes watched as I explained Oak Isle, the Treasure Pit, and how I worked on the wreck of Randall's ship in the future. It was as if the whole room was holding its breath when I told them of the vase and how I had opened it, only to be caught in a sand storm and carried through time.

They heard each Apache name, discovered each pang of loneliness I'd suffered in Mexico City. I told them of Angelica and how I'd run from her, fearing I was falling in love. I explained my fear of changing the future, my decision to finally take my place at sea, the place I knew best because of my university degree in piratical history. I told them of my training in medicine and how I'd worked with the ship doctor, only to be pressed into service by Randall when he attacked us.

Confessing to every murder I'd committed under his rule made me feel sick. There was no judgement in their eyes, though. They understood what choices I'd made and the consequences that had followed. When I finally arrived at the point where Samantha had shown back up in my life, I stopped. It felt like it had been hours. Maybe it had been. Either way, I felt a lightness that I hadn't before. The air around me was filled with acceptance. For the first time since I'd arrived in Paris, I felt like I was part of the brotherhood again. Looking up from the table, I glanced around, seeing the supportive faces around me. Samantha was smiling sadly, her hand clutched in Tristan's. Beside me, Abella stared at me with tears in her eyes.

"*Merci*, Monsieur Bell. I am sure it was not easy for you to share all of that." Bevard, staring at me evenly, regarded me for another moment and then turned to his right, where Tristan was sitting.

"Monsieur O'Rourke. Would you care to pick up from there?"

Tristan spoke of The Order's attempt to corner Randall in London, but it had been a distraction from the real objective of the Black Knights. While The Order was looking for them in England, they had stolen away Samantha. The travesty had not been discovered for several days, during which Abella had been shot and left to die in Sam's room. By some miracle, the bullet had only grazed her, though, and she had managed to bandage herself enough that she was still alive when Tristan arrived.

"And what did you tell him?" Bevard asked, addressing her for the first time.

"I told him that his wife had been kidnapped," she said, her voice shaky. "And described the men the best I could remember."

"Could you describe them for us again, now?"

"Um." She looked around nervously, twisting her

hands together under the table. "*O-oui, Monsieur*."

Silently, I took one of her hands, squeezing it reassuringly. "It's okay," I muttered loud enough for only her to hear. "No one is here to judge you, just to listen."

Nodding, she squeezed back, holding on tightly, and cleared her throat. "I saw Thomas Randall. He was in the front of the group. At the time I didn't know his name, but I would never forget his face, nor the way he talked to Samantha."

She delivered her part of the tale quickly after that, grasping my hand under the table the entire time, her fingers trembling every so often.

Others were called upon to give their story, Captain Lomas speaking for a time, Tristan answering questions every now and then as well. Finally, Bevard turned to Sammy, smiling kindly.

"Would you tell us what happened to you?"

She hesitated at first, clearly pained by having to relive it all again. Whenever she fumbled, she would look to me for reassurance, finding whatever it was she needed to continue in my face. By the time she had finished, Tristan had joined in her tears, the pain they shared together obviously very real to everyone in the room. The worst part had been Rachel—their unborn child. Abella had cried freely as Sam spoke of burying the baby, knowing that her father would never get to see her.

After the entire tale had been recounted, Bevard sighed, closing his eyes. All was silent for several minutes, before he stood and began pacing. "Let us reconcile the things we can."

"The treasure. We know it is safe in the mountain,

guarded by the Apache. I have also decided there will be a special team dedicated to protecting it as well. It will be a team unlike any of our others, as it is not sea-bound. I will announce the particulars, as well as those assigned to said mission after I have pondered it longer.

"*Dáinsleif*—the Norse sword that the Apache gifted to Samantha. Where is it now?"

"At our home, here, in Paris," Tristan answered. "Kept under lock and key. A weapon that can not be put away until it deals a killing blow is not something we want others to get their hands on."

"I agree. You may lock it up in the Temple, should you so wish. I trust that you will protect it with your very lives." Bevard sighed, rubbing his face.

"Captain Lomas. Tell me more of this ship that Randall escaped with."

"*Skíðblaðnir*," Lomas replied. "An enchanted vessel. It will carry anything, no matter the weight or size. The vessel is also capable of travel over water, land, and air. It may be folded to fit inside a mere pocket. Randall could walk the streets of Paris with it and we would be none the wiser. It is also worth remembering that the snake got away with the belt of Thor, so not only can he escape easily, but he will be ten times stronger than any one man, so long as he is wearing the garment."

Pursing his lips, Bevard sat again. "It would appear that our foe has managed to outsmart us yet again."

The entire room shifted uncomfortably at that, glances of worry exchanged among each other. A few moments of silence passed while Bevard thought with his eyes closed and then he stood.

"Captain Lomas. You and your crew are given one week of shore leave. You and I will reconvene at that time to decide what path you should take now that your previous mission is fulfilled. I thank you all for your participation today and remind you that this meeting is being held in the strictest of confidence. Do not speak with anyone outside of this room about the things you have heard today. You are dismissed."

The crew rose practically as one, saluting and moving to leave the space. In less than a minute, only myself, Abella, Tristan, and Sam were left in the room.

"I apologize, my dear, for the hardships you have faced in this time. When we last met, I'd hoped that your trials were at an end." Smiling gently, Bevard patted Sam's hand.

"Thank you," she said, hiccupping after her emotional retelling.

"Mark Bell. I'd never in my life thought I'd meet one time traveler, let alone two." Grinning, he examined me once more. "You had quite the story to tell."

"Ten years is a lot of time to cover," I replied smoothly, leaning in my chair. Abella's hand still rested easily in mine, neither of us having let go as we listened to the harrowing tale we had lived through.

"If you should so desire, there is a spot here for you, among The Order. You may carry the brand of a Black Knight, but you are no scoundrel, that much is certain." He watched me intently and I felt myself stiffen some at the offer.

Abella, sensing my sudden distress, squeezed my hand, smiling as she watched.

"I had planned to ask for him to join my crew, should ye still be thinking I'm deserving of a ship, Grand Master." Tristan grinned at me as well, the formality of the meeting dwindling into nothing between the five of us.

"Pffft." Bevard rolled his eyes, shaking his head. "Deserving. Of course you're deserving, soldier. You're one of my best men."

Tristan blushed at the compliment, coughing to cover up his surprise.

"Monsieur Bell is more than welcome to join your crew, should he wish. We have plenty of opportunities for him, if he feels his place is among the Knights. He would be a perfect fit for the new team I wish to station in this Arizona, as you called it. The Apache are already friendly with him and trust him. It would make matters much easier when it came to setting up a partnership with them."

Abella sucked in a sharp breath that only I heard, her grip on my hand tightening even more. Grimacing, I pulled my fingers out of her grasp, rubbing them gently.

"To be completely honest, Grand Master, I don't know what I would like to do." Frowning, I stared at the people around me. "For the longest time, all I could think of was finding a way to get home, to my own time. I know now that it isn't possible, at least not in any way that I'm aware of. Pandora's Box is at the bottom of the Treasure Pit, where it will stay until Samantha finds it in our own time.

"I left the Apache because I felt like I didn't have a purpose. I suppose I did the same thing in Mexico City. I don't want to feel useless here, too." Sighing, I smiled tightly. "I guess what I'm trying to say is, yes. I will join The Order."

A general murmur of happiness coursed through the room, though Abella seemed more worried than happy. It made me want to laugh; I knew she was thinking of the new team in the desert. She'd shared with me on our journey to Paris that she'd found the place horrible. It was very clear she was imagining what it would be like to live there full time at this moment.

"I would also like to stay with Samantha and Tristan, if it really is my choice," I added. "I was never much of a desert rat to begin with."

This made them all laugh, Abella especially. Relief washed over her features and she slumped back in her chair, as if she'd been waiting on the edge of her seat for my answer. "You will make a wonderful crewman," she said seriously. "Perhaps, even a doctor again, if you wanted."

"Maybe," I agreed. "I guess we'll have to wait and see what Captain O'Rourke wants me to do."

Looking over at him and Samantha, I felt my stomach twist. What was I doing, agreeing to go everywhere with them? I should have been staying away, learning to let go of my feelings. Instead, I was allowing myself to be deluded into the idea that Sammy still needed me, that I could still love her and not feel like it was killing me every day.

Tristan had asked for my help, though, hadn't he? He wanted me to be part of his crew. He wanted me to see Sam every day. He wanted me to help pull her out of the hole she was in. I was only doing what her husband wanted.

Grimacing, I tried not to show my sudden discomfort to the group. I was still walking a dangerous line when it came to Samantha and no one seemed to be noticing—only Abella. She always caught on to my thoughts about Sam and was somehow clued in when I was feeling upset or aggravated. She didn't approve of how I felt, I was sure, but she'd never said anything to me about it directly, choosing to let me find my own way down my path to self-destruction. For some odd reason, I had a feeling she would be there at the end, too, offering a hand to help me out of the pit once I'd hoisted Sam out ahead of me.

Frowning, she stared at the pair as well, biting her bottom lip. The look she gave me as she turned her attention to me was one of warning. *Don't mess up*, it said. *Don't act selfish and ruin what they have.*

"We'll have the initiation ceremony in a week, then," Bevard was saying, oblivious to my reservations and the warning Abella was giving me. "Until then, you all have shore leave as well. Enjoy your time off!"

Kneeling, I made sure to keep the great sword in my grasp steady, the point resting on the ground in front of me. Both hands rested on the hilt, the pommel and blade guard forming a cross across my face. An old sheet had been draped around my shoulders, meant to recreate the tabard of The Knights Templar from the age of the Crusades.

"The Grand Master will anoint ye with the oil, then," Tristan continued, standing before me in demonstration. "On yer forehead, shoulders, and chest, in the sign of the cross, savvy? While he does so, I will utter a warrior's prayer, as your guide through the initiation ceremony."

"What then?" Staring up at him, I resisted the urge to laugh. It felt like we were playing pretend, not preparing for my entrance into a secret society. This was a normal room, not a sacred, hidden space. Everything about this space was as plain as it could be, with a burning hearth, couches and seats to rest in, rugs on the floor, and green paint highlighting the walls around us. Behind me, the entrance to the hallway sat. To my right, a large window, looking over the outside world like some magic mirror waiting to tell a story.

And yet, it still somehow felt like the special place we imagined it to be.

Tristan, standing in front of the fireplace, nodded. "The Master will bid ye rise and introduce ye to the congregation as the newest member of the Brotherhood. After that, ye'll be a Templar for the rest of yer days." He smiled, offering his hand to me as I got up. "Any questions?"

"Was there always this much ceremony involved, or is this something you started in the past three hundred years?" Samantha, seated by the window in her combat training clothes, crossed her legs and folded her arms, eyeing her husband curiously. It wasn't the first time she'd butted in to our rehearsal, nor, did it seem, did she have any intention of stopping her inquisitive mind soon.

Regarding her with caution, Tristan cleared his throat. "Aye. I suppose it has always been done this way. Why do ye ask?"

"I'm just wondering if it will change at all in the future. Slavery will be illegal. Perhaps the portion detailing how new recruits are no better than slaves would be omitted. It also seems a bit redundant, asking three times if he understood what he was committing to. Would they really allow someone to back out at that point? When equality is finally recognized as a basic human right across the board, will they honor that truth? Will The Order finally allow women to join their ranks? Or will it always be a group of mysterious men, determined to keep the fairer sex from destroying their eternal man cave?" Snorting, she shook her head, peering out the glass pane beside her.

Tristan remained silent for a moment, closing his

eyes and placing his fingertips on the lids—a sign of him trying to control whatever it was he'd been about to say—before folding his hands together and looking at her once more.

"Samantha. I know ye do not approve of how many things are in this time, but ye must give the rest of us the chance to come to yer same conclusions. Yer time is hundreds of years away. That's decades worth of people evolving their minds and discovering new ideas. Centuries worth of change and progression. Ye can't demand that everyone fall in line with ye now. It doesn't work that way, lass."

"I don't need you to tell me how things work," she replied, rather sharply, turning her steely gaze on him once more. "I'm reminded of my place every day, thank you."

Sighing in frustration, he crossed his arms. "That's not what I meant, and ye know it." Turning to me for assistance, he tilted his head in her direction, a slight pleading in his eyes. I didn't know why, but he always seemed to think I had something to say that would get her to immediately drop the subject, especially when it came to matters of the future.

"I think what Tristan is trying to say is . . ." Floundering, I stared at her, trying to decide where I was going with the conversation. "The world needs time. Even in our century, there are still struggles with equality and acceptance. We've come a long way, but only because of the backbone that was built for us by history. We need to let the people of today build us our world of tomorrow. They aren't ready to be as progressive as we would like. Yet."

Raising an eyebrow at me, she turned her attention

to the window once more, arms still folded tightly across her body.

Glancing at Tristan, I shrugged, not thinking there was much more I could do to help the situation. Sam was in one of her moods again. It was easy enough to tell she was upset she was being excluded from the ceremony, happening in three days' time.

At first, she had asked most of the questions, seemingly fascinated by the whole process. Soon after, she apparently realized it was going to be a male only affair. I wasn't sure if she'd come to that conclusion herself or if Tristan had informed her, but either way, she had taken to tearing down the pomp and circumstance of it all whenever she had the chance. Her feelings were hurt, I realized, but there was nothing I could do about it. Technically speaking, we had already broken the rules by telling her how an initiation occurred. The information was supposed to remain secret and was sacred among the men, but Tristan hadn't even blinked when she asked him how it all came together.

The longer I watched them, the more I realized that the pair didn't have many secrets between them, if any. Their relationship was an open book, with everything shared. As long as I could remember, I'd hoped for a relationship like that. Seeing them sharing that made me wonder if I would ever find someone I trusted as much as Sam to share my life with.

Surprisingly, it was getting easier to be around her. I'd thought that it would be pure torture, watching her love someone else, but it was calming to my nerves. There was always a reminder she wasn't mine to pursue. Sure, I still loved her, but I could breathe easier now, sleep through the night, and look at Tristan without feeling an extreme amount of prejudice toward him.

The silent space between us all seemed to be growing more tense with each passing second, Sam staring out the window, her foot bobbing quickly in the air. Tristan, staring at her, frowned, the expression seeming to somehow deepen on his face, a dark cloud covering his eyes. Not knowing what to say or how to keep the impending argument from breaking out, I took to examining the ceiling, chewing on my bottom lip, my hands fiddling with the sheet draped over me.

"Tea time." Abella's voice in the doorway drew our attention, a tray of pretty china cups covered in hand-painted, blue flowers and a matching pot held in her hands. She curtsied quickly, the brown dress and her long, white apron brushing against the wood floors as she did so. Moving through the sitting room with ease, she set the tray down on the coffee table Tristan and I had moved to the side of the space, busying herself with filling the cups.

A breath of relief slipped from me and I smiled, wondering how she always managed to have perfect timing. Had she been waiting in the hall? Or was she just that lucky? The tension eased some as she moved around, apparently oblivious to the high emotions she'd walked in on.

"Madame Fairfax has informed me that dinner will be served at five in the afternoon. Cook has prepared a lovely feast for this evening, with the hog Samantha picked at market yesterday." Turning toward her lady, Abella held out a cup and saucer, waiting for Sam to take it.

"We've been smelling it all afternoon," I offered, beaming at her as she flashed me a smile. "I can't wait to taste it."

"I agree," Tristan replied wholeheartedly. "It will be a welcome respite from the cabbage and beans, though Cook prepares those as well as any in his profession I've met. Sam?"

His wife had yet to take the offered drink, staring at it with a blank expression. Blinking, she seemed to come out of her own thoughts, her features falling. "Abella did all the picking. I just told them where to send it." Her tone had gone from angry to tired and she rubbed a hand over her face, rising from her seat. "I have a headache and think I'll lay down for a while. Excuse me."

If Abella was affronted by being ignored, she didn't show it, pulling the cup away and holding it close to her chest. She curtsied, moving away as Sam rose and left the room.

Watching as she disappeared into the hall and then up the stairs, I felt a pang of sadness for her. I'd often seen her shut herself off from others when she'd been a prisoner on Randall's ship. It was one of her most used self-preservation techniques, but I'd never expected to see her use it here, among her friends and family. I'd thought she was doing better, going out with Abella, laughing over cards with Tristan, cutting down her practice time in the courtyard. Clearly, she was still suffering with her invisible wounds, though. Any delusions I'd had that my presence was helping her were just that—delusions.

Taking the sword from me, Tristan fiddled with the pommel for a moment, taking a deep breath as he watched the street outside. After a moment, he turned to Abella and I, smiling tightly. His formed seemed to deflate, a sadness overcoming him, and his expression fell. "If ye'll excuse me," he said quietly, taking his leave and following his wife.

"Have they been fighting again?" I asked Abella, moving to close the door to the room so our conversation would be private.

She shook her head. "I'm afraid it's something more that they are both struggling with."

"Do you know what it is?"

She smiled sadly, nodding. "The babe, Rachel. If she'd not passed away in the womb, she would have been born sometime in this past couple weeks. It's created much tension between them, but not out of anger. They are mourning."

The realization washed over me like a cold shower and I dropped my head, cursing myself for having not realized. All the activities we'd been doing, the time I was spending at the house, Sam's moods, it all made sense now that I knew what was going on. What if I had said something careless, making it worse for the pair of them? It hadn't even occurred to me that their joint despair would be made fresh because of the date.

"Is there anything I can do to help either of them?" Crossing the room, I picked up a cup from the tray, motioning for her to join me on the couch.

"I don't think so. They want their daughter, Mark. Tristan has never even seen her." Her eyes teared as she spoke and she looked at the glass she held. "I should have been there. I promised Monsieur O'Rourke I would watch after his wife for him. I should have insisted the ruffians take me with them, too."

"Abella, no." Setting my drink down, I reached for her, cradling her face in my hand and forcing her to look at me. "They wouldn't have taken you. Do you hear me? They would have killed you. Hell, they left you for dead when they came for her. If you'd insisted you come along, you would have been dead for sure and we wouldn't even be having this conversation.

"And what could you have done, if you were brought along? You would have been a prisoner. The men would have raped you repeatedly and there wouldn't have been anything I could do about it. Randall could've killed you just to scare Sam. The chances that you would have made it out alive in that situation are next to none."

The tears trembled past her eyelashes and slid down her face, wetting my hand as I rubbed her cheek with my thumb. What I said had scared her some, but she still shook her head, wanting to argue.

"Regardless of what would have happened to me, I would have been there for Samantha. It was my job to take care of her and I didn't do it." She hiccupped, trying to pull away, but I wouldn't let her.

"There was nothing you could have done," I replied roughly. "I was there, and there was barely anything I could do. I couldn't stop them from attacking her. I couldn't stop Rachel from dying. I'm not just trying to make you feel better. I'm telling you the truth. Nothing could have been done, by you, me, or anyone else to change what happened. Not even Tristan could have stopped the miscarriage if he'd gotten there in time."

Scooting closer, I placed my other hand on her

140

face, holding her steady as I spoke, wiping the tears away as they fell. "Besides all that, if you hadn't been here to tell Tristan what happened, he might not have ever found her. You are a hero in this story, Abella. You survived a gunshot! You helped track down a pirate, the leader of the Black Knights! You fought side by side with The Knights Templar and didn't even hesitate! You nursed many men, myself included, back to health. We would have died without you—I would have died without you, and on more than one occasion."

The statement seemed to surprise the both of us and I stopped short, staring into her wide eyes, her tears having slowed to an occasional droplet here and there. "I would've died without you," I repeated softly, laughing in spite of myself. It had never occurred to me that she was the reason I was alive until just now. "I owe you my life, Abella. You may not have been able to save Sam, but you saved me. That's a debt I'll probably never be able to repay."

Hiccupping, she blinked, setting her cup to the side and touching my hands with her own. "It was nothing. You needed help and I gave it. I don't want you—or anyone—to feel that they owe me a debt. I only did what was right."

"There are many people who wouldn't have done it." Grasping her fingers in mine, I rested our hands in our laps, staring at them in contemplation. "I don't know if I ever thanked you. I'm sorry for that. It should have been one of the first things I did, when I was shot and when I almost drowned." Staring at her face, I smiled, feeling a strange swirl of emotions. "Thank you, Abella. Thank you for saving my life. Thank you

141

for being there when I needed you. Thank you for being my friend."

She laughed slightly, her face turning red, and then cleared her throat, turning toward the door. She seemed uncomfortable for some reason, like she didn't know what else to say. "I have chores I need to do," she stated, her tone almost regretful. Her youthful face was sad when she turned back to me, her lips trembling. "I don't want to leave you in here alone, though. Or have you stop saying such nice things to me." She laughed again, her hand fidgeting against my own.

For once, I agreed. Not wanting her to leave either, I tightened my hold on her, smiling. "Stay here, then. We haven't talked in a long time, not like we used to. Sam won't mind if you don't help with the chores. You're not an actual servant here. I'm surprised to see that you act like one."

"I enjoy the work." She shrugged, peering at the closed door once more. "Sam is always telling me I don't have to help if I don't want, but I am hired to be her maid. It's not fair to the other servants if I don't do my part. Besides, it's all I know." She frowned then, looking at me as if she were suddenly ashamed of herself. "I'm not a Lady, like Sam. I don't attend Court regularly and the dresses I helped make for years were never ones I meant to wear myself. In my most desperate hour, the only place I had to turn was the streets and the grace of God. I'm not meant to live the life of someone higher. I'm happiest here, doing work with my hands and staying out of the politics of those around me."

Nodding, I smiled softly, understanding what she

was saying. "I'm no Lord," I offered. "This life we live now is one that I'm not familiar with. However, should you ever be in your most desperate hour again, you can feel comfort in knowing that you can come to me. You may not be a Noble Lady, but you are a woman of great worth."

The door opened suddenly before she could answer and we broke apart, a wave of heat washing over me, Abella rose quickly, smoothing her dress and wiping any remaining wetness from her face in a rush.

Tristan, having not noticed the two of us together, shut the door behind himself, sighing. Turning, he smiled at the both of us, as if he'd been hoping we were both still here. "She's fine. The headache will pass with rest." It sounded a bit like a white lie, his nose twitching some, but I didn't question him. When he saw that we weren't going to press for more details, his shoulders relaxed and he nodded. "Mark, would you like to go over the ceremony again?"

Glancing at Abella, who had also turned a light shade of pink, I smiled. "I would love nothing better."

Yawning, I covered my mouth, looking around the space in mild awe. The amount of building the Templars had managed to hide underground was staggering, to say the least. Even more impressive, they had somehow kept anyone from discovering it.

The room I stood in now was a marvel of engineering and design, somehow managing to replicate the feeling of being in a large cathedral. Giant, stone pillars twisted up from the cobblestone floor, flowing into the arched ceiling like water. Tapestries hung over the walls, candelabras lighting the space every few feet. Just ahead of me, a pair of gigantic wooden doors waited, locked until the initiation ceremony would begin. The hum of hundreds of men sounded lowly from the other side, filling me with an excitement I'd yet to feel when thinking of joining up.

Beside me, Tristan waited with his eyes closed, mouth moving along to some silent prayer he'd been reciting since arriving at the center of the Temple, where the most sacred of duties were carried out. He wore plain clothes under his long tabard, the large red cross of The Order stretched across his chest and back.

It looked every bit the same as it did in history books, marking him clearly as a Templar. The leather belt around his waist also housed a sword, long and heavy, like the ones we had practiced with. I'd never thought of him as a highly religious man, but, watching him now, it was clear that he had a relationship with his God, whomever or whatever it might be. He took his position as a Knight seriously and with reverence, something he had bid me do as well.

Glancing at my boots, I felt somewhat naked next to him. I wouldn't be given a tabard or sword until the ceremony was underway. All I had with me at the moment were my boots, pants, and shirt that I'd usually worn on board the ship. Tristan had said this wasn't the place for finery and to dress as I would for comfort. Titles and wealth did not matter in this place and showing them off was considered in poor taste.

I was the only recruit coming in tonight. When the clock struck midnight, Tristan would usher me through the doors and into the fold, guiding me through the steps and requirements of the ceremony until we reached the Masters. After I answered their questions, I would be passed on to the Grand Master, to complete the process. Every Templar who was close enough to attend would be there, watching. It made me feel something akin to stage fright, but I knew in my gut that it would all turn out fine.

"Are ye ready, *a dhuine*?"

Staring over at Tristan, I nodded, swallowing hard. "Are you?"

"Aye. I thank ye for the honor of letting me be yer guide in this endeavor."

"It's not like I knew anyone else who could do it,"

I muttered, eliciting a laugh from him.

"I suppose that's true. Still, it is my great pleasure to do so." Somewhere overhead, a bell began to ring, signifying that midnight was upon us. Crossing himself, Tristan turned toward the door, squaring his shoulders, ready to perform his duty. The hum of voices on the other side dimmed to nothing, everyone ready for the ceremony to begin.

Taking a deep breath, I watched the entrance, waiting for it to open so Tristan could lead me inside. One minute passed, and then another. Fidgeting, I looked to my guide for answers, but he seemed just as confused as I was.

Suddenly, sound came roaring through the space, the doors flying open with a bang, revealing chaos in the inner Temple. The men were scattering around the room, holding blades to one another, shouting in everyone's face. I couldn't hardly see past the few men in the front, stepping back in alarm as a fist fight broke out.

"Ye there!" Tristan yelled at the man who had opened the doors and was trying to escape out into the waiting area. "What's happened?"

"The Grand Master!" He stuttered, pointing to the back of the room were several ceremonial curtains should have hid the Masters and Grand Master. "He's dead! Murdered on his seat!"

Shocked, Tristan froze, the expression on his face melting into one of horror and disbelief. Gazing into the space ahead of us, though, he seemed to gather himself, shaking his head, and then leapt into action. "Get inside and close the doors," he ordered, grabbing me by the arm and propelling me forward. "Do not let a single soul leave, either of ye!"

The fight just in front of us was spilling into our space, the men rolling across the ground, pummeling each other. Someone drew a knife, brandishing it defensively, trying to stay out of the muck of the match.

"Inside!" Tristan roared, striding into the midst of the argument and kicking one of the men in the stomach. "Get yer arses moving!"

Whether it was the tone of authority in his voice or the murderous glare in his eyes, the men listened, seeming to come to their senses as they picked themselves up. As soon as we were all in the inner Temple, he pulled the doors shut, locking them tight.

"Wait here," he said to me, looking me hard in the eye. "Do. Not. Move. Ye'll understand in a moment."

Frozen in uncertainty and mild fear, I peered over the room, trying to make sense of it all. It appeared to be much like the waiting room outside, save the stone pews that were set into the floor. A set of stairs rose up at the head of the room, resting beneath a faux stained-glass widow that was illuminated from behind by candlelight. I could see the spot where I would've stood during the ceremony, as well as the hidden seats of the Masters. If it hadn't been for the riot occurring in front of me, I would have thought we were in a place of sanctuary and peace.

"Order!" A voice boomed over the racket, the firing of a gun catching everyone's attention. At the head of the room, up the steps and in front of the white sheets, a man held his pistol over his head, smoke curling from the end. "There will be order in this Temple!"

147

A few of the scuffles continued, one so close to us that Tristan grabbed one of the rabble-rousers and yanked him back, breaking up the fight.

"Listen to the Master," he hissed, pointing toward the man on the steps.

"How do we know the Masters ain't the ones that killed Bevard, eh?" the man hissed, pulling himself out of Tristan's grasp. "How do we know it wasn't you?" He glared at Tristan with disdain and distrust, eyeing him like he was no better than dust.

"Shut yer mouth," Tristan growled, letting just enough threat slip into his tone that the man stepped back.

The crowd settled some and I was able to catch a glimpse of several men moving the long curtains around peering behind them. Blood had soaked the ends of one and for a split second, I thought I saw the Grand Master, seated on a padded chair, his sliced open neck available for all to see. Before I could assess if that was what I was actually viewing, though, the crowd shifted again, still arguing and fighting with one another.

"It was someone in this room," I said to myself, surprised. Suddenly, I understood why they all were fighting—they were accusing each other of doing the deadly deed. Friends were turning on each other at the drop of the hat, desperate to discover the traitor among their midst.

"Order!" The Master yelled again. "You dolts! Do you not realize that by fighting you have helped the traitor hide his blade? The blood of Bevard was the only mark we had to catch him with!"

The men weren't listening, though. They were still

shouting, shoving, accusing. Huffing in annoyance, Tristan began shoving his way through the group, trading a punch here and there with anyone who thought of getting in his way. When he finally reached the steps, he had blood spatter on his white tabard and his chest was heaving. He didn't want to talk to the crowd, though; instead, he made his way to the curtains, disappearing behind them for a moment. When he returned, he crossed himself, a pained expression on his face.

The gun fired again, the bullet hitting the ceiling and sending rock chips raining down on one corner.

"Enough!" The Master's face was red and wild, his voice booming through the space so loudly that the men actually stopped to listen to him. "All of you! Put your weapons away and prepare to give a statement. You will not leave this room until your statement has been recorded! Anyone caught trying to leave beforehand will be arrested and put in the tower." Fuming, he looked over the group, disgust on his face. "When I find who did this, I will gut you like a pig myself." Spitting on the ground, he motioned to the exit in the back of the room, right where I was standing. "Line up! If you fight further, you will be taken care of. Save your accusations for the recorders!"

A few men pushed through the crowd, taking their spots at the doors, firm expressions on their faces. They had gathered paper and quills from somewhere along the way, ready to fill the Master's order.

"What about the Grand Master?" The shout had come from the middle of the room, the asker unknown, but the Master nodded all the same, glancing behind him and crossing himself.

149

"He is among the angels now. Once we have given our own account of our activities this evening, myself and the other Masters will take him to rest and inform his wife and daughter." He paused, clearly upset by the prospect of having to tell the family that their husband and father was dead.

"What then?"

Turning to the three other men on the steps, the Master made a questioning gesture toward them.

"Not to be unkind, but . . .we must vote," one of them hesitantly replied, his French accent thick with sadness. "The Order cannot continue on without a leader, especially when the Black Knights are so active and among us."

This caused the group to shift uncomfortably again, glancing at each other in suspicion. My mind raced as I watched them all, the tension in the room making the hairs on the back of my neck stand on end.

"More information will be spread through the usual channels, as we make it available," the first Master added. "But, yes, there will need to be a vote."

Murmurs swept through the crowd at that, causing him to hold his hands up for peace. "Please. Let us focus on the matter before us."

The crowd was ignoring him now, though. Some of the men were making their case as to why they should be the new Grand Master, others were arguing about the motives of the murder.

"Black Knight!" someone shouted, another gunshot ringing in the air. The man in front of him fell, clutching his chest, and the chaos erupted once more.

Tristan, appearing out of nowhere, came to stand by me. "This is madness," he stated, glancing around the room in disgust. "Someone in here has murdered our leader and they will walk away without a single ounce of regret. The statements will do nothing; the Masters are floundering. They are too shocked to see that the murderer is slipping away right before their very eyes."

Another shot rang from the Master's gun, but it had no effect this time. Men were now swarming the steps, yanking down the ceremonial curtains, crowding around the dead man's body, trying to get a better look. The Masters were soon employed in fighting as well, all semblances of order disappearing in the blink of an eye.

"We should go." Tristan's voice was quiet, his head tilted toward mine. "No good is going to come of this."

Nodding, I turned toward the exit, feeling shock continue to take hold of me. We were in the middle of a madhouse, blades and bullets flying. It would be a miracle if they didn't all kill themselves right now.

"Monsieur, I cannot let you leave without a statement!" One of the guards by the door shouted at us as we approached him.

A pair of Knights staggered across his path, desperately trying to rip each other's hair out as they growled obscenities at each other. Bumping into the guard, they didn't even pay him any attention, continuing on with their petty fight.

"Get off me!" The guard screamed, kicking one of the men in the shin and then clobbering the other over the head with the clipboard he'd meant to record statements on.

The two men did move away then, not because

they were being attacked by someone else, but because their general stumbling caused them to do so.

Straightening his tabard, the guard, swallowed, clearly looking shaken, and then stared at Tristan and I again. "Names!" he barked. "And be quick about it! God willing, we will all be away from this place and home in our beds before dawn!"

"That doesn't seem very likely," I muttered, earning a glare from the man.

"Tristan O'Rourke and Mark Bell," Tristan told him roughly. "We were the Guide and Initiate waiting outside the doors."

Nodding in understanding, the guard scribbled our names down and where we had been. Then, he unlocked the door, opening it a crack for us. "God be with you," he said seriously. Glancing over the blood washed space, he sighed. "And with us as well."

"I know you were one of Bevard's favorites," the man, Joseph McKinley, said, staring at Tristan with kind eyes. "And, while I cannot promise that you will be given the same level of inclusion and trust, I can promise that you will keep your position as captain. You need a new ship, yes?"

Tristan, sitting across from the man, his form clad in the finer fashions of France, sipped his tea slowly, nodding. His eyes never left the Templar's face, though, his gaze narrowed and slightly distrusting.

"How does a Man of War sound?" McKinley grinned, leaning forward in his excitement. "Think of it—the entire sea at your command. No more robbing pirates and playing the part of a thief. You would be a king in the ocean."

"Hmm." Setting his cup and saucer down, Tristan rose, straightening his dark green jacket. "I thank ye for thinking of me, McKinley. Ye have certainly given me much to think on. Mark as well, I'm sure." Smiling at me, he acted as if he were trying to keep from laughing, his lips pressed into a thin line and a mischievous glint to his eyes.

"Can I count on your vote, then?" McKinley

stared at us in earnest, still seated in his chair.

"I don't think I can say as to who my vote belongs to, yet," Tristan replied, sighing. "I do not speak for Mister Bell, but I would assume he feels the same."

"I do," I butted in, voicing my opinion for the first time. "It's too soon for me to know who I can trust."

"Too soon for anyone to know, really." McKinley grimaced, shaking his head. "Bevard, poor man. Have you heard how his wife and daughter are handling it?"

"I have not, but I imagine they are overcome with grief." Tristan sighed as well, rubbing his face.

McKinley, seeming to feel that his time here was up, rose and bowed. "Thank you for allowing me into your home. With any luck, I will attain your votes when we gather to cast ballots in a week's time. I bid you both good day."

Striding to the door, he pushed it open, startling Samantha and Abella on the other side. "Ladies." Dipping his head in acknowledgment, he took off, leaving us all in silence.

"That's the third one in two days," Sam finally said, hurrying to the window. "Though, he may have been politest about it."

"The most dishonest and willing to offer bribes, ye mean." Tristan snorted, joining her. Placing his hand on the small of her back, he fiddled with the ties of her red bodice, seemingly unaware that he was doing so.

"You mean the offering of being the captain of the Man of War?" Abella asked, hovering just inside the doorway.

"Aye, I do. That ship already has a captain, savvy? Which means if McKinley is voted in as Grand Master, he intends to change around the positions of leadership. It's not technically out of his realm of power to do so, but it will not sit well with the men. Many of them will lose their positions, their pay will be affected, and they will most likely remove him again." Shaking his head, he looked at me. "I don't know what ye plan to do with yer vote, but I will not be casting mine for McKinley."

"I'm surprised I was given a vote at all," I confessed. "I'm not even a member, yet."

"But you would have been, which is why they allow ye to have a say. Yer initiation was held off due to circumstances beyond yer control."

"This whole thing is ridiculous." Samantha turned, addressing both of us. "They still have no idea who killed Bevard. What if you vote the traitor in as your new leader? Has no one thought of that risk?"

"It's all they can think about." Rising from my seat, I shook my head, moving to pour myself more tea. "No one trusts anyone. Last night, we heard that a brawl broke out in one of the pubs on the other side of the city. The Knights were locked in the Bastille. It's unclear if they're going to be released any time soon or not."

"What is The Order thinking?" Sam turned to her husband, sharing her concerns with him. He replied in kind, the two of them branching off into their own conversation about what they thought would be best.

Glancing over at Abella, I smiled, raising my cup in thanks for the tea she'd provided us with. She grinned in return, nodding her head in acknowledgement.

"*Mademoiselle?*"

Caught off guard, she turned toward the doorway, summoned by one of the other servants. *"Oui?"*

"Une autre lettre est arrivée pour Monsieur O'Rourke."

"Merci, Annaliese. Je vais le prendre maintenant."

Annaliese, one of the shy kitchen maids, appeared in the doorway, handing over a folded piece of paper with a wax seal on it. She curtsied when she saw me watching, her face flushing, and then ran off, disappearing.

Abella stepped into the space, eyeing the letter with curiosity. "It's another message from The Order, I think." Stopping beside me, she watched Sam and Tristan talking, their conversation mumbled between them now.

"Ye can open it, Mark, if ye want," Tristan said, apparently still listening to what the two of us were saying as well. "Ye're as much a member as I am, as far as I'm concerned."

Nodding, I took the item in question from Abella, trading her for my glass in the process. As I popped open the seal, I noted the cross in the wax, suddenly thinking that the members of such a sacred and holy order weren't acting very appropriate to their calling. Fighting in public, openly campaigning against each other, and all before the previous Grand Master was in the ground.

Laughing, I looked at the letter. It was in French, which I did not speak. Motioning for Abella to come closer, I held it out for her to read. "I don't understand any of it."

She chuckled as well, leaning over my arm to read

the contents. "Bevard is to be buried in four days' time at Calvaire Cemetery. The King has heard of his advisor's death and sends his condolences to friends and family, but will be unable to make the services."

"Not surprising," I mused. "Bevard wasn't a major character of the Court, was he?"

She shook her head. "No, I don't think so. Still, it is a great honor to his memory that the King himself would send condolences on his behalf."

"We'll need to attend the funeral, of course," Sam said, she and Tristan having stopped their conversation to listen. "Are the black dresses clean, Abella?"

"*Oui, Madame*. I will air them right now." Curtseying, she turned quickly and left, leaving my cup in my hands.

"I think I need some air myself." Shaking her head, Sam glanced toward the window again, as if she expected yet another Templar to arrive on her doorstep, determined to convince the men in her life that one of them was the right man to lead them. "It might also be a good idea to write to Madame Bevard and her daughter, Gloria. This week has probably been the worst of their lives." She sighed then, picking up her skirts as she followed after Abella, worry on her face.

"Aye. I'll join ye in just a moment, lass." Taking another sip of his tea, Tristan slowly sat back down, a thoughtful expression on his face. Then, glancing at me, he shrugged, as if at a loss. "Who will ye vote for, Bell?"

Surprised by the candidness of his question, I sat as well, lips pursed. "I don't know," I replied honestly. "You're more informed than me. You know these men and The Order better than anyone else, in my opinion. I've not had the years you do, making friendships and trusts, learning who can be taken at their word and who can't. I would as soon vote for you as the Grand Master than any of the men who've come begging for votes."

"Me?" He seemed shocked and unsettled by the thought. "No, I wouldn't think so. I'm naught but a wee lad when it comes to concerns of The Order. Young and foolish. There are many a man who are more qualified and able than I would be."

Shrugging, I chuckled slightly. "I don't know any of them."

He stared at me quizzically, like he didn't think I was being serious. "I'm no Grand Master, Mark. The treasure I oversaw was compromised. Twice now, the man who challenged me to battle got away with nary a scratch on him. I can't even protect my wife from being abducted—how in the world would anyone think I could be trusted to run The Knights Templar?"

"Have you forgotten that you still managed to keep your treasure hidden and protected? That you uncovered a whole ring of Black Knights in Mexico City and brought them to justice? In your quest to rescue your wife, you not only united many Templars, but you managed to find and save a portion of the treasure that had been missing for hundreds of years. Randall got away, yes, but he's missing a hand now. On top of all that, everyone *knows* you didn't kill Bevard—you were locked outside the room, with me. You are the only option that everyone is sure is not a Black Knight."

"By that logic, ye have as much a chance of being voted Grand Master," he argued. "Ye were there with me! Ye're older as well, which would make ye preferable, out of the two of us."

"But I'm not a member of The Order, yet," I reminded him. "And I do wear the brand of a Black Knight. I'm not stupid. I know that will make many men never trust me, no matter what I say or how many times I share my reasons for joining with the enemy. All I'll ever be in this organization is a plain, entry level man." Seeing that I'd caught him, I smiled, raising an eyebrow. "You might want to prepare yourself, Tristan. You very well could be voted in."

Crossing himself, he muttered something under his breath and rose to his feet, the option I'd presented him with having clearly never crossed his mind. "I pray it doesn't happen," he said, his voice suddenly sounding dry and thick. "I must refuse if it does."

"Why?" He'd caught me off guard now and I frowned, wondering why he would turn down such a position of power and honor. Surely, it would be a distinction to his family, who had served The Order since it first began during the crusades. Technically speaking, he was royalty as well. It made sense to turn to him as a leader; he would have held that position had fate not changed the path of his family.

"Samantha." He appeared slightly panicked, glancing toward the door, as if he thought saying her name would cause her to appear. "I can't be away from her that much. Not yet. She's still so hurt, so . . . lost. If I were to be voted Grand Master, I don't know that she would ever recover."

Staring at me, he swallowed hard, a glint to his eyes that I'd never seen before. "I can't help her," he said softly, his voice breaking some. "I don't know how. She spirals so far from me, shutting herself off, and it's all I can do to try and keep her with me. The nightmares—I had already planned on killing Randall, but I will do it with joy now. The things she has said in her sleep, the words she's had with me when she's awake . . ." He swallowed, his gaze turning down to the floor for a moment. "Ye know. Ye were there with her."

Clearing his throat, he stared at the window again, moving to stand just in front of it. "The child—Rachel. It is so strange, the amount of pain I can feel for a being I have never met or even laid eyes on." He laughed slightly, and I had the sudden impression he might be crying, which was why he'd turned away. "Sometimes, I think I feel her spirit with me," he continued. "But I don't know how or why. What business would a baby have with haunting people?"

The confession made my heart ache for him. It was the first time I'd ever really considered what it must be like for Tristan, the events of the past several months. Sure, I'd been aware he was hurting, that he was suffering with Sam, but I'd never stopped to consider him by himself. I was always concerned with Sam and how she was feeling, wondering and hoping that Tristan was taking care of her right.

Now, as he stood before me, though, I realized that he had his own wounds that needed nursing. Was Samantha taking care of him, too? Or was she taking all he offered her and giving him no comfort in return?

Here, with the perfect opportunity to talk to him about how he was feeling, I faltered, not knowing if I should try or not. Would he want to share his troubles with me? In the end, I knew it didn't matter if he did or not. He needed someone to talk to, and I was the only person here now.

Clearing my throat, I rose, trying to think of what I could say to him that would help. Downing the rest of my tea, I set the cup on the table and folded my arms, coming to stand behind him. "Perhaps," I started slowly, wanting to make sure I got the words right. "It's not so much a haunting as it is a visit. You're right—why would a baby need to haunt anyone? But this isn't just any baby. It's your baby. Tristan's baby. Rachel Dawn O'Rourke. Rachel never met her father. Her spirit may be trying to reach out to you for that reason. Maybe she's trying to comfort you as much as you're trying to help Sammy. Or, it could be that she wants you to know she loves you. Do you ever get that feeling when you feel her around?"

He laughed, a humorless sound, and responded without turning around. "I tell ye I'm being visited by a spirit and ye don't think I'm mad? Ye don't want to rush me off to church or call the priest to come cleanse the house?"

"Why would I think you were crazy?" I asked, taken aback. "You have no reason to lie to me about this. There's nothing you could gain from telling me. Honestly, I don't even know why you would share it with me, given our relationship." The conversation was taking an uncomfortable turn, and I suddenly wished I hadn't brought up our common interests.

He did look back me then, his eyes red and a smirk on his face. "Ye mean the fact that ye're in love with my wife? Aye, I probably shouldn't have given ye such ammunition against me. Try as I might to hate ye, though, Bell, I find that I enjoy yer company and conversation. Perhaps it is my curse, to always have a constant reminder of the life Samantha could have had without me and the horrors she faced when I didn't protect her."

Biting my cheek, I stared out the window, nodding. His words had both hurt and helped me, causing feelings of confusion and resentment in me. I didn't want to be a reminder of the worst time in Sam's life, nor did I think I deserved his friendship after I had so openly declared my emotions. It wasn't my aim to be alone in this time again, though, and I was pleased to hear that he enjoyed having me around, even if it meant his attempts to hate me had failed.

"Do you honestly think that Sam would have been happier in her own time?" I asked, choosing to ignore all the other things he'd said.

"She wouldn't be hurting." His answer was simple, but there was so much pain in it that I paused, sympathy rocketing through me once more.

"I disagree." Speaking softly, I watched a man walking down the street outside, his jacket pulled tight around him, breath puffing from his mouth like a cloud of smoke. It was easier to say what I needed to when I didn't look at Tristan, I realized, mostly because my opinion was the truth and it hurt me to admit it.

"Samantha was alone in our time. Her mother had passed away and The Pit took her father. I was only a simple friend. We didn't even know each other all that well. There was no boyfriend that I knew of, no prospects of settling down that she seemed to have. If she had stayed there, she would've been lonely and sad. I saw it setting in after Michael—her father—died. She was stressed, upset, and trying so hard to keep herself together. Simply put, she was hurting.

"Here, she has you, though. You put her back together, Tristan, gave her a family to love and care for. She's cracked now, yes, but she has you to help pick up the pieces. Will she ever be the same? No. It's foolish to even think that she'll be the same as she was before. The death of a child will mark her forever. It will mark you forever. But, you've been marked together."

Breathing deeply, I glanced over at him, watching as a tear rolled down his cheek. I knew it was a show of great trust on his part, to let me see him like this and to talk with me about what was troubling him.

"Why do ye want us to work through it together so badly?" he finally asked, turning to meet my gaze. "She does so much better when ye're here. Ye help her in ways I cannot. Ye could take her from me, if ye wanted. I think ye know that."

Laughing outright, I smiled, rubbing my chin. "I love her, but she loves you. As much as I would like her for myself, she wants you, Tristan. And I want what she wants, no matter the cost to myself."

Snorting, he wiped his face, blushing slightly. "Aye, I suppose she has picked me, hasn't she? It hasn't felt much like it lately. Ye've been like her savior, coming from nowhere to pull her from the muck and set her on her path again."

Surprised, I practically gaffed at the statement, staring at him incredulously. "You've got to be joking. I'm not any kind of savior, simply a guy who was in the right place at the right time. She loves you, Tristan. Go to her. Talk it out. Share how you've been feeling—all of it. Tell her you're hurting as well and she needs to recognize that. If anyone is going to pull her out of this, it's going to be you. I'm not her hero. You are. Don't forget that."

He gave me a small smile, opening his mouth to reply.

"*Monsieurs? Oh—excusez-moi.*" Abella had appeared in the doorway, cutting off whatever he'd been about to say. Immediately realizing she'd interrupted something, though, she curtseyed, turning to leave.

"Wait," Tristan called, clearing his throat and moving toward her. "What is it, Abella?"

She hesitated, looking to me as if making sure it was okay to intrude, and then spoke again. "Samantha was wondering if either of you would like to join her in the courtyard for dueling practice."

Nodding, Tristan smiled, appearing as if nothing had occurred between us. "Aye. Tell her I will be there shortly."

Curtsying again, she quickly left, giving me one last glance of hesitation.

"Abella is good for Sam, too," I noted, moving to the couch I'd been sitting on earlier.

"She's a bonny lass," he agreed, moving to face me. "And she likes ye."

"Excuse me?" I asked, staring at him in surprise.

"Abella has taken a shine to ye." He chuckled, clearly amused I hadn't come to the same conclusion. "If ye ever decide to abandon Sam, she would make ye a good companion."

"I'm old enough to be her father," I retorted, suddenly wishing we could return to our conversation about his feelings, instead of talking about someone else's admiration for me.

"So?" he pressed. "Ye're old enough to be mine and Sam's father, too. It is that way with many in this time. Is it not in yers?"

"No." My reply was strong and rough, my face flushing as I turned away. "It's frowned upon. Abella isn't even considered a legal adult yet in my time. I would go to prison if I had a . . . a . . ." Why was it so damn hard to say relationship?

My skin was flaming red by now and Tristan laughed, apparently pleased with how uncomfortable his comment had made me. "Aye," he continued, folding his arms. "Still. She would make any man a fine companion, indeed."

Leaving me with my embarrassment, he strode out of the room, his spirits appearing to be considerably lifted at my own expense.

The funeral procession moved slowly through the tiny cemetery, the large number of people who'd shown up for the services clogging the area. Members of the King's Court had come to pay their respects, as well as many of The Order. It appeared Bevard had been well liked in the French society, the sheer amount of bodies that had come to pay their respects surprising me.

At the head of the group, beside the casket that was being carried through the throng, Madame Bevard and her daughter, Gloria, slowly led the way to the freshly dug grave, their faces covered with black veils and tissues in their hands. I'd not had the chance to meet them yet, but Sam whispered to me that they were nice enough. It was our combined hope that they would be taken care of, now that they had no head of the household. Tristan assured us The Order would assist them, though, even if they had no idea of its existence.

Finally reaching the late Grand Master's resting place, the group crowded around the shallow hole in the ground, the chill in the January air seeming to add to the gloominess of the affair.

Speaking in French, a priest began to pray, placing

a hand on the casket as he spoke. After a few moments, I found my mind wandering, as well as my gaze.

It was a relatively small graveyard, boxed in on three sides by the surrounding buildings. The graves were covered with stones, some of them sporting statues or intricate carvings. There were the characteristically large and tall headstones that populated any old burial ground, trees swaying gently overhead, and yellow, dead grass on the ground beneath our feet. Overall, it felt like a nice place to be put to rest. Part of me couldn't help wondering if the tiny area would stand the test of time, or if it would be destroyed or lost over the years. I'd never had much interest in the history of cemeteries, though, especially ones in Paris, and had no inkling of what the fate of this place would be.

Sighing, I stole a glance at Samantha on my left. She had her hand wrapped around Tristan's arm, her head on his shoulder, eyes closed as she listened to the preacher speak. She didn't understand any of what was being said, either, but she seemed at peace somehow, like her spirits had been lifted by coming. Her black dress blended into the fabric of Tristan's jacket and pants, as well the crowd of mourners, though we all stood away from the throng. Adjusting her position slightly, she moved to the side, revealing Abella sanding just behind her.

Feeling my breath catch in my chest, I tore my eyes away from her, staring hard at the priest. Her image seemed burned in my mind, though. A simple, black gown, covered by her light cloak, curly hair pinned up by her face. She was listening to the sermon with rapt attention, her eyes never straying from the ceremony in front of us.

Ever since Tristan had told me he thought she liked me, it had been hard to be around her. I couldn't stop thinking about what I'd done, if anything, to encourage such feelings. She knew how I felt about Sammy, after all. I'd thought she and I were only friends, lending a hand to one another when we needed it, joining together to help our common friend in her time of need. Never in a million years would I have thought Abella had a crush on me, or that I could ever return the affections for her.

She was a child! What business did she have with developing feelings for a man in his forties? She was what, seventeen now? Stealing another glance, I gulped, suddenly suspecting everyone here could read my thoughts on my face.

Of course, she had no idea of the turmoil Tristan had created inside me. How could she know I stayed awake at night, thinking of ways to dissuade her, to show there were others much more worthy of her affections. Every young man I saw in the street suddenly became a possible suitor for her, to distract her with.

At the same time, if I was honest with myself, I didn't want her attentions turned elsewhere. It wasn't out of romantic inclinations for myself, but because I cared for her in a different way. She was a woman who had saved my life and been my friend in a time when I desperately needed one. What if, God forbid, the young man who came to steal her heart was cruel? What if he was destined to give her a life of sadness, loneliness, and fear? What if he wasn't a young man at all, but some old pervert, bent on making her his play thing? No, it would be better to keep her away from something like that, to keep her safe, as I always had.

Abella's safety was always one of my top concerns, I'd come to realize. Whether it was the life debt I owed her or my duty as a man, I'd sworn to myself at some point that I would let no harm come to her. That oath included any actions I could take against her, such as shattering her young heart when I told her I would only ever love Sammy.

Still, she had said nothing to me of her feelings. Maybe Tristan had only been teasing me, trying to make me nervous. If that were the case, it had worked. I could scarcely be in the same room with the girl before I felt my face flushing and had to excuse myself.

All around me, the group muttered an amen, the priest's service concluded. Coming back into the present moment, I shook myself, shoving my concerns about Abella from my mind once more.

One by one, those in attendance moved forward, to pay their respects to Bevard and his family. Some of them touch the casket, others went straight to the wife and daughter, hugging them and muttering quietly. When it was my turn, I hesitantly stepped forward, feeling out of place. I'd only met the man once, after all, and had never even spoken to his family. I didn't even know if they spoke English or not.

Resting my hand on the wooden box, I smiled weakly at the women, inclining my head toward them. "I'm sorry for your loss. He seemed a great man, when I met him."

Madame Bevard sniffled behind her handkerchief, bowing her head to me as well. "*Merci, Monsieur.* Your words are most kind."

Stepping away, I watched as Samantha and Tristan moved forward, taking a little longer to pay their respects. Abella stood behind them, silent, playing the part of a servant once more.

Sighing, I watched her, an unfamiliar ache in my chest. It wasn't pleasurable, suffering with such discomfort around her. Gone were the days of my sharing every whim with her, of telling her my emotions and having enriching conversation. Now, all I could see was a woman I needed to distance myself from, if not because of our difference in age then because she was from a different time than my own.

I would not risk changing the future for my own happiness. A relationship with anyone from this time would create a whole new line of people, possibly corrupting everything I knew about my own time.

Glancing away as the group turned around, I watched the line of people slowly leaving the cemetery now, clumped in little groups, whispering together. A sadness hung in the air, as was usual with funerals, but it seemed to penetrate everyone to their core today. Perhaps it was because the man they laid to rest had been murdered. Maybe it was the gloomy, cold weather. Either way, I suddenly found myself wishing I was home in front of the fire, alone with my mind.

"Are you feeling well, Mark?" Sam appeared beside me, placing a hand on my arm. There was worry in her voice and eyes. "You look very pale."

"I'm fine," I assured her, smiling weakly. Patting her fingers, I carefully stepped away, putting some distance between us. The action caused me to almost run into Abella, who had appeared on my other side, and I froze, trapped between the two of them. Clearing my throat, I stared at Sam, trying to sound convincing. "Only tired. I've had a hard time sleeping with everything that's been going on."

Tristan, coming up on her other side, nodded as he took her hand. "Aye. Myself as well. The vote will be finished tonight, though. God willing, we can put the whole ordeal behind us."

"God willing," she echoed, beaming at him.

"Will you be staying for dinner, Mark?" Abella's quiet voice drew my attention and I looked back at her, feeling the odd clenching of my chest again. Her eyes were hopeful, I thought, as she watched me, waiting for my answer.

"I don't think so."

Any disappointment she felt, she hid well, merely nodding. "I'll make sure to let Cook know, then."

"Ye aren't staying to eat?" Tristan asked, overhearing our conversation. "Why?"

"I want to go home and gather myself before tonight," I lied, pleased with how quickly the excuse had come to me.

He nodded, accepting the reason without question. "I think that is wise. Tonight will be an evening of much change, in yer life and in the life of The Order. It will be good to have some time alone with yer thoughts beforehand."

Samantha sighed, watching me with searching eyes. "I don't think you'll change too much," she said, laughing slightly. "At least I hope not."

Blushing, I stared at the ground. Part of me was desperately wanting to flee the group, to feel some peace and to let my heart settle. The other part was content in talking with Sammy this way and believing

I was an important part of her life.

Pulling at my necktie, I made a face at her, meant to display my discomfort. "Don't worry. I'll still be the same selfish, stubborn brute you've always known."

She laughed at that, shaking her head. Moving forward, she and Tristan started toward the street, their voices quiet as he spoke to her, their path interrupted almost immediately by someone wishing to speak with them.

"I think, member or not, Mark Bell will always be a man of great courage and honor," Abella said softly. It wasn't clear if Samantha even heard her, but I peered over in shock, surprised that she would complement me so. Her eyes met mine with warmth and she smiled, her expression one of peace and acceptance.

"I think you grossly exaggerate my better qualities," I replied just as softly.

"No." She shook her head, gathering her skirt in her hand as she stepped forward to join her Lord and Lady. "I was there. It is you who forgets who you truly are."

The chapel inside the Temple was silent—a stark contrast from the last time I'd been here. Hundreds of men sat in the stone pews, watching as the Masters conferred at the head of the steps before them, the light from the faux stained-glass window shining on them like a rose-colored beacon from God. All around me, signs of the battle that had raged here sat openly, for all to see. There were a few bullet holes in the stone pillars, some of the benches broken in spots. It was apparent someone had been in here, repairing things, but the work wasn't done yet. The only stark difference I could see was the white curtains at the head of the space. They were bloodless, for one, and they had all been pulled back, revealing the chairs that the leaders of The Order would inhabit during ceremonies.

In addition to the steps leading up from the pews, there were two more set of small stairs. On the first level, four chairs sat. Tristan had mumbled to me that the Masters would take their place there. The second level housed only one chair, large and ornate. It was the seat of the Grand Master, decorated with the cross of the Templars, gold leafing, pearls, and all other sorts of finery. It was, by far, the finest thing in the entire space.

I couldn't help but wonder how they had cleaned it, after Bevard's blood had washed over it. Was the cushion replaced? Was it the same seat they'd used since the crusades? Now wasn't the time to pick Tristan's brain about it, though, so I remained silent, watching the Masters with everyone else.

I was the only person without a tabard, dressed in my brown breeches and white shirt, waiting to be initiated into the secret sect. The ceremony couldn't take place without a Grand Master, though, and so, we had all gathered to tally the vote that had been cast for the office.

"Who did ye vote for?" Tristan asked quietly, leaning toward me.

He was nervous, I realized, his fingers tapping on his leg as he watched the proceedings.

"I voted for you."

His head snapped over, glaring at me with wide eyes. "I told ye not to!"

"And I told you, I don't know anyone else well enough to vote for them!"

The man next to me gave us a disproving glance, but swallowed uneasily, as if he were also nervous about the results. Then again, who wasn't? Bevard's murderer was in the room with us right now and we still had no clue who it was.

"Let's hope the rest of the men have enough brain in them to cast their vote correctly," Tristan muttered, his attention returning to the top of the stairs.

Shooting him a glare, I shook my head, also turning to watch the Masters again. They had several slips of paper in front of them, spread across the alter. They arranged the votes into groups, which I assumed were sorted by candidate, one of them keeping track of the number in a book he held tightly. They all seemed apprehensive and tired, as if keeping The Knights Templar from killing each other for a week had been more work than any of them expected. Finally, they stepped away from the sheets, grouping together to discuss.

Mutters began in the pews around me, the men eager and impatient to hear the results of the vote. After a moment, the Masters formed a line in front of the alter, raising their hands for peace.

"The results have been tallied," one of them said. He was tall and bald, his pale skin wrinkled with age. His French accent spread through the space with ease, though, and I recognized him as the Master who had declared we would have to vote on the night of Bevard's murder. He held the notebook in his hands, his eyes scanning the crowd.

"That's Master Francois," Tristan whispered, nerves practically rolling off him, his eyes never leaving the man who was speaking.

Nodding, I watched Francois with rapt attention, feeling the importance of the occasion. It was like watching every reality television show competition combined, except this would have real life consequences for all of us.

"When I call the name of the new Grand Master," Francois continued, staring at all of us. "He will rise and join us at the altar. There, he will remove his tabard and sword, becoming like new to The Order. He will join our initiate outside and prepare himself to take on the duties of our leader. When the clock strikes midnight, he will take part in his second initiation and be awarded the title of Grand Master, should he accept it."

Silence spread through the space, the tension in the air palpable. It felt as though I could scarcely draw a breath, so anticipated was the answer we had all be waiting for.

Taking a deep breath, Francois glanced at the other three Masters, as if asking for them to share their strength with him, and then stared back at the congregation. "Joffrey Davies."

A murmur of mixed emotions swept through the room. I could hear surprise, anger, excitement, and even worry in some of the whispers. Beside me, Tristan remained still, his gaze seemingly far away as different emotions passed over his face.

"Who is that?" I asked him quietly, peering around to see if Davies had stood yet. "He didn't come visit us, did he?"

Shaking his head, Tristan blinked, looking at me. "I don't think I've ever met him. I'd heard rumors that he was campaigning, but, no, he never came to speak with us."

Finally, a man rose from the middle of the room, a smile on his face as he strode into the aisle. Brown hair, cut short on the sides and long on top like my own, had been swept out of his handsome face. A light stubble covered the bottom half, his eyes bright under full eyebrows. He was young, somewhere between mine and Tristan's ages I would guess, and the smile on his face was one of determination and acceptance. I couldn't see much under his tabard, but he appeared to be in good physical condition, his form that of a fighter.

A thousand thoughts seemed to race through my mind as he strode to the head of the room and up the stairs. Why would the group pick someone so young to lead them when they had many seasoned members? What had this man done to gain favor with so many of the Knights? Why had he decided not to campaign personally to Tristan and I? What kind of leader would he be? And, most of all, was he secretly Bevard's murderer?

Upon reaching the Masters, Davies removed his belt and sword, laying them across the altar, followed by his tabard. He wore the simple clothes of a crewman underneath, the dark gray of the fabric almost blending into the stones around him.

"You accept the call from your fellow Knights?" Francois asked him.

"I do." His voice carried the ring of a tenor, but

had a surprising amount of authority to it. It carried through the space with ease, sounding like that of a leader.

Francois nodded, motioning for him to step outside. Then, searching for myself and Tristan, waved for us to go as well. "When the clock strikes midnight, gentlemen."

The doors shut tight behind the three of us, dulling the murmur of the men on the other side. They had all watched as Davies left the room, whispering among themselves. Each face had worn a different expression, the pick for the new Grand Master clearly surprising many of them. It made me wonder how many votes he had actually received and how divided the men had been to begin with. The Masters had created many piles when they were tallying the vote. Had Davies only won by a few?

Stopping in front of one of the tapestries on the wall, the Frenchman crossed himself, gazing at the portrayal of the first Knights of The Order, muttering what appeared to be a prayer for strength under his breath. "Forgive me," he said, turning his attention to us. "I imagine I will be poor company for the next several minutes."

"Ye are called to a great duty," Tristan replied, inclining his head. "I'll not fault ye for turning to the Masters of old for guidance."

"I won't, either." Watching him, I felt like I wanted to ask all the questions swirling through my mind, but refrained.

"To be called so young to an office that could hold a lifetime's mark of duty, should ye do it right, is a great honor and burden," Tristan offered, smiling tightly.

"*Oui*, I am young," Davies responded, noticeably catching the tone of interrogation in Tristan's voice. "Not much older than yourself, I would assume. God has called me forward in the work, though, and I must answer. What is your name, good man?"

"O'Rourke, Monsieur." Bowing slightly, showing respect to the candidate, Tristan never took his eyes of the man, an air of distrust flowing from him.

"*Oui.* Tristan O'Rourke. This is your companion, Mark Bell, I assume? I've heard of both of you. It would appear you've had quite the year, and an exciting year before that." Davies laughed slightly, nodding. "I thought of paying you a visit during this past week, but I'm afraid I did not have the time. Many of the men kept me tangled up in pubs and on the streets, speaking about my plans and ideas for the future. I look forward to meeting with you again in the coming weeks and sharing them with you. Now, *excusez-moi. Je dois me préparer.*"

Turning away, he focused his attention on the tapestry again, kneeling before it as he prayed. His voice was barely discernible, head bowed in reverence, his attention focused fully on the task he was about to undertake.

Motioning me to the other side of the room, Tristan watched him with curiosity, studying him. "What do ye think?" he asked me quietly, the sound not traveling far enough for Davies to hear.

"He seems nice enough," I replied, shrugging.

179

"He's praying."

"Aye. Methinks he is dedicated to the task at hand."

"He's young. If the claim that the men kept his company to hear his plans is true, he's probably seen as a man of the people, a leader who will take counsel not only from the Masters, but from anyone in The Order." Watching the man as well, I pursed my lips. Tristan said my next thought before I could even open my mouth.

"It could all be for show. He could have murdered Bevard in cold blood, hoping to take over power. A Black Knight could be right here, in front of us, and we'd have no idea."

"It took a lot of skill and secrecy to murder the last Grand Master, though. I doubt he could have done that on his own, let alone win the vote afterword."

Tristan nodded, his eyes narrowing and expression darkening. "This is true. If that be the case, we have much more to worry about than just one Black Knight among our midst. It will be a whole colony of them, and where there's a colony, Thomas Randall is sure to be."

The bell overhead began to chime midnight and Davies rose, his expression flat as he turned toward the great doors. As soon as the ringing finished, they opened, revealing the Templars on the other side, all standing and waiting for him to enter.

"We will wait here," Tristan murmured to me. "Davies must go first."

Without further prompting, the Frenchman strode inside, walking down the aisle with his head held high. When he reached the steps, he was stopped by the first of the Masters, Francois.

"Joffrey Davies. You have been called into the service of Almighty God. What is your response?"

"A man can do no greater service than that to his God," Davies responded.

Moving to the side, Francois allowed him to move forward. After a few steps, he was stopped by the next Master, a man Tristan had said was named Campbell.

"The calling of a Templar is for life. Do you knowingly and willingly accept this call, with no force from any soul to do so?"

"I do."

Passing up the next couple steps, Davies halted in front of the Master who had been trying to bring order to the group when Bevard was discovered murdered. I knew now that his name was Abbey.

"Our secret allegiance with God is just that—secret," Abbey started, staring down on him with a blank stare. "Will you keep our organization hidden from the world, or risk hellfire for sharing the truth of our mission?"

"I will keep the secret, or my own life be forfeit."

Permitted to pass, Davies reached the last of the Masters. It was Fazil, the only man not from Europe in the group. His Arabic accent sounded exotic and strange next to the others, his gaze seeming fiery and dangerous as he looked upon the young man.

"You have stated that you join our brotherhood freely, of your own will, in the service of God and with the intention to keep His secrets for life. Do you still swear that all of this is true?"

"I do."

The other three Masters slowly joined Fazil at the

altar, creating a small semi-circle around Davies.

"Kneel," Fazil ordered, watching as Davies did so without question. His form seemed even smaller in the indentation in the floor once he was inside it, the space meant to symbolize the grave and his lifelong commitment to the cause.

I was fairly familiar with the ceremony up to this point, Tristan and I having practiced it many times in preparation. It was slightly different, since Davies was already a member of The Order, but it had calmed me some to see that I remembered how things went and I felt confident that my own initiation would go smoothly. Now, however, I was curious to see what would happen. I had no idea what went into swearing in a new Grand Master.

"You kneel before us now, already anointed and blessed in the service of God Almighty. Today, the angels have picked your path. You are called to the position of Grand Master, by your peers and your Heavenly Father. How do you respond?"

"I am but a man, who still has much left to learn in this life. I will fill the office of Grand Master to the best of my abilities, though, and with the blessing of God, the angels, and those who surround me now."

"Do you swear to fight tyranny, protect those in need, and remain loyal to the cause for the entirety of your life?" Francois asked.

"I do."

"Will you guard your Knights with your life and soul, dedicating yourself to servitude in their names?" Abbey asked.

"I will."

"Are you dedicated to following the mission God

gave us at our start; to protect His treasures and the treasures of the world, while spreading the truth of His word across the face of the planet?" Campbell stared hard at him as he asked, as if he didn't trust Davies could do the job.

"I am."

Fazil cleared his throat and sighed, examining the man with a blank expression. "I must ask again. Do you knowingly accept this office, of your own free will? Do you understand the work that will be required of you? Can you lead this great Order to the fulfillment of God's desires?"

"I can and I must," Davies responded strongly. "I accept this calling, with all of my heart and soul. God has called me and I kneel before you on this day to answer."

A brief whisper flitted over the crowd at that. Apparently, Davies had gone off book in his reply. Instead of being frowned upon, though, the answer seemed to have pleased many of the congregation.

"Rise then, and take your place among us." Fazil offered his hand to Davies, helping him to his feet.

The group moved up the steps, to the ornate throne, and stopped just before it. Campbell, moving behind the seat, emerged with a new tabard that was the reverse of everyone else's. The white cross on the red fabric seemed to shine like the sun as it was pulled over Davies head. Abbey revealed a new, black belt, securing it around Davies waist with ease. Francois then emerged from behind the throne with a sword that outshone every other blade in attendance. The hand guard was all swoops and swirls, cocooning his fingers with elegance. Carefully, he offered it to Davies, bowing slightly.

Taking the sword, Davies carefully placed the point on the ground in front of him, holding the blade steady as Fazil approached, a bowl in his hand.

Dipping his fingers inside, Fazil carefully anointed Davies, touching two fingers to his forehead, collarbone, and each shoulder. He muttered a prayer in his native language as he did so, the words barely reaching Tristan and I at the rear of the room.

Finally, the entire process finished, the Masters stepped away, and Davies sat on the throne, his face triumphant and radiating as he stared out over everyone.

"Praise be to God and long live the Grand Master!" Fazil yelled.

The entire congregation echoed the phrase, Tristan included, as the white curtain was let down, hiding Davies from view. Slowly, the Masters took their own seats and the sheet covered them as well. For a moment, all was still, and then, almost as one, the congregation turned to look at me.

"Yer turn," Tristan said, smiling.

Swallowing hard, I nodded, breathing in a long breath. After a moment, Tristan stepped into the space, myself following just behind him.

Stopping in the middle of the aisle, Tristan spoke to the group, his voice echoing off the stones around him. "I bring a man of good honor and skill to join The Order of The Knights Templar," he proclaimed.

"And who is calling?"

The voice came from behind the curtains, one of the Masters making the inquiry.

"Tristan O'Rourke, for Mark Bell."

"Proceed," the disembodied voice replied.

Turning to face me, Tristan drew his sword, placing the tip on the ground before him. "Do ye join our brotherhood of yer own free will and with the understanding of what will be required of ye?"

"I do," I responded firmly, feeling the beat of my heart increase under the stares of those in attendance.

Nodding, Tristan motioned for me to continue forward with him, bringing me to the foot of the stairs. All at once, the curtain hiding the Masters moved away, and the four of them took their place on the steps, as they'd done with Davies.

Francois smiled at me, his expression much friendlier than it had been mere moments before. "Mark Bell. You have been called into the service of Almighty God. What is your response?"

"A man can do no greater service than that to his God." My mouth felt dry as I spoke, my hands practically shaking as I watched him, but he nodded and moved to the side all the same, bidding Tristan to take me forward.

Campbell waited just ahead, his demeanor also much nicer than it had been when swearing in the Grand Master. When he spoke, his voice had an almost cheerful ring to it, as if he had no greater pleasure than inducting me into the society. "The calling of a Templar is for life. Do you knowingly and willingly accept this call, with no force from any soul to do so?"

"I do."

Campbell grinned, stepping to the side and motioning for me to continue down the line to Abbey. Tristan, standing by my side as always, nodded, leading the way.

"Our secret allegiance with God is just that—secret." Abbey started as soon as I reached the step in front of him, as if he were eager to get the meeting over with. "Will you keep our organization hidden from the world, or risk hellfire for sharing the truth of our mission?"

"I will keep the secret, or my own life be forfeit." A sense of calm was starting to overtake me now, the beating of my heart slowing as I was bid to proceed to the top of the steps, where Fazil waited for me. He was the only one who gave me the same stare he'd given Davies, his voice strong and loud as he spoke to me.

"You have stated that you join our brotherhood freely, of your own will, in the service of God and with the intention to keep His secrets for life. Do you still swear that all of this is true?"

"I do."

The other Masters gathered around me, as they had before, except this time Tristan stood on one end, separated from them by about a foot. "Kneel before the Masters, friend," he instructed me, motioning to the indentation in the floor. "Know that ye make this oath on yer own grave, forfeiting yer life to the cause from this moment on."

Doing as he said, I knelt in the long rectangular hole, looking up at the five of them.

"We Masters have found you worthy," Campbell spoke, gazing out over the crowd. "It is now left with the Grand Master to decide your fate."

The curtain moved then, revealing Davies on his throne, and I felt a smidge of the nerves I'd pushed to the side return.

Rising from his seat, the Grand Master slowly

descended the stairs, sword in hand. Stopping on the other side of the altar, he waited for the Masters to part, so I could see him, and then spoke.

"Mark Bell. You are presented here today by Brother O'Rourke and have been found worthy by the Masters to partake in our quest. I must ask you one final time—do you join this brotherhood of your own free will and with the knowledge of what will be required of you?"

"I do."

"Then rise and put on the mantle of God."

Getting to my feet, I stood in the hole, watching as Davies procured a white tabard, belt, and sword from inside the altar, passing them to Tristan.

Moving quickly, but carefully, Tristan dressed me in the attire, grinning widely as he did so. When he was finished, I was the same as every other man in the room.

Joining me in the symbolic grave, Davies dipped his fingers in the bowl he now held, the oil inside dripping off his skin as he reached for me. As he anointed my body, Tristan muttered the words to the Warrior's Prayer, asking for my safety and loyalty in return for my life given to God.

Davies, finished with his task, smiled and motioned for me to turn around. "Brothers, accept the new addition to our cause: Mark Bell. Praise be to God and long live The Knights Templar!"

"Praise be to God and long live The Knights Templar!" I shouted with the rest of them, feeling as if the weight of the world had suddenly been cast onto my shoulders.

Seated at the round table, deep in the bowels of the Temple, I had the distinct impression that I perhaps had not quite known what I was getting myself into when I promised myself to The Knights Templar. At the very least, I hadn't considered what a change in leadership might do to The Order, and now that I was staring such a situation in the face, I kind of wished I had declined the invitation to join in the first place.

The most distinct difference so far was the chairs around the table. Under Bevard's leadership, they had all been the same, resting around the table with no specific head. Now, Davies sat in a seat much larger than the others, with arm rests and cushions, the wooden frame etched with symbols and artful designs. His form was clad in the finer clothes of the French upper class, his appearance giving him the vibe of royalty without the crown. The tapestries on the walls had been changed, displaying different battle scenes now, rather than the mostly peaceful renderings that had resided in this room before.

It had also dawned on me, as I walked through the halls on my way in, that there was less light to see by, but the space had been thoroughly cleaned, scrubbed until shining like new. Guards clothed in all black were stationed throughout the interior now, instead of only at the door. The stood watch like heavenly sentinels, unmoving and unresponsive to any attempt to speak with them. Overall, the entire temple suddenly had the air of a military base, instead of the calm and peaceful atmosphere I'd experienced when Bevard was here.

While the changes alarmed me some, they made sense as well. The Order was facing an outbreak of Black Knights. There should be more guards, more force in general applied to the situation at hand. Bevard's murderer walked free in these rooms, his identity still a secret from the rest of us. Davies was trying to paint himself as an undisputed leader in a time where tensions were running high and loyalty was at an all-time low.

Unfortunately for him, though, there weren't many who seemed willing to give him their entire trust, just yet. I didn't think he blamed any of the men who were hesitant to share their knowledge with him, due to the circumstances of his advancement, but he was obviously frustrated and tired, the proof of it showing on his face.

"I have a fairly good understanding of the events that took place on Oak Isle," he said, after having listened to Tristan explain everything that had happened with the Treasure Pit. Curiously, though, he hadn't mentioned anything about Sam being a time traveler, and Tristan hadn't said anything about it, either. "There are some rumors, though, about your wife." He paused, regarding Tristan through narrowing eyes, and then waved his hand, brushing off whatever he was about to say. "But, I will save that for later.

189

What I am most interested in is hearing about how Monsieur Bell came into the picture and the lost treasure in the Americas."

"You didn't hear beforehand?" I asked, surprised.

Davies, giving me a slight look of annoyance, shook his head. "No. Your meeting with Bevard was ordered to be kept classified for the time being. Unless they were in the room, the only souls who know what happened on this latest voyage are the ones who partook in it."

Tristan shot me a glance that warned me to be silent, and he sighed, focusing on Davies again. "Randall kidnapped my wife."

"*Oui*, I know that. Everyone knows that. You came bursting into the Temple like a bat out of Hell, demanding you be given a ship to go after them with. The only reason you got one was because Bevard favored you so. If I had been in charge then, you wouldn't have been able to go off on your silly retrieval mission and I wouldn't be left dealing with the number of men who were killed in the process." Shifting in his seat, Davies exhaled in annoyance. "I'm not interested in the specifics of that—I want to know about the treasure. What was in it? Did Randall take anything from it? Why was Monsieur Bell dragged into the whole affair, especially after all of my men had taken oaths during their initiation ceremony to not share the secret of our group with anyone?"

Tristan's face flushed, anger crossing his features for a moment before his expression went blank.

It occurred to me then that Davies thought the story of Samantha being from the future was fake. He didn't see the wisdom in going after her, of saving her from Randall, because he thought she was just a woman who had been exaggerated. She was of no importance to him whatsoever.

Flushing myself, I cleared my throat, addressing him sternly. "I was the doctor aboard Randall's ship. I took care of Madame O'Rourke when she was kidnapped. Eventually, I was inducted into the Black Knights." Rolling up the sleeve of my jacket, I displayed the brand on my arm. "Of course, I only joined so I could spy on them. Samantha was the one who told me about the Templars. She insisted they would be coming to save her."

"Of course." Davies rolled his eyes. "Do you keep no secrets from your wife, Monsieur O'Rourke?"

"No, sir, I do not," Tristan replied coldly. "But I never told her I was a member of The Order. She figured that out herself."

"Really?" Davies sounded skeptical.

"She's much smarter than you give her credit for," I butted in again. "Strong, too."

"I don't care." He sounded bored again, leaning back in his fancy chair with a sour expression on his face. "What about the treasure?"

"With all due respect, Grand Master, ye're asking the wrong men. Captain Lomas knows more about that treasure than even Bevard did." Tristan's reply was rough, but respectful. "He's the one you should bring in if ye want to know the truth of it."

"*Oui*, but Lomas and his men were called in early by Bevard, just before his death. They shipped out two days before he was murdered, so I have no opportunity to ask him about the treasure, now do I?"

"That's a shame," Tristan replied easily. "I

suppose ye'll have to wait, then."

Shoving to his feet, Davies slammed his hand on the table, screaming at Tristan. "Tell me what you saw in the treasure vault! Tell me where it was! I order you, as Grand Master, to tell me!"

Flinching away, I looked at the man in shock, desperately trying to think of a way out of this situation.

"I'm sorry, Grand Master," Tristan replied coolly, inclining his head some in respect. "But I never saw the treasure and I don't know where the vault is. Lomas was the man who discovered it all."

Not expecting him to tell an outright falsehood, I stared at Tristan, sensing I was in a meeting with pirates once more. They were ruthless and did whatever was needed to get what they wanted, not caring who was injured in the process. Tristan was effectively throwing Lomas under the bus, but wouldn't Davies find out the truth soon enough?

The realization of what was happening began to settle over me. Tristan didn't trust Davies, so he wouldn't tell him anything that wasn't already general knowledge in The Order. He wouldn't mention that Samantha was a traveler, out of the hope that Davies wouldn't ever try to take advantage of her. That was also most likely why he hadn't said anything about me travelling as well. He was playing his part as a pirate, protecting his treasures and refusing to withdraw in the face of a new threat.

Swallowing, I closed my mouth and took a deep breath. I'd been a pirate before, too, as well as a spy. This was a game I was very much familiar with.

"It's true," I stated, folding my hands and setting

them on the table in front of me. "Randall released Madame O'Rourke before he went in search of the vault. Tristan stayed with her. He never saw anything of importance."

"And what about yourself?" Davies asked, huffing as he sat back down. "Did you mysteriously not see any of the treasure, either?"

"No, I was in the vault," I confessed. "It was a small cave, inside the mountains. Much of it had been raided by the natives, and passing travelers, though. There were some gold pieces and a few gems. Anything of significance was already gone."

Davies eyes narrowed as he studied me, distrust written on his features. "You're lying," he finally said, spitting on the floor beside his chair. "Both of you."

"Accuse us all ye wish," Tristan snapped. "When Lomas returns, he will tell ye the truth of it, though. I imagine Bevard sent him off so quickly in the hopes that he would be able to track down some of the missing artifacts."

Trying not to smile, I silently applauded Tristan. He'd made Davies pause in his accusations, the realization that Lomas's sudden departure did indeed match with our stories causing the Grand Master to fall silent.

"I will be calling in other members of your crew to verify and expand on your story," Davies finally said. "In the meantime, I have your new orders."

Motioning to one of the guards at the door, Davies stood, watching as the man exited the space, closing the door behind himself.

Pulling two rolls of paper from his jacket, he eyed us before rolling the forms across the table to us, folding his arms. "You're both being assigned to our privateering vessel, the *Isobel*."

"Don't you need legal papers from the king to captain a privateering vessel?" I asked, surprised. Pulling my paper toward myself, I broke the seal on it and glanced over the first few lines. I was assigned as a rigger, meant to climb the ropes of the ship and help with the sails. It was quick work, and often hard, but I could do it.

"You do." Davies smiled wickedly, a bit of fire in his gaze. "If you're the captain."

Surprised, I glanced at Tristan, who's face had paled some as he looked at his orders.

"I'm being demoted?" he asked, staring back at Davies calmly. "May I ask why? Have I done something to offend ye, or spoken out of turn in the few days since we first met?"

"I have more of a need for riggers than I do captains, at the moment, Monsieur O'Rourke. That, and you managed to burn and sink the last ship The Order saw fit to give you. Not to mention the fact that the treasure you were entrusted with was compromised and your actions regarding your wife have been childish at best. Bevard may have thought you were ready to captain a vessel for him, but you are not ready to do it for me. Does that answer satisfy you?" Davies smiled again, obviously enjoying his belittling of the man.

"Aye," Tristan answered, a level amount of respect to his tone. "It does." His eyes flashed, the only sign of the anger that had silently filled him.

"Of course, along with the demotion, your pay is going to be cut. I've already sent word that you and

194

your wife are to be moved to smaller accommodations, which you will be able to afford on your salary. With things as they are right now, The Order can't afford to keep paying for you to live like the high-born members of society."

That was the tipping point for me. "You do know that Tristan is an Irish clan prince, right?" I asked, aghast at how my friend was being treated. "He's not some pauper off the street. Even if he were, he's done a lot of good work for The Order, and so has his wife. They literally are high-born members of society, as you put it. It doesn't seem right to treat them in such a manner. It's downright rude and disrespectful, if you ask me."

"I'm not asking you," Davies responded sharply. "You are also being removed from the home Bevard settled you in. The Order is not required to find you a new place of residence, though, as you have no family and will on board our ship for most your time. If you would like an apartment in the city, you will have to procure it yourself."

Sitting down, Davies folded his hands together, staring at the ceiling. After a moment, he looked to the door in annoyance. "Where is that guard?"

Right on cue, the entrance opened and the man in question appeared, towing another person behind him. Trying not to stare, I glanced over the man, wondering who he was and what he was doing here.

It was apparent right from the beginning that he was Scottish, the blue, green, red, and black kilt around his waist giving that away in an instant. He wore plain boots and a white shirt as well, a gun belt slung over his shoulder and a sword at his hip. A tartan sash rested across his other shoulder, hidden partially under his long, brown and gray beard. Fierce eyes stared at us, his bald head reflecting the light of the candelabras overhead. I would have guessed he was in his fifties, but there was still a youthfulness to him that made me think he could have been in his late forties, too.

"Grand Master," the Scot said, inclining his head as he stopped just to the side of Davies. "Ye asked to see me?" There was an obvious amount of distaste in his tone, his entire body practically screaming that he had no respect for the man in front of him now.

"Captain MacDonald" Davies remained seated, looking over him with a frown. "It's been some time. It doesn't look like you've done very well since last we met."

"And it looks like ye managed to worm yer way through that pile o' shit ye call a brain and get yerself voted in as leader of this damn circus."

Choking on the air, I hurriedly disguised my laugh into a cough, covering my mouth and trying to appear as apologetic as possible. Tristan did no such thing, though, chuckling under his breath at the comment.

"Ye two know each other?" he asked, giving them an amused smile.

"We ken each other, right," Captain MacDonald replied, frowning. "Davies used to be a rigger on my ship. If ever there was a man meant to stay on land, it's this lad here. Doesn't ken the difference between one knot and the next, let alone how to handle a blade properly."

"Shut up, old man," Davies growled, shaking his head. "I didn't ask you here to belittle me and make a fool of yourself."

"Then what am I here for?" Captain MacDonald frowned, making a noise that only a Scotsman could, clearly highly annoyed with his current situation.

"Meet Tristan O'Rourke and Mark Bell. They're your new riggers."

A wave of recognition washed over me, and I peered at my orders again. There it was—Captain MacDonald's name. We were indeed supposed to be working under him now.

Taken aback, MacDonald stared at the two of us and then at Davies. "But I don't need any more riggers."

"I don't care." Davies smiled evilly. "They're yours. You're here to brief them on your mission within The Order and the destination of the treasure you transport."

Offended, MacDonald stepped back, eyeing Davies. "No."

Davies, acting as if he were ready to blow his own brains away, slammed his hand on the table and glared up at the captain again. "Excuse me?"

"They already ken the mission. We protect the treasure. I willna tell them the destination, though. That's a need to ken piece of information, and they dinna need to ken." He snorted, folding his arms, apparently readying himself to have a showdown right then and there.

"I need to know," Davies growled. "Bevard's map was enchanted so that only he could read it. He died before he could pass it on to the next Grand Master."

"Sounds like a personal problem."

The two men stared at each other, tempers rising, until Davies finally broke.

"Damn it, MacDonald, just tell me where you're taking the treasure!"

"How do I ken ye're not the wee bugger who slit Bevard's throat in the first place, eh? I'll not be telling ye anything, Davies. I ken ye. I wouldn't trust ye with a pet rock." MacDonald snarled, leaning toward the Grand Master, his hands forming fists.

"Fine!" Throwing his hands up, Davies, shook his head. "Fine, don't tell me. I'll find it eventually. I can't fault you for being cautious until the murderer is found." He frowned at Tristan and I. "The *Isobel* leaves port in five days' time. Gather your things and tell your women goodbye. You won't be seeing them for several months, at the least."

Surprised once more, I felt my eyes widen. That was so soon and a long time to be away. Now that Tristan wasn't captain, he wouldn't be able to bring Samantha along as he'd planned. They were going to be split up once more, forced to be apart yet again.

Glancing at Tristan, I saw his face become even more pale, the same realization seeming to cross his features.

"You may go," Davies said to all of us, covering his eyes with his hand. "All of you."

"Aye," Captain MacDonald replied, glancing at us. "We leave with the early morning tide in five days. I expect ye on board the night before. Dinna be late, or I'll lash ye myself."

"I don't understand what's happened." Samantha stood in the hallway, her sword in one hand and a look of shock and dismay on her face. Around her, servants worked to tidy the house, a small pile of trunks slowly gathering by the front door. "Why are we being put out?"

"Davies is trying to make a statement," Tristan replied, frustrated. Tugging at the cloth around his neck, he ripped the garment off, throwing it on the pile of their belongings in anger. "Because I was so close with Bevard, he's pushing me to the bottom of the barrel, so to speak. It lets everyone else know that he won't be continuing the relationships the last Grand Master fostered."

"Where will we live?" Her voice came out as a squeak, her eyes round as she watched him. "Does he mean to make us live in the streets until we leave port?"

He flinched, glancing at me with a pained expression. Apparently, whomever had beaten us to the house to tell the servants they were moving had neglected to mention that Tristan had been demoted.

"We won't be leaving port, lass," he said, still

watching me. Then, taking a deep breath, he turned toward his wife.

Her face fell as she studied him, whatever expression he was wearing alerting her to the arrival of bad news.

"I've lost my position. Davies took the leadership from me and has stationed me on another ship, as a rigger." He spoke quietly and quickly, but he might as well have shouted, the way the statement affected her.

The sword slipped from her hand, clattering to the floor, and her knees buckled. Falling back, she caught herself on the small table behind her, knocking the vase full of flowers that had been sitting on it to the floor and shattering the glass. Tristan was beside her in an instant, holding her up, one hand at her waist and the other in her hair.

"It will be fine," he said, trying to reassure her. "Only a few months. I'll be back before ye know I'm gone. Abella will be here with ye—it won't be as awful as it seems."

Shoving away from him, she straightened her shirt, her hands shaking as she continued to stare at him with wide eyes. "It will not be fine," she choked out, backing against the wall. "The last time you left me here I—I was—" Tears gathered in her eyes, one rolling down her cheek. Wiping it away angrily, she turned to me, as if asking for help.

Shaking my head, I declined coming to her aid. There was nothing I could do for her in this moment, nothing that would ease her spirits or make her believe everything would be fine when Tristan and I were gone. She had every right to be as upset and afraid as she was now. She was being put from her home, her husband taken from her, and the man who had abducted her before was still at large. If it were to happen again, I wouldn't be there to protect her. The world she lived in now was a terrifying one.

Abella, frozen on the stairs above her, seemed to be reasoning with herself, her shoulders settling decisively as she peered over the railing. "You are not the woman you were the last time your husband was unable to take you with him, Samantha." Gracefully, she moved down the steps, quickly, her attention turned to her friend and employer. "You have survived Hell on Earth and come out stronger than ever. What was all your sword practice for, if not to defend yourself when attackers come again? Why do you make yourself get out of bed every day, if not to face the world and prove that you are stronger than the trials given to you? The Samantha O'Rourke I know does not need a man to make her feel safe. She makes herself feel that way. She has walked through time, lived among pirates, battled demons, and conquered evil itself!"

She tucked a hair behind Sammy's ear, and smiled, her expression encouraging. The gesture didn't have its intended effect, though, and Sam moved away, shaking her head.

"I can't do it, Abella," Sam said sadly, another tear rolling down her face. Her hands went to her stomach this time, though, and I instantly felt the pain she still suffered with over Rachel. "I can't lose them both."

"Ye aren't losing me, Sam," Tristan rushed to say, moving close to her once more. "Never, ever. I'll only be gone a few months at most. I'll send word whenever I can. I'll have Mark with me, to make sure I stay away

201

from trouble."

She glanced at me again, lip trembling. Slowly, she nodded, taking several deep breaths. "You'll take care of him?"

"With my life," I promised.

Abella sighed in relief, stepping away from the pair of them, hovering by the door and the growing pile of their belongings.

Tristan, laughing slightly, wiped the tears from her face. "I don't think I need anyone's protection, love. But, if it will make ye feel better, I promise to do nothing without consulting Mark on the matter first."

"You'd better," she said, bossily. "I know you Tristan O'Rourke. You are not a man to wait to do anything, if you can help it."

Chuckling again, he wrapped his arms around her, resting his chin on the top of her head. Only then did he let the worry and sadness cover his own features, his eyes closing as he held her close. "We have five days," he whispered to her. "Five whole days."

Feeling like I was intruding, I turned, heading down the hall. When the cold, fresh air of the courtyard touched my face, I sighed in relief, feeling my own overwhelmed emotions swirling inside me. Stepping into the dirt and dried mud, I slowly ambled along, thinking.

It was a cruel trick of fate, to have Samantha show up in my life, only to be just out of reach. Now, she would be even further; an ocean would be between us. Even worse, I would still be forced to think of her every day when I saw her husband.

One could only hope that the distance would aid me in shutting those feelings off, the hard work of a ship taking up all my time and thought.

"You are troubled as well."

Glancing behind me, I spied Abella, standing in the doorway, her hair blowing gently around her face. She looked as if she'd been helping in the packing, a light sheen of sweat on her neck and chest. Wiping her hands on her apron, she peered at the sky, as if trying to judge the clouds overhead. After a moment, she stared at me, silently judging me as well.

"Would you go for a walk with me?"

The question was abrupt, catching me off guard, and I simply stared, not knowing what to say. I'd been trying to distance myself from her, after all, but it seemed cruel to turn her down now, just before I was to leave on the *Isobel*.

"Don't look so conflicted." She laughed. "It's only a walk. We'll be back before the carriage arrives to take them away."

Blushing slightly, I nodded, clearing my throat as I pulled my jacket around me tighter.

Reaching back through the doorway, she grabbed her cloak off the hook there, sliding it around her shoulders, and strode out into the muck of the courtyard. Her yellow dress seemed to be the only bright and happy thing in the space, save her face.

As we trekked down the alley and onto the street, she smiled at the people around us, offering salutations to a few of them. "I find that exercise does a busy mind good," she stated to me, her pace quick and direct. We passed houses alongside us, and people hurrying through the streets, a carriage rolling by every now and then.

"I suppose it does," I agreed.

"Well, why don't you tell me about yourself, Mark Bell. The most I've ever heard of you was when we met at the Temple and you shared your story with the group."

Surprised, I laughed, having not expected the conversation to move in this direction. "What do you want to know?"

She remained silent, thinking, and then smiled, glancing over at me. "Where were you born?"

"In the colonies."

Stopping in the road, she raised an eyebrow at me, not pleased with my answer. "Half-truths are not going to work today."

Snorting, I motioned for her to keep going, coming to stand closer to her as I spoke. "Maryland," I said softly, peering around to see if anyone was listening. "I was born in Maryland, on a military base called Fort Detrick."

"Your father was a military man?"

Smiling, amused, I shook my head. "My mother. She was a doctor, working in the cancer research department." Seeing that she didn't quite understand, but that she got most of my meaning, I laughed again at her surprise.

"She was part of the militia?"

"The army," I corrected her. "And, yes. Women can enlist in my time. The government paid for her to go to medical school and then stationed her at Fort Detrick, where she could best use her degree."

Wonder filled her features and she stared across the street, her pace slowing some. "Samantha has often told me that women are more privileged in your era," she confessed. "But I don't think I ever realized what

204

exactly that meant. I mean, being part of the military, going to medical school, working as a doctor—those are all things only afforded to men, now. I can't even imagine what I would do with so many options for my life."

"Whatever you want?" Chuckling, I couldn't help but feel a tinge of sadness at her reaction. Abella would never have the opportunity to go to medical school, even though she had an affinity for the practice. She would never own land, vote, or have a major say in the running of her country, all because she'd been born in a century that didn't truly value what a woman could provide.

I'd always thought that it made sense, the way women had been treated in the past. It was a more violent time, full of dangers and hardships. Women were the only option for our species to continue growing. Of course, the men would protect them. They would keep them at home, where they could care for the young and stay safe. It was a biological instinct that couldn't be ignored.

Now, though, I realized I'd had an asinine view of the past. Women were just as influential and important in this year as they were in my own. Abella had stood among men and defended herself just fine. She was smart, self-sufficient, and brave. She didn't need anyone to protect her, let alone a man. If there was biology involved, it was her own instinct protecting her and nothing else.

"Tell me about University," she persuaded, interrupting my thoughts. "What is it like in your time?"

"To be a student or a professor?"

205

"Both. And what is it like to live in the history that you studied so thoroughly?"

With each answer I gave her, she had another question, keeping our minds occupied as our feet traveled the roads of Paris without a care. The sun slowly set, and the lamps lining the avenues were lit by men carrying torches. Our laughter echoed off the cobblestone streets, our arms entwined as we continued over the river and through old city walls. Before I knew it, hours had passed, and still we walked, visiting with each other.

Gradually, the clouds overhead opened, dumping their icy wetness on us. Snickering together, we ducked inside the closest establishment. It was an inn, crowded with people eating and drinking before the fire.

"I'm starving," I confessed, smelling the delicious feast that had been prepared for those willing to pay. "What about you?"

"Food sounds delightful." Removing her cape, she shook the water droplets off it, folding the fabric and pressing in against her midriff.

Squeezing ourselves into a corner far from the warmth of the hearth, we flagged down one of the mistresses wading through the crowd and ordered two plates from her. She left us with a couple glasses of rum and a promise to return soon.

Watching the dining hall, Abella smiled, her face flushed from our adventure together. "Look at them," she said, nodding to the group. "They are all so happy. Not a care in the world. They have all they need for the night. Food, drink, a warm bed to sleep in, and a companion to share their thoughts with."

Nodding in agreement, I took a long drink of the rum, licking my lips when I'd finished. "This is the type of place Sammy would love. Not a hoop skirt in sight."

Shocked, I stared at Abella with wide eyes.

"What is it?" she asked, alarmed.

"Sam," I said slowly. "I've not thought of her for some hours now. That hasn't happened since . . . I don't know when."

"Oh." Breathing a sigh of relief, she laughed again. "I thought something was wrong." Pausing, she seemed to consider something. "I hope they aren't worried about us. We vanished on them. I didn't mean to stay out so long, but I was having such a good time talking with you."

"Me, too," I agreed. "It was . . . relaxing." Smiling at her, I felt the strange flip of my heart, a sensation that had normally been reserved for Sam. Suddenly, I felt very sad to be leaving her behind, wishing that we had more than just five days to talk like we had tonight.

At the same moment, I was acutely aware of how old Abella was. I would never be able to forget how much of a gap there was between us—twenty-eight years. It may have been normal for couples in this era to be so far apart, but I didn't know if I could get past that.

And I was still in love with Samantha.

What would it be like, though, I wondered, to love someone else? Would they feel they were my second choice? Would I feel that way about them? But, how wondrous our life would together would be! For, if I were to love someone else, it would have to be a love to eclipse what I felt for Sammy. I loved her more than

207

the moon and the stars. To feel more than that for someone else would mean that I'd left my entire self behind, that I'd found a love as bright as the sun. It would have to warm my entire body, steal my thoughts from me, and make me unable to exist without the woman who caused such strength of conviction and adoration.

I didn't know if such a love existed.

"What are you thinking about?" Abella asked, bringing my attention to the moment at hand. Her eyes shone as she smiled at me, her dark hair untied and hanging around her face. It was a beautiful look on her, her pale skin glowing in the dim firelight.

Seized upon by an urge to ask questions I shouldn't, I grinned, leaning forward. "What would you do if you loved someone who's heart belonged to another? What would you say to them?" I asked slowly, curious to hear her answer.

Pursing her lips, she considered me for a moment, eyes searching my own. "It would depend," she finally said.

"On what?"

"On whether the person I loved truly belonged to another person. If so, I would say nothing. It's not my place to disrupt the lives of others to satisfy my own selfish needs."

Feeling slightly chastised, as if she'd been directly referring to my affection for Samantha, I picked up my cup, taking another long drink.

"If they did not, though," she said quietly. "If they did not belong to another, if their heart was their own to give freely, to remove from the affection for someone else, then I would say—" She paused, looking down at her hands in her lap. After a moment, she laughed slightly, shaking her head, and rose from her chair, leaning across the table.

Before I realized what was happening, her lips were on mine, soft and warm. It was a simple kiss, one that wouldn't incite songs or retellings of the moment, but it made my heart stop, my body freezing as her hand touched the side of my face. I didn't even know if I was kissing her in return, so surprised was I by the sudden movement, my breath caught in my chest.

Pulling away, she studied me evenly, searching my eyes. "Pick me. Choose me. I know I am not—them—but I love you so. And I am here. I will always be here. Choose me."

She sat, clearing her throat, a deep blush spreading across her face as she looked down at her lap again.

Leaning back in my chair, I regarded her with surprise and confusion. "I don't think we're talking about a rhetorical situation anymore," I stated, my mouth dry.

Snorting, she shook her head. "Were we when you asked me to begin with?" She stared at me pointedly, lifting her glass to her lips. Her hand shook slightly as she grasped it, an underlying nervousness to her entire being.

"No, I guess we weren't." I felt acutely aware of her, sitting there on the other side of the table. Her breath was quick, eyes anxious for me to say more. The tantalizing flush of her skin made me feel even more thirsty and I gulped down another drink, not knowing what to say.

Silence stretched between us, lasting past when the mistress returned with our food and refilled our cups. Inside, I was screaming at myself to say something, but I couldn't seem to get my mouth to work. Halfway through the meal, I finally set my silverware down and sighed, looking at her apologetically.

"I shouldn't have asked," I said, awkward and unsure. "I apologize. I don't know what I was thinking."

"I shouldn't have kissed you." She blushed again and then kept going. "You were thinking about Samantha and how you feel for her," she said, compassionately, working to cut the small piece of meat she'd been given. "You love her. I know that."

"I do." I said it quietly, afraid of hurting her, but was surprised to see her shrug and look at me the same she always had.

"I don't expect you to change anything for me, Mark. You are your own person. You've loved Sam for as long as I've known you. At this point, I don't even know if you are capable of untangling your heart from her. As it stands, you are destined to be unhappy as you watch her love someone else."

"Aren't you doing the same to yourself?" I pointed out. "If you truly feel that way about me?"

She shook her head, smiling at me. "The difference between us is I choose happiness, Mark. My romantic life does not dictate the joy I feel in other parts of my existence. I can face unrequited love and still smile through the day. Maybe, someday you'll realize that you have that same choice, as well."

"The choice of happiness with you, you mean."

"No. Being in a romantic relationship does not guarantee happiness. But choosing it for yourself?

That is true joy. You have that choice. Happiness for just you."

The house was quiet and dark when we returned, the carriage I'd hired to bring us back making the only noise in the night as it pulled away from the front door. Rain still pattered lightly, making the road slick and slippery and the air that much colder. Where the conversation with Abella had somehow managed to keep me warm earlier in the day, her silence now made me feel all the more alone.

Walking down the street to the alley, we looped our way around the house and into the courtyard. Each step I took, I felt as if I'd made some grave error in not returning her affections. What could I say to her, though? Both of us had laid our feelings in front of each other and there had been no resolution to the situation.

Opening the back door, Abella went inside first, disappearing into the black of the kitchen without a word. Sighing, I rubbed a hand over my face, trying to decide if it was worth it to wake the carriage driver and have him take me home. Sam and Tristan wouldn't mind if I stayed the night, but I didn't know if Abella wanted me around.

Suddenly, she screamed, the sound muffled by

something, and I barreled through the doorway, searching every direction for her. When I finally caught sight of her in the darkness, her form barely visible in the light from the coals of the fire, a thousand thoughts passed through my mind.

She was being held, a hand pressed over her mouth, the man who had grabbed her doing his best to keep her from fighting. Despite his best efforts, though she was putting up quite the struggle.

At first, I thought Randall and his men had come again, breaking into the house and seizing her. Then, when I realized the man wasn't trying to kill her, I thought he was a thief, who had gotten it in his mind to rape one of the servants. Several other scenarios raced through my mind as I rammed myself toward him, a growl on my lips, fists raised to strike.

"About time ye show up."

Spinning around, I looked at Captain MacDonald in surprise as he lit the lamp on the table beside him, throwing the situation into clearer light.

"Valentine, let the poor girl go," he said to the man who'd grabbed Abella. "We dinna have the time to be playin' cat and mouse." Rising, he straightened his kilt and motioned to another man who had appeared in the doorway behind me.

"O'Rourke will be down in a moment," the man said, leaning against the molding, the dark leather of his outfit blending into the night around him. He held a knife in his hands, turning the blade over and over, playing with it like a seasoned professional.

"Thank ye, Dagger. See to it that the carriage is ready, would ye?"

"What's going on?" I asked, watching as Abella

213

shoved away from the gangly man called Valentine.

"We're shipping out tonight," the Scotsman replied. "Seeing as how Davies saw fit to give ye and O'Rourke to me, I thought it best ye be on board."

"Tonight?" Confused, I glanced at Abella and then to the captain. "Why?"

"Davies is a sneaky rat, that's why." Watching me with a grim expression, he sighed. "We have to leave before he can assign anyone else to the crew to spy for him. I'll not be having my treasure compromised, not if I can help it."

"What is the meaning of this?" Tristan shoved his way into the kitchen, Samantha close behind. "Why do you come into our home in such a manner?"

"It's not yer home any longer." MacDonald snorted. "The only reason yer still here is these two—" He motioned to Abella and I. "Off gallivanting through the city, causing ye to have to wait for them to return."

Dagger appeared in the doorway again. "Carriage is ready."

"Very well. Let's get on our way then." MacDonald motioned to his men and they all headed to leave. "Ye two say yer goodbyes. Ye'll not see yer womenfolk for some months to come."

Taking the lantern with him, he nodded to the four of us and followed the other two, going into the courtyard, leaving the room in darkness once more.

A stunned silence filled the space for a moment, the words of the captain setting in slowly.

"Tonight?" Samantha whispered. "Now?"

"You had five days," Abella echoed, her voice flat.

214

Not responding, Tristan grabbed Samantha by the hand, pulling her into the hall after him. Their footsteps stopped just out of view, his voice murmuring to her gently—saying his goodbyes.

Realizing that I had no choice other than to follow my new captain and leave, or stay and be punished, I stared at Abella, the weight of our earlier conversation crashing down around me. Could I pick happiness for myself? I didn't know. All I knew right then was that Sam was currently with her husband and I was with a woman who'd said she loved me. We wouldn't see each other for who knew how long, and I could possibly die before we ever set eyes on each other again. It may have been the sudden urgency of the mission I was now sworn to follow, or even the rum I'd had at dinner, but I couldn't find it in myself to listen to any of the reasons I had for staying away from her in that moment.

Striding over, I pushed her hair out of her face, wrapping an arm around her waist. "Forgive me," I whispered, not knowing if I was talking to her, God, Samantha, or myself.

Pressing my lips against hers, I closed my eyes, savoring the feel of her skin on mine. I'd caught her off guard, her form freezing the same as mine had when she'd kissed me. Her hair was soft in my fingers, though, her cheek warm under my palm. Pulling away, knowing I had most likely already crossed a line I shouldn't have, I looked at her shocked expression.

She grabbed me, pulling me toward her, our lips meeting once more. This kiss was different from the others, though. It felt alive and exhilarating, like I was taking the first real breath of my life. Every other thought in my mind melted away, until there was only her and her touch, her fingers on my face, her body against my own. When we finally broke apart, it seemed as if I'd been broken down to nothing and rebuilt entirely by her, a part of me now forever tied to her.

Resting my forehead against hers, I rubbed my thumb over her lip, breathing deeply. "Be safe, Abella," I muttered. "Don't get yourself into trouble."

"You're the one who needs to worry about trouble. I will be fine. Promise to write me, even if it's only once." She toyed with the kerchief around my neck, loosening the knot like she'd seen me do so many times.

"I promise."

"Will it be like this when you return?" she asked, hesitantly. "With us, I mean."

Sighing, I closed my eyes, grimacing. "I don't know." Stepping away, I frowned apologetically. "Time will tell, I guess."

Pressing her lips into a thin line, she nodded. "I understand."

Shaking my head, I took her face in my hands again, wanting to reassure her. "You don't. Whatever this is, what we're doing right now, I *want* it. There's too much to deal with right now, though. I can't answer every single question in your head and mine right at this moment. My captain is literally waiting for me outside. I need time to process this. You do, too."

She smiled slightly, pleased with what I'd said.

"I will write," I promised again. "And we will figure this out. I just need time first."

The door opened again and MacDonald's head

216

popped into view. "Let's go," he ordered. "We'll miss the tide if we dinna hurry our arses along."

Releasing Abella once more, I grabbed her hand, kissing her fingers, and turned to leave, glancing down the hall at Tristan and Samantha. He was kissing her goodbye, wiping the tears from her eyes, and then he was striding toward me, a hard expression on his face.

She met my gaze behind him, her hand raised in farewell. For the first time since I'd found her in this time, I didn't feel so helpless at the thought of being without her again.

Turning to the kitchen, though, I suddenly found myself wondering how I would make it by without Abella to talk to and reassure me of things. She smiled at me and I stared at her once more, my heart hammering in my chest.

"Move along, lovebirds," MacDonald ordered, his voice gruff. "We haven't got all night."

Tearing my eyes away from her, I watched as Tristan turned away from his wife once again, leading the way out.

No sooner did I step outside, did the exit close behind me, and I faced the carriage waiting for us to climb inside. Dagger sat beside the driver, a bored expression on his face. Valentine was peering at us from his seat inside, moving over as MacDonald climbed in beside him. Without question, Tristan and I took our places across from them, closing the entrance and remaining silent as we lurched forward, leaving the courtyard quickly.

"You've a beautiful wife, Monsieur," Valentine said to Tristan, his voice surprisingly low. "She will miss you while you are gone."

"Thank ye," Tristan responded stiffly.

"And you," Valentine continued, seemingly unaware of the uncomfortable air between us all. "Your companion is very beautiful, too, Monsieur Bell. Quite the fighting spirit. I was afraid she would bite my finger off before she realized I didn't mean her any harm."

"In the lass's defense, ye did grab her in the black o' night and try to keep her from screaming." MacDonald grinned in the dim light, his eyes thoughtful as he watched the two of us. Silence surrounded us once more, the wheels outside clattering over the streets, the driver urging the horses on.

"I suppose I should explain myself," he finally said, leaning back in his seat. "Though, ye both listened right well for having just joined the crew." Laughing once, he crossed his arms. "It will do ye good to act the same in the future."

"Captain doesn't take kindly to rule breakers," Valentine offered.

"No, I do not. Nor, do I spies."

"We are no spies, Monsieur," Tristan interrupted, his expression guarded.

"Any dolt could see that." Waving a hand at him, MacDonald leaned forward again, lowering his voice. "The two of ye were only assigned to my crew as a punishment for the difficult time Davies had when he worked as one of my riggers."

"Punishment?" Finding my voice, I raised an eyebrow. "We did nothing to the man."

"Not yer punishment. Mine." He snorted, shaking his head. "O'Rourke here is starting to get a reputation for losing treasures. Bell is a strange man who's assisted the enemy. Davies thinks that giving the both of ye to me will somehow lead to my own demise and him discovering where my part of the treasure lies."

At a loss for words, I stared at him, my mouth slightly open in surprise. After a beat, I gathered myself, clamping my lips together and sucking in a deep breath.

"If Davies was one of yer riggers, why does he not know at least the general area of your treasure port?" Tristan asked, choosing to ignore the slight insults that had been thrown at us. "He did ask where it was when we first met, did he not?"

MacDonald's grin was one of amusement and annoyance. "Aye, he did. I dinna have access to the port when he was under me. We were only a layover for the treasure. Once every half year, we would meet with the flagship of our section and pass over the items we carried."

"The *Isobel* is the flagship now, then?" Tristan pressed.

"We are." The Scotsman sniffed, staring us down again. "I expect ye both ken yer places on the ship and have worked in the role before?"

"Yes," I responded.

"Me as well." Tristan still sounded as if he didn't trust anyone around him, his body still next to me, a strange sense of nervousness and anger coming from him.

"Good. I run a tight ship. Everyone has their place and role. If ye don't fill yer duties, ye will be punished. As riggers, ye'll be expected to maintain the sails and ropes. On occasion, ye will assist in the galley and with swabbing the deck. Those are chores every member of the crew takes part in, on a rotating schedule.

"It would behoove ye to know, coming from a pirate vessel, there is no voting on my ship. My word is law and will not be questioned. This is for two reasons, the first being that our legal papers to privateering are in my name and any vote that would remove me from office would make the vessel turn pirate in the eyes of the French government. The second is for yer safety. I have sworn to do my duty and protect my crew—this includes the two of ye now. If I give an order ye dinna like, ye'll have to accept that it was for yer better good. Do ye understand?"

"Aye, Captain," we replied, recognizing he was using his authority over us to address us now.

The carriage skidded to a stop, the sound of water lapping the shore outside reaching my ears. Grabbing the handle of the exit, MacDonald pushed it open, hopping out like a man much younger than he was.

Confused, Tristan went after him. "Are we sailing the river to Rouen?" he asked, stopping short as something in front of him caught his attention.

"Aye, we are," MacDonald replied, laughing.

Sliding from my seat, I exited the ride as well, gaping as I looked at the river in front of us. "How did you get it all the way to Paris?" I asked, staring at the galleon waiting in the shallow harbor. "The Seine isn't deep enough to bring ocean craft in this far!"

"As ye can see, it is. It took some work, and we canna leave until the tide comes in, but we got her in. We were trying to make the vote and I dinna want to leave her so far away, should something happen to her while I'm in the city on business."

"It's the rain," Dagger muttered behind me, his

blade still in his hand like a play thing. "There's been so much of it over the past year, the river is flooded. We wouldn't have made it otherwise. Captain knows this, which is why he decided to try it in the first place. He didn't want us to miss having our voice heard."

"I pity the fool who doesn't possess yer understanding and tries his hand at it blindly," Tristan said, a hint of admiration to his tone. "I never would have been able to do it with my ship."

MacDonald made a Scottish noise, striding toward the gangplank and motioning for everyone to follow. "Tide waits for no man and we have no time to lose. Every man to his station!"

Staring at the wide, open ocean ahead, I sighed, feeling more at home than I had my entire time in Paris. There was something about the fresh air, sunshine, and the gentle rocking of the waves below that made my spirits lift and put my mind at ease.

"There she is," Tristan said beside me, examining the expanse as well. "A sight for my sore eyes."

"Bell! O'Rourke! Stop hanging around and get to work!" On the deck below, Dagger shouted at us, fulfilling his duties as Quartermaster in making sure we were holding up our end.

Unwrapping my arm from the rigging ropes I'd settled myself into, I began the climb down, stopping to check a knot here and there. It had been three days since we left Paris, moving slowly down the river and onto the ocean. Now, as we left the coast behind us, the

221

wind pushing us forward with ease, I found myself wondering how long we would be gone and what treasures we would behold before we set our sights on France once more.

"Bell," Dagger called, motioning me over. "You're on galley duty tonight. Go and relieve Smithy, would you?"

Nodding, I adjusted my course, taking the stairs to the second deck. Hammocks hung across the space, this floor of the ship being the crew quarters. The ceiling was a large, metal grate, which could be removed if necessary, creating a pit in the center of the top deck that opened into the quarters. In the middle of the space, pushed up against the starboard side, the galley sat, dried meat and herbs hanging around the beams and tiny counter that blocked it off into its own little space. Coals from breakfast's fire still glowed in the hearth, the wood around it blackened from smoke and flames.

Smithy—the man whose main job on the ship was carpentry and blacksmithing—was nowhere to be seen, but it was no matter. Striding into the place, I began glancing around, surveying what I had to work with for the evening. There were the normal staples of the ship, like oats, beans, and jerky, as well as flour and salt. Eggs sat cradled in a basket, the hen that had birthed them already dead and eaten. More livestock was held below, the crew's source of milk and fresh meat for the foreseeable future.

Moving around the galley, I decided to make a skillet type meal, with the beans and some of the beef that had been brought aboard in Paris. I grabbed the dish I wanted to use and set it in the coals, ready to get to work.

Behind me, a pan clattered to the floor, catching me off guard. Spinning around, I looked to see what had happened, only to feel like the breath had been knocked out of me.

Holding a finger to her lips, Abella's eyes begged me not to say anything. She was dressed like the other men on the ship, her hair tied up in a bun, her hat having fallen off in her attempt to catch the pan she'd knocked over. Crouched beside the table the fire sat on, she breathed quickly, staring me down with a determined expression.

"What are you doing here?" I hissed, crouching down as well.

She shook her head, staying silent, and then slowly reached up, taking some old bread off the counter. Then, smoothly and without sound, she slunk off into the depths of the ship, where I couldn't see her.

Samantha O'Rourke

The hold stank, which didn't bode well for the rest of the trip. If it was already smelly, and we had only been on board for three days, how much worse would it get over time?

Sniffing delicately, I glanced up, certain I was right below where they were holding the animals. The stench from their feces was strong and I suddenly wondered if the small amount of salt water I'd been crouching in was pee.

Grimacing, I quickly moved to the side, holding onto the large, tied down boxes stacked around me for balance. Of course I was under the animal pen. Nothing had been stored beneath it, but cargo lined the entire area, leaving the perfect place for Abella and I to stow away. We were hiding among shit, literally, but it would have to do.

Suddenly, Abella appeared through the small crack between the containers. There was bread in her hand and the bottle I'd given her to fill with water sloshed around her neck, held in place with a rope.

"Were you seen?" I whispered, meeting her in the middle of our tiny space.

She grimaced, answering without saying a single word.

"Damn," I muttered under my breath.

Silence stretched between us, the faint sound of a goat filtering down from overhead. What were we going to do now? There was nowhere for us to hide that they wouldn't be able to find. We could lock ourselves in the brig, but that would simply make it easier for them to catch us. France was only a day behind us. It wouldn't be too difficult for them to drop us on a random shore like the stowaways we were.

Finally, I sighed, rubbing my face. There was nothing to do but accept it and prepare to defend our decisions to the captain and crew. Hopefully, they wouldn't be as angry as I expected them to be— Tristan, especially. Turning to Abella, I resolved to be ready for anything that could be thrown our way.

"How long till they find us, do you think? I was hoping we wouldn't be discovered until we were too far out to sea for Captain MacDonald to turn around and drop us off."

She shook her head, looking past the boxes and in the direction of the brig. It was dark, here in the bottom of the ship, but the bars of the ocean prison could dimly be seen, thick and menacing in the background. Neither of us had been on a ship with an actual brig before, not one that we'd seen anyway. It was a constant reminder of all the laws we were breaking, and a promise of what would happen to us if we were caught.

"It was Mark," she finally said, turning her attention toward me again. "In the galley. I'd waited until the cook left to use the head, but Mark showed up before I could get anything to eat. I'm sorry, Samantha."

Shaking my head, I laid a finger across my mouth, falling silently into thought once more. After a few beats, I spoke again. "He recognized you?"

"Without a doubt. He asked what I was doing here, but I didn't answer." Leaning against the container behind her, she thumped her head against it in anger, frustration on her features. "All of that work and they're going to just take us back."

"I'm not so sure," I replied slowly, still thinking. "Mark might not say anything about it. He would know how much trouble we would get in. He might be punished for it as well, if they think he helped us get on board."

"How could he have? He was with the captain the entire time."

"Trust me," I said, smiling grimly. "They never think a woman managed to do something by herself. They'll blame him, or Tristan."

The thought of my husband made me pause. It was very likely Mark would tell him he'd seen Abella. My presence on board would be assumed, as well. I would probably see both before the sun rose tomorrow, whether we were caught or not.

"What should we do?"

Peering at the cargo around us in the dim light, I sighed again, feeling like there had to be something we could do to keep from getting caught, even if it was just long enough for us to be thrown in the brig for the remainder of the journey, instead of returned to France. As I examined everything, a slow sense of despair and acceptance settling over me, my eyes finally landed on our salvation.

"We'll make it that much harder to be discovered."

Motioning for her to move aside, I went to the box she'd been leaning against, touching a slat that was sticking out slightly further than the others. With some effort, I managed to pull it away from the rest of the container, revealing the inside. It was full of cloth, and I smiled.

"Help me with these other boards," I said quickly. "Pull them away, but make sure not to break them."

After a few moments—and more than a couple winces over how much noise we were making—we removed the boards on the bottom of the container, opening a space just large enough for the both of us to sit inside. Once we removed some of the fabric, stowing it between two of the other cases, we began working on a way to quickly put the boards back in place. The process took longer than the undoing of the thing, but finally, after half an hour, we had managed to climb inside and close the opening. Anyone who came searching wouldn't even know we were there.

"Here," Abella whispered, ripping the bread she'd stolen in two and offering me a half. "It's not much, but it will do."

Nestled in the cloth, warm and somewhat dry, I munched on the stale piece, silently praying that my plan would work. I couldn't get caught and sent back to Paris. Every fiber of my being knew I had to be with Tristan. Bad things happened when we weren't together.

Frowning, I let my mind travel to the edges of the thoughts I didn't dare touch, the ones that filled me

227

with such pain and misery I wished I could take a blade to my brain and cut them from me. They were surrounded by a wall of anger and fear, locked tight behind a door of denial and self-loathing. It was like there was a vast desert inside me, those memories hidden in the deepest, darkest part of the hot hell. I didn't dare cross the barrier and go through the entrance without Tristan at my side. Sometimes, even when he was with me, I couldn't face those moments. It was too much too soon.

Still, a single name managed to pass the divide I'd placed to protect myself. Sucking in a sharp breath, I squeezed my eyes shut, trying to stop the image from coming. It was no use, though.

Rachel. My beautiful baby Rachel. I could still remember what it felt like to hold her tiny body in my hand, her skin so pale and translucent. Her eyes were shut, as if sleeping, her fingers curled together in a tiny fist. I would've given anything to see her take a breath, to hear her cry, to find any signs of life in her, but, no. She had been too small, too early. There was no way she would've lived even if she'd been born alive. It was better she'd passed away inside me, warm and surrounded by my love, instead of in the cruel world I brought her into.

Sniffling, I pushed her memory away, searching for something, anything that would save me from having to relive the heartbreaking moments I'd had with her.

That was when he appeared at the surface. His face, dirty and sinister, a smirk on his lips, black, greasy hair hanging around his pasty skin, shining at me through the darkness, like a challenge to come and find him.

Thomas Randall.

Embracing the rage that flowed through me, I suddenly found myself wishing we would be caught hiding. At least then, when I was in the brig, I could practice sword play again, or work on building my strength. Here, in the box, there was nothing I could do but plot all the ways I would kill him when I got the chance. Every day, I cursed myself for not taking the opportunity to do so in Arizona. I'd been so weak from captivity, though, and concerned with keeping him from his goal, I hadn't ended him when I should have.

I wouldn't make that mistake again.

Resolving to not let my time go to waste, I slowly began to picture the pressure points on the body, going over the options of attack and how I would get into position to use them against the person I fought. When I'd finished with that, I settled on the organs, mentally kicking and punching, fighting my way through every scenario I could think of.

"Abella!"

Torn from my pretend battle, I froze, hardly even daring to breathe as I listened.

Mark's voice hissed in the silence quietly, his tone somewhat angry. His footsteps sounded close, but didn't stop outside our box. "I know you're down here," he whispered, a frantic edge to his tone. "Why? What are you doing?"

There was a cramp in my hip, but I didn't dare move to stretch it, not while he was here. My companion remained silent as well, not a single movement coming from her direction. Unable to see in front of me in the space, I didn't know if she was asleep or not. For a moment, I considered revealing our position. It was only Mark, after all. He was one of my best friends. I didn't trust him not to give us away, though, and remained silent, hoping our hideaway would remain a secret.

He whispered a few more times, the sound fading into the abyss and I relaxed, a feeling of safety coming over me. After about five minutes, he passed by again, this time quickly and without staying quiet.

Knowing he had given up for now, I closed my eyes, ready to let sleep take me. He would be back, certainly, but we were still safe until then.

My earlier rage having been quelled by the sudden interruption, I found my thoughts drifting once more, settling around the only person who could ever really make me feel at peace.

Tristan. The picture of his face had often been the only thing that kept me going. Sometimes, when he was sleeping, I would watch him, memorizing every detail of his appearance, locking the image away for any occasion we might be apart from each other. His hair hung in his eyes a bit now, grown out while we were separated these past months. Light and curly, I found I was somewhat partial to the longer style. It gave him the youthful look that was missing from his battle-hardened visage. When we'd returned to Paris, he'd cut most of the locks off, but I'd managed to convince him to keep some of the darling pieces.

Green eyes that shone like the stars in the sky always came next in my memory. I'd stared into them so many times, it was impossible to forget them. His nose, long and thin, led down to lips that were soft and warm, his skin smooth and tan from a life at sea. The rest of what I'd locked away were little things, like the way his cheeks dimpled when he smiled big, or the way he scratched his chin when he hadn't shaved in a while, the stubble itchy and bothersome. The slight beard made him look even more dashing, though—a fact he knew—and so he usually kept a light dusting of facial hair, well-trimmed and thoroughly handsome. Many a woman sighed when they saw him, taking in his muscled physique and breathtaking appearance. Only I was granted the privilege of being his wife, though, of loving and supporting him through this mess of an existence we called life.

Frowning, I silently cursed myself for somehow coming full circle, back to my bad memories and away from the ones I so desperately wanted to be lost in. Shoving the images of my captivity aside, I tried to focus on anything else, desperate to keep myself from going down the path that would lead me into nightmares once I fell asleep.

Images flashed through my mind in a rush as I tried to distract myself. One second I was marrying Tristan on the beach, the next we were dancing at our reception. After that, he was kissing me below deck, the two of us hidden in the darkness of the ship he helped run. Then we were in the gardens at The Palace of Versailles, strolling arm in arm, taking in the scenery.

If I tried hard enough, I could hear his voice in my head, low and husky, as I imagined his fingers brushing across my cheek.

"I love ye, Sam." His voice was as much a comfort as his face.

Sighing, I settled myself further into the fabric,

letting the cargo wrap me in a cocoon of warmth and safety. Abella's breathing was slow and even, now, obviously telling me she was asleep, as I'd suspected.

Hoping to join her peaceful state, I slowly counted backward from one hundred, focusing on the numbers, until I faded away into the deep, lost in a world that no one had yet been able to save me from.

The darkness was suffocating, pressing in on all sides, crushing me with its weight. The odor of sea salt and sweat smells hung in the air, mixing with the tart scent of my own terror. That, coupled with the soft swaying motion of a vessel at sea, was the only indication that I was not where I should be.

Pressing myself into a corner, scratching along the wooden walls to try and get my bearings, my body trembled as I peered into the black once more, trying to see any type of exit. Only the void greeted me, though, not a single thing in sight around me. It was like being locked in a haunted house, when the hair on the back of your neck stands on end and your breath comes quick, every fiber of your being knowing that something is about to happen. I needed a weapon of some sort, even a tiny blade to protect myself, but there was nothing. I was alone in my breeches and shirt, my bare feet cold on the damp floor.

And then he was there, looming out of the shadows, his sickening grin giving me the urge to vomit.

"Samantha," he said, his voice patronizing as he shook his head. Long, black, greasy hair swung in front

of his features and he pushed it back, out of the way. The action brought his face into sharper focus and I recoiled, wishing I could melt through the wall and into the ocean, to freedom.

"Shhh." He raised a finger to his lips, chuckling as he bade me remain quiet. It was then that I noticed the blade grasped in his other hand, the tip pointy and sharp. He held it out lazily, gesturing for me to rise. The red of his shirt was like blood, the black of his pants fading into the space around us.

Gathering my bearings, I stood. Still, being trapped in this corner wasn't stopping me from glaring hard at him "I hope you burn in Hell." My tone was more bitter than I'd expected, but I meant every word. Thomas Randall was the scum of all the earth and deserved to rot for the things he'd done.

"Don't be like that. I thought we were getting along so well." He smiled, leaning in, eyes devouring me hungrily. Slowly, he guided the knife toward me, resting the edge along my face as he stepped forward, closing the space between us.

"Get away from me," I snarled, shoving at him.

He didn't budge, not even a tiny space, as if I hadn't even touched him. Instead, he slid the blade down my skin, almost cutting my neck, the blade catching in the fabric of my shirt as it moved across my chest and came to rest over my stomach. Resting his cheek against mine, he inhaled, sighing with pleasure before pulling away to study me.

"So beautiful," he murmured, his free hand playing with a strand of my hair.

Jerking away, I turned my head, trying to put any space I could between the two of us.

"And feisty!" Chuckling, he grabbed my jaw forcefully, turning me to look at him again. "Chosen by the gods, naturally. Tell me, Sammy, do you miss your own time?"

"Leave me alone," I growled, shoving him. "Tristan will come for me, and when he does, you'll wish you'd never been born."

He snarled, bringing the blade against my throat in an instant. "He's not coming," he spat. "Not here. In this place, you are mine."

He kissed me, his mouth attacking mine with rage and strength, body pressed against mine like a stone I could not move on my own. Scrambling, I clawed at his flesh, my scream muted beneath his crushing embrace. The more I struggled the more ferocious he became, though, the blade at my throat pressing into my skin and drawing blood. In an instant, I realized there was nothing I could do to escape him.

Trembling with fear, I slammed my eyes shut, mind racing as I tried to grasp onto anything that would help me. Slowly, an awareness filled me—I was dreaming.

"This isn't real," I muttered against him, still trying to push him away. "This isn't real!"

Tears flowed down my face, my neck sticky with the few drops of blood that had rolled away from the small cut he gave me, and I was suddenly screaming at him, pounding him with my hands.

"It's not real!" I cried, feeling the edges of my consciousness starting to fade out. "You're not real!"

Breaking away, he stared at me with madness in his eyes, a crazy giggle sounding from his breathless form. "On the contrary, dear Sam. It doesn't get more real than this. "

"Samantha!"

Abella's voice hissed at me through the darkness, her hands pressed over my mouth as she struggled to keep my form from thrashing around.

Still confused and gripped by the nightmare, I lashed out, panicked. It was as if Randall were still there, holding me down, forcing me through his disgusting display of dominance. Flailing, desperate to regain some kind of control, I felt my knuckles connect with jaw bone, the pressure on top of me lessening as she leaned away.

"Ouch!" Slapping me hard, she put her hand over my mouth again, sounding breathless as she spoke. "Sam, it's me, Abella! You're going to get us caught if you don't stop!"

Slowly, her words started to make sense to me and I stilled, the inner turmoil of my episode hot and bubbling just under the surface. Her weight on top of me was suddenly comforting, as was the smell of the sea and wooden crate around us. I tenderly touched the fabrics next to me, counting to five as I forced myself to breathe deeply. After a few more moments, the panic attack subsided and I collapsed back against the floor, a few tears of relief rolling down my cheeks.

"Did I hurt you?" I finally asked, clearing my throat roughly to try and ease the soreness and clogged feeling it had.

"Only a little," she whispered back. There was no

malice or offense in her tone, but I felt bad all the same. "What about you? Are you okay?"

Touching the spot where she'd slapped me, I winced, the area still smarting some. I didn't think it would leave a bruise, though, and I sighed, silently cursing myself over the whole ordeal. "It's fine," I answered, moving to adjust my position some. "How long?"

"A minute or two. The sound woke me and I did all I could to wake you up. It took a moment to do—someone may have heard above."

I didn't need to see her face to know she was worried about the possibility. We'd managed to stay hidden in the hold for another four days since Mark saw her in the galley. The odds of us being returned to France now weren't very likely, not if Captain MacDonald wanted to stay on schedule, at least, but I felt it was better for us to stay out of sight for as long as possible. Abella had agreed, promising to do all she could to keep the secret.

We'd come up with a new plan for survival, trying to keep to ourselves. Before, we would take turns sneaking out to steal a tiny bit of food. It had to be enough to keep us from starving, but not so much that it was noticed. While the crew slept at night, we would hurry to the head and relieve ourselves, one keeping watch while the other did her business. Now, though, we didn't dare take from the galley until it was black as night and the crew slept in their hammocks beside it. The head was abandoned as well, replaced with an old bucket that looked to have once housed pitch. It wasn't the most glamourous—or well scented—lifestyle, but we were making it work.

Or, at least, we had been. Until tonight, I'd been lucky enough to not be visited by terrors. Thinking I'd only been plagued with them while at our home in Paris, I'd relaxed, thankful that I didn't have to see my captor's face each time I closed my eyes. It was clear to me now, though, that we should have gagged me each time we slept, as I'd planned to do when we first stowed away. It was too late now, though.

There was a sound on the other side of the hold, where the hatch was. Men's voices flittered through the space, followed by the barking of dogs.

Feeling a slight chill rush over me, I froze, eyes growing wide. It hadn't occurred to me that there might be dogs on board. They would sniff us out in minutes, despite our position beneath the animal pen. It wouldn't matter that we'd hidden ourselves in a crate, being extra careful to make sure nothing was out of place.

What if the hounds were trained to attack on sight? Were we about to be maimed? Killed even? A million images of people attacked by animals flashed through my mind, my heart racing as I listened to the sounds get closer. Would it be better to surrender? I didn't know what to do.

Reaching through the darkness, I found Abella's hand, trembling and cold in my own. She was probably thinking much the same as I was, jumping slightly as a bark sounded mere feet away from us.

"Over here!" a man's voice yelled, summoning the rest of the group toward us.

Thinking quickly, I tried to guess what would be worse; should we stay in the box and hope they would pass by us, but have nowhere to run if they did discover our position and the dogs attacked? Or should we reveal ourselves now, giving us ample space to try and escape any kind of attack?

Deciding in an instant, I pushed against the boards we'd removed, letting them clatter to the floor, splashing into the water outside. Before I could scramble out, though, a huge, furry thing jumped on top of me, pinning me down. To my surprise, it licked my face enthusiastically, laying down on top of me to cuddle. Beside me, Abella was receiving the same treatment from a second dog, crying in surprise as she was blindsided by the shaggy beast.

"It's a pair of women!" The sailor sounded surprised, his comrades gathering around him.

"Not just any women," a voice said, full of annoyance and distaste. It was one I recognized, despite still being mauled with love. Dagger sighed, the frustration we'd caused him evident in every sound he made. "That's O'Rourke's wife and her maid."

Calling to the dogs to come away, he peered into the box, staring at the two of us with a frown as he held the lantern in his hand over our forms. He appeared much the same as he had when I'd seen him in Paris, wearing all black and a belt that boasted at least eight knives around his waist. His beard had grown some, his head covered in a makeshift turban to help protect from the sun, and the bridge of his nose was slightly sunburned, but those were the only differences.

"*Madame*," he said, his voice tight even though he nodded his head as a sign of respect. "Were you aware you chose our most expensive batch of cargo to soil and destroy?"

Laughing slightly, I shook my head, sitting up

slowly. "I wasn't thinking about cost when I picked it, Sir. Or should I say Quartermaster? That is your job on this ship, is it not?"

He grinned, apparently somewhat pleased with my easygoing response. "Yes, it is. However, sir will do just fine. You are not a member of this crew. I wouldn't expect you to address me as one."

Staring, I waited for him to say something else. The pleasantries would end soon enough. We were stowaways, after all. They would have rules for how we needed to be dealt with. It was also almost certain that an undesirable punishment awaited Abella and me soon.

Pursing his lips, he moved away from the entrance, taking the light with him. "Come on, then. I expect you'll have to come with me. Captain is going to want to see this, I'm certain."

Scooting from the box without any further prompting, I stood and stretched, wincing slightly at the brightness of the flame in the glass case Dagger held aloft, lighting the area. Abella followed after, stretching as well, and then fell still, watching the men around us with some uncertainty. Besides the Quartermaster, three other men had come to help capture the intruders. The dogs—big, hairy, gray, and somewhat ugly—danced around their feet, sniffing everywhere, begging to be shown more attention.

"That's enough," Dagger said to them, holding out his hand. In an instant, the two hounds sat, paying strict attention. Without even glancing at them, he grinned at Abella and I, inclining his head. "*Madame, Mademoiselle.*" Motioning for us to go ahead, he stepped aside, clearing the small pathway to the hatch on the other side of the room.

Smiling tightly, I nodded, going in the direction he indicated. It was somewhat surprising that they hadn't clapped us in irons. One of the men who'd accompanied him had been carrying the handcuffs, alerting me to the fact that they'd intended to arrest whomever they found. Why hadn't they done it to us?

As we moved through the hold and to the next deck, the reason became increasingly clear. We were Ladies. I'd been a guest of the King at Versailles and was technically married to a prince, even if Tristan had no lands and his family hadn't reigned in Ireland for a few generations now. Dagger was choosing to treat us as he would if he'd encountered us on the street. Everything he said was increasingly polite and diplomatic. He even asked after our general health and well-being.

Staring pointedly at the main brig as we came up from of the hold, I stopped, forcing him to pause behind me. The jail covered the entire deck, stretching across the ship menacingly. Unlit lamps hung from beams every few feet, waiting for the time they would need to be used. These cells were mostly the same as the secondary brig in the hold, but they made me more nervous, for some reason. In the dark, you could pretend that you weren't a prisoner. Here, with lamplight to show a different story, you always knew where you stood. "Will Captain MacDonald put us in there?" I asked Dagger, not looking to see his reaction.

"It's not my place to say what the captain will and won't do," he replied.

"Would you, if you were captain?" I turned and folded my arms.

His nose twitched, as if I'd amused him and he blinked, staring me down. "I'm not the captain. Shall we continue?" He motioned to the next set of stairs, and continued to watch, as if he expected me to bolt.

Abella, sliding her hand into mine, leading the way this time, mounted the steps with her head held high, despite the shaking of her fingers. The gun deck

242

came into view, the long cannons tied and waiting for the moment they would be needed. Not hesitating, Abella continued onward. As we leveled out on the next deck, she marched through the hammocks of the crewmen, already familiar with this floor and what it had to offer.

Surprised, several of the men who'd been resting sat up, watching as we strode through them. There were more than I expected, more than we'd ever had on Tristan's ship anyway. It was much like when we'd been aboard The Order's Man of War, with her huge crew and giant ship. The *Isobel* wasn't as large, but it felt like she had just as many men aboard.

And then I saw him. Rising from his hammock, the wonderfully green eyes I'd memorized so well studied me with a mixture of elation and horror. It was as if I'd just dragged my fingers through his hair, the locks sticking up and windswept. The image made me wish I could touch him, my hands aching to feel his short beard and touch his face once more. I wouldn't stop at his face, though, choosing to shove the open neck of his dirty and wrinkled, white shirt to the side, so I could trace the saber scar on his shoulder, rediscovering more of his body. Our lips would meet then, and I would ask him what he had been doing to scuff up the black pants and boots he was wearing. There was pitch on them, so he would most likely explain whatever work he had been doing, if only to make me quiet so he could kiss me again. As I drank in his appearance like a woman who had been dying of thirst, I noticed other tiny things, like the rope burn on his left hand and the sunburn on his cheeks. It was so relieving to see him again, I found myself at a loss for words, my heart skipping a beat as I finally gazed on my husband once more.

"Samantha?" He sounded so shocked, so caught off guard, that it almost made me want to laugh. Mark hadn't said anything to him, clearly.

"What are ye doing here?" He stepped forward, hesitating slightly as he stared past me, to the escort of men watching him. Frowning, he stared at me again, his face flushing some. "Have ye lost yer mind, woman?" His tone was angry this time, embarrassed even. "What were ye thinking, stowing away?"

"An excellent question." Captain MacDonald's form appeared on the other side of the grate overhead. "And one I would verra much like to hear the answer to. Get up here, the lot of ye."

"Aye, Captain," Tristan responded with the other men.

"Bell!" MacDonald shouted. "Get down here, now!"

Swallowing hard, I moved with the rest of the group, coming up on the top deck and blinking in the bright sunlight. A cool breeze brushed past and a small spray of water came with it, lighting gently on my skin. Looking around at all the open space, I felt as if I could breathe fully for the first time in a week.

Captain MacDonald was waiting in front of the entrance to his quarters, arms folded. He was as striking as the first time I'd seen him, the red of his kilt bright and as menacing as the expression on his face. Around him, the crew was gathering, Mark standing in front of them, a frown on his face. As soon as Abella and I reached them, the crew formed a ring around us, the dogs excitedly circling around the captain.

"Fergus, Hamish, settle." He made a movement with his hand and the pair sat, holding still as statues, panting as they stared forward. Studying them now, I realized they were Scottish Deerhounds, which meant they were probably the captain's pets and not the ship's anti-stowaway system. That was why they had been so friendly and loving instead of attacking us on sight.

"Madame O'Rourke, Mademoiselle," he started, addressing us both with a healthy dose of annoyance. "What are ye doing on my ship, pray tell?"

Remaining silent, I glared at him. There was nothing I could say that would stop whatever he was about to do to us. It would be better if he just got it over with, so we could all move on with our lives.

"Stowing away is a highly punishable crime," Captain MacDonald continued, his eyes seeming to blaze as he watched me. "I could have you flogged. Prison is a viable option, as well. Ye would make a nice slave, methinks, too. Or I could throw ye overboard right now and not think about it for a second longer."

Tristan made a distressed noise in the section of the crew to my left, and fidgeted, obviously not willing to let any of those options come to pass. The captain ignored him, though, his steely gaze remaining on me.

"Ye've cost this ship money," he continued. "No doubt ye've stolen the clothes ye're wearing." He looked at our pants and shirts with a raised eyebrow, distaste in his expression. "And the food will have been compromised. Suppose we all starve to death because ye had to take our food. They'll find our shriveled and sun dried bodies in a few months and it will all be because ye two ate our food."

245

"Oh please," I scoffed, breaking my silence and rolling my eyes as I folded my arms. "You have plenty of food. More than enough, actually. I used to work in a ship's galley, so don't bother trying to tell me different. These are my clothes, too. I didn't steal anything I didn't have to. If you're trying to make me feel guilty, it's not working. I suggest you give up now."

He didn't even look taken aback that I'd responded to him so. His crew, however, seemed scandalized, as if they couldn't believe the words that had come from my mouth. Tristan only sighed, staring at the sky in defeat. Mark, on the other hand, unsuccessfully tried to hide his smirk, his gaze focused on the floor.

"Ye are on fragile ground, Madame," MacDonald responded, a slight growl to his tone. "Ye're presence here has endangered my crew, cost our vessel money, and stands to create discord among my men. These are things I canna let stand. Do ye mean to tell me ye dinna care about the effects of yer actions?"

Remaining silent, I stared at him, not wanting to give him the satisfaction of another answer. He was trying to goad me into a reaction of his choosing and I wouldn't do it.

"Ye've stranded yerselves on a ship bound for war!" He yelled then, his face flushing with anger. "Stuck on the ocean, with a crew that canna stop to protect ye when the battle wages on around ye."

"We don't need your protection," I spat back, my defenses rising. There was nothing I hated more than being treated like a helpless woman. "We're more than capable of taking care of ourselves!"

"Says the woman who spent the better part of a year as a captive to one of the worst men of our time." His words were cold and cruel, his expression mean. "How many men died because ye weren't able to defend yerself, eh? How many souls fell to the wayside because ye couldna be bothered by the rules? How many more will suffer because ye refuse to stay in yer place?"

Stepping forward, my hand struck the side of his face before I even considered what I was doing. It smacked hard, leaving a bright red mark that disappeared into his beard. Breathing heavily, fighting back tears, I glared at him, wishing he could feel all the pain his few words had dredged up inside me. I knew how many men had sacrificed themselves to save me. They were part of the reason I was here. They had fought for my place, for me to stay at Tristan's side, fighting against the evils of the world. It was a dishonor to their memory to stay home, sitting on my butt, not doing anything. I had been saved for a reason, traveled through time for a purpose, and I was not about to let one pompous old man tell me any different.

I wanted to say all of this and more to him, to scream and shout, to pound into his brain all of my motives for stowing away on his ship. Instead, I was so angry I couldn't find the words, a single tear breaking free and rolling down my cheek. Brushing it away furiously, I continued to glare at him, not an ounce of regret for my actions coming to the surface.

Rubbing his face with a frown, he stepped forward, looming over me. "Ye're a liability that I dinna want. Spoiled. Selfish. And ye'll be dropped on the first sight of land I see."

"It won't matter," I shot back, finding my voice in an instant. "I'll just stow away again. And again. However many times it takes for you to realize that I do not intend for this ship to go anywhere without me. Not as long as my husband is on it."

"Aye, yer husband." As if my words had alerted him to Tristan's presence, he turned and frowned at him. "How long have ye known she was here, O'Rourke? When did ye sneak her on board?"

"I was unaware of her presence, Captain." Tristan frowned, looking at me in worry. "Had I known, I would have brought it to yer attention immediately."

"Immediately, ye say?" MacDonald laughed, shaking his head. "I dinna believe ye." Then, turning to Mark, he sighed. "Bell? How did ye get them aboard without anyone seeing?"

"I didn't help them stowaway," Mark said, clearing his throat. "I didn't know they were here, either."

Snorting, MacDonald shook his head, turning to me again. "Dagger," he called, motioning for his quartermaster. "Ten lashes. Each."

Abella whimpered beside me, her hand still tightly wrapped around my own.

Dagger, coming to stand beside me, hesitated slightly, as if he didn't think lashing us was such a good idea. He was a loyal sailor, though, and took my arm, pulling me from the circle.

"Dagger," MacDonald said again, causing us to pause. "Not the women, ye dolt. Their men."

Suddenly panicked, I yanked away from the Quartermaster, turning to look at the captain once more. "They didn't know, I swear!" My heart was racing in an instant, fear for Tristan and Mark filling me, the knowledge of how painful a lashing was flitting through my memory. Randall had lashed a crewmember once.

The man died.

"I dinna believe a word that comes from yer mouth," the captain replied smoothly, motioning for Mark and Tristan to go with Dagger.

Abella sobbed beside me, clinging to me like she would fly away if she let go. Her eyes were wild and scared as she gazed at Mark, her face red and wet.

"I swear!" I yelled, watching as the pair slowly walked to where they had been ordered. "They didn't know! It was all me. I came up with the plan and convinced Abella to come with me. I didn't tell them what we were doing because I knew they would try and stop us. Please, you have to believe me—they didn't know!"

"Even if they dinna have a clue, as ye insist, someone still needs to be punished for yer actions."

Staring at the captain with what was surely a crazy stare, I opened and closed my mouth, trying to find a response. "I'll do it," I finally said. "I'll take the lashes. All twenty."

Abella gaped at me in surprise, her grip tightening even more.

"Sam, no!" Tristan hissed.

"Sammy, don't," Mark added, a strain to his voice as well. "You can't handle that many."

"I think I know what I can and can't handle!" I snapped, glaring at him. Turning to the captain, I held my head high, trying to suppress the out of control feelings inside me. "I'll take the punishment."

Captain MacDonald studied me evenly, a strange expression crossing his features for a second. Then, he sighed, a wave of exhaustion crashing over him. "No," he said softly. "Ye canna take the lashes. It was yer decision to sneak aboard and watching yer husband take the brunt of the beating will be yer punishment. I'm sorry, lass."

Shocked, I watched him a moment longer, then peered around the crew with pleading eyes. Behind me, a man appeared from below deck with the whip, its many leather tails hanging in the wind lifelessly. For a brief moment I felt some thankfulness for the fact that there was no glass or rock woven into the threads, like the one Randall had used. This one only had knots tied into the braided leather, as far as I could tell. The seriousness of the situation came back in an instant, though, Abella gasping and trembling beside me as she looked at the weapon.

Dagger, taking the whip, turned to the captain once more, his mouth a thin line, and then motioned for Tristan to come forward.

Doing as asked, stepping in front of the Quartermaster, Tristan removed his shirt and turned, displaying his back to his discipliner. He then knelt on the ground, gazing at me with a tight smile. "It'll be alright, lass," he said softly. "I've had worse. Ye know that."

Tears freely rolling over my face, I looked at the captain. "Please," I whispered. "Please let me take them. He's been hurt enough because of me."

"No, Samantha," Tristan said again, his voice strong and sure.

The words seemed to affect MacDonald more than

anything else I'd said to him, his face a mixture of emotions. For a moment, I thought he would agree, or call off the whole thing entirely, but he didn't. Shaking himself, he frowned, his voice sounding like it was full of hurt emotion as well. "This is the punishment for crewmembers who don't follow the rules," he said, failing to keep his tone even. "And even if he truly dinna ken ye were here, he's still responsible for ye. I'm sorry. No."

Turning to one of the men, he motioned toward Abella and I, moving toward his quarters. "Take them to the brig." He gave the impression that going through with the flogging was as much a punishment for him as it was for the rest of us, which only made me angrier. Before I could say so, though, he disappeared through the doorway, his dogs trailing behind him.

The man MacDonald had ordered to take me away nodded, motioning to a few others in the group and moved forward, grabbing me by the arms.

"Tristan!" I cried, trying to meet his gaze as they dragged me away.

"It will be fine," he said again, his voice firm as he watched me go.

Dagger raised the whip and brought it down across his back sharply, and Tristan flinched, sucking in a quick breath as his eyes widened. In a split second, the second stripe spread across his back, Dagger wasting no time in executing his orders.

I could still hear the sound of the leather cutting into him as I was carried away and locked below deck.

Abella hiccupped, her face red and swollen from crying. She seemed smaller than ever before, huddled in the corner, her knees drawn against her chest, arms wrapped around them. Long, black hair, that had been tied up in a bun, had come loose at some point, and was now sticking to her skin, making her look like she was a homeless, crazy woman.

"Do you think they're alright?" she asked me quietly, staring at the floor in front of her.

Sighing, I turned away, leaning against the bars of our cell, hands wrapped around them tightly. I'd done a fair amount of crying myself and sniffed, wishing there was something I could do to ease the heavy feeling of my heart. "I don't know," I responded, my voice barely a whisper.

"They didn't scream," she offered, a hopeful tone emanating from her. "And ten lashes aren't too many, I guess. They should be fine, *oui*?"

Staring at the empty cell across the way, I weighed her words. By all accounts, the boys should be fine. Of course, their backs would be cut and bruised, sore for the next little while, but, overall, there was no need to worry too much about what had happened. It wasn't my concern for their general safety that bothered me, though.

"I knew there was a possibility they would be blamed and punished," I confessed, unable to keep my thoughts to myself any longer. "But I thought it would be something like laying new pitch or having to clean the head for a few weeks. I never thought they would actually be hurt because of me." My voice broke at the end and I started crying anew, gripping the metal in my fingers as tightly as possible. The action made my hands ache, but I couldn't stop. It seemed as if I would fall apart completely if I let go.

Tristan had been through so much already because of me. Mark, too. Hadn't I done enough? Why hadn't I realized this was an option when I'd snuck on board?

It was because such a punishment never would have happened on a pirate ship, I realized, at least not the ones like Tristan and I had been on before. The crew would revolt and vote to remove the captain from office if any of them were physically harmed by his order. This wasn't a pirate ship, though; it was a privateer vessel, which put it on par with the navy and their rules. The navy regularly punished their crewmates in this manner, if I remembered correctly. It was one of the reasons so many men turned from the military to piracy—they weren't treated the way they thought they should be.

"You couldn't have known, Samantha. I know they will not hold it against you. They both love you with all their hearts. Neither of them would have let you take those lashes, even if the captain had agreed to let you do so."

Surprised by the sadness in her voice, I glanced

back, watching as she wiped her face.

"I should have offered to take them." Frowning, she peered over at me, lip trembling. "I couldn't find my voice when I needed it—when you and Tristan and Mark needed it. All I could do was cry and be scared."

Wanting to offer some comfort, I went to her side, sitting on the floor. "It's okay to be afraid," I reminded her. "It happens to everyone. I felt that way, just now."

"But you said something," she insisted, wiping her face angrily this time. "I said nothing! My own father almost succeeded in cutting my own hand off and I was too afraid to face the cad. My friends needed me and I wasn't there—again."

Wrapping my arm around her shoulder, I sighed, leaning my head against hers. "Tristan and Mark wouldn't have let you take the punishment either. We were outvoted this time."

Silence stretched between us then, Abella still sniffling as my mind swirled around a few key thoughts. How injured had the two guys ended up? Were they in a lot of pain? If not, why hadn't either of them come here yet—or anyone, for that matter—to let us know the outcome? Was this part of MacDonald's punishment, too, keeping us in the dark when it came to the wellbeing of the men we loved?

Glancing at Abella, I considered revising the last thought. It was fairly easy to watch her and know she cared for Mark, but did she love him? The few times I'd seen them together, I'd thought he was partial to her as well, which made me oddly jealous at times. I'd never returned his affections or encouraged him, but it still felt like I was losing him to her, somehow. Perhaps it was because we were such close friends, or the fact that we were from the same time. There would never be anything romantic toward him inside me, but I wanted him to be a part of my life still. Watching the way he smiled when she entered the room had made me uncomfortable for some reason.

I didn't think he even noticed he did things like that around her.

Pushing the pair from my mind, I focused on Tristan again. He would come see me now, if he could. The ship's physician would most likely examine him and dress his wounds, if Captain MacDonald had any sense of propriety, but he would come to me after that. More than enough time had passed for that to occur, though, and still he hadn't arrived.

A tingling string of worry grabbed hold of me and I sighed, staring over at the empty cell across from us once more. Overhead, the sounds of rushed footsteps and orders being called to different people were muffled down toward us.

Would the captain keep them from coming to see us? Could he be that much more cruel than he already was?

"Batten down the hatches!" Dagger's voice reached us clearly, as if he were standing right next to us, shouting. "And get to your stations! The wind is in our favor. We'll be on the pirates within the hour!"

It was then that I realized the hurrying and talking I'd been hearing before wasn't just normal ship chatter; a ship flying a black flag had been spotted and His Majesty's Privateers were now on the hunt for their prize. Panic seized me for a second; Tristan was hurt. He wouldn't be able to defend himself as well if things went south. The rest of the crew wouldn't be concerned with watching after him. They would most likely shut him in a room and hope for the best.

Or, worse, they would expect him to fight in his weakened and pained state. Even worse than that, the blockhead would probably insist he fight because I was on board. He would want to protect me, without realizing that he was the one who needed protection right now.

Desperate, I strained to hear what else was being said. Would they let us out? Maybe I could convince them to let us stay with Tristan and Mark, where we could all protect each other. I didn't care if I had to go back to the brig afterword, as long as I was able to make sure we were all okay in the meantime.

"What about the women?" It was a voice I didn't recognize, just outside the hatch to the brig deck.

"Captain said to keep them in the cell. They'll be safer there."

The wooden door in the ceiling slammed shut without another thought, the sound of the latch securing tight echoing through the space. We were left in almost complete darkness, with only the light from the one torch that had been lit by our cell to guide us.

Swallowing hard, I tried to focus. Something had to be done, but what?

"Pirates?" Abella asked, seeming to have gained better control of herself. Rising from the floor, she straightened her shirt, taking a deep breath.

Nodding, I glanced at her. "We need to get out of here. They think they're protecting us, but if the ship is overrun, we'll be sitting ducks. Besides that, Tristan and Mark are hurt. They might not be able to fight at all. We have to help them."

"How? We're locked in and the bars are too close together to slip through." She shrugged, but the way she held herself told me she was ready to do whatever it took to follow me in this plan.

Thinking quickly, I took in everything around me. There had to be a way to escape without the keys. The hinges proved to be impossible to crack, though, and there was nothing to try and pick the lock with. Finally, I landed on an empty torch, mounted on the beam beside us, just outside the cell.

"Can you reach that?" I asked, pointing to the object. She was smaller than me and had a better chance of being able to grab it.

"*Oui*, I think so." Striding over to the corner, she stretched her arm across, the tips of her fingers barely brushing the torch. Grunting, she struggled to get closer, this time almost hooking the very tip of it. She fell back for a moment then, brushing her hair from her face, a determined glare in her eyes as she stared at the empty container.

Trying once more, she pressed herself against the bars, her head turned to the side in an attempt to give her more reach. It still wasn't enough, though and she growled, reaching as far as she could. "Push me," she ordered, straining against the bars.

Responding instantly, I stood behind her, using my own body weight to push her into the rods. Just as I became worried that I was hurting her, she let out a victorious cry and knocked the torch from its bearings, watching as it rolled across the floor to us.

"It's too big to come in," she said, watching as I reached through and picked it up.

"That's fine," I responded, slowly moving toward

the door, passing the object between hands as I maneuvered around the poles. "It doesn't need to come in."

Finally, upon reaching the door and the lock on the outside of it, I said a silent prayer to anyone who was listening and raised the heavy wood and metal carrier as high as I could. Slamming it down, I smashed it against the lock, trying to break it. A loud, clanging sound echoed, the lock holding strong.

"Damn," I muttered. It always seemed so much easier in my head.

Raising the makeshift club once more, I continued to clobber the door, over and over again. If it hadn't been for the ensuing fight above, I was sure someone would have come to see what we were doing. As it was, it seemed no one could hear us with the hatch closed and their minds on the enemy.

After ten minutes, a sweat soaked collar, and a few smashed fingers, the lock clattered to the floor, broken. A rush of adrenaline burst through me and I threw the door open, stepping into freedom and the planning phase of our next motions.

"We need weapons," Abella stated, thinking along the same lines I was. "Do you think they found the ones we hid in the hold yet?"

"I don't know. I hope not." Grabbing the lit lantern off its peg, I led the way down the stairs and into the hold, looking around with a sense of urgency and confusion. It had always been dark when I was here before. I'd never really noticed the way things were stacked and tied, or where certain things were kept.

"This way." Stepping around me, she made quick work of darting through the containers, not concerned with how different it all seemed now. She had been the one to hide the blades when we first snuck on, too, and knew how to get to them.

It had been a bit of a hassle, bringing the swords along, but I hadn't wanted to be without one, should the need arise. I'd been in that situation before and didn't plan on doing it again. In the end, though, bringing them on board with us had proved mostly easy, and Abella insisted they were well hidden without much effort on her part.

Stopping in front of a pair of barrels, she pulled the lid off one, revealing a large amount of rice. After dragging her hand through it a few times, she revealed the two weapons, handing mine to me.

"How long has it been, do you think" I asked, wiping some of the dust off my blade on my pants.

"Over half an hour?"

"They should be attacking soon. We need to find Tristan and Mark now."

She nodded, taking a deep breath, and then closed her eyes, as if steadying herself. "Alright. I'm ready." Glancing at me, she nodded, sliding her blade into the belt around her waist.

Zig zagging through the cargo, we made our way to the stairs, not bothering to be quiet or sneaky along the way.

A loud boom sounded overhead, the ship rocking slightly to the side before it leveled out, and we both froze on the steps, listening intently. Another crash went off, and then another.

"It's starting," I said, moving onto the brig deck. "They're firing the cannons." Hurrying up the next set of stairs, I undid the latch on the underside of the hatch, cracking the door open and peering into the world above.

I'd expected to see the same scene I'd lived so many times since my arrival in the past. The crew would be scurrying around, loading weapons, some even painting their faces, all readying to attack the ship that they desired to capture. There would be a sense of excitement in the air, anticipation on the faces of each man. Together, they would prematurely celebrate their victory, laughing and ribbing each other in glee.

Instead, I was greeted by a somber feeling. Every person I saw appeared grim and was frowning, almost reluctant as they went about their duties. Quick hands worked at the cannons, four men to a gun. On the steps leading to the crew deck, one man—who I assumed was a Mate—relayed orders from above.

"Hold your fire!" He shouted, his hand above his head, his attention turned to whoever it was that was yelling directions from above.

The ship bucked some, breaking through a wave as she sped through the water, and then leveled. To their credit, the crew didn't even flinch, all of them steadying their cannon and weapons, silently waiting to continue.

"Fire!" The Mate dropped his hand, shouting with

ferocity.

One after another, the guns were lit and shot forward, expelling the cannonballs with a surprising amount of force. The wheels on the bottom of the weapons rolled in reaction, pulling away from the small windows, until the ropes that kept them in place caught them and forced their direction to change. The men around them helped as well, pushing the cannons into place and loading them once more, ready to fire when ordered.

Carefully closing the hatch over my head, I shut out the precision planning and battle going on above us and turned to Abella. "We're going to have to wait until they board the ship to leave," I told her. "There's a Mate on the stairs ahead of us and it's more organized than I expected."

A revelation came to me then, and I laughed, locking the epiphany away for future moments when I thought I knew how this ship worked.

"What is it?" Abella asked, confused by my reaction.

"I keep thinking this is like the ships I was on before, but it's not. These men aren't pirates. They're privateers. I'd always thought privateers were a form of legal pirate, people who'd sworn to help the crown but they were just trying to escape the noose. These men aren't that way, though—Captain MacDonald isn't like that. He has a commission from the King to fight in his name and to try and keep order on the sea." Smiling, I shook my head, several thoughts tying together the more I thought about it.

"But the captain is a Templar Knight. Isn't he a pirate in that right, and in the fact that he must rob the ships he takes to secure his treasure?"

"I don't think so." Sitting on the steps, I folded my arms, watching her. "He's the only member in the entire Order who has privateering papers. That says to me he is concerned with following the law. I imagine The Order had a hard time getting the papers as well, seeing as how MacDonald isn't even French. Someone had to convince King Louis to sign him into navy service. Why go through all that trouble?"

"The Order must find him very valuable," she supplied slowly, thinking about it herself now. "Otherwise, they would have found someone else to be a captain for them. He must have done something, or know something important to them."

"And he would follow his rules with absolute authority." A tinge of bitterness crept into my tone and I mentally kicked myself. "He can't risk losing his Marque of Authority from the king. The laws he sets here can't be forfeit for any reason."

It took her a minute to digest that, her eyes suddenly widening as she realized what I was saying. "The lashes were a mercy." Wonder filled her tone. "If the Navy finds stowaways on board, they either press them into service or get rid of them. We can't be pressed because we're women—"

"And disposing of us would have caused an uprising in the crew, with Tristan and Mark at the head of it." Pressing my lips into a thin line, I sighed, angry with myself for not realizing all of this before. Had Tristan? Was that why he was so calm about the whole affair?

"He must have known that they would fight back if he tried to lash us," Abella added, chuckling slightly

263

herself. "So he gave the sentence to them, to appease the need to follow through with punishment, to save us from harm, and to give Tristan and Mark the peace of mind brought by knowing he hadn't harmed us."

I'd come to the same conclusion myself. While I would have preferred to keep thinking of the Scotsman as a horrific brute who loved to abuse power, I had to admit that these revelations had cleared his name somewhat in my mind.

"That explains why everyone is so grim up there, too," I finally said, standing and putting my hand on the latch, hoping to catch another glance at the action above. "They're navy men. I never thought to ask, but they might not all be Templars. If not, we're sailing with a group of soldiers ready to lay down their life for King and country. I don't think they take much pleasure in killing."

Pushing the door open a smidge, I took in the scene on the gun deck. It was a fair amount busier than it had been a few minutes ago, owing to the fact that the enemy vessel was now close enough for a boarding attempt. Both sides had stopped firing on each other, the up and down motion of the water swaying the boats from side to side.

Faintly, I could hear shouting above, the words floating down softly as the men loaded their own pistols and pulled swords from scabbards.

"Surrender now and yer lives will be spared," Captain Macdonald shouted, addressing the other ship. "I imagine ye're low on supplies and it's been a cold few years. I give ye my word that ye will be treated kindly on my ship, with food enough to fill yer bellies, blankets to keep ye warm, and a promise that ye will face a fair trial in Saint Domingue when we make landfall in Hispaniola."

There was a moment of silence and I thought the pirates might have been responding to him, shouting over the waves. Suddenly, the sound of a cannon firing blasted through the air and all the men standing in my field of vision hit the deck, covering their heads.

Dropping the door shut, I grabbed Abella and cowered, flinching as the ball from the pirates cracked through the hull above us, scattering wood chips across the floor with a pattering noise.

Another beat of quiet followed, and then the world exploded into action above us.

Shouts and gunshots were exchanged overhead, feet slapping against the floor, the entire crew suddenly moving. With a surge of energy, I threw the hatch open, not worried about being seen, and hurried into the chaos.

This was like my fights with pirates. Instead of being grim and mellow, Captain MacDonald's men were fierce and ready for battle, charging the stairs and through the cannon windows with vigor, ready to finish what they had started.

The pirates from the opposing vessel were boarding the *Isobel* as well, splitting the groups in half, skirmishes taking place on both vessels. MacDonald had been right about them being low on supplies, though; the men I could see appeared to be wasting away, their forms red from the cold and faces pinched from hunger.

"Don't kill anyone you don't have to," I said over my shoulder to Abella, drawing my sword. "I think the captain wants to help as many as possible."

"All right."

Without another thought, I ran forward, bringing up the rear of the crew. We flooded the steps, charging through the crew quarters and onto the main deck, where we scattered, each person finding their own opponent. It seemed that many of the privateers had taken to swarming the other boat, while the pirates amassed on this one. They were vastly outnumbered, but were putting up a surprising fight.

Turning to my right, I caught sight of Captain MacDonald facing a large man in tattered clothes, their blades stinging each other quickly and with the expertise that only came from years of practice. The captain was duel wielding weapons, though—a large, aged hammer was clutched in his other hand. He would thrust with his sword and quickly follow through with a wave of the hammer.

In the blink of an eye, another pirate appeared, behind him, a dagger clutched in his hands. Raising it high, he snuck toward the pair, his intent to kill MacDonald when he wasn't looking obvious.

Darting forward, I yelled, catching their attention, but didn't stop there. Before he even knew what was happening, the second pirate was fighting with me, fumbling to unsheathe his own sword, tripping and slipping across the deck. When he finally got his bare feet under him, he growled menacingly, probably trying to scare me.

Laughing, I settled into the stance I knew best, inviting him to come at me, if he dared. His eyes widened in distaste and annoyance, and he raised his blade to meet mine.

Spinning to the side, I stepped close, elbowing

him in the spine. Apparently, I was faster than he'd expected. Watching as he adjusted his speed to match my own, I let my mind go to the calculating place I so often practiced sword play from. It was like watching a movie then, studying his steps and finding my own to counter him. We were a hurricane of jabs and clanging metal, dancing around the deck as we battled. After a few moments, I realized he might not be trying his best to kill me and a wave of anger overtook me.

I was so tired of being treated differently because I was a woman.

Shouting, I put in more of an effort, driving him back as I hacked and chopped. He wasn't able to block every hit this time, receiving a cut on his arm and the thigh. While I was careful not to kill him outright, it was a struggle to try and wound him enough to stop him. I'd never thought I'd be in a situation where I didn't want to kill whoever it was I was facing. All of my finishing moves were kill shots.

Someone bumped into me and I turned, barely avoiding being crushed by a falling Captain MacDonald. He either slipped or been knocked down, but I didn't care just then—the hammer he'd been wielding had fallen to the ground beside him.

Grabbing the handle of the surprisingly heavy mallet, I grunted, swinging it to my front and up with all the force I could muster. The head connected with the jaw of my opponent, knocking him backward. When he fell to the ground, he didn't rise, but he continued to breathe. Satisfaction settled over me and I smiled, feeling accomplished.

"Look out!"

Turning at the captain's cry, I just managed to get

my blade raised in time to block the blow coming from the same tall man he'd been fighting this whole time. The pirate was bloody and half crazed, but determined, it would seem.

Swinging the hammer, I hit him in the face, wincing as I heard the sound of his nose cracking beneath it. Just like his fallen brother, he stumbled, crashing to the ground, becoming still at last.

Breathless, I set the hammer on the deck and extended a hand to MacDonald, who was watching me like he couldn't believe what he was seeing. All the same, he took my help, getting to his feet with little difficulty.

Picking the mallet up, I extended the handle to him, smiling triumphantly.

He stared at me a moment longer and then turned to the rest of the ship, raising an eyebrow. I looked as well, smiling as I saw Abella expertly subduing her own partner, a blade at his throat as he threw away his cutlass in surrender. The rest of the pirates were doing so as well and I sighed.

The fight was over.

"I've never seen a woman fight like that." Dagger appeared beside the captain, his shirt cut and blood running from his ear, but he was otherwise unscathed. "Least of all a couple of Frenchwomen."

"I'm from the Americas," I replied smartly. "And any Frenchwoman could fight like Abella if she took the time to learn and practice as she has."

"Aye," Captain MacDonald agreed. "Give a woman a weapon and she'll send ye to yer grave with it if she must."

"You've seen a woman do something like that?"

Dagger asked, unbelieving. "Why haven't I ever heard about it?"

"I have," he confirmed, sheathing his blade and setting the hammer on the ground, head first. "A gentleman doesn't kiss and tell, Dagger." He grinned, but there was a sadness to it. It made me think he didn't want to talk about fighting women any longer and I cleared my throat, ready to change the subject.

"Where are Tristan and Mark? Did they fight? Do they need tending to?"

The men stared at me with blank expressions, as if they hadn't expected me to flip so suddenly.

"Where is my husband?" I pressed, suddenly frustrated.

"We've taken the enemies ship, Captain!"

Drawn by the hailing of one of his crew, MacDonald shook himself, turning his attention away from me.

"Very well. Take their surviving crew to the brig, Mister Roberts. Prepare the fallen for burial."

The man nodded and saluted, turning smartly and barking orders to those around him.

"Tristan?" I asked again, crossing my arms in impatience.

"Here, lass."

The sound came from the stairs leading below deck and I turned, smiling as I saw him at last. He had definitely taken part in the fight and seemed tired, but he was standing tall, clearly not as hindered by his lashing as I'd feared.

"Ye should have stayed below deck." Chastising me as I rushed to him, he smiled anyway, knowing full well that there was nothing he could have done to stop me. "Are ye hurt at all?"

Shaking my head, I wrapped my arms around his waist, gingerly trying to feel if he'd been struck there. He didn't flinch at my touch, though, and so I leaned against him, inhaling the scent of him and feeling a peace wash over me that I missed whenever we were apart.

"I'm good, too, if you were wondering."

Mark's sarcastic tone made me laugh and I peered over my shoulder, watching as he crossed the gangplank between the two vessels.

"Sore," he continued. "But fine."

"That is good to hear." Abella stepped in front of him, blocking his path and threw her arms around his neck, hugging him tightly.

Flinching slightly, he laughed, untangling her from himself. He didn't let go of her hands, though, and smiled as if he were truly happy to see her. Once again, I felt that strange sense of jealousy toward the pair of them. It was a happy envy, as I was truly grateful to see the two getting along so well, but it made me face things I didn't like about myself.

Turning my attention back to my husband, I put the uncomfortable thoughts from my mind and kissed his cheek before laying my head on his chest.

"Should we take the ladies to the brig as well, Captain?"

It was the Mate who had asked for orders earlier, his tone uncertain as he stood between the four of us, staring at his commander, who had taken up residence by the helm.

MacDonald studied us, pursing his lips and then shook his head. "No, Roberts. I dinna want them there with that lot. Ye can put them in my cabin for now. They can stay there until we land in Hispaniola and they're set ashore."

The color drained from my face at his words and I stepped away from Tristan, boiling mad. "What?" I demanded. "You're still going to leave us there?"

"Ye're still stowaways, are ye not?" He stared at me with a blank expression, as if waiting for me to somehow make a fool of myself.

"I just saved your life!" I reminded him. "We fought with your crew against pirates!"

"And it was very impressive, I'll admit. But not necessary. Ye put yerselves in danger and could have endangered my crew yet again." He sighed, rubbing his face and I was distinctly struck with the thought that he found me very tiresome.

"We didn't, though. We fought well and helped your crew." Staring at him hard, I stepped forward, hands curled into fists.

"The fact still remains that ye are here by unlawful means and will be put ashore in the Caribbean. Good day, Madame O'Rourke."

He motioned for Roberts to take me, turning his back on me.

Shooting the Mate a death glare, I focused on the captain, trying my hardest to keep from screaming in rage. "I don't care how many times you take me off this ship," I stated, surprised by how calm my voice sounded. "I will find a way on. Even if I have to sneak onto another boat and chase you, I will find a way back here. It might take days, it might take months, but you can be sure that it will happen."

Glancing over his shoulder, he gave me a

271

withering look, supreme annoyance on his features, and then threw his hands in the air. "Fine. Meet me in my quarters and we can discuss your terms, Madame, since you seem so intent on holding me hostage against my better judgement."

The captain's quarters were somehow like all the others I'd seen, yet nothing like them at the same time. All of the usual things were there—bed, desk, bookshelves, maps, navigation tools, and the large window overlooking the rear of the ship, boasting magnificent views of the sea and all her wonders. But there were also comfortable reading chairs, dog beds in the corner, a tartan blanket folded over the end of the bed, herbs hanging in front of the windows to dry, plants growing in containers that had been tied down around the walls, pictures of landscapes and people displayed on every surface, and a pot of soup boiling over in the fireplace on the right hand side of the room. It felt so distinctly like a small Scottish home that I found myself taken aback, having not expected it to be so personal and welcoming.

Roberts deposited me inside, Abella quickly pushed in behind me, and closed the door, leaving us without another word.

Slowly, I took in everything, still in awe of all he'd managed to gather. Pausing in front of a small picture on his desk, I tilted my head to the side, studying it. The ability of whoever had drawn it wasn't at a professional level, but the portrait was still well done. It was a woman with long red hair, her slim figure clothed in a white dress, purple heather in her hands. She was smiling, standing in front of a brick hut surrounded by trees.

"Isobel."

Captain MacDonald's voice broke through my thoughts and I jumped, having not noticed that he had entered. He was standing in the doorway, his dogs at his side, watching me with an odd expression.

"I'm sorry?"

"That's this ship's namesake, Isobel." Moving inside, he shut the door and ordered the dogs to go lay down in their beds, next to the chair that Abella had seen fit to settle in.

Leaving his hammer by the entrance, he strode to the fireplace, using a rag to pull the boiling soup from the fire and set it on the hearth. "It's not a verra good likeness of her—I did it myself—but it's enough. Enough for me, anyway."

"Is she your wife?" I asked, curious.

He laughed, shaking his head. "No, just a lass I knew, a long time ago. She was a stubborn and independent as yerself."

My heart fell at his words, the tone of his voice telling me all I needed to know. "Was?" I asked quietly, moving to the chairs on the left and sitting by Abella.

"She's dead." He paused, swallowing hard. After a moment, he rose, moving to his desk and taking a seat behind it.

"I'm sorry for your loss."

"*Oui*, very sorry, *Monsieur*. It must be hard, losing

274

the one you love." Abella frowned, looking over at the dogs.

She didn't know what else to say, I realized, and was uncomfortable. The captain seemed to pick up on that as well.

He cleared his throat, shaking his head. "It's been thirty years. My old heart has had plenty of time for condolences and well wishes. Thankfully, that's not what we're here to discuss." He sighed then, his earlier tiredness and annoyance returning as he moved his chair to face us. Stroking his beard, he stared for a moment and then stood. "What exactly are ye wanting me to do, Madame O'Rourke? I canna very well allow ye to stay on board as a guest. Privateering is dangerous business and I have secrets I must keep for The Order."

"First, you can stop calling me Madame," I replied roughly. "Samantha, or Sam, will do just fine."

He smiled, amused, and then motioned for me to continue.

"I don't want to stay on board as a guest. Do you Abella?"

She shook her head beside me. We had already discussed how we would try to convince him to let us stay before we ever even climbed aboard.

"Ye want to go ashore, then?" He looked confused.

"No. We want to join your crew."

Silence stretched between us, his eyebrows raised high as he stared at us in disbelief. "Have ye lost yer minds?" he finally asked. "Ye can't join the crew!"

"With all due respect, Captain, we can." Sitting straighter I swallowed, hoping that my argument would convince him. "If we had been men caught stowing away, you could have pressed us into service as punishment. I request that you do that to us now."

"But ye're women!"

Raising a hand to stop him from continuing, I watched him evenly. "Women who just proved they can hold their own in a fight. I've lived among pirates before, disguised as a man and as myself. I know how a ship works and how to do my part on it."

"I've also traveled on ships before," Abella added. "I may not know as much about how to sail, but I can work in the surgery, or the galley. I follow orders well and can do any chore, so long as I'm shown how to first."

"As can I. I'm quite familiar with the galley and how to cook for a whole crew." Smiling, I tried to guess if we were convincing him yet or not. "We've both fought for The Order before, myself on several occasions. Abella was part of the siege in Arizona and the reason that many of the men of your Order returned home instead of being left for dead in the desert."

"And Samantha was the key consultant in the construction on Oak Isle. She fought Thomas Randall there—and in Arizona—and has been one of the biggest advocates I know for protecting the treasures of the Templars from him."

"Ye mean she was the reason Randall managed to have a go at either of those treasures in the first place," MacDonald argued. "If not for her, they would both have remained safe and undiscovered."

"Randall would have found a way," I replied coldly, not liking how he'd turned that part on its head. "He is ruthless and uncaring. He means to discover all the treasures, no matter the cost to him or those around him."

"Or the world." Abella had mumbled the reply, but we all heard it.

"And ye think all this makes ye eligible to have on my ship, with my men?" He shook his head, frowning. "I have a rule, one that I follow to the letter. Nothing that could cause harm to my men can be allowed to happen. There is no dying on this boat—not unless I go first."

"How are we compromising that rule?" Frustrated, I huffed, leaning against the chair.

"Randall has a tendency to find ye, no? Who's to say he's not on his way to ye right now, ready to kill the lot of us?"

The question stung some and a trickle of fear jumped through me. It took a second to gather my bearings—a second that he noticed.

"Even if he were, it wouldn't have to be a danger to your crew." Looking him in the eye, I lifted my chin, trying to show how resolute I was on the matter. "I would kill him before he even had the chance to lay a finger on any of them."

"Ye're certain of that, are ye?" He laughed slightly, smiling. "A feisty one, eh?"

"*Oui*. Feisty, like your Isobel."

I could have kissed Abella for the comment. It seemed to hit him harder than anything else we'd said to him and he paused, glancing over at the picture on his desk once more.

"Aye. Like Isobel."

Sighing, he seemed to consider our words and then nodded, turning his attention to us once more. "Fine.

I'll press ye into the crew."

"Yes!" Standing in triumph, I grinned, feeling an excitement rush through me.

"However," he said loudly, giving me a pointed stare. "When we arrive at the treasure port, ye must stay on the ship."

"You don't trust us?" I asked, taken aback.

"It's not that." He grimaced, sitting back in his chair. "The port is protected year round by . . . well . . ." He tapered off, seemingly at a loss for words as he stared out the window. A beat passed and he blinked, gazing back at us. "They dinna take kindly to unexpected visitors, that's all. Since ye're technically not part of the crew commissioned by The Order, I expect they'll not be happy to see ye."

"Fine," Abella agreed. "We'll stay on the ship. Anything else?"

He nodded, stroking his beard in thought. "Aye. Ye'll both work the galley and the surgery, since ye said that's what ye ken. Ye'll have chores, too, just like the rest of the men. I willna be givin' ye any special treatment because of yer gender."

"I think that's fair and preferable." Grinning, I couldn't help but feel like I'd won all around. I would be with Tristan, at sea, doing work, and feeling useful once more.

Captain MacDonald stood, motioning to the door. "Get on with it, then. Ye have dinner to cook for the whole crew and a brig full of prisoners to attend to."

"Yes, Captain." Dipping my head as a sign of respect, I continued to smile, feeling like the world was finally getting back on track.

Hurrying out the door, followed closely by Abella,

I ran right into Tristan. Grabbing onto him for support, I accidentally touched the lashes on his back and he sucked in a sharp breath, eyes widening.

"Sorry!" Letting go, I stepped away, filling with guilt for hurting him yet again.

"What happened?" he asked, brushing the incident aside. "What did ye talk about?"

"We've been pressed into service," I told him excitedly.

"We're your new cooks and doctors," Abella added happily.

"What?" Mark appeared behind Tristan, concern on his face. "He's pressed you into service? Has he lost his mind?"

"Excuse you," I said sharply. "I had to convince him to do it. It's the only way we won't all be split apart."

"A dangerous way," Mark argued. "You could get yourselves killed!"

"It won't be any use arguing with her now, Bell." Tristan grinned as he watched me. "She's gotten her way and knows it. The women can protect themselves well enough, we both know that. Now, we should just be grateful that God has somehow seen fit to bless us with their company once more."

Mark gave him a patronizing stare and then glared at Abella as well. "I'm sure you helped her argue her point, too."

"I did." She stared at him defiantly, as if daring him to say anything about it.

Sighing, he shook his head. "Why couldn't you just stay safe, in Paris? Why do you both have to put yourselves in the path of endangerment?" His voice

279

lowered and he leaned in, practically giving her a death stare. "You promised me, Abella!"

"I promised I would be safe," she shot back. "Not that I would stay in Paris!"

"You and I both know I was asking you to stay there!"

"And we both know that you only kissed me goodbye and made me promise to stay because you weren't able to do it to Sam!" Huffing, she shoved past him, anger rolling off her as she disappeared down the stairs to the lower decks.

Mark watched her go, staring with an open mouth, and then snapped it shut, turning and walking away from Tristan and me.

"They're getting along nicely," Tristan whispered.

Still shocked over the argument I'd witness, I turned to him, frowning. "You're just happy to see Mark getting pushed around."

"Maybe." Grinning, he took my hand. "I don't have much time. Dagger will be expecting me in the rigging. Half our crew will be taking over the pirates' ship and sailing to Hispaniola with us. I'll be spending double the time working. Come away with me now, for just a moment?" He kissed my hand, giving me his most swoon worthy smile and I felt myself blush.

Taking that as an agreement, he turned, his fingers intertwining with my own, and headed toward the crew deck.

Leading me down the stairs, past the hammocks and men scurrying about in their various duties, Tristan pulled me along, hugging the wall. No one paid us any attention, including Abella, who had taken up residence in the galley and was moving things around, most likely planning what food she wanted to make. I felt slightly guilty for not going to help her right away, but remained silent all the same. I hadn't had Tristan to myself in a week—I hadn't even been able to talk to him. I needed to hear his voice for more than a few seconds at a time, to feel his skin on mine, to simply be with him and breathe.

Stopping in front of a slightly opened door beneath the captain's quarters, he smiled, peering inside, and then slid through the gap, guiding me in behind him. He turned the lock and sighed, moving to face me once more.

"Come here." His voice was rough as he pulled me closer, his mouth finding mine in an instant. He kissed me like a man dying of thirst, and I responded in kind, throwing my arms around him tightly.

Flinching, he pulled away, a grimace on his face. "My back," he reminded me.

"Oh, I'm so sorry! I wasn't thinking." Releasing him immediately, I stepped away, feeling horrified that I'd somehow managed to hurt him again. It was like I wasn't thinking straight. Was the universe playing a game with me, trying to see how many times I could unintentionally break him?

Putting the thoughts out of my head, I sighed. "Can I see?" I asked softly.

Nodding, he gingerly faced the other way and removed his shirt, revealing several angry red lines webbed across his skin. There were cuts in a few places, but nothing bad enough to need serious attention. Bruises were slowly appearing as well, marring him with dark splotches.

"Is it bad?" Carefully, I touched one of the lines with the tip of my finger.

Glancing over his shoulder, he grinned, shaking his head. "Not as bad as ye'd expect. It hurt when I was getting hit, but it's more of a dull ache now. It does sting when ye touch it, though."

Pulling my hand away, I frowned. "I'm sorry, Tristan. I didn't mean for this to happen."

Moving to face me, he took my hands in his and kissed them. "It's fine, Sam. I know ye didn't intend for anyone else to take the fall for ye, but I'm happy to do it, if it means ye remain safe and unharmed."

Brushing my hand across the saber scar on his shoulder, I tried to keep the tears in my eyes from falling. How many more scars would he earn because of me? How many of them would I be able to see? How many would be on the inside, jagged and painful, but hidden from the outside world—from me? Would he always feel as he did now, pleased and willing to

282

torture himself on my behalf? Or would he finally wake up one day and realize I wasn't worth all the trouble? Would he see I was broken, lost in a time I still didn't fully understand, and aching for the family Death had stolen from us? Stopping, my palm rested over his heart, and I sighed, looking him in the eye.

His eyes held a world of understanding in them. There was so much love on his face it practically made my heart melt. The expression he wore was one that said he would never blame me for the things that had happened. He already saw I was shattered and instead of running, he was slowly picking up the pieces and putting me together again. "It doesn't matter how many scars brand me," he said softly, placing a hand on the side of my face. "Or how many obstacles we face. So long as it means you are with me until the end. That's all I want, Sam. Ye and me, together. We'll get through anything that way."

It was almost painful, how well he knew me and my thoughts. Laughing slightly, I nodded, a tear escaping my eye. "You aren't mad I stowed away?"

His thumb brushed over my cheek, his other hand rising to wipe away the tear. "Mad? Never. Surprised? Aye, ye caught me off guard. I should have expected as much from ye, but it didn't occur to me that ye were as resourceful as to get on a ship ye'd only heard was leaving an hour before. Ye're a bucket of surprises, woman, did ye know that?"

Cradling my face, he leaned forward, resting his forehead on mine. "But when I saw ye being brought to meet the captain, it was the same as every other time I lay eyes on ye."

"Oh really?" I chuckled once, feeling more at

283

peace than I'd been in months. "And what is that?"

He made a humming sound, his eyes closing as he exhaled a long breath, as if he were reliving the moment right then and there. "It's like staring at the sun. Utterly blinding and breathtaking. Then, all at once, ye realize that ye're staring at the center of the universe, the one thing that keeps ye steady and grounded. The one thing ye would surely die without."

My breath caught at his words, another tear breaking free and cascading over his hands. I didn't know what I'd done to deserve such a loyal and adoring companion, or why he was sticking with me after everything I'd put him through, but I loved him so much. I loved him more than I thought was humanly possible, more than the moon and the stars, more than the life that flowed through my own body. He was my strength and my rock, my closest friend, my greatest ally and advocate.

"I love you," I whispered fiercely, putting my hands over his own.

"And I love ye."

Closing the rest of the distance between us, his lips covered mine, moving with strength and passion, heat rolling off his body. Slowly, he guided me backward, his chest pressing against my own.

Sliding my hands down his arms, I delighted in having him like this again. The world had been so messy and broken for so long, but here we were, just a man and a woman on a ship, somehow falling even more in love than we'd been at the start.

Grabbing his waist, I anchored myself to him, feeling a sense of excitement as he pushed me against the wall, his entire form against my own now. His fingers tangled in my hair, his breath quickening as he pulled away, choosing to lightly suck on a spot just above my collarbone.

Groaning, I tilted my head to the side, giving him better access. His movements made my heart race and skin flush with wanting. If the smile he gave me when he caressed my lips once more was any indication, he was very aware of that fact.

"Do ye want me, Samantha?" The question was laced with heavy seduction, purring from him with all the tease in the world. His lips fluttered over my cheek, then my neck, chuckling as I fidgeted beneath him.

"What do you think?"

His teeth grazed my earlobe, his warm breath causing my flesh to ripple. Grinning, I recalled other times that he'd teased me, and the very nice benefits said episodes had reaped.

Capturing my lips once more, his tongue tasting me, he hummed, his hand slipping under the hem of my shirt and moving to rest on my breast. He massaged it lightly, nipping my bottom lip, and then put his mouth by my ear once more.

"Tell me ye want me. Tell me all the ways and places you want me to touch ye. Tell me how to make ye mine." The whisper was rough and highly arousing, making me feel like I might melt into a puddle right then and there.

"I'm already yours," I replied breathlessly, holding him to me.

He nodded. "Aye, and I yours. Until the end of all time."

Taking his time, he kissed me again, tasting and feeling my mouth, his touch gentle and loving. His hands caressed my body, bringing life back to me, filling me with everything I needed to survive.

"I'll never get tired of this," he mumbled against me, smiling some.

"What, sex?" I asked, laughing and pushing my fingers into his hair.

"No, ye. I'll never get tired of ye like this, or any other way. I could spend the rest of my life in this spot, holding ye in my arms and it would be a life well lived."

A knock sounded at the door, someone clearing their throat loudly, and I sighed, realizing our time together was at its end.

"Give me a minute," Tristan called, still leaning against me, his eyes locked on mine.

"Your arse better be in the rigging in a minute," Dagger's voice said from the other side.

"Aye, Quartermaster, I'll be there. I'm only showing my wife the surgery."

Dagger snorted, the sound of his footsteps moving away from the front of the room. "I know exactly what ye're doing. Two minutes O'Rourke. That's all you'll be getting from me."

"How generous," Tristan mumbled, causing me to laugh as he grinned at me. "But why rush something that should be done slowly and delicately?" He nibbled my neck once more, licking it lightly. "Pleasurable things should never be rushed if ye can help it. Don't ye agree, lass?"

Caressing him in response, I let my hands do a little wandering of their own, giggling as he groaned. "You tell me."

"We should rush it," he said seriously, grabbing

my wrists and holding them over my head. "Just this once, aye?"

Two minutes later, he pecked me on the cheek at the bottom of the stairs, quickly dashing up the steps and disappearing from view.

Sighing happily, I was smiling as I joined Abella in the galley. She had started reorganizing the food, something already simmering in the coals, and was chopping an onion to add to the dish. It took me a beat to realize her tears weren't because of the vegetable in her hands.

"Let me take that," I said quickly, grabbing the knife and onion and setting them aside.

She gave me a pitiful stare, one full of pain and annoyance, her lip trembling, and then straightened, as if refusing to allow herself to be upset any longer. "I cry when I'm angry." Her tone was defensive and clipped and she turned to the boxes she'd stacked on the floor.

"I can see that." I wasn't exactly sure what I should say, or how to let her know it was okay for her to vent to me, so I remained silent, taking over the chopping I'd stolen from her.

After a few moments, she slapped her hands on the counter and gave a disgruntled sigh. "I can't believe he spoke to me that way. I thought he would be happy to see me, after, well . . ."

"He kissed you." The strange jealous twist gripped my stomach and I frowned. I hadn't known they were that close, not until she threw it in his face a few minutes ago.

"*Oui*. More than once. I thought he truly cared about my safety, but as soon as we were discovered and I saw him staring at you, I knew it hadn't meant as much to him." She turned to me, her eyes watering, and laughed, shaking her head. "He only had eyes for you. It was like I wasn't even there."

She went to the boxes, taking the items and returning them in a more organized manner. "I thought he was realizing you will never be his. I thought he was opening up to accepting a different life." She paused, staring at her hands. "But he only wanted me because I was close to you. It's always been you."

She glanced at me once more, tears still on her cheeks. "I'm not you, Samantha. How can I ever compete with the idea of the woman he loves, when she's always standing right next to me?"

Frowning, I crossed the tiny space, wrapping my arms around her. "I didn't have any idea you felt so strongly toward him," I confessed. "And it breaks my heart to know that I've been hurting you without intending to."

"I don't blame you," she said instantly. "It's his own fault. I've made it very clear how I feel for him. I told him he could choose his own happiness. I never thought that he would choose to keep loving you, though, and suffer."

"Maybe he was just worried about you," I offered. "Sometimes anger can be hiding deeper feelings. He might have been scared when he saw you on board, concerned for your wellbeing."

"Then why was he kind to you and mean to me?" She pulled away, shaking her head. "If that were the case, he would have spoken to you as roughly."

"He took the lashings for you," I reminded her.

"He had to. The captain ordered it."

Feeling awkward, I remained silent again, not knowing how to respond. After a minute, she sighed, sounding defeated.

"He promised he would write me. Now I wonder if they were just empty words."

"If Mark promised he would do something, then he will do it." Staring at her seriously, I nodded. "That's a promise you could take to the bank." Putting my arm around her shoulder once more, I sighed as well. "I'm sorry that I'm causing so much conflict in your life, Abella. I don't know what to say, other than it will all work out the way it's supposed to. That's a pretty bad piece of advice, but it's all I've got."

She laughed, wiping her face, and smiled. "It's helpful, all the same."

"I'm glad to hear it." Sensing it was the opportune moment to change the subject and get her mind off her own romantic woes, I stepped away and gestured to everything around us. "What are we cooking and what can I do to help? We have a lot of people to feed tonight."

The distraction worked. Abella's face morphed into one that was busy with the task at hand and in a few moments we were making bread and salting meat.

Life settled into an easy routine. It wasn't lost to me how much more comfortable I was at sea, or how much happier I was with Tristan always nearby. We had taken to sleeping in the surgery, which afforded us all the privacy we needed, on a pallet we'd created ourselves. My nightmares were few and far between, and when they did arrive, they were short lived and experienced without much consequence on my end.

While some of the men didn't seem too pleased that there were now women on the crew, they left us alone for the most part. I wasn't sure if Tristan and Mark had said anything to them, or if it was because of the sword fighting display we'd put on during the pirate fight, but I was grateful to not always be harassed by those around me.

Captain MacDonald interested me more and more every day. While stern, he was very kind and open to suggestions from his crew. The men—who I also discovered to be Templars—loved him and could do nothing but sing his praises. He was quiet when on his own, though, as if he were continually lost in some memory he couldn't seem to shake. The melancholy manner of his expressions made me think that he was very sad, though, maybe even lonely, and I couldn't help but wonder if it had anything to do with his Isobel and her death. No one on board seemed to know anything about her, other than the fact that the ship was named after her.

"It's not strange to any of you, the fact that he cared about this woman enough to name a ship after her, but he won't tell you anything other than she's been dead for thirty years?"

Mark shrugged, snacking on some crunchy bread from the day before, leaning in a relaxed fashion against the counter. "Not really. It's his business, he doesn't have to tell any of us about her if he doesn't want to."

"Well, Abella and I are curious, that's all." Hesitating, I realized I'd mentioned the one subject Mark didn't like to talk about—Abella. It was the same with her. She didn't want to talk about Mark anymore and the pair avoided each other like the plague. Currently, she was in the surgery, doing who knew what, having fled after Mark approached the galley. Tristan was in the rigging, unable to come to my rescue this time, and I swallowed, trying to decide if I wanted to attempt to push the issue again.

I did.

"You should go talk to her," I said quietly, pushing the coals in the fire around with the poker. "Her feelings are hurt. She thinks you're using her to get to me."

He snorted, giving me a patronizing look. "I don't need her to get to you. Case in point, I'm with you now and she had nothing to do with it."

"You're being mean," I replied, feeling somewhat

291

angry at his flippant reply. "And you led her on. I didn't think you were that type of guy."

"I did no such thing!" He had the audacity to appear offended. "I kissed her, yes, but I told her I needed time to sort things out. I was very clear on the fact that I didn't know if anything would happen between us."

"And then you kissed her," I interrupted. "And promised you would write her and told her to be safe. Those are contradicting statements, Mark."

"Just butt out of it, Sam. I don't need you, of all people, telling me how to run my love life."

Annoyed, I dropped the spoon I'd been using to stir with and rounded on him, hands on my hips. "Apparently, you do," I shot back. "Because you're doing a bang up job of it yourself!"

"She's almost thirty years younger than me, Sam!" The phrase burst from him like a rocket, his eyes wide and expression hurt. For a beat, he acted as if he wished he'd not said anything, surprise flitting across his features. His voice softened then, a tone of self-loathing filling it, the words he spoke coming slowly and painfully. "Thirty years. Do you know what that does to me? What that makes me? It's—"

"Disgusting?" Smiling in spite of myself, I nodded, my earlier annoyance dissipating some. His reservations made sense to me now, but I felt he was missing one rather large point. "Yes, in our time it would be. You would be called a cradle robber, pedophile, and all sorts of other names. They'd send you to jail if anything ever happened between you. But you know what? It isn't like that in this time. Love does not see age the same way. It's more than common for men your age to marry and love women Abella's age. Age is only a number here."

He laughed once, staring at me in disbelief. "So you're saying that I should just let it go and put everything I know to the side, ignore how bad these emotions make me feel, and just get over it?" He shook his head, disgusted, and stood straight, putting the bread on the counter. "I can't do that."

"No," I said, grabbing his arm as he moved to leave. "I'm saying that if that's your reason for being so hard on her, you need to tell her. She deserves to know that your reservations have nothing to do with her personally. She deserves to be happy, too, Mark, and to move on if she wants. You can't just kiss her and then throw her to the wind because you're uncomfortable, not if you want to be a good guy."

He snorted, not pleased with what I had to say. "I'm not throwing her to the wind. God, this is just like high school! Everyone is snooping around my business and there's a teenage girl crying somewhere because I broke her heart. Does it never end?"

Smiling in spite of myself, I released his arm, sighing. "High school or not, I want you to be happy, too," I said softly. "You're one of my best friends, Mark. I don't want to see you suffer any more. Why can't you let yourself be happy?"

He stared at me, his jaw clenching and unclenching, eyes full of emotion.

"Sails ahead!" The cry came from above, drawing the attention of all those on the crew deck.

"Pirate?" asked Dagger as he sat in his hammock.

There was a pause, everyone waiting for the answer, an air of anticipation hanging over us all.

"It's the flag of Jean Bart," Captain MacDonald's voice called.

The men relaxed at that, going back to whatever it was they had been doing before. Mark made an odd noise in his throat, nodding as he turned to me.

"Do you know who Jean Bart is?" I asked him under my breath, hoping his particular knowledge on pirates would help fill the blanks I was experiencing now.

"French privateer," he whispered quietly. "And a famous one at that. Did so well that King Louis made him a member of the aristocracy and named him an Admiral in the navy."

"We've caught him a little earlier than intended," MacDonald continued above us. "But it's of no consequence. Hopefully he has the time we need to get our treasure out of his hold and he isn't in a rush."

"He's a Templar?" I whispered in surprise.

Mark shrugged. "I don't know, but it sounds like there's treasure on his ship either way."

"O'Rourke!" Captain MacDonald's voice barked once more, grabbing our attention.

"Aye, Captain!" Tristan's voice sounded distant, probably because he was in the rigging.

"Not ye, O'Rourke, yer wife."

Some of the men laughed, and I could practically hear the humor in the Scotsman's voice. Tristan's laughter could be heard as well, and I smiled, happy to hear him so at ease and joyful once more. The sea had done us both good, as I'd known it would.

"Aye, Captain?" I called, stepping from the galley and heading for the bottom of the stairs, wiping my hands on my pants.

"Ye and yer maid are coming aboard Bart's ship with me. He likes a good story and it will be distraction enough while the men move the treasure."

"Captain Bart needs distracted from that?" I asked, surprised. "He's not a Templar, then?"

Shaking his head, he smiled. "No. A great man and service to his king, but not part of The Order. The man is as blind as a bat when it comes to what he's really carrying in the hold. Still, our frequent meetings have made him a good friend of mine. It's not him that needs the distracting, though; I could do that myself. No, ye're to be a distraction for his son."

"I see." Frowning, I stared at him for a moment. "A pair of breasts for him to look at?"

He snorted, amused. "Aye, I suppose ye could say that. I dinna doubt ye'd put him in his place if he ever gave ye reason to, though, lass. I just need ye to talk to him. He keeps sneaking around my crew, eavesdropping and trying to find out what's really going on. If I bring two women aboard, though, he's sure to stay close and leave everyone else be."

Shrugging, I sighed. "I'll tell Abella." Turning toward the surgery, I started walking away, only to pause at his next comment.

"There's dresses in one of the crates in the hold, if ye want to appear more lady like."

"Is that a suggestion, or an order?" I called over my shoulder.

"An order, woman. I canna very well take ye on board lookin' like the sea hardened sailors ye do now, can I?"

"You could, but I doubt it would be enough of a distraction for such a simply pleasured man as the admiral's son."

More laughter followed that and I smiled. I was happy to do my part to help, even if it meant putting on a dress. Sure, it made me feel more like a commodity than a useful member among the crew, but this was a job I could do and everyone knew it. Hopefully, Abella would see it the same way.

Moving in to the surgery, I watched her for a moment, going over the bottle and bandages in the case on the table. It was a good stock of supplies, along with some surgical instruments, but not anything that needed as thorough an inspection as she was giving.

"Everything alright?" I asked, breaking her concentration.

"Hmmm? Oh, yes." Glancing at me, she smiled, a vial of some herb clasped in her hand. "I was just trying to remember all the uses for these. Mark could probably tell me better, but I don't want to ask him."

Remembering my very recent conversation with him, I decided to give her a gentle push as well. "You should," I replied casually. "He might enjoy the break from the ropes."

"Perhaps." Returning to the case, she set the vial down, picking another and staring at its contents with narrowed eyes.

Feeling like she was trying to be aloof on the subject on purpose, I frowned, knowing I wasn't going to be able to get through to her right now. The only thing that would pull her from the focused task in front of her would be new commands from the captain to follow.

"Captain MacDonald has given us some new orders. Another privateer ship has been spotted—Jean

Bart's. We're to find the dresses in the hold and change into them, so we can go aboard with him."

She looked up at me again, surprised. "Jean Bart? The war hero?"

"That's the one. Do you feel like distracting him and his son while the rest of the crew moves the treasure off his ship?"

She blinked, as if she were caught off guard by everything I said, and then nodded, putting the medical supplies to the side. "Of course. Did Captain MacDonald say where the dresses were in the hold?"

"No, but I imagine we can ask."

Leaving the surgery, the two of us sought out Dagger and got directions to the crate we needed. An hour later, I found myself dressed to the nines, my hair pulled away from my face and covered with a large hat. Abella looked much the same, the dress she wore now more decorated and fashionable than any I'd ever seen her wear. The blue and yellow fabrics of our skirts seemed to brighten the deck as we stepped out into the sun, ready to do our part.

The two ships were now drawn close, the men employed with the task of lashing the vessels together and securing a gangplank over the open water.

"Ye two look right beautiful," Captain MacDonald said, coming to stand by us. He'd changed into a clean shirt and kilt, his beard freshly washed and trimmed. "I'm sure Bart and his son will be pleased to see ye."

"Thank you," I replied cordially. "You look very nice yourself."

"Ye noticed, did ye?" That seemed to please him very much for some reason. "Aye, well. I canna meet an old friend looking like a sea dog myself. My mother would hang me from my toes and spank me with a switch."

The image he painted was so clear, I laughed, looking at him in surprise. He'd never said anything of his family before. In fact, for the first time, he seemed to be in a genuinely good mood. He and Bart must have been fine friends indeed, if he was this happy to see him again.

The gangplank smacked into place, creating a walkway between the two boats and grabbing our attention once more. With a start, I realized I recognized one of the sailors on the other side, his face one I hadn't seen in over a year.

"John! John Butler!" Grinning widely, I waved across the water, watching as he turned to me in surprise. He was wearing the same white shirt and black pants I'd always seen him in, his skin tan and scarred, a few teeth missing from his smile. However, he was handsome as well, and I had many memories of his friendship and assistance from when I'd first arrived in this time. He had been Tristan's Quartermaster and fought at the battle for Oak Isle. We'd not seen each other since then, as he'd been injured and sailed back to France on a different ship.

"Sam?" His voice was full of shock as he climbed onto the gangplank, staring at me like he was seeing a ghost.

"Get over here," I called. "Give me a hug! It's been too long!"

Like a man chased by Hell Hounds, he crossed the boards, hopping down onto the deck and wrapping his arms around me.

"Thank the gods," he said, somewhat breathless. "Is Tristan here with ye, too?"

"Why wouldn't he be?" Pulling away, I studied him questioningly. What I'd thought was just shock at unexpectedly seeing an old friend was more than that, I realized now. John seemed genuinely relieved and thankful to see me, like he'd thought something terrible had happened to me. "What is it?" I asked him, eyes wide. "What's the matter?"

"Nothing," he rushed to say. "Only that, well, I thought ye both were dead."

"Dead?" Shocked, I stared at him with wide eyes. "Why would you think that?"

Blanching, I wondered if he'd thought Randall had killed me instead of kidnapping me. I'd always thought most of The Order had known the general events of what happened in Arizona. Did John not? Was the story not as well circulated as I'd previously imagined?

But, no. He'd said he thought Tristan was dead as well. Everyone would have known he was alive, especially after all the meetings he'd had to attend in Paris. He'd been front and center at the initiation ceremony of the new Grand Master—there was no way anyone could have mistaken him for dead.

"Ye mean, you don't know?" John frowned, nodding. "Of course ye wouldn't. Ye weren't there."

"What are you talking about? What don't I know?"

He peered around, as if searching for someone, his eyes passing over Captain MacDonald and Abella behind me. Finally, he sighed and stared at me again.

"Yer house burned down, Sam. The whole thing is a pile of rubble. By some miracle, the stables in the rear managed to survive and yer neighbors didn't suffer any flames, but everything else is gone. When they found bodies, we all assumed it was Tristan and ye."

Mind reeling, I tried to digest what he'd said. "Stables?" I managed to sputter. "You mean the old house, the one with the servants, burned? Not the new place they were sending us?"

He frowned, seeming just as confused as I was. "New place? There was no record of ye being moved anywhere else. We—what was left of Tristan's old crew—searched to see if ye could be anywhere else. Davies himself said it was the only house ye had."

Shaking my head, I closed my eyes, refusing to hear what he was saying. "No, Davies kicked us out of that house. He told Tristan The Order couldn't afford to keep us in such a nice place anymore and we had to leave. We were supposed to go that night, but Captain MacDonald came and snuck Tristan and Mark out early."

"I don't know what to tell ye, Sam. I went to the man myself. He said no such thing to me."

Still rattled, I tried to think of anything else I could ask him. "How did the fire start?"

He hedged, looking around once more, and I realized he was searching for Tristan. He didn't want to tell me what had happened; he wanted to tell Tristan and let him break the news to me.

"Just tell me," I urged. "You're making me imagine all sorts of horrible situations."

"It was intentional," he replied quietly. "There where witnesses who saw three men break in with torches and set the place ablaze. Yer friend Mark . . .

I'm sorry, Samantha. His house was burned as well. We weren't able to find a body."

"John!"

Tristan appeared overhead, grinning like a fool. "I didn't know ye were on Bart's ship!"

John smiled tightly and nodded. "Aye, friend, I am. It's good to see ye alive and well."

Stepping away, I turned to Abella and Captain MacDonald, feeling like I might lose my sea legs for a moment and vomit my breakfast over the railing. "Someone tried to kill us," I said weakly, knees wobbling beneath the heavy dress. "All of us."

The ship suddenly felt like it was spinning, my ears ringing loudly as I gripped the railing, fighting tears. Someone had died in the fire, most likely one of the maids, maybe even all of the people who had been working for us and living in the house. The thought made me feel even sicker. The more I went over what I'd just heard, the harder it was to breathe and stand, my knees buckling underneath me.

Captain MacDonald was by my side in an instant, slipping his arm around my waist and holding me steady. "Monsieur O'Rourke," he called over his shoulder, watching me with an even stare. "Yer wife needs some assistance, methinks."

"I'm fine," I replied, weakly, stumbling as I tried to stand on my own.

Tristan's hands were on me then, concern on his face as he held me. His touch helped ground me, the spinning slowing as I stared at his eyes, inhaling deeply as he coached me along.

"Take her into my cabin," MacDonald was saying behind me. "Lay her down and let her rest. There's some whiskey in the desk that will help her find her bearings."

"It's alright, lass." Tristan's voice was like a prayer to my lips, his strong arms hauling me into the air and keeping me close to his chest as he carried me away.

I wanted to resist, to say I needed to follow my orders from the captain and go on to Bart's ship, but I couldn't find the words. All I could think was that someone had tried to harm me and my family, again, and it was very likely they would have succeeded if we'd been there.

Taking me into the captain's quarters, Tristan laid me down on the bed sitting beside me for a moment, his hands gripped in mine.

"Abella, sit," he said, motioning to the chairs behind him.

I hadn't realized until right then that she'd followed us in. Glancing over, I could see tears falling down her face, fear in her eyes.

"He said there were b-bodies. The other servants—Annaliese, my friends—they're all . . ." She covered her mouth in horror, squeezing her eyes shut as she turned away from us. Leaning against the desk, her shoulders shook as she made sniffling noises, crying over the lives that had been lost.

"What's going on?" Mark suddenly appeared in the space, the door slamming shut behind him as he took in the three of us with wide eyes. "What's happened?"

Abella, turning toward him, hiccuped, her eyes bloodshot and starting to swell. The two stared at each other for a moment, a million expressions seeming to

KAMERY SOLOMON

pass over the both of them, and then Mark turned his attention to Tristan and myself.

"Are you hurt?" he asked, stepping forward. "What can I do to he—"

"She almost fainted." Cutting him off, Tristan stood, nodding toward Abella. "The lass just discovered her friends have been killed in a house fire. Our house fire."

Confused, Mark glanced at Abella, hesitating again, as if he didn't know which direction to go. "Your house fire?"

Sitting up slowly, I took a deep breath, hoping the spinning in my head would stay away. "Someone lit our house on fire. Everyone inside was killed. Apparently, the same thing happened at your house."

His eyes widened even more. "When?"

"It would have had to be the night we left on this ship," Tristan interjected. "Before we moved to our new homes and before anyone realized we were already gone."

"But Davies said we weren't moving when John talked to him. Do you think he changed his mind and was going to tell us in the morning?" I stared at my husband with worried eyes. It was clear what he was thinking. I was thinking it, too. But I didn't want to be so fast to condemn a man, not when I'd never even met him.

"I think the wee bugger tried to have us killed, if that's what ye're getting at," Tristan responded with a growl. "He's lyin' to the other Templars about it, too."

"Why would he do t-that?" Abella hiccupped, wiping her face with her hand.

"What does he stand to gain from killing us?"

Mark added, glancing at her one more time.

Tristan frowned at both of them, and then sighed, rubbing his face.

"He's a Black Knight," I offered quietly, putting my hand on his knee. "And we're the biggest obstacle the Black Knights have had to face so far. Getting rid of us is a business move for him."

Tristan remained quiet, watching me with sad eyes.

"That's what you're thinking, isn't it?" I pressed.

"Aye, Sam. It is. I don't have enough proof to know for certain, but that is a possibility. I don't want to believe we voted a traitor in to lead us, though. Not yet."

"There are a lot of other options," Mark interjected, folding his arms. "It doesn't have to be Davies. I mean, sure, he's lying to the other Templars about our living situation, but that could be for any number of reasons."

"Like what?" Watching him with a frown, I tried not to show my annoyance when he couldn't come up with an answer.

"It could have been Randall," he finally said. "He hates all of us. He could have easily gotten some of his wacko followers to go torch our houses."

"Ye have a point," Tristan agreed. "But this doesn't seem like something Randall would do. He's always been very upfront and likes to take his enemies himself, so he can see them go."

"Yeah, but every time he tries to do that to the two of you, he has to run away with his tail between his legs. Maybe he just got tired of losing and thought it would be better this way." Mark shrugged, clearly not convinced Randall wasn't the perpetrator of the crime. "He's been unusually absent from the front lines of his cause lately. I think it's a safe bet to say he's licking his wounds and trying to take care of his mess with as little effort as possible."

"Ye don't know the man like I do." Frustrated, Tristan stood, running a hand through his hair. It wasn't until that moment that I realized how bothered he was by this turn of events. He seemed shaken, worried even, and it made me feel that much more upset by it.

"I think I do," Mark shot back. "You knew him when he was still trying to save face. I've worked with the monster that he is now. It doesn't seem like a far stretch to think he finally got tired of you chasing after him. This was an easy target. I mean, come on, Tristan. You stayed in the same house he broke into before. You might as well have put up a sign inviting him in. You could have tied Sammy to a chair and left her on the front porch for him and it wouldn't have been any easier than this."

Angry, Tristan rounded on him, his face flushing. "Aye, you'd like that, wouldn't ye? Then ye could swoop in and save my wife again, be at her side when I should be. Maybe ye'll get lucky and be able to attend the birth and death of another one of my children, so ye can lord that over my head later."

"Stop it!" Rattled by his words and the fight unfolding in front of me, I got off the bed, grateful to find my legs felt fine now. "Both of you. Someone tried to kill all of us and you're going to fight over this?"

Turning to Tristan, I smiled tightly. "What

happened was awful, but we can't change the past. I thought we were both doing better, here, on the ocean. If not, this is a conversation you need to have with me, not a fight you need to have with Mark."

I then glared over at Mark, taking in his heated stance and the frown on his face. Folding my arms, I sighed, knowing I needed to stop this argument before it got even more out of hand. Tristan was still hurting and blaming himself for what had happened to the baby and me. I didn't need Mark rubbing salt in the wounds by insisting Tristan wasn't doing anything right. "I'm grateful for the help you gave me, Mark. But, if you're going to use it to try and tear my family apart even more, I will leave you behind faster than you can blink."

Raising my hand as he opened his mouth to interrupt, I continued. "I don't think that's what you were trying to do just now, but still. We need to focus. The fact our homes have been burned could have nothing to do with what happened before. It's in the past. Let it stay there."

He frowned, giving me a stare that said he didn't much like being called out by me, and then turned, heading toward the door. "Let me know when you have the proof you want of who did it," he said casually, leaving the room with a frustrated air.

Shaking my head, I turned toward the bed and Tristan, doing my best to keep my head together and not break into the worried woman I really was.

Tristan, relaxing in his chair some, looked at me with sad eyes. It was an expression I'd seen many times in Paris, whenever he'd been feeling especially upset about Rachel.

"Abella," I said, without looking over to her. "Are you feeling well?"

"Better," her soft voice replied.

"Do you think you could go ask the captain if he's still in need of our assistance? I would like to talk to my husband alone for a moment."

She sniffed, and I could hear her footsteps following after Mark, the door opening and shutting softly behind her.

Silence stretched between us for a moment, the two of us simply staring at each other. If there was a pin to drop, we probably would have heard it hit the floor clear as day.

"Talk to me," I finally said, sitting beside him.

"He's right." There was a note of acceptance to his tone I hadn't ever heard before when we had this conversation. With a start, I realized he was starting to believe he couldn't protect me. He'd always asserted that he didn't need to, but he wanted to. If he were now openly admitting he couldn't do it, though, what did that mean?

"He's not right—"

"He is." He laughed lightly, a sound that was in no way funny or endearing. "I can't protect ye, not from Randall. Not from whoever the bastard is that tried to roast us in our beds. Our home has been violated and destroyed twice now, and I was away in each instance."

"I wasn't there this time," I said softly. "I was here, on this ship, with you."

"Not by any of my doing," he retorted. "If ye weren't so stubborn and insistent, ye'd have been there. It would have been yer body they found in the ashes."

He sighed, rubbing his face, and snorted, shaking his head. "I would have missed my child's *and* my wife's funerals. What kind of husband and father am I?"

"A damn good one." Leaning forward, I wrapped my arms around his neck, pulling him toward me. "The best of the best. The love of my life and the most caring man I've ever had the pleasure of knowing. I would be lost without you. I *was* lost without you."

He shook his head, the words not getting through to him. "Still. This is not what I imagined my life would be like. I didn't think it would be so hard, or painful." He smiled sadly and shook his head. "There's been plenty of joy as well, but it seems like the hurt clouds over all of it. All I can think of is how much it stings, of how . . . alone it makes me feel. Even on this ship, surrounded by the crew and with a job to do, I feel as if I've been abandoned, sailing through an empty sea, living a life with hardly any purpose at all."

"I love you," I said softly. "We'll get through this together. Always together, like you said. We can beat anything that comes our way, so long as we have each other. You will never be alone."

"Aye, we have each other. But are ye not closed off as well? We're a broken pair, Samantha. I know I'm not the one who suffered the pain of losing a child physically, that ye've known the horror of it and can recall it at any given second. But I feel like I would give anything to have those memories, just to know that she was real and I was there to see her, to hold her, and to say goodbye. I will always carry those regrets. You sit before me now and say we can move on, that we still have each other, but it feels like there is a hole in my heart now. Life is not what it was before."

"And it never will be." My lip trembled as I watched him, tears filling my eyes. "We lost something we never had, something that can never be replaced. We lost our child. But, we lost her together. I intend to patch ourselves back up together, too."

Nodding, he rose from the chair, moving to sit beside me on the bed. As he wrapped his arms around me, he released a great, shaky sigh, as if he'd been holding in what he'd just said for years and a weight had finally lifted off him.

"I'm sorry I got angry with Mark," he mumbled, resting his head against mine. "I was only upset because he was right. I should have taken more precautions to protect ye once we returned home."

"I'm sure he only fought back because he was shocked by the fact we all could have died. Stress does things to people, makes them act in ways that they normally wouldn't."

"Aye. I'll speak with him when I get the chance and apologize, though."

Silence stretched between us for a moment, his warmth wrapping around me like a blanket. The peace was short lived, though, as I found my thoughts drifting toward what Mark had said about our arsonist.

"Do you think it could have been Randall?" I asked quietly, staring at the chair in front of us.

He paused, as if he weren't sure what to say, and then sighed again. "It could have been. Mark was right about that, too. I was never close with Randall and I've not spent months at sea with him as a blood thirsty captain. He very well could have decided to try a

310

different approach to killing us."

"But that doesn't take into account the fact that Davies lied about us moving to another residence. Why would he do that? He has nothing to lose or gain from telling everyone he was having us moved."

"I agree. There is much to think about and discuss before we return to Paris. It would seem we have many enemies and I'm not sure how to face them all."

A knock at the door drew our attention, and we turned to see Captain MacDonald letting himself in.

"I apologize for my intrusion," he said politely, walking to his desk. "Are ye feelin' well, Madame O'Rourke?"

"Much better," I replied, nodding. "Thank you for your help and the offering of your room for my recovery."

"Think nothing of it." Waving his hand, he opened one of the drawers, revealing the bottle of whiskey he'd mentioned before, and took a swig. The action seemed to be stressful, as if he were greatly agitated by something and seeking some release from the drink in his hand.

"Is everything alright, Captain?" Tristan asked, picking up on the feeling as well.

"No. But it's not anything to bother yerself with at this moment." Sitting in his chair, MacDonald took another drink, corked the bottle, and put it back in the drawer. "We are untethering ourselves from Jean Bart and moving on, though, if ye are able to head to yer station now."

"What about the treasure?" I asked, surprised. We hadn't been in here long enough for the crews to carry it over, had we?

Captain MacDonald grunted, making me think I may have lighted upon the source of his annoyance. "It would appear, there is none." His reply was short and sounded angry, but he stared at me as if we were having a conversation about the weather.

"How can that be?" Tristan asked.

Captain MacDonald shrugged, rising once more and going to the window. "I dinna rightly ken. I received the distinct impression that the treasure was there, but they'd been ordered not to give it to me."

"Why?" His words didn't make sense to me. The Order worked like clockwork. The treasure transports were their most important task. Why would anyone try and mess that up?

"That is a question that remains to be answered, as well," MacDonald replied thoughtfully. "But I intend to discover the truth of it."

"Are you enjoying your time at sea, Samantha?"

Randall smiled at me, his eyes bloodshot and skin pale. He looked unwell, like he hadn't slept in days and was slowly becoming some undead thing, dark and scary. His white shirt was spotted with sweat stains and wrinkled like it had been shoved in a drawer for some time. Dark, stringy hair was pulled away from his face, tied with a leather band at the nape of his neck. Overall, I was getting the impression that he really was sick with something, but I couldn't tell what.

Seated across the table from him, I kept my fists firmly in my lap, my wrists bound together, trying not to lash out and attack him. Our gazes were riveted on each other, my own conveying all the hatred and disgust I had for him.

"Tristan will come for me," I said, enjoying the sickened expression that crossed his face. Our meetings were falling into a pattern now. It didn't take long for me to realize I was dreaming. All I had to do was irritate him enough to get him to attack me in some way and I would wake up.

"Let him," he replied smoothly, placing his arms on the table and leaning forward. "I want him to come."

"Why, so you can try and fail to kill him again?"
Refusing to back away, I sat straight as a board, not
flinching as his face came closer to mine. "You should
give up. Evil never wins over good."

He paused at that, frowning. Leaning away, he
watched me with his exhausted eyes, mouth pressed
into a thin line. He seemed almost as if he were on
drugs then, a crack addict who had been without his
latest dose and was now suffering the consequences.

"There is no good and evil, Sammy. No right and
wrong. Simply one man's perspective. You think me
bad, but all I want to do is save the world from itself.
In my eyes, you're the one stopping the salvation of
every person. You're the one mucking up plans and
causing failures. You're my evil."

"I'm not the person who sacrifices his own men to
get what he wants, who burns entire villages to the
ground for sport, who murders joyously, or who thinks
it's okay to force himself on others. You may think I'm
evil because I stand in your way, but good will always
stand in your way. There is no salvation for a world
ruled by you, only death and destruction."

Laughing, he shook a finger at me, either highly
amused by my words or very bothered by them. "I've
seen where you come from, Sammy. Did you know
that? The gods speak to me now and they show me
things. They tell me that you're dangerous but greatly
powerful. You've managed to pass all of their tests, but
you stand for everything they are against."

"I don't know what you're talking about." His
ranting scared me some, the strength of his conviction
evident in everything he'd said. I'd known the man was

314

crazy before, but he sounded like a certifiable maniac now.

"You and I are chosen," he said, licking his dry lips excitedly. "Me from a place of devotion and submission, you from one that was defiant and murderous. Every day, people from your time are killing one another in the name of love and freedom, destroying lives without a single thought except for how it will benefit themselves. You raise your leaders high, only to tear them down with magnificent force when they don't do as you ask. You say you are good, but you are from an era of murder, rape, lies, and faithlessness. How could you even know what good is? The people in your time can't even talk to one another without fighting. And it's only going to get worse. You use your magic and your machines to destroy one another, claiming it's for the better good, when, in all reality, you want to be the one in control. In the end, you're unable to see that you were never in control, but a slave to the very destructive patterns you claimed to hate."

"And you're better than all of that?" I asked in disbelief. "You, who are a murderer and a liar?"

"I am faithful!" he shouted, eyes wide with anger. "I have never sought to make myself more than I am. I have always been devoted to the cause of the heavens, to cleansing the earth of the wicked that will birth your time and ideals. Why do you think the gods granted me my life, healing my hand when you so hatefully cut it off?"

"You have always wanted to be better than you already were," I growled, leaning forward. "That's why you've been stealing the blood of the gods in the

first place. That's why you didn't die in that cave. You managed to get lucky and fall in their essence. The gods weren't saving you—you are a victim of circumstance."

"You're wrong," he whispered. "They've chosen me. God Almighty Himself had chosen me before these new gods ever did. I am meant to save this world."

"You're meant to be locked in a mental institution."

His hand flashed out, striking me across the face. The ring on his hand cut me slightly, a drop of red splashing on the table between us as he leaned in close and growled in my face. "I am meant to be the new god. Nothing you can do or say will change that."

Starting, I sat in bed, my cheek still tingling from where Randall had slapped me. My breath was coming quickly, my heart racing, and I peered around the dark surgery in a panic, trying to regain my bearings.

"Sam?" Tristan's hand rested on my arm, the shadow of his form rising next to me. "What is it?"

"Nothing," I whispered, breathing deeply. "Just another nightmare."

"Not as bad as the others?" he asked. "Ye weren't screaming."

"No, I wasn't."

Gradually, my pulse slowed and my breath evened, a sense of safety and peace washing through me. Gently, I laid down, cuddling into Tristan's embrace. He pulled the blanket over my shoulders, kissing the top of my head, and gently caressed my face.

"Sam?" he said in surprise. "Ye're bleeding."

"What?" My face was still sore as I touched it gently, shocked to find it was sticky with warm blood. "How . . .?"

Sitting up, I fumbled with the blanket, untangling myself and moving toward the coals in the fireplace. "Did I scratch myself, you think?"

"Let me see." Taking my chin, he turned my face toward the fire. "It doesn't look like a scratch, I don't think. Are ye wearing a ring? Maybe ye caught yerself with it when ye woke and didn't realize because of the dream."

Showing him my bare hands, I shook my head. "Nothing. Are you wearing any?"

"No."

Sighing, I rose, going to the box of medical supplies and getting some clean rags. Carefully, I wiped my face the best I could, feeling the small cut with my fingertips. It wasn't very big or deep, but it bled a lot. All I needed to do was put pressure on it to stop the bleeding. It would be fine.

"I was cut by a ring in my dream," I said slowly, thinking about the strange conversation with Randall. The nightmares were becoming less like torture sessions and more like a talk show where Randall would spout off all sorts of nonsense. I didn't know why they were taking such a strange turn. Perhaps it was simply me trying to move on. The terrors had started as memories of what had happened to me, and then moved on to events that had never occurred. Now they seemed like visitations. It was like the Randall in my mind was getting weaker and scared, pulling away and keeping to himself. If anything, I was hoping it was a sign I would soon be done with the nightmares altogether.

"Sails, starboard side!"

The muffled cry from above kept Tristan from responding, the two of us looking up in surprise. Normally, the night watch didn't call any ships they saw nearby, preferring to wait until morning to see what flag the vessel was flying.

"Hard to starboard!" Captain MacDonald's voice roared. "She's tryin' to ram us!"

Footsteps pounded overhead, and sounds of the crew suddenly waking and rushing to their stations came to life around us.

"O'Rourke!" The door burst open, revealing Dagger standing there, his shirt undone and feet bare. "To the rigging, quickly! We're being attacked!"

He didn't need telling twice. In an instant, Tristan was disappearing up the steps as he took them two at a time.

Turning to me, Dagger motioned for me to come as well. "I need you to—"

The ship suddenly veered to the side, the force of the movement causing us both to stop what we were doing and hold on to the nearest object to keep from falling. I found myself in Dagger's arms, the two of us holding onto the doorway in a slight panic, until the force of the motion lessened enough for us stand normally.

Releasing me and clearing his throat, Dagger straightened his shirt. "Go to the brig and warn the prisoners of what's happening. They should all be awake after that. Take Abella with you."

Nodding, I dashed through the rows of hammocks, dodging men and piles of things strewn everywhere as I hurried toward the galley. Abella slept in the hammock closest to the kitchen, as it had been empty upon our appointment to the crew. To my surprise, I found Mark with her, his palm on her cheek, fingers twisted in her hair as he whispered something to her. She was nodding, her own hands on his chest. She was out of sorts, and I suddenly realized she must have fallen when the boat turned. Mark was checking to make sure she was okay.

"Abella!" I called, not really caring if I interrupted them or not at the moment. "We have orders from Dagger to check on the prisoners below. Are you okay?"

Tearing her eyes away from him, Abella nodded. "*Oui*. I am well." Disentangling herself, she darted toward the stairs leading to the decks below.

"She's good," Mark said as he passed by, headed for the rigging as well. "She fell out of the hammock and hit her head, but it's fine. I sleep right next to her and saw the whole thing."

"Oh really?"

"Yeah. Why do you think she's so mad at me? She thinks I'm trying to babysit her." He grinned over his shoulder before disappearing from view as he headed toward the main deck.

Everyone was shouting above as the cannons were being loaded in the darkness, which seemed to be pressing in from all sides. The only light was a dim glow from spontaneously placed lanterns, the rest having been dampened to conserve supplies.

319

Stumbling slightly, I made my way to the gun deck, ducking out of the way as other members of the crew shot around me, hurrying to their battle stations.

Suddenly, the ship rocked again, breaking over a rough wave, and I felt my stomach turn unpleasantly at the sensation. This was no time to get sick, though, and I pressed on, finally joining Abella in the brig.

"His head is split open, Samantha!" she yelled, her hands thrust through the bars of one cell. She was desperately trying to stop the bleeding from a large cut on the pirate's head, his mates not doing anything to help.

Glancing at the other men, I realized there were several injured. They hadn't been warned of the turn and must have been thrown around like baby dolls, crushed against the walls and bars of their cells.

"What's going on?" one of them yelled. "Who is attacking us?"

"Someone tried to ram us," I said loudly. "That's all I know."

"Good! We'll be free in no time." A few of the pirates laughed at that, some of them acting absolutely gleeful in the dim light.

"Or you'll all be dead at the bottom of the ocean," I yelled, effectively silencing them. "In the meantime, everyone with an injury, move to the front, by the bars. Abella and I will assist you the best we can."

Thankfully, the prisoners listened, shuffling around until they were organized and I could better see what was wrong with each of them. Most seemed to have sprains or small cuts, but a few—like the man Abella was trying to help—and been badly hurt and needed assistance right away.

"Abella, go grab the needle and thread from the surgery. Grab the whiskey from the galley, too."

Taking her place, I ripped the bottom of my shirt off, wadding it and placing it on the cut. "What's your name?" I asked the older man.

"M-McGregor," he stuttered, his hands shaking as he tried to help me hold the cloth over the wound. Blood covered his face, giving him the appearance of one going to meet Death.

"McGregor, do you know that head wounds usually bleed the worst?"

He tried to nod, his lip trembling, and I smiled encouragingly.

"You're going to be fine, I promise."

Abella returned a moment later, arms full of ratty bandages and other supplies. "Here's the whiskey," she said, handing the bottle to me as she passed. "I'm going to clean a wound a few cells away."

We each worked quickly, stitching and administering whiskey for pain. After half an hour, it seemed we'd caught the worst of the ailments in time and the prisoners would survive the trip to Hispaniola, provided the rest of us did.

Rising, I wiped my hands on my pants, noting the blood under my fingernails, and sighed. "I think that's everyone," I said to Abella, joining her at the foot of the stairs. She'd been gathering all the dirty rags for washing, throwing them in the box we'd kept them in when clean.

"We should probably go check the rest of the crew, see if any of them were injured," she stated. "See if there's any more information on what happened."

Suddenly, the cannons began firing in earnest, the

sound deafening as each gun shot. The air overhead filled with smoke, and we were rolling again.

The side of the boat scraped and moaned, shaking and rocking, knocking everyone to the ground. Lamps fell from their brackets, darkening as they hit the floor or eagerly burning at the beams they smashed against. Above, guns rolled out of place, taking the men who manned them along for the ride. Beneath us, I could hear some of the cargo in the hold tipping over, smashing to pieces with a loud bang.

Ears ringing, I looked around, dazed, trying to understand what was happening. Prisoners were crying out, the men upstairs shouting and swearing. Abella was lying flat on her back beside me, staring at the ceiling like she'd never seen one before. Slowly, I realized we must have been rammed by the other ship, the collision causing us to spin in the water.

"Reload!" Dagger yelled overhead, his voice breaking through the confusion. "It wasn't a direct hit! They've swiped the end of the starboard side. We've still got a fighting chance in this battle!"

Shaking myself, I pushed to my feet, turning toward a small fire a few feet ahead. It wasn't a bad blaze, but would become one if not taken care of. Desperate, I glanced around, trying to find something to douse it with.

Spotting one of the prisoners in a nearby cell, I ran over to him, pushing a hand through the space between the bars.

"Give me your jacket!"

"The hell with ye," he said groggily, holding his head.

Frustration ripped through me and I growled, suddenly feeling very done with my whole polite, privateer manner. In the blink of an eye, the pirate side of me shone through, and I snarled, letting all the anger I felt drip through my tone. "Damn it man, give me your jacket or we'll all burn into Davy Jones' Locker!"

Surprised, he stared at me with wide eyes, his fellow cellmates reflecting his expression. After a beat, he shrugged off the coat, handing it over without another word.

Wasting no time, I tossed the heavy fabric on the flames. Stamping my foot on top of the smoldering pile, I coughed, covering my mouth and nose with my sleeve in an attempt to breathe easier. After a moment, the smoke was all that was left of the miniature blaze.

"They're coming around, hold steady!" Dagger yelled.

My mind was in a panic. Having never been faced with this situation before, I didn't know what to do, or where I should go. I knew I could be of more help than standing here, yelling at pirates, though.

Moving toward the stairs, I helped Abella to her feet, motioning for her to come along. We darted along the steps, ducking out of the way of the gun crew, and surveyed what was happening on their deck.

A few of the cannons had rolled from their spots

and were being pushed to their windows, while others frantically loaded the balls into the front, trying to peer over the dark waters and catch a glimpse of the incoming vessel.

Finally, I spotted Dagger, cramped into a corner, hastily trying to get a wick to light. He seemed annoyed more than anything, but I could tell the midnight attack had shaken him.

"Something's wrong," I said to Abella, still watching him. "Dagger's worried."

She frowned, studying him as well. "What do you think it is?"

"I don't know."

Pushing through the mass, we hurried to him.

"Dagger!" Catching his attention, I closed the distance between us, trying to ignore all of the questions running through my mind and focus on just the important ones.

"The prisoners are fine," I told him. "A little beat, but we took care of it. What can we do now?"

He glanced at me as if he had no idea who I was for a moment and then shook himself. "Right." Passing the wick he'd finally lit off to another man, he ushered us out of the way, speaking quickly. "Get to the hold and search for any damage to the hull on the starboard side, particularly around the stern. If we're taking on water, find Smithy as fast as possible and show him . He'll tell you what to do from there."

"And if the other ship boards us?" Abella interjected, her tone calm and calculating.

He hesitated, glancing past us to the men nearby, and then came closer, whispering quietly. "I don't know. It's the *Iron Fist*—a Templar ship. They were our next treasure trade, but we were supposed to wait until morning, so we could feign the fight for any crew that aren't members of The Order. I have no idea why they've attacked us for real or what their plans are, should they board us. At this point, I would say be ready to fight for your lives. *Iron Fist* won't go down without giving us everything she's got."

Shocked, it took me a second to wrap my mind around what he was saying. First Bart's ship had said there was no treasure and now our second meet up was attacking us? A sickening feeling filled my stomach. Was this the work of The Black Knights? Was their reach really that far, that they could destroy our entire route with hardly any effort at all?

"Go now," Dagger said, breaking me from my thoughts. "If we're taking on water, we need to stop it fast. Iron Fist is aiming for us again. We can't sink before we discover what's going on."

Nodding, I turned, sprinting back to the steps. It didn't matter what implications this whole affair could have—like the fact we could all be branded as traitors if we fought and couldn't prove Black Knights had been involved. Right now, I needed to find if there were any holes in the ship.

Practically jumping the stairs, I grabbed one of the lanterns from the brig and threw open the hatch to the hold, halfway thinking I was about to find it already under water. A breath of relief passed through me as I set eyes on mostly dry wood. Everything seemed okay, if not a little worse for wear. Hopping to the floor, I held the light high over my head, looking in the direction of the stern. That was where the secondary brig was, lost in the darkness, waiting for someone to come and fill her dark cells.

Swallowing hard, I hurried down the tight aisles, stepping around crates that had fallen and items that lay askew across the floor. Finally, I reached the wall, the right side seemingly fine. There was very little water coming through, and anything that was leaking could be fixed with pitch.

Another great sigh of relief left me and I turned to Abella, laughing. "It's fine," I said. "You and I could fix it ourselves right now."

A great crack sounded through the hold and I flew back from the wall, slamming against the bars of the secondary brig. My lantern broke on impact, showering me with glass, the fire going out and plunging us into darkness. The containers around me shifted, falling and crashing against each other. Abella screamed, and I heard her bang into the cell door beside me. It popped open with a loud moan, depositing her inside with a thud.

The ship swayed from its second impact with *Iron Fist*, but remained tilted to one side, as if stuck on something. Thankfully, the starboard side continued to hold, despite the creaking and groaning. It appeared our attackers hadn't been going fast enough to break us.

Gingerly, I pushed away from the bars, trying to get a clear footing in the tilted space.

"Abella?" I called, feeling around, blind. "Are you alright?"

She didn't answer and my heart quickened, fear filling me.

"Abella?" I called again, louder this time. "Where are you?"

In the silence, it was as if I could hear my own heartbeat screaming at me, like a drum pounding in my ears. When I finally found the entrance to the cell, I practically threw myself in, using my hands to reach out and find her.

At last, my fingers brushed against skin, and I released a cry of relief. It was her arm, stretched across the floor at an odd angle. Gently, I felt up the bone, feeling her dislocated shoulder. The pulse in her neck was strong and steady, though, giving me all the comfort I needed in knowing she was still alive. Feeling the rest of her body, I searched for other injuries, but could find nothing other than a bump on her head.

"You're going to be okay," I told her, trying to shake off my own nerves in the pitch black. "I'm going to find some light and come back for you. You'll be safe here."

Moving as quickly as I could, still thrown off by the tilted position of the ship, it took much longer than I would have liked to find my way back to the stairs.

Pushing open the hatch, I was instantly assaulted by a barrage of yells from the prisoners. They were cheering a battle of their own, the two men going at each other with swords and insults. With a start, I realized it wasn't the prisoners themselves that were fighting, but a member of my crew and a man I didn't recognize.

Suddenly, I knew we'd been boarded by the *Iron Fist*. A fight for our lives was taking place, and if what I was watching now was any suggestion, it was going to be a brutal one.

Ignoring what was happening, I made my way to

the gun deck, staying close to the walls. I'd left my sword in the surgery—a rookie mistake, damn it—and was desperately trying to get there without being noticed. A few men were dueling here as well, the hull of the *Iron Fist* visible through the windows. It was so close I could have reached out and touched it if I wanted. Starting once more, I realized the reason the ship was still tilted on its side. Our mast must have gotten caught in the rigging of the other ship, anchoring the two together. It would be impossible to get free without sending someone up to cut all the lines.

Frowning, I thought of Tristan and Mark, both riggers. If anyone was going to try and cut us loose, it would be one of them.

As I came to the crew deck, I slipped, landing hard in a puddle of blood. The dead eyes of the man that the gore belonged to stared at me with an emptiness that made my soul seem to chill. He was a member of my crew, one of the able bodied sailors, I thought. Someone had run him through and cut his throat, leaving him on the ground without a care in the world.

"What do we have here?"

The sneer made my blood boil and I turned to look at the man who had chosen to call me out.

He appeared the same as any other man who would have been on this ship. Plain clothes, a single sword, and a gun to defend himself with. He didn't have the cruel air I'd seen exhibited by so many other Black Knights. In fact, he seemed taken aback by my presence, as if he were horrified to find me in such a position.

"A lady?" he said in surprise. "That changes the

narrative somewhat, doesn't it?"

"Not in my book," I replied.

Taking the dead man's sword, I got to my feet, making sure to never glance away from my opponent.

"I don't want to fight you," he said hesitantly.

"I'm a member of this crew. If you're here to fight them, you're here to fight me."

He laughed, thinking I was joking, and then stilled. "You're serious? Blimey woman, do you not know who you're sailing with?"

Taken aback myself, I raised an eyebrow. "The Order of The Knights Templar. Do *you* know who you're sailing with, Black Knight?"

He snorted, offended by what I'd said. "Watch your tongue. I'm no Black Knight. It's the men on your ship who are the traitors."

"What?" Staring at him like he was stupid, I laughed. "You're kidding, right? None of these men are Black Knights. I should know, I'm married to one of them. Tristan O'Rourke. Perhaps you've heard of him and the endlessly long list of things he's done to fight back his enemies and keep the Templar name clean?"

Pointing the tip of his blade toward me, a dark mask fell over his face. "Now I know you're lyin'," he said, stepping forward. "Tristan O'Rourke and his wife are dead. Captain MacDonald has been found guilty of the murder of Grand Master Bevard. He and his Black Knight crew slipped away in the middle of the night, speeding off to claim the treasure they've been hoarding. And you're in on it. Woman or not, I can't let a Black Knight get away."

Jumping forward, he jabbed his blade toward me,

missing as I spun out of the way. My response was a swift cut across his shoulder, the blade digging into him with much more force than I'd intended. Blood spurted from the wound and he howled, yanking away. Angry, he circled around, slipping slightly in the gore around us.

Not wanting to waste any more time than was necessary, I leapt forward, our blades clanging against each other. We hacked and stabbed, each trying to get the upper hand, desperate to claim the spot of winner.

Doubt crept into my mind as I fought. If what he had said to me was true, this man was not a bad person. He was a Templar who thought he was protecting what was most sacred to his cause. He didn't realize his information was wrong.

I couldn't kill him, I realized. He was innocent. Killing him now would be no better than murder, even if it was in self-defense.

Changing tactics, I shoved him, bringing the hilt of my weapon up and cracking him over the head with it. He slumped to the floor without another movement, unconscious.

Out of breath, I turned, shrieking as another man came running at me with a sword. A gunshot sounded through the space and I jumped, watching as he fell to the floor.

Dagger stood on the steps, a cut on his face and the smoking gun in his hand. "Are you hurt?" he asked.

Shaking my head, I turned toward the lower decks. "Abella is. She's in the secondary brig, unconscious."

"How many men between here and there?"

"Maybe half a dozen of ours, eight or so of theirs."

"Good."

Looking back at him, I watched as he pulled one of the many blades from his belt and offered it to me. "Can you climb the rigging?"

"Yes."

"Then take this and get up there. We have the fighting mostly under control, but we need more people working on the ropes so we can untangle ourselves without cracking the main mast in half. I'll get to Abella, I promise." He wore an expression of trust and I realized in that moment that Dagger didn't just tolerate my presence on board; he accepted it without question. I was one of the people under his protection and guidance. It didn't matter to him that I was a woman.

"I'll do my best." Taking the blade, I nodded, moving past him to the main deck.

Most of the fighting had stopped, as Dagger had said, a small group of the enemy gathered in a circle in front of the captain's quarters. They'd been tied together and were being guarded by four men with rifles. A few other sailors aimed firearms over the railing and shot at the other ship, but it appeared most everyone was employed in trying to cut the vessels apart. Both sides had scores of men in the ropes, sawing and cutting away anything they could get their hands on.

Grabbing the set of ropes nearest to me, I hauled myself up, climbing until I reached a spot where the two ships had become entangled. A sail flapped in the wind, which ship it was from unclear at the moment. It sounded like thunder, booming every time it blew out to its full capacity, and I shivered, suddenly scared.

I cut through the lines with ease, marveling at the

sharpness of the blade Dagger had given me, and moved on to the next spot. After a few moments, I felt the ship shift beneath us.

"She's movin'!" Captain MacDonald's voice called as we started to pull away, the masts scraping against each other with a loud whine.

Wrapping my arms around the ropes tightly, I closed my eyes, feeling like I was on some horrible ride at an amusement park. Something snapped beneath me, wood splintering into the air and stinging against my skin, and then we were free, standing straight in the ocean again.

Shouts from the *Iron Fist* sounded across the way, someone ordering what men were left to abandon the fight and sail ship away. It didn't seem like there were very many of them left to control the vessel, but it slowly started to fade away, leaving us alone in the night, with our damaged sails and rigging, and floors washed with blood.

Captain MacDonald slammed his hand on his desk. "I want to ken who the dog is that accused me of bein' a murderer! Where did yer orders to attack us come from? Eh? Answer me!"

The four prisoners in front of him remained silent, staring at him with uncaring eyes. None of them had said a single word in the hour they'd been in the captain's quarters, all of them choosing to glare at us like we were the scum of the earth.

"Do ye honestly and truly think me a Black Knight?" Captain MacDonald frowned. "It goes against my own personal code! I've spent my entire time in the service trying to emulate all that was peace and fairness. Why would I kill Bevard? He was the man who recruited me. One of my oldest friends. Anyone with a brain could see that."

"Maybe that's the problem with The Order lately," Tristan grumbled. "It's severely lacking in brains."

Smiling, I hushed him, putting my hand in his. He'd taken high offense to being listed as a member of the Black Knights and believed with even more conviction that Davies had been behind both the attack on us and now this one. Even Mark had come around and agreed that it had to be the new Grand Master.

Staring at the prisoners, the captain grimaced. "None of my crew was supposed to die, not unless I'd done everything possible to keep them alive first. I was supposed to be the first one to fall. Now, because ye couldn't be bothered to stop and explain why ye were attacking, I have five bodies I must put to rest. Five men who will never see their homes again, or their families. Five sets of people who will be in mourning, because ye were too damn riled to listen to reason. Keep yer pride if ye want, refuse to acknowledge ye did something wrong, but their deaths are on ye. Judgement will fall on ye eventually."

The men shifted uncomfortably, his soft words effecting them more than his earlier shouting. They all remained tight lipped and silent, though, refusing to speak to the man they had branded a traitor.

He gave them a steely look, leaning on his desk. "If ye won't answer me, I'll have no choice but to turn ye in as pirates when we reach Hispaniola in a days' time."

The men still didn't respond.

Sighing, the captain shook his head. "Get out. All of ye." Waving his hand, he dismissed us all as he sat, gazing through his window in thought.

Moving to follow the group, I sighed, wondering what else we could run into before we made landfall. What if there were more people waiting for us on the shore? What if the lie about MacDonald's loyalties had spread through the entire Order? The Templars would do everything possible to try and stop him.

"O'Rourkes, ye two wait," Captain MacDonald said, catching us before we left. "I need to speak with

335

ye."

Letting the door shut behind us, we waited for him to say whatever it was he had planned.

"When we land in Hispaniola tomorrow, I want the two of ye to take charge of the prisoners and deposit them in the prison. Since most everyone thinks ye dead—"

"It will be easier for us to get in and out unnoticed," Tristan finished for him. "Aye, Captain. We can do that. Do ye require us to find someone to help fix the ship, too?"

"No." Pursing his lips, he intertwined his fingers, staring at us seriously. "I want ye to return as soon as ye can. I've no idea what force, if any, will be waiting for us in Saint Domingue, but I intend to disappear before they get the chance to attack us."

"You don't think they will listen to reason?" I asked, surprised. "Or that we'll be able to prove our innocence to them?"

"The men we battled before were not interested in talking, so no, I don't think they will listen."

Tristan looked at him, curious. "What do ye mean by disappear?"

"I mean we'll go somewhere that they cannot. We will skip our last treasure meet up and go straight to the source with what we have. With the extra protection there, even if they did manage to find where the cache was, they would never be able to get in."

"And where is this impenetrable location?" I asked, skeptical.

Captain MacDonald stared at us, as if studying everything we had to offer, and then nodded. "It is time to tell ye, I can see that. I canna rightly keep it from ye any longer. Or Bell and the maid. Ye've all proven yerselves many times over."

His mentioning of Mark and Abella caused me to think of them again with some worry. Abella's shoulder had been put in place with little effort, but she was still in a lot of pain from being thrown around. Mark had been the one to doctor her, acting half angry and half worried about her as he worked. He was with her now, watching as she slept, making sure that she didn't do anything to further injure the joint he'd tied down.

Rising from his seat, Captain MacDonald brought my attention back to the present as he pulled a roll of paper from one of the desk drawers and spread it open for us to see. It was a map of the Caribbean, with various marks here and there, but nothing striking that I could see.

Pointing to the edge of Florida, he hummed, as if trying to decide what to say. "There is an area here." His finger drew across the map in a straight line, out to a tiny island. He then dragged the point down again, toward the islands of the Caribbean.

As he blocked out the triangle shape, I felt a light bulb of recognition go off in my mind. Without even thinking about it, I laughed, peering at him in disbelief. "The Bermuda Triangle?"

Captain MacDonald raised an eyebrow, turning to me with a small smile. "I've never heard anyone call it that. Perhaps The Devil's Triangle, or even Davy Jones' Locker, but never that." He stared at me for a moment, the map seemingly forgotten, and then sat back in his chair.

"Ye are a well learned woman, Samantha

O'Rourke. Perhaps the rumors I heard of ye were more than gossip, eh?"

"That depends on what you heard," I replied, blushing slightly.

"Are ye a witch?" He asked in a very unceremonious manner, but with no condemnation. There was only curiosity in his tone and in his eyes as he waited for me to reply.

"I am not."

"Pity. I kent a witch once. She was the most interesting person I ever had the privilege of knowing. I would suppose that means ye're a time walker, then?"

Staring at him evenly, I smiled, remaining silent.

"Well. What do ye ken of this triangle, time walker?"

Glancing at Tristan, I shrugged, suddenly feeling put on the spot. "Superstitions, really. Whole ships go missing and are never found. Airplanes, too." Pausing at the strange expression the captain gave me, I opened my mouth to explain and then decided against it. "There's a lot of theories on what happens, but no concrete proof. Magnets have been blamed, as well as clouds and ocean currents. Some think that there is paranormal activity in the area, or even extraterrestrial. Time loops have been suggested as an option, too. So many people travel through the area unharmed, though, it's not really believed that something is actually occurring in the triangle."

"True. The triangle houses many shipping lanes from different countries."

"Is this the place Columbus mentioned?" Tristan asked, butting into the conversation. "Where he saw the fireball and strange lights?"

Thrown off by the sudden change in conversation, I broke away from the explanation I'd been giving. "What are you talking about?"

"When Randall took ye, I spent most of my time on the ship reading about the Black Knights who had gone in search of treasure in the Americas, trying to find some connection that would bring me to Randall faster. In one of Columbus' journals, he mentioned a fiery orb that crashed into the ocean. The next day, he saw odd lights in the sky. I was only curious if this strange place was home to those occurrences as well."

"It is." Pulling our attention to him, Captain MacDonald, tapped the triangle on the map again. "It's also the home of our treasure port."

Staring at the map, I tried to wrap my mind around this new piece of information. "It's not the craziest thing I've heard," I finally said. "There's not a whole lot more than water there, though, and all the shipping lanes, like you said. How do you hide it? Where in the triangle is it safe?"

"It would appear that the superstitions ye carry in yer time are not all that untrue," the Scot said slowly, glancing between Tristan and me. "But not necessarily right, either."

"Ye mean magic?" Tristan asked, not quite following.

"Something like that."

Rising, the captain moved to his window, staring across the ocean. "The natives in this area have a story. They claim there is a fountain somewhere in these islands that can heal any wound and restore youth to those who drink from it."

"The Fountain of Youth, aye. I'm well acquainted

with the tale." Tristan watched him with complete focus, clearly committing everything that was being said to memory.

Captain MacDonald looked over his shoulder to us. "It's not a story." Gazing through the window, he sighed, folding his hands behind his back.

"That's where the treasure is?" Shocked, my mouth popped open, my mind quickly trying to make room for not one but two mythologies that were now being changed to fact in my head.

"The people who lived nearby the fountain kent what a precious and sacred thing they held in their possession. They believed it to be the blood of their gods that saved them and gave them eternal youth. But, as with all things, the power was craved by those who should not have it."

His words streamed into an effortless retelling, creating a picture of the civilization that had dedicated itself to guarding The Fountain of Youth. They grew a large navy, fought neighboring peoples, and conquered much of the world around them. While they were feared among their enemies, the civilization lived in a practical utopian society, advancing farther than the rest of the world in the areas of science and mechanics. It seemed that they would forever reign in peace and with a strong fist.

"However," Captain MacDonald said, moving to his seat. "It is God's will that there be opposition in all things. The civilization was met with a force so strong and evil, it destroyed everything they thought they knew about life. Realizing what danger they were in, and still wanting to protect the fountain, the people did the only thing they could. They asked the gods to sink their city into the ocean. It is said that in a single day, the entire civilization was swallowed by the sea, never to be seen again."

"Hold on," I said, unable to keep from interrupting him any longer. "You're not talking about the city of Atlantis, are you? Because *that* might be the craziest thing I've heard."

His smile said it all.

"Let me get this straight," I said, feeling like I'd been slapped repeatedly and was now trying to win a spelling bee. "The treasure port is in The Fountain of Youth, in The Lost City of Atlantis, in The Bermuda Triangle?"

Shaking his head, Captain MacDonald held his hand up for me to stop. "The Fountain of Youth is the treasure the Atlantians protect. It is considered part of the wonders housed in the city, but is separate from the items we bring them."

"The people are still *alive*?"

Tristan made a sound of surprise next to me as well, clearly having not expected that tidbit of information.

"How?" he asked. "If their city is at the bottom of the ocean, how can the people still be living? How can we get the treasure to them?"

"It's a tricky thing to describe." Sighing as if he were suddenly very ready to go to bed, MacDonald sat in his chair, rolling the map shut and placing it in its drawer. "And one I dinna ken if I can adequately sum up. It will all make sense when we arrive, though. Can ye trust me until then?"

Nodding, I remained silent, thinking of all the things he'd said to us and what I'd learned. The

Knights Templar were turning out to be a much more invested and mythological group than I could have anticipated. For a moment, I wished for the simpler time when I'd thought Oak Isle was the only treasure cache they kept.

"Tristan?"

Glancing at my husband, I saw him watching the captain with a questioning expression.

"Ye said there is a gatekeeper," he started. "Have ye ever even been in to the city, Captain?"

MacDonald frowned, sadness crossing his features for a split second before he cleared his throat. "I haven't. There is . . . a complication. It keeps me from passing through the gate and into the city."

"Have any of yer men? Or any of the crews before ye?"

"No Templars have set foot in the place, if that's what ye're getting at."

Surprised yet again, I stared at him. "How do you know the treasure is truly safe, then?"

"As I said, lass. It will all make sense when we arrive. Ye'll just have to trust me until then."

I couldn't quite place the strange, gurgling noise I kept hearing. It was like someone was choking on something, but I was the only one here.

Warm lamplight washed the deep brown wood of the surgery with light, making it feel almost homey. A few tall crates were stacked in the corner, the long table I often used for examinations resting in the middle of the floor.

The gurgling noise sounded again and I rose from my pallet on the floor, the hem of my shift brushing across the top of my feet. The white fabric was warm and hugged me around my hips and breasts, tank top sleeves leaving my shoulders bare. I loved the feel of it. Clothes weren't like this in Tristan's time. They were rough and scratchy, unless you paid really good money for them. Even then, it never quite managed to feel like the clothing from my own time. Apparently, manufacturing the items in mass amounts did something to the fabric that made it seem softer to me. Whatever the difference was, though, I could tell this shift was something I could have picked off a shelf at a name brand store. It was so smooth and silky, with the faint scent of strawberries and crème on it. It made me think of mornings when I would make oatmeal and watch cartoons, while Mom was still alive.

Once more, the gurgling caught my attention and I pulled my mind from the memories I so pleasantly recalled.

"Hello?" I called, looking around the empty area.

A knock beat behind the crates, the choking noise intensifying.

Panic flooding through me at the sound, I hurried to the corner, trying to move the crates with little success.

"Hold on!" Throwing my whole weight against the box, I grunted, sliding across the floor, until I finally managed to move the heavy block a bit.

Peering through the crack I'd created, I saw someone on the ground, their body twitching, the sounds they were making growing in earnest.

Desperate, I threw myself against the blockade once more, struggling to make a space big enough to slip through. After what felt like a lifetime of trying, I had managed to make a small pathway.

Squeezing myself into the miniscule place, I wiggled through the crack, trying to remember if I knew how to do the Heimlich maneuver, CPR, or anything that might help. It all felt like a haze as I went over it, not sure anything would be able to help whoever was in need of assistance on the other side.

Finally, I broke into the tiny cavern behind the boxes, practically falling right on top of Thomas Randall.

Blood gurgled from his mouth, his eyes wild as he gagged. Legs twitching beneath me, he made a wild grab for my wrist, shaking horrifically. The gore *bubbling from his throat had covered his chest and the floor beneath him, staining my white nightgown with angry, dark red splotches.*

Screaming, I tried to pull away, but his grip on me was so tight, it felt like he was bruising my wrist with his fingertips.

"Help . . . me . . ." He coughed violently, spraying me with grime, his eyes pleading as he stared at me. "Help."

Try as I might, I couldn't get him to let go of me, my screams echoing over the top of his pleas, the entire scene a picture of red and terror.

"Samantha!"

Coming out of the nightmare, I shrieked, wrestling with whoever was on top of me. I could still smell the blood in the air, Thomas Randall's fingers still pressing into my skin, their rough nails digging in and leaving marks. In the darkness, it was as if he were still there in every single way, the gagging sound of his dying ringing in my ears.

"Sam!"

Slamming my hands above my head, Tristan straddled me, breathless. He acted as if he'd just been in a fight for his life, resting his forehead against mine for a moment as he caught his breath.

"It's me, love," he said softly. "Only me. We're in Saint Domingue, remember?" He continued to murmur, going over the events of the day, explaining how we had turned all of the prisoners over to the city warden in Captain MacDonald's name, quietly slipping away before anyone could ask us questions. The inn we were in was on the outskirts of town and ran by a shady couple, but they hadn't asked for names. All they wanted was cash and we gave them plenty. We would slip away at dawn, traveling the coast until we met up with the *Isobel*. Then, we would be on our way to Atlantis, to discover yet another portion of the Templar's treasures. Only, this time, there was no immediate threat to beat, no rush to get there first.

There was no Thomas Randall here, no gore, no terror to express. Only the warm bed and my loving husband, trying to lull me into the relaxed state I'd been at moments before.

Taking a deep breath, I blinked a few times, feeling more tears roll down the side of my face. My heart was still hammering, skin tingling, the night terror slowly fading from my mind.

"I'm okay," I whispered, wiggling underneath him. "How bad was I shouting?"

"I half thought the Devil himself had arrived and was dragging ye to Hell," he joked, rolling to the side. "Scared the life right out of me when ye started up."

"Sorry." Slightly embarrassed, I sat up, wiping my face. It was frustrating, the fact that I was still having nightmares centered around Randall. They weren't even fear based all that much anymore, but odd conversations I had with him. Sometimes he would try to force himself on me—an occurrence that had never happened when I was his prisoner—but I never felt like I couldn't defend myself. I knew I was dreaming. Randall seemed to know I was, too.

"Do ye want to talk about it?" Tristan asked

quietly. "Ye don't have to if ye don't want to." His fingers danced gently over my skin, tracing circles on my arm, tickling me slightly.

Scooting over, I snuggled against his side, his arm under my neck and my head on his shoulder. Laying my arm over his stomach, I gazed at his face, smiling.

Tilting his face to meet my own, he kissed me gently, holding me close. "It feels nice to have ye in a bed again, instead of on the floor or in a hammock." He chuckled, resting his head on mine.

Making a noise in agreement, I closed my eyes, wishing away the remaining tendrils of the nightmare. Tristan, seeming to know that I was still bothered, remained silent, holding me in the darkness.

After a while, when I finally felt fully detached from the dream, I sighed, a sense of peace coming over me. "I dreamed he was dying," I said softly. "Horribly. Painfully. All he could do was ask me for help."

Not answering, Tristan kissed my forehead, his fingers twisting in my hair.

"Where do you think he is?" I asked. "What do you think he's doing? The fact that we don't have any solid idea of what he's planning makes me nervous. He could be in the room right next to us and we would never know until he came barreling in, guns and blades blazing."

"I don't know." His response was soft, thoughtful. "To be honest with ye, I find I don't think of Randall so much as I did before. Dwelling on yer own bloodlust isn't really the best idea, if ye get my meaning."

"I do. Planning all the possible ways to kill someone can turn you into something you aren't."

"This is true." He paused. "I was so consumed

347

with catching him before, I lost ye in the process. He came in and took ye right from under my nose. It made me realize I wasn't paying attention to the things that I should be. On the crossing to Arizona, I used to promise God every day that I would focus more on ye if he would just let me have ye back." Glancing at me, he smiled, squeezing me lightly. "And here ye are."

Grinning, I pecked him on the lips, basking in the safety of his arms around me. "How do you do it?" I asked, curious. "How do you keep from thinking about him?"

Shrugging lightly, he frowned. "I tell myself not to think of him. It doesn't always work, but I've found, over time, it gets easier to put him away and live in the present."

"I wish it was that easy for me," I replied, halfway teasing. "I would lock him in a box for the rest of time."

"I wouldn't blame ye." His voice softened as he spoke, taking on a sad quality, his form going still beside me. "I don't know if I could lock away the memories that you suffer with. Being threatened personally, having him move to cut the child from your belly without even a second thought for what he was doing. I can't imagine being locked below deck and then forced to come and spend time with the crew that took ye. Being bound and dragged through the desert like a common animal. Beaten. Holding yer dead child in yer arms and leaving her in a place far from home."

His voice caught and he cleared his throat roughly. "No. I think I would have nightmares as well. Those aren't things ye can lock in a box right away and shove out of sight. They'll stick with ye, until ye've suffered with them so much, ye have no choice but to put them away or go mad."

"It's nice when you have an extra pair of hands to help you shut everything out." Smiling, I hugged him tightly, wanting him to know I was grateful for all of his support. It had been a long few months, with both of us still holding on to the baggage that threatened to drown us. Together, though, we'd managed to stay afloat. As more time passed, I was sure we would find ourselves on dry land again at some point.

Scooting away some, he laid on his side, propping himself up with his elbow. Holding my hand to his bare chest, the corners of his mouth turned up, eyes brushing along the length of my body.

"Ye're so brave, Sam. I knew if from the first day I met ye, but I never could have guessed exactly how much ye could withstand. I'm a better man just from knowing ye."

"I remember the first time you said that," I replied, laughing. His words had brought to mind a very fond memory of when we had first been thrust into each other's company. "In your grandmother's garden. You took me there after dinner and gave me this whole speech, telling me how brave I was. That was the first time you told me you loved me."

Grinning, he nodded. "And I still mean it as much today as I did then, if not more. I will follow ye to the end of the earth, woman, no matter the cost or pain it will cause me. The only thing worse than hurting with ye is hurting because I'm without ye."

I suddenly felt like crying, his words having touched me in a way that made me realize just how much he loved me. We had been through so much, but we had been through it together. That's how we would be, forever—always together.

Placing my hand on the back of his neck, I met him in the middle of the space between us. His lips were warm and soft, his body pressing against mine as we slid together under the blanket. The warmth that cocooned us only helped to speed my heart rate, my breath catching as his teeth nipped at my bottom lip.

Suddenly, Tristan rolled over, trapping me beneath him with a devilish grin. Slowly, he lowered, pressing against every inch of me, his lips brushing along my neck. His fingers wrapped around my own, holding my hands, making me his prisoner for the moment. Teeth grazing my skin, he sighed contentedly, lifting his head to look at me with smoldering eyes.

Releasing my hands, he slid his fingers down my arms, brushing over my shift. He didn't stop there, though, drawing a line down my sides until he had the hem of the fabric in his hands. Sitting up, he put his hands on my skin underneath it, pushing the fabric out of the way as he felt my body. His palms were warm and tender, caressing me with such softness I was practically melting beneath him. Every movement he made caused me to feel like I was slipping further into a hazy dream of euphoria.

He slid the fabric all the way up my body, cupping my breasts as they came into view, the shift momentarily forgotten. Leaning forward, he layered a few kisses between his fingers, nipping and sucking as he felt like it. A soft groan came from him as he straightened once more, still touching my chest.

Arching my back, I pressed into his touch, silently

urging him to continue his exploration of me. In response, he grabbed the shift and pulled it completely off, tossing it somewhere on the floor, before laying over me again.

I didn't know what was different about that night, especially after the months we had been reunited, but something changed as he caressed me. We seemed to be growing closer together than ever before, like the string that had connected us had been twisted at some point and was now unraveling. For the first time since I'd been returned to my husband's loving embrace, I felt as if we were both truly beginning to heal from the trauma that had separated us and scattered the pieces of our hearts across the sea. No longer were we trying to fix ourselves alone, simply leaning on one another to get by. Instead, we moved forward hand in hand, gathering the shards of our past and mending them as one.

"Well," Mark said, leaning against the railing and looking out over the open ocean, his off-white shirt ruffling gently in the breeze. "We're officially in The Bermuda Triangle."

Abella minutely crossed herself, fingers brushing across the brown, laced bodice she wore over her own white shirt. The action brought a smile to his face, though he pretended to have not noticed.

Watching the two of them, I felt a sense of healing in their relationship. It wasn't anything romantic, from my guessing anyway, but they seemed to be friends again, speaking easily with one another and acting as they had on the crossing back to France. Apparently, somewhere between the fighting and Mark putting Abella's arm in a sling, they had at least managed to patch up some of their relationship.

Putting my friends odd feelings from mind, I stared at the horizon. "What do you think the odds of us traveling through time are?" I asked Mark, trying not to laugh at the absurdity of the question.

He glanced at me with a somewhat amused expression. "I'd say pretty good, since we've already managed to do it once."

Tristan snorted, his hand grasped in my own. "I've traveled this lane more times than I can count. The worst that ever happened was skirmishes with pirates—and I was the pirate doing the skirmishing."

"Still," Mark said, sounding somewhat disbelieving. "Atlantis is here somewhere. We'll be at her gate before nightfall, if Captain MacDonald is to be believed."

"He hasn't given us any reason not to believe him," Abella said softly, her gaze still riveted on the horizon. "I just wish he would have explained how it all works better."

"It's always a little rough on the new crew."

Turning, we all looked at Dagger, standing behind us in his usual black, numerous blades in the belt around his waist. His turban was somewhat undone, pieces of the fabric hanging around his face and looping above his shoulders. He was watching the water as well, an easy air about him.

"But it's not anything to worry about." Waving a hand in dismissal, he shook his head. "The hardest part is convincing yourself to believe everything you're seeing."

"What do you mean?" Mark asked, stepping forward to the front of the group. "How hard is it to believe what's right in front of your face?"

"You're quite the skeptic, why don't you tell me?" Dagger grinned. "I don't want to ruin the surprise."

"Will Captain MacDonald be the one to barter with the gatekeeper for our entrance into the city?" Abella asked, her question surprising me. As everyone turned to her, she raised an eyebrow. "*Ce qui?* Samantha said the captain has never been in the city, as there is a complication keeping him from going. I'm simply wondering who we are entrusting our fates to. What will happen if they can't convince these Atlantians to let us in?"

"The complication doesn't keep the captain from going into the city," Dagger replied hesitantly. "No Templar has ever entered the city, so far as we know, but we can easily approach the gate. However, I will be the one to speak with the Atlantians, as Captain MacDonald is unable to approach the gate."

"Why?" Confused, I watched him with a guarded expression. It felt like someone wasn't telling us something, besides all the things about Atlantis they weren't sharing.

He hesitated, glancing between each of us and then sighed. "There's a woman who waits on the beach every time we come to make our delivery. He knows her, but doesn't want to speak with her, so he doesn't leave the ship. I do all of the negotiating and moving of the treasure. Captain usually stays in his cabin. The gatekeeper will join him there more often than not, once I make all the necessary arrangements. The only time I've ever seen the captain set foot on the beach is if the red head is nowhere to be found."

Something in my mind connected together and I blinked, feeling like I'd been clubbed over the head. "Isobel?" I asked. "Isobel is in Atlantis?"

"He told you about her?" he asked, surprised.

"I saw the picture he drew of her in his room. He said the ship was named after her and that she was dead, that's it."

"How can a dead woman be on the beach at Atlantis?" Mark asked, some anger in his tone. "What aren't you telling us?"

"Someone is lying about something," Tristan agreed. "And that doesn't sit well with me."

"No one is lying about anything."

Captain MacDonald's voice drew all our attention away from Dagger, the four of us turning to find him in front of his quarters. He'd been growing increasingly distant and the tired air around him grew the closer we got to our destination. Now, it seemed he would rather be anywhere else in the world than here.

"Get in here, the lot of ya. I'll explain." He nodded at Dagger. "Get the drums ready. We'll be at the center within the next hour or so. Start hailing them now, though, so we don't waste time sitting there."

Dagger nodded, turning on his heel and leaving us in silence.

"Do ye want to ken what's going on or not?" Jerking his thumb toward his room, the Scot went in himself, leaving the entrance open.

We filed in behind him, confused and quiet, myself feeling like we had stepped on some toes by asking too many questions. The captain was upset, that much was clear, and I didn't like feeling like it was my fault.

"Atlantians are a . . . magical group," he stared, not even waiting for the door to shut behind us. "Their society is shamanistic in nature. Ye ken what a shaman is?"

"A spiritual leader," Mark replied, folding his arms. "They claim their power comes from the earth itself and her creatures. They are very nature minded and centered."

"Aye, they are. They're also highly rooted in spirit

355

magic. They call on the spirits to protect them and guide them through life." The captain sighed, shaking his head. "Dagger was telling the truth. Isobel is the woman on the beach."

"But you told us she was dead," Abella said quietly, no judgment in her tone. "What purpose would a lie like that serve?"

Captain MacDonald stared at her, his lips pressed into a thin line. For a moment, I thought he was angry with her, his rage boiling beneath the surface, but then he answered, his voice cracking in pain.

"It wasn't a lie," he said mournfully. "Isobel is dead. The woman on the beach is a ghost, waiting for me to come accept my punishment for causing her death."

A stunned silence filled the space. I didn't want to believe that what he'd said was true—how could I? But the pain in his voice and the heartbreak on his face couldn't be disputed. The man truly believed the woman was his avenger, come to take her revenge on him. There were even tears in his eyes, his jaw working furiously as he turned away from us, clearing his throat.

"How?" Tristan finally asked. "How can that be?"

MacDonald responded without turning around. "When the shamans asked their gods to sink Atlantis to the bottom of the ocean, they moved the entire civilization into the spirit realm, where they could protect it without fail. The gate isn't just a gate to the city. It's a gate to what they call The Web of Life, where everything is connected and suspended in time. It's where the shamans go to commune with their spirit guides. Any soul can appear there, should they wish it."

It was starting to make sense, why he hadn't told us all of this before. He sounded like a madman. It would have absolutely been better if we'd seen it for ourselves.

"And ye believe Isobel is there to speak with ye?" Tristan asked. "To condemn ye?"

"Wouldn't ye?" The Scotsman turned to us, his eyes red with misery. "If ye had the chance to see the person who killed ye?"

"You killed her?" Watching him with renewed caution, I studied his face, his expression falling even further as he turned back to the window.

"I might as well have."

More silence followed, everyone trying to absorb the explanation.

"So Atlantis is in the spirit realm," Mark finally said. "That would explain why no one has ever found it. How do we get there, though?"

"The drums," Captain MacDonald replied simply. "Shamans use drums to help put themselves in a trance. We do the drumming and their guards transport the ship to the edge of the realm, where we can safely make land and deposit the treasure."

"Guards?" Abella, who seemed to be having the easiest time digesting what he was saying, wore a questioning expression. "What do you mean guards? Surely, if there were a ship resting at a set point, people would have noticed them by now."

"Another shaman secret," he replied softly. "They aren't in a ship. They're in the water. They're the fish."

Mark made a noise of understanding at that, nodding. "The Apache are shamanistic as well," he replied, smiling at my questioning gaze. "They believed that if someone were to gain enough trust from the spirits and the earth around them, they would be able to merge with it. A shaman could become anything, like an animal."

That sparked some recognition in my mind. "You mean like Skin Walkers?"

He half smiled, looking at the floor. "That's a bit of a derogatory term for it, but yes, like that."

"So the Atlantians developed trust with the fish?" Tristan asked, disbelief on his face.

"It would appear so." Captain MacDonald turned around, looking at all of us with his sad eyes. "So, now ye ken why Dagger must do the negotiating for us. I trust the man with my life. I would expect ye to do the same."

"Of course," I replied, no longer worried about that part of our plan. "But what about you?"

"What do ye mean?"

"You loved Isobel," Abella stated, frowning. "And I'm willing to bet she loved you, if she's waited all these years, trying to speak with you. Why not talk to her?"

"Do ye ken what it is like, living without the person ye loved more than anything else for twenty-five years, only to find them on a beach in the Caribbean?" He laughed, clearly upset by the whole situation. "For five years now, I have watched her sit there through every transport, waiting for me to come to her. Believe me when I say this—any love that woman had for me died with her. I can tell from her face that she means to lecture me and call me to judgment." He frowned, shaking his head once more.

"I dinna want to spoil my memory of her with such things. I ken what I did, but I'm not ready to face her and accept it yet. Can ye blame me for that?"

"No." It was Tristan who spoke this time, stepping forward and placing a hand on the captain's shoulder. "No. I may not have lost the woman I loved to death, or have been separated from her as long as ye've been from yers, but I know what it is to lose the one ye love. Ye face no judgment from me, or any of us, I would guess. Thank ye for telling us the truth. I know it wasn't easy for ye."

The captain nodded, taking a deep breath. Then, staring at everyone, he let it out slowly, defeat on his face. He walked to the window, staring across the ocean.

On the deck outside, drums began to play, the beat starting slow and soft. It began to grow in intensity and volume the longer they played. It was a sure sign that in a short amount of time, we would be seeing the things we'd been told about.

"Ye can go now. I've told ye everything." Captain MacDonald sounded as if he were breaking inside, his voice shaky as he watched the water. "I would verra much like to be left alone now."

Standing on the deck, I watched as a few members of the crew sat in a circle, drums of varying sizes resting in front of them. They beat the instruments with sticks or with their hands, some of them wearing wristbands with little bells on them that jingled with every movement. The beat was steady now and monotonous, the sound of it seeming to drill into my brain. It felt like I was slowly drifting away from the present, the rhythm somewhat hypnotizing.

Still, the world was the same around us. I didn't think we'd done any traveling, or that magic-people-fish-things had come to take us to the edge of the spirit realm. Everyone was calm and relaxed, lounging about, listening to the drums. It was the first time I'd seen the crew not really doing anything.

The whole situation made me feel like I had sand in my boots—uncomfortable and like I needed to shake the feelings away, but there was nowhere for me to sit and take care of the nuisance. Most of all, I felt nervous. What did they mean by "traveling?" The last time I'd been transported in a magical fashion, it had hurt like hell and I'd almost drowned. It wasn't really an experience I wanted to relive.

The longer I stayed silent, letting the thoughts in my head battle it out, the more I realized I needed to talk to someone about what was happening. It was the only way I would find some peace until whatever was going to happen was finished. Taking Tristan's hand in mine, I muttered under my breath.

"Do you feel any different?"

He shook his head. "Would we, though? What if traveling is like falling asleep? One moment we're here and the next we're not." His thumb brushed the back of my hand, his voice low and soothing. He didn't fool me, though; I could tell he was nervous as well, his thoughts stuck on the same track as my own.

Mark, seated on the ground beside us, leaned against the inside of the hull and whispered quietly. "We haven't gone yet."

"How do you know?" Abella was standing on the other side of him, staring at the water. She sounded anxious as well, rolling her injured shoulder slightly in its sling, an expression of discomfort crossing her features.

"They're still drumming."

No one replied. After a beat, he seemed to realize we didn't understand what he was saying and he elaborated.

"It helps your brain focus," he said softly. "If you listen long enough, it puts you in a bit of a trance state. I used to watch the Apache do it."

Looking at the crewmen, their forms hunched over the instruments, hands keeping a steady movement, I frowned. "It's not just to sound cool or make you feel intimidated, then?" I asked, shifting from one side to the other. I still didn't know how I felt about all the

361

information I'd been told, or if I could even believe the whole mess. Spirits, shamans, other worlds . . . it felt like I was being sucked into a fantasy.

"Everything serves a purpose," Mark replied, watching the drummers with mild interest. "This is different from anything I ever saw in Arizona, though. It's . . . special, I think."

The explanation didn't really help my nerves at all. I didn't know how everyone else could seem so relaxed and carefree. Was it only because they'd "traveled" before? Surely, if it was a painful process, they wouldn't be smiling and laughing, tapping their feet to the beat and nodding their heads along to the rhythm.

Suddenly, the drummers stopped, one final beat ringing through the air with an ominous thud. It was as if the entire ship vibrated with it, a strange wave of air sweeping past us. I could see it rippling through the water, a small wave rolling away, like we'd suddenly set down from above and disturbed the calm sea. The boards beneath us groaned slightly and everything seemed heavy all at once, like a crushing amount of weight was suffocating the life and light from everything.

Panic seized upon me in that instant, memories of almost drowning in the Treasure Pit filling my mind. I hadn't been able to breathe or tell which way was what, water crushing me from all sides. Rocks had cut into my skin as I was swept past them, white hot pain shooting through my body. This pressure was like that, crushing me, robbing me of air, burning me from the inside out—and then it was gone.

Sucking in a deep breath, I grabbed onto the rail

behind me for support. My stomach rolled, threatening to get rid of my breakfast, and I closed my eyes tight, head spinning. All the same, something felt different to me. I couldn't tell what it was, but I knew without a doubt that we had moved from one realm into another.

Carefully, I opened my eyes, staring in wonder at the deep blue color of the ocean below. I'd never seen that hue before, so incredibly rich and complex as it moved back and forth. A flash of pink moved into my view and I gasped, reaching behind me and blindly grabbing Tristan.

"Look!" I whispered.

I had never seen something so terrifying and beautiful at the same time. The tail was pink and green, with streaks of purple and spots of gold, dancing through the water. Fins flashed in the light, like they were covered with a layer of glitter, shining in the sun like jewels. Scales flowed seamlessly into skin, dotting the waist of the woman and spreading up over her chest. Long, blonde hair billowed around her face, almost like it was dancing to music I couldn't hear. She was gorgeous, even with the many scars that marked her form. They were angry, white streaks and puckered lines, webbed over her tail and skin. A long spear was clutched in her hands. Cold, black eyes stared up from the deep, shining from her attractive face like an omen of dark things to come.

"It's a mermaid," I whispered. "The shamans are mermaids!"

Peering out further, I could see that there were more of the creatures, all of them swimming to the ship, like a small army, come to take us hostage. Some of them had barbs, like a lionfish, the long, thin needles giving the impression that they could kill with one strike. A half man, half squid creature crawled toward us in a terrifying manner, a pitchfork like object in his hands. Another one had claws like a crab, while I spotted another with shark like teeth. Several of the creatures had what looked like scaled armor covering their arms and chests, sea shells forming elegant helmets on their heads.

The more I watched, the more in awe I felt. Each one was as unique as the creature they emulated. Even the weapons they carried seemed specific to each person, like they had been made specifically for them. I could have studied the sight for days and still never discovered everything there was to notice about them.

Slowly, the ship began to move, the mass of transformed beings seeming to guide it along. The action suddenly drew my attention to the other things around me, and I stared in awe, not sure what to feel or think. Everything seemed more concentrated, colors glowing like I'd never seen before, sounds tinkling by like music. The air smelled like rain, but there wasn't a cloud in the sky. It was as if I were hyper aware of everything around me, each sensation magnified one hundred times.

It was immediately clear why the crew hadn't acted out of sorts about coming. There had been a brief moment of pain, but it felt *good* here. The air practically gave me a high as I inhaled, warmth wrapping around me. I felt almost invincible, like every cell in my body was bursting with light and life, my energy rising, mind clearing, and a total sense of revitalization taking over.

Turning to Tristan, I sucked in a sharp breath. He

looked the same as he always had, but there was more contrast to him. There was an entire universe of color I'd never seen in his eyes, and his tanned skin seemed to glow slightly in the pink and orange light of the setting sun. His hair moved gently in the breeze, and when he spoke, it sounded like there were deep bells in his tone, a sense of music coming from him that I'd never heard before.

"Sam," he said in surprise, staring at me with wide eyes. "Ye look . . . well, the same, but—"

"Different," I interrupted, laughing. I could hear the tinkling in my own voice as well. "You do, too. It must be something about this place."

He nodded, breathing deeply, a smile of satisfaction gracing his features. It seemed ten times more inviting and happy than normal, and I laughed again, feeling explicitly joyful for no reason whatsoever.

Glancing past him, my gaze swept across everyone else, taking in their enhanced features and pleasant expressions. Mark and Abella were still staring at the water, whispering to each other, their excitement almost glowing around them like an aura.

With a start, I realized I *could* see their auras. I could see everyone's. They weren't big rainbows or clouds of color, like I'd always imagined, but light, almost invisible, shimmering air surrounding everything. The auras where what gave the air its glitter-like quality and made everyone seem like they were glowing. They didn't necessarily show me what everyone was thinking or feeling, but more marked us as living, breathing creatures.

"There," Tristan said, drawing my attention to him

as he pointed in the direction we were moving. "Do ye see it?"

Observing where he indicated, I saw a tiny island, not even big enough for our entire crew to camp on for the night. A thick stand of palm trees covered it, with a white sandy beach leading down to the ocean. There were a few driftwood logs and grass growing in patches, but other than that, there was nothing.

Mark and Abella, having finally torn themselves away from the sights in the water, joined us, eyes wide in awe.

"I can see every thread in your shirt," Abella said in wonder, touching my shoulder lightly.

"Aye, there is much to be seen and felt in this place. Something is missing, though." Tristan frowned slightly, still studying the island.

Inspecting the land, I instantly realized what he was saying. "Where's the gate?" Confused, I shared a glance with the three of them.

The sound of a door opening behind us caused us all to turn, watching as Captain MacDonald emerged from his quarters. The red of his kilt was dark, like blood, the hammer in his hand almost vibrating with a strange energy I'd never seen before. It was like the wood was as alive as the rest of us, buzzing with a magnificent force of purpose. It made the captain seem all the more fierce, his visage battle hardened, as if he were readying himself to go to war.

It was then that I realized something else had been missing from the island—there was no red headed woman, waiting for her lover to return and speak with her.

Pausing, Captain MacDonald nodded at the four

of us, smiling slightly. "It's a bit of a shift in perception, eh?" When we didn't answer, he laughed lightly, brushing a hand over his beard. "Dinna fash. Ye'll get used to it. The hard part is returning to our realm and realizing the world isn't as beautiful as it was anymore."

"I can't imagine ever wanting to leave this place," Abella replied, staring at him with wide eyes. "It feels so perfect. How do you and your men do it?"

Amused, he shifted the hammer from one hand to the other. "Perhaps it's with the knowledge that we'll return in the future, or the sense of honor and duty we hold with The Order. Whatever our reasons for leaving, I'm sure ye'll discover yer own when the time comes."

"Captain, Zaka has appeared on the beach." Dagger, calling from the helm, pointed to the tiny island.

Glancing back, I sucked in another sharp breath, catching sight of a woman standing in front of the stand of trees. Her skin was dark and tattooed with gold symbols, long dreadlocks reaching to her waist. Colorful patterns adorned her dress, feathers fanning out from her shoulders. Despite still being a small distance from the ship, I could see the wisdom in her eyes, as well as the aura spreading around her. It moved exactly like the hammer that Captain MacDonald held and I was suddenly curious as to where it came from and what the jittery movement of the air around it meant.

"The Gatekeeper." The Scotsman sighed, as if considering his options, and then nodded. "I will approach her this time, Dagger."

"But, Captain—"

Captain MacDonald held a hand up, silencing him. "It is a great favor we are asking. I should be the one to do it." He didn't seem particularly happy about the decision, but there was an air about him that was different from when we'd spoken to him earlier in the day. He seemed resolved and confident, though I thought I caught a glimpse of fear shivering beneath the surface as he looked toward the shaman and her stand of trees.

"Sam." Tristan's soft whisper drew my attention to him and he pointed at the beach once more.

A woman with long, flowing red hair was now sitting on one of the driftwood logs, wearing a white dress. She stared forward, her spine straight, watching the ship with a neutral expression. Captain MacDonald had been lying when he said his drawing of Isobel wasn't very good. It matched her almost perfectly, down to the curve of her chin and the dainty look of her fingers. There was only one thing about her that was different—she had no aura. The air around her was plain and empty, the absence of the life-like shimmer clearly letting anyone who saw her know she was dead, a spirit waiting on the beach.

"It's really her," I breathed, feeling fascinated and scared at the same time.

"A spirit," Tristan murmured, the same awe and caution in his tone.

A splash alerted me to the dropping of the anchor, and before I knew what was happening, Captain MacDonald was in a long boat, rowing toward the island at a steady pace. The mermaids swarmed around him, some of them beaching themselves as he made landfall. Isobel stood as his feet touched the sand, but remained where she was.

Keeping his attention focused ahead of him, Captain MacDonald held a hand out to her, as if asking her to stay there for a moment, and then approached the gatekeeper.

"What do you think he's saying to her?" I whispered, the entirety of the crew watching him.

"He'll have to explain what's happening in our world, I imagine," Mark answered softly, leaning forward and putting his elbows on the rail.

"I suppose he'll have to convince her to let us all in the gate," Tristan added. "What that will take, I don't know."

Captain MacDonald turned around then, surprise on his face, and waved at us.

"She's agreed to let us through," Dagger said in surprise, still standing at the helm.

"That quickly?" Abella asked sharply, disbelief in her tone.

"Everyone, to the boats." Dagger, seeming to snap from his shock, started moving, ordering the vessels brought up and for everyone to get onboard.

Scrambling, the men did as he asked, all of us loading into the tiny crafts and lowering ourselves into the water. Around us, the mermaids slipped through the surf, some simply staring at us as we moved forward. One of them, the strange octopus one, surfaced right beside Dagger, causing everyone in the boat to jump.

"We will guard your ship," he said in a throaty tone, his accent thick and almost like that of the islanders I'd met on Hispaniola.

369

"Thank you," Dagger replied weakly, apparently no accustomed to speaking with the warriors.

We cut through the water easily, the shamans making a path for us as we rowed ourselves to the shore, bewildered and surprised. Until this moment, I didn't think any of us had actually expected to be let into the city. We had all hoped it, and told each other that it would happened, but I was realizing now that everyone had been skeptical.

Cautiously, we moved across the beach, pulling the boats from the water, until we were all standing in the sand, an anxious air about us all.

"Welcome," Zaka called, her voice booming through the area. "Don't be shy. I won't bite you, though I can't say the same for some of my friends." She laughed when we all remained silent. "Come, come! We have much traveling to do still and many things for you to discover. You are expected."

"We are?" I asked, not able to help myself in my continuing surprise.

"Yes, Samantha," Zaka replied, a knowing expression on her face. "All of you. The spirits told us of your arrival some time ago. We've been waiting most excitedly."

This comment seemed to relax some of us, while putting others more on edge. Unfortunately, I was in the second group. I couldn't help but remember the last time I'd talked with a priestess. The conversation had ended in a generous amount of vomit and an opium headache from hell.

Whether she realized what impact her words had or not, the gatekeeper turned her back on us then, waving her hands high above her head. Suddenly, the palm trees began to twist and shake, bending until they formed an archway. A path unlike anything I'd seen before stretched out on the other side, no sign of the ocean or anything familiar gracing the trail. It was simply a long tunnel, leading down, the end of it disappearing from view.

"This will take you from the edge of the spirit realm into the heart of it," Zaka said, facing us. "Shall we begin?"

The group faltered, whispering amongst each other. Finally, Captain MacDonald stepped forward, nodding.

"Will!"

Isobel's voice made him freeze, his body turned away from her. Her pleading tone made even my heart hurt for her. It was clear she desperately wanted to speak with him, but for some reason she didn't force him to listen to her.

"You don't have to converse with any spirit you don't want to," Zaka said softly, watching him. "You know this. I've told you many times. Isobel will only approach you if you let her."

Captain MacDonald nodded slowly, his shoulders slumping some. "I ken. Yer promise on that is the only reason I was able to come speak with ye myself today." His voice was soft, hurt even. Then, straightening, he seemed to find the resolve he wanted. "Lead the way, Zaka. I'm not here to speak with any spirits, just yet."

"What a very Will thing to say."

Isobel met my stare with a frown, annoyance written all over her face. Apparently, what Zaka had said was true, though. The spirit sat on her log, staring at the ocean, her arms folded tightly across her body.

A tear ran down her cheek and she brushed it away angrily, unable to say what she wanted to the man she had loved.

Turning to the captain, I saw that he had flinched at her words, but refused to look at her all the same.

"This way," Zaka stated, stepping into the tunnel and began moving along the path.

The crew followed apprehensively, filing past the captain until only he, Tristan, and I were left. Catching his eye as I passed, I glanced at him questioningly.

Smiling sadly, he motioned for me to continue, following us into the tunnel as it closed behind everyone. "Now isn't the time, ye ken? She may not like it, but I have to take care of my crew first."

Tall, ominous trees surrounded our path, their heavy branches weighted with vines and leaves, some of which were bigger than my entire body. The roots spread across the ground like spider webs, camouflaged underneath other strange plants. It felt more like we were wading through the jungle instead of walking through it.

Wiping my hair off my sweaty forehead and out of my face, I stared in awe at the strange birds peeking down at us. Snakes lazily wrapped around the limbs of the plants, watching the procession with sleepy eyes. In fact, animals of every kinds seemed to be peering at us from their resting places. Some of them I recognized, but others were like things from a dream. Lightning bugs floated here and there on the air too, some of them apparently giggling together. The only thing that stood out to me was the same thing I'd noticed about Isobel—they had no aura. We were surrounded by spirits, this strange land filled to the brim with life and yet lacking that one thing entirely.

Glancing over my shoulder, I suppressed the shudder that tried to creep across me at the sight of the red headed spirit leaning against a tree behind the group. She'd been following us slowly, keeping her distance and remaining quiet, but I could tell that Captain MacDonald was acutely aware of her presence. He was tense and kept his eyes forward, his hand gripped tightly around the handle of his hammer. Now that we were moving deeper into the spirit realm, the strange shimmer around it had intensified, making it almost impossible to look at the thing without squinting.

"Why does it do that?" I asked him, pushing a branch to the side as we followed the end of the group. Tristan was beside me, but Mark and Abella had moved farther into the crowd, listening as Zaka told them some story about spirits who lived here.

"Hmm?" Captain MacDonald glanced at me questioningly and then the hammer in his hand. "Oh, Sheila? It's magic, lass. Ye canna see it in our realm, but it's hard to keep secrets in this one, ye ken?"

"Magic?" Surprised, I stopped, staring at the weapon with newfound interest. "You mean like a wand, or something?"

Laughing, he shook his head. "No. It's enchanted to protect its owner. No one who means me harm can take it from me. That's how I kent ye dinna intend to do anything to me or my crew when ye were discovered. Ye took her from me during that first fight, do ye remember?"

Smiling broadly, I nodded. "I do. I never would have imagined fighting with a mallet would be so exciting."

That made him chuckle again and he motioned for me to continue, using the hammer to push some bushes aside for me.

"How did you come across it?" I asked, curious. "Was it the witch you knew? What did you say about her? That she was the most interesting person you'd ever had the privilege of knowing?"

Peering back, I saw as his face fell, a shadow crossing his features. In the background, Isobel stiffened as well, her own expression matching his.

Understanding filled me and I bit my lip, regretting I had asked at all. "Oh."

"Aye," he replied roughly.

Tristan, clearing his throat, took my hand, pushing me ahead of him as we climbed a small hill, the group moving into a single file line as the foliage became denser around us.

The conversation died after that, everyone trying to catch our breath as we followed Zaka deeper into the jungle. Shadows flitted about us, a strange humming to the air, and I slowly found myself wondering if we would be lost in this place for eternity, always walking and never reaching our destination.

Finally, the trees broke apart, revealing the start of a wide river. There were long boats on the shore, all without paddles or means of directing them. They appeared more like plain, hollowed logs than the elegant designs I would have expected. Twelve men could easily fit in one of the small vessels and we filed into three of them.

"Interesting," Mark said as he sat behind me, Abella taking the seat by his side. "Look at these carvings." He pointed to some hieroglyphics on the inside of the hull. The markings swept along the inside of the boat, covering every surface but the benches we sat on. They must have been a mixture of languages.

375

Some I recognized—like a few Egyptian marks by my foot—and others were completely foreign.

As we examined the marks, a soft glow seemed to seep into them, lighting up with the same fuzzy haze that surrounded the captain's hammer. The magic filled the air, the writing glowing bright white, and then the boats gently moved forward, gliding across the water.

The entire group remained silent as we moved. The water was teeming with fish and even a few mermaids who stopped to watch as we passed by. Zaka stood in the nose of the first boat, facing forward, unmoving. Her hands were held at her sides, palms facing forward and I had the impression that she was concentrating, using her power to direct all of us through the realm.

After a while, large cliffs rose in the distance, ominous and foreboding. The closer we got, the more apparent it became that the waterway was going to cut through them.

"Do you think that's where the city is?" I asked Tristan quietly, clutching his hand in my own.

"I don't know, love," he whispered. "I hope so. Being here in the open makes me feel uneasy, like I'm being watched."

Nodding, I stared toward the heavens, catching sight of a black face with a bird's beak staring at us. "Well, we're definitely being watched." My mutter caused him to shift uneasily, the cliff face rising above us.

"Zaka."

Captain MacDonald's voice filled the air, a strong sense of curiosity and caution to his tone. He wasn't in our boat, or the shaman's, and I rose slightly, trying to see him over the heads of everyone. When I finally found him, I saw that he was staring over the edge of his boat, as were the men around him.

"What is *that*?"

Curious, I peered into the water just beyond the edge of our own vessel and sucked in a breath. The black machine was just like the pictures I'd seen, the design outdated and long left in the past. "It's an airplane!"

Scanning the crystal clear water, I saw more aircraft, resting peacefully along the bottom of the river. They looked as if they were brand new, frozen in time and forgotten in this place.

"Airplane?"

The word was foreign to most of the people around me, many of them muttering it in confusion and leaning over the edge in bewilderment. Tristan, on the other hand, practically threw himself to the edge, peering into the liquid with wild eyes and excitement.

"Truly?" he asked me. "That's an airplane?"

"An old one," I told him, laughing. "But yes. They're mostly the same in my time, but the machinery is different, more advanced."

"This is something from yer time." Wonder filled his voice as he turned to me. "I'm seeing something from yer time. Something I thought I would never lay eyes on. This is . . . incredible, Samantha." His gaze returned to the airplane, a strange sense of fear and apprehension about him. "Ye told me about it, but I don't think I ever realized just how advanced a time ye were from. And this is old, ye say!" Swallowing roughly, he considered me again, emotion I hadn't expected filling his face. "Ye gave it up, for me. Ye gave up flying for me. Ye abandoned a world filled with things like this to be with me?"

Struck by his words, I felt my reply get stuck in my throat, tears gathering in my eyes. Nodding, I smiled. "That world didn't have you," I said softly. "I can live without flying and without machines. But I can't live without you."

Grabbing me roughly by the neck, he pulled me forward, crushing my mouth with his own in a show of passion I hadn't felt from him in some time.

Behind us, someone cleared their throat uncomfortably, a slight snicker brushing past my ears from the other side. Blushing, I pulled away, grinning all the same.

"What's an airplane?" Abella asked, confused.

"People in the future are able to travel by air, like birds," Mark told her. "In machines like this. This one isn't for travel, though. It's a fighter plane, from around the World War II era, I would guess."

"I think so," I agreed, turning to inspect them again.

His words didn't seem to make much sense to her, but she nodded, scrutinizing the craft below. "So many of them," she said slowly. "How did they end up here?"

Mark frowned as I looked at him, his attention turning to the flagship of our little group. "Yes, how did they get here?"

Zaka glanced over her shoulder at us, smiling. "Sometimes, things and people that shouldn't be here get caught in the triangle. More often than not, they manage to break free, but some of them are brought to this place."

"What happens to the people?" Glancing at the empty cockpits, I swallowed hard, thankful that there were no skeletons inside.

"They are welcomed into the city." Shrugging, she continued to guide us along the waterway, the planes disappearing from view as we rounded a corner of one of the cliffs. "They are dead in their own time, but we offer them the chance to continue living in the service of the spirits."

"And if they refuse?" Mark sounded highly skeptical as he asked.

"They are left to their own. There's much more to the spirit realm than what you see here, Mark Bell. Atlantis is not always what a soul is seeking. We do not keep those who wish to wander from doing so."

The rocks opened around us then and the group took a collective gasp. Where we had hoped to see the city was a graveyard of ships, the broken and battered vessels leaning against rocks and submerged in the water. Some of them looked like galleons or other ships that would be sailing in Tristan's time. Others were closer to my own time, or even older than the both of us. Ripped and tattered sails hung lifeless, the boats seeming to silently wail of the horrors and tribulations they had felt. Propellers dug into the riverbed, gleaming in their unmoving state. Fish swam through shattered portholes, sand covering some ships almost completely.

"How can all of this be here?" I asked, staring at it all in awe. "From so many times and so many different places?"

"The Web of Life encompasses all times and life," Zaka replied.

"Everything is suspended here, like Captain MacDonald said," Mark muttered behind me.

Slowly, we navigated around the ship graveyard, twisting and turning through the canyon, watching as all sorts of crafts passed by in varying states of disarray and perfection. The more we saw, the more I realized just how many people must have disappeared to this realm.

A shudder passed through me. It was one thing to visit here of my own free will, but to be trapped? I didn't know if I would have been one of the souls content with staying in Atlantis. There had to be more than this after death, especially if there was truth in all things. What about Heaven and Hell? What about reincarnation and all the other thoughts and ideals about death and what came after life?

Suddenly, the cliffs opened up around us, the river turning to a large lake. Ahead, the most magnificent city I'd ever seen rested, shining in the light of dusk like a beacon from another world. Waterfalls cascaded over the edges of the city walls, tumbling across the ridges of the pyramid shaped civilization. There were buildings on each level, as well as gates and guards, magic buzzing in the air. Music also flitted past my ears, a hum of voices joining the symphony of sounds. Plants drooped their limbs over the walls, painting the white glare with a soft green. Animals appeared here and there, some minding their own business, others watching us with interest.

"Zaka!"

The call drew my attention to the side and I saw another boat much like ours, several fishermen holding nets waving at us. Fish held still in the trap, seeming as if they had voluntarily been captured.

"Welcome!" they called, smiling like we were their long lost friends, returning home at last.

"Look at the top of it," Tristan said, pulling my attention back to the city.

A large geyser was shooting from the top of the city, the source of all the waterfalls and the lake and river we'd just sailed on.

"The Fountain of Youth," I said in awe.

Zaka, lowering her hands, turned to face all of us, a huge smile on her face. "Welcome, my friends, to the City of Atlantis."

A tall guard, his skin dark and tattooed, nodded to us as we sailed by, through the opening in the wall. As we passed the thundering waterfalls and crept into the outer part of the city, I felt yet another wave of amazement wash over me.

There were waterways, like every iconic picture of Venice, Italy, spreading between the buildings. Stone pathways crept here and there, but it seemed like most everyone traveled by water. The people stopped and waved at us as we came by, laughing and acting the happiest I'd ever seen a group behave.

The spirits mixed freely with the people. Some of them seemed to be part of families, laughing and helping with the chores, while others appeared to just be there, studying everyone in silence. Their lack of an aura made them stand out like sore thumbs, but their presence didn't seem to bother anyone in the slightest.

The shamans themselves were just as colorful as Zaka, their language sounding very choppy and guttural. Whenever they spoke to us, though, it was in English, with a perfect knowledge of the language.

Slowly, we drifted to one of the stone pathways, many different trails leading away from the main hub by the water, their final destinations a mystery.

"I'm afraid this is where my time with you ends." Zaka smiled, beckoning for us to leave the boats. "Choose the path that speaks to you the most. It will lead you where you need to go. Tonight, when the moon is high in the sky, we will gather at the head of the Fountain and the spirits will speak with you. Until then, enjoy our city and the treasures she offers you."

Ambling from the boats, our group stood there, somewhat awkward, watching as she guided the vessels away. In a matter of seconds, we were left alone, not a soul appearing to guide us further.

"Well," Captain MacDonald finally said, sounding somewhat strained. "Ye heard the woman. Meet at the fountain tonight." He paused, frowning slightly, and looked around. It seemed that everyone noticed Isobel was nowhere to be seen. After a beat, the captain nodded to himself, shouldered his hammer, and started along one path, leaving the rest of us behind.

With some muttering and whispers, the crew slowly dispersed, choosing which trail they wanted to follow, disappearing into the depths of the city.

"Any of these call to you?" Mark asked, watching as everyone left our foursome alone.

"Not really," I admitted. "I feel like I'm going to get lost if I go anywhere."

"I think that may be the point," Tristan replied, smiling slightly.

Taking my hand in his, he kissed it and then tucked it under his arm, picking a path and leading me away. Mark and Abella followed slowly behind, the silence cocooning us.

Tall, white buildings stretched every which way, the walkway twisted and narrow. It seemed that everything was empty, no signs of life peeking in the windows or doors, no close sounds reaching our ears. As the sun continued to set, throwing long shadows over everything, I wondered what spirits wanted to speak with us, what story they would share. I'd seen movies with shamans in them before, where they met with the spirit of a bear or another majestic creature and learned valuable life lessons. Would this be something like that?

Eventually, we found ourselves in the midst of an open air market, the sounds and smells of the city encasing me with warmth and excitement. The vendors sold items like shark teeth, precious gems, and animal totems, everything laid out to be examined. Tree branches wove together overhead and a few people had hung wind chimes from them, as well as necklaces and pieces of fabric. It felt like a swap meet almost, with smiling faces and eager buyers all around. After a while, though, the overwhelming amount of it started to give me a headache and Tristan led me away, leaving Mark and Abella with a man who dealt in rare coins—as if things from the legendary city weren't already rare enough.

"It looks like there's a garden maze over there," Tristan said, motioning outside the marketplace. "It should be quieter with the hedges. Do ye want to have a look?"

Nodding, I smiled, tightening my hold on his arm. Glancing at the sky, I frowned. "The sun takes a long time to set here."

Laughing, he stared up as well. "Aye, I'd thought

that myself. The days must be longer here. I don't think it's the same as where we come from."

We entered the hedge maze, pretty flowers sticking out of the bushes everywhere and lightning bugs hanging in the air once more.

"How much time do you think has passed in our realm?"

He shrugged, brushing the petals of one of the flowers as we passed. "I can't rightly say. I suppose we'll find out when we return, aye?"

"I guess."

We turned right, taking a different branch of the maze, and I silently hoped he would remember the way out. An image of shamans descending on the maze to rescue us entered my mind and I giggled, both amused and horrified by the thought.

"What is it?" Tristan asked, grinning.

"Oh, nothing. I was just thinking—"

We'd reached a dead end. The hedge rounded in front of us, stone benches resting along the foliage. In the center, was a statue of a woman holding a jug, which rested on her shoulder, water pouring from the container into the pool beneath her. I could see someone sitting on the benches on the other side, a couple with their heads bent together. Turning to watch as we entered the clearing, they remained silent, smiling lightly.

My apology for intruding on them stuck in my throat as I stared. It felt like my heart was going to explode from my chest, if it would only start beating again. Tears filled my eyes, my lip trembling, my body anxiously trying to remember how to breathe. For an instant, I thought my legs would give way beneath me and I grabbed onto Tristan with both hands, my nails digging into his skin. When I finally was able to speak, it was barely a whisper, tears rolling down my face.

"Mom? Dad?"

They looked just like I remembered them, even though it had been years since both of their deaths. The only thing they lacked were glittering auras, the absence of the cloud marking them as spirits. Mom's dark hair curled over her shoulders, her happy eyes filled with moisture as she stared at me, her familiar and kind smile breaking my heart. She was wearing her favorite red dress, the one that tied in the back and had matching lace on the shoulders. Most of all, she didn't seem sick, like she had the last time I'd seen her. She was healthy and glowing, no sign of the disease that had killed her.

Dad, on the other hand, had hair that was as crazy as it always had been, the blonde strands practically standing off the top of his head. He wore his work jeans and t-shirt, his most common outfit when he'd been alive. He was still tan, fit, and smiling, the grin he had always saved only for me covering his features.

Breaking away from Tristan, I ran to them, arms wide and laughter bubbling from me, my tears making it almost impossible to see them. Rising, they hastened to join me, arms also flung wide as tears streamed across their faces. Wrapping me up in a ginormous hug, their bodies pressed lovingly against me. I felt I must be dreaming, or imagining their presence.

"Is it really you? Are you really here?" Sobbing, I clung to them, refusing to let go, fearful that they would disappear if I did.

"It's us, Sammy," Dad responded, chuckling as he

squeezed me tighter.

"It's so good to see you, pumpkin." Mom kissed my forehead, wiping some of the wetness from my face as she pulled away some to observe me better.

"How?" Glancing between the two of them, I couldn't help the grin on my face. "How are you here? How did you know *I* would be here?"

"We're here because you needed us to be," Dad replied softly. "You called us. We've been waiting for you to arrive."

"Oh, Sammy." Mom put her hands on the sides of my face, smiling sadly. "You've been through so much. You're so strong, so much stronger than I ever hoped you would have to be."

Beaming through my tears, I put one hand on top of hers, the other still holding onto Dad's arm. "I've missed you both so much."

"We were never far away," Dad said softly. "You know that, don't you?"

Fresh tears rolled down my cheeks and I nodded. "I know."

"You had someone there to help you whenever you needed it." Mom peered away from the two of us. "Someone who loves you as much as we do and was willing to hold your hand and walk the path with you."

Looking over, I saw Tristan, standing awkwardly at the mouth of the passageway, surprise and happiness written on his face.

Grinning at him, I chuckled, wiping away the new tears. "Mom, Dad, this is my husband, Tristan O'Rourke. Tristan, these are my parents."

"I gathered that," he replied, chuckling slightly in his shock. "It is an honor to meet both of ye, Michael and Lucy." He acted as if he didn't know what to do, keeping his distance as he continued watching us.

"What, no hug for your father-in-law?" Dad asked, breaking the awkward air between them with a teasing tone.

Grinning, Tristan strode over, joining our embrace without question. He kissed Mom on the cheek, flashing me a happy expression, and laughed, his face flushing somewhat. "This is not something I ever thought to experience," he finally said. "Meeting my wife's parents, I mean."

"You were calling us, too," Mom spoke, stepping away, taking my hand as she spoke to him.

"Well, not us specifically," Dad added, stepping away as well. "You were both calling the one we've been with for the past little while."

"And who is that?" I asked, confused.

They both smiled, a knowing glance passing between the two of them.

I felt like there was some secret they weren't sharing. Their faces shone with happiness and excitement, but they said nothing, ignoring my question.

"Hello."

Turning to the mouth of the pathway, I jumped slightly. There was another spirit there, a young woman wearing a long, white dress. Her dark hair was tied at the nape of her neck, hanging across her shoulder and falling to her midsection. She was a delicate woman, seeming only a few years younger than myself, a dainty grin covering her features. An excitement seemed to surround her, her hands clasped together as she bounced in place a few times. Her green eyes shone brightly with anticipation—green eyes I knew all too well, because they were Tristan's.

Mouth going dry, I stared at her, noting all the things that stood out to me. She had my nose and Tristan's lips, as well as his long fingers. Her hair and frame matched my own, but everything else was such a mixture of the two of us that it took my breath away. I knew who she was, without a doubt, but I was too afraid to voice it, on the off chance that I was wrong. I didn't know how I knew, or what made me so certain, but watching her was making my heart break all over again, as well as filling me with a strange sort of happiness.

For a moment, we simply stared at each other. I was at a loss for words. When someone finally did speak, the sound of it undid me the rest of the way, an onslaught of tears rushing across my cheeks once more.

"Are you . . . Rachel?" Tristan asked hesitantly, his voice catching.

She smiled even wider, nodding. "Hi Dad. Hi Mom."

Racing toward her, we wrapped her in our arms, crying and laughing at the same time, our daughter locked in our embrace at last. It felt as if I would burst as she hugged me, pulling us both close to her, her voice ringing in our ears. I almost didn't notice when we all collapsed to the ground, holding each other tightly, together for the first time.

My hands touched her face, her hair, desperation filling me. It seemed like this was all a dream, but no. With each touch, I knew she was real, she was here, and she had grown into everything I could have ever hoped for her to be.

"I was worried you wouldn't recognize me," she confessed. "But Grandma and Grandpa said there was no way you wouldn't. I guess they were right."

Pulling away, I rested my fingers on her cheek, staring into her eyes with wonder and confusion. "How?" I felt myself asking again. "How are you here, like this?"

"Spirits are allowed to choose how they want to appear," she explained. "It's easier for me, like this. I don't feel like anyone has to take care of me." She looked past me, to Mom and Dad, and grinned. "But there were a few people who wanted to help take care of me and keep me as part of the family anyway."

Glancing at my parents, I felt such a swell of love for them, as well as gratitude. It was comforting me to know that my child was in their care, even if it meant they had passed on without me.

Rachel touched my face, and drew my attention to her. "You've been so upset because of what happened," she said, the first sign of sadness crossing her features. "It wasn't your fault. I knew you needed my help, to hear from me, but I didn't know how to get to you."

Staring at Tristan, she took his hand, squeezing it gently. "And you were so distraught that you never got to meet me. You blame yourself for not being there to protect me, but it wasn't your fault, either."

Taking a deep breath, she grabbed my hand as well, taking on a somber air as she spoke. "It wouldn't have mattered if Mom wasn't kidnapped, or if Dad had been there to protect us. I was never supposed to live. I know that now, as a spirit, and I've accepted it. I hope both of you can accept that truth as well, and let yourselves move on."

Shocked, I remained silent, not knowing what to say.

"How can you know that?" Tristan pressed, holding on to her as if she were going to disappear at any second.

Smiling slightly, she sighed. "It's difficult to explain, what happens when a spirit goes home, but I know, without a doubt. There was nothing either of you could have done to save me."

Shaking my head, I felt like her words had only added more weight to the burden for me. "That means it was something wrong with me, with my body," I said fearfully. Peering at Tristan, I saw he was thinking the same thing I was.

"We might not ever have children," he said slowly.

The statement hung in the air like a black cloud of death and despair, instantly killing my dreams of having a family.

Nodding, he swallowed, blinking away more tears in his eyes as he took my other hand. "It will be alright, as long as we have each other. That's all that matters to me. If we're meant to have no living children, I can survive that so long as ye're by my side. I don't need little ones running around, especially if trying to get them is going to hurt ye so badly."

Rachel shook her head. A slight laugh came from her and she gazed at the sky, sighing. Finally, she met our gazes again. "I have a few sisters who would debate that," she said quietly, her eyes shining.

Her words didn't make sense for a second. Staring

at her blankly, my brain scrambling to understand what she'd said, I blinked. Then, all at once, her meaning struck me and my mouth popped open, more moisture gathering in my eyes. "Sisters?"

She nodded, her own eyes wet again.

"Ye have sisters?" It was like Tristan had been clubbed over the head. "As in, more than one?"

"As in, your daughters, who are here in the spirit realm, anxiously awaiting their chance to live on Earth, with you." She grinned lightly, her voice filling with compassion and insistence as she continued. "Don't give up on them now, not when you're hurting over me. They love you. They want to come be with you. You will have children. You will have a legacy. And you will be more loved than you ever thought possible."

He seemed to be at a loss for words, clutching her hand in his as he pressed his lips together, overcome with emotions once more.

She cried as she watched him, practically beaming. "I love you, Daddy," she said softly. "And I always will."

Tristan sucked in a pained breath, moisture in his eyes and shook his head. "And I love ye, Rachel Dawn O'Rourke. Always have, Always will. I didn't need to see ye to know that."

He wrapped his arms around her, holding her tightly for a few minutes, his shoulders shaking. Even though his face was hidden from me, I knew he was crying all the tears he'd held back over the months, simultaneously saying hello and goodbye to his daughter. When they finally broke apart, his face was red and he wiped his sleeve across it, chuckling slightly.

She turned to me, her face wet but beaming "Mom," she said, her voice shaky. "I know what you went through because of me and I'm sorry. I want you to know, though, it means the world to me that you did it. I've caused you so much pain, but I love you more than anything. Thank you for being my mom, even if it meant you had to suffer for it."

"I would do it again in a heartbeat," I answered, and it was the absolute truth. "My life is not mine without your memory in it. I love you, Rachel. Don't ever forget that."

Wrapping her arms around me, she hugged me tightly, her chin on my shoulder. "I won't. I can't. I remember what it felt like to be alive, inside of you. I could feel your love for me even then. I will carry it with me always."

"Samantha, honey." My mom's voice timidly spoke. "It's time to go, sweetie. There are others who need to speak with you tonight. Our turn is finished."

Hugging Rachel tighter, I shook my head. "No. Anyone else can wait. I'm not ready to let go yet."

Gently disentangling herself from me, Rachel sighed. "You do have to go talk with the others. There is much you must learn, and much you have to prepare for. I'll always be with you. Both of you. But, I have to leave now."

"Will we see you again before we leave?" I asked, suddenly desperate.

Shaking her head, she stood. "Not this time. Maybe, someday. But I must leave you with someone else now."

"Who?" Tristan asked, mirroring my fear of never

KAMERY SOLOMON

seeing her again.

"Don't worry yerself, lad," a voice said from behind us.

Turning, I saw an old man wearing a suit of armor covered by a tabard of The Knights Templar. He had a scraggly beard and wild eyes, his Irish accent lilting through the clearing. Somehow, he'd managed to enter the clearing and station himself in front of the fountain, grinning at us like a crazy old coot.

Straightening his tabard, he moved toward us, tipping his head toward Mom and Dad as he passed them. He stopped a few feet from us and offered his hand to Tristan. "Yer great-granda is here to answer all yer questions and impart some wisdom on ye."

"I have to go now," Rachel said softly, drawing our surprised attention back to her. "But I'll always be with you, I promise." Leaning in, she kissed us each in turn on the cheek, smiling through the moisture that had gathered in her eyes again. She stood, moving next to Mom and Dad, taking their hands in hers. The group gave us one last grin in farewell, and then moved away, disappearing through the hedge and vanishing from our sight.

"Wait!" I called, not ready for them to go. "Come back!"

"It's alright, lass," Tristan's great-grandfather said. "Their time with ye is finished. As hard as it is to say goodbye, it is necessary. All things must end, in life and death."

Glaring at him, I held in the retort I wanted to fling in his direction, my heart raw and frayed from the unexpected interactions.

"I don't mean to be rude," Tristan replied, his tone clipped. "But ye are not my great-grandfather."

"I suppose not, technically," the spirit answered easily. "Not the first generation. I thought ye might be overwhelmed if I listed all the years between us when

I introduced myself, though." Shaking his head, he stepped forward, offering his hand to Tristan and pulling him up. "Allow me to do so properly, now. I am Cathal O'Rourke, the first of yer ancestors to join The Order of The Knights Templar."

A beat of silence hung between the three of us, yet another shock stinging into my already overwhelmed mind. Finally, Tristan nodded, a long breath escaping him, and he turned, helping me to my feet as well.

"Why are ye here, and not my parents?" He stared evenly at Cathal, no judgment in his eyes. He was curious, I could tell, but I also wondered if he was secretly hurt that his own mother and father hadn't come to meet him as mine had.

Cathal smiled gently, motioning for us to follow him. "Yer parents wanted to be here, lad. Unfortunately, the message we need to share with ye is not theirs to give, but mine alone. Perhaps, someday, ye might meet with them again. But it will not be on this day."

Taking my hand, Tristan remained silent, leading me into the maze behind his grandfather.

"What's the message?" Curiosity rippled through me. I was trying my best to not be overwhelmed by all the visitations and things we were learning. Most of all, I attempted to keep the feeling of Rachel with me. Everything she had said had done much to heal my heart and aching body. I didn't want to ever lose that feeling.

"My grandson will have told ye I partook in the Holy Crusades, aye?" Cathal spoke as he followed the hedges, twisting and turning through the maze with ease.

"Yes."

"That wasn't the only thing I did for The Order."

"What else was there?" Tristan interjected. "I didn't think the Templars did much more than fight and gather treasure in those times."

"That is true. It was an early time in The Order, full of learning on all sides and discoveries that would make ye wide eyed and speechless if ye knew the extent of them. Still, there were many secrets we kept, even from others in our ranks. I was the guardian of one such secret."

He paused, having come to the exit of the maze, a wide, open pathway resting before us. It boasted views of the jungle and river, as well as the almost completely set sun. Pinks and oranges filled the sky, streaking it like the Arizona desert at sunset. The picture was breathtaking and awe inspiring, causing us all to simply stare, taking it all in.

"This place was another one of the secrets we kept. Discovered by an unsuspecting knight, simply trying to do his duty. The shamans traded the knowledge of this place with him in exchange for protection from extinction. When it came time to hide our treasures here, they welcomed us with open arms."

Clearing his throat, he turned to us, grinning. "Of course, I never knew about it while I was alive. I was dead nearly two hundred years before anyone other than the Grand Master knew of this place's existence. Still, I stood here, in this very spot, when the treasure first arrived. I wasn't the only spirit in attendance, naturally. I don't think I'd ever seen such a sight in my entire life. And I'd been to Avalon many times during my time among the living."

Stepping away, he moved toward the right, heading for a set of stairs that led up to the next level of the city. Tristan and I stared after him, his words slowly absorbing into us.

"Avalon?" Tristan said slowly. "Ye mean . . . the home of the old religion? The Isle of Apples? I thought that place was only a story, told to wee ones in their beds."

Cathal peered back at us, a sparkle in his eyes. "Oh, it is much more than that, lad." He climbed the stairs, not checking to see if we were following, and disappeared at the ledge at the top.

"Avalon?" I murmured to Tristan. "Like . . . Merlin and King Arthur?"

"Aye, Sam. That's the one." Tightening his grip on my hand, he hurried us after his kinsmen, practically dashing up the steps.

"That was the secret ye kept for The Order? The location of Avalon?" Stopping beside the man, Tristan, stared at him hard, waiting for the answer.

"It was," Cathal said easily. "A secret our family kept for The Order, more like. Over time, due to rivalries and usurping of power, we were removed from the knowledge of the place. There hasn't been an O'Rourke in Avalon since my four times great-grandson. He was the first man to transport treasure there, on the ship that fled Paris during the scourge of the Black Knights in the thirteen hundreds."

"Why are you telling us this now?" I asked, breaking into the conversation. "If Avalon is another treasure haven for The Order, that means there are already men who protect it and keep its location a secret. Are you asking Tristan to insist he be added to that detail?"

"The man is a captain without a ship or port to call home, is he not?" Cathal shook his finger at me, biting his lip. "But, no. That is not what I'm asking." Taking a deep breath, he turned to Tristan again, his eyes steely this time.

"Avalon has fallen."

The statement floated there for a second, bold and dangerous, but somehow confusing as well. It sounded like the title of an action movie, exciting and enticing, but I couldn't help the sick twist in my stomach as he continued.

"Black Knights protect the borders now, and the treasures she keeps—the relics of our people and our past—have been compromised. Ye must save her, Tristan. Ye must rescue her from the clutches of those who would use her powers for harm and destruction. The Isle of Apples is calling out for her people to protect her and ye are the only one left who can answer the call. Bring O'Rourke back to her shores and show the world what it means to have Merlin's favor and The Lady of The Lake's power. Fill the shoes that the great Arthur of Camelot once did and bring peace back to yer homeland."

Overwhelmed, Tristan stared at him, floundering for words. After a few beats, he managed to get out one word. "Homeland?"

"Aye, lad. She is in Éire. Avalon rests on the shores of Ireland, the land of yer people and the home of yer blood."

Glancing at me, as if asking for help, Tristan seemed to be falling into a pit of sorts, everything he'd learned today squishing him into a tiny space of panic and doubt. I was sure the expression I wore looked much like his. I wasn't ready for Tristan to be called away on some special mission. We weren't even done with our current assignment!

"Why Tristan?" I asked, watching Cathal as I voiced my inner confusion. "Why not any of the other Irishmen in The Order? Is it just because he's an O'Rourke? Or . . ." The color drained from my face and I met Tristan's gaze once more. "The Black Knights. Thomas Randall?" I whispered. "He's taken over Avalon?"

"No." Cathal's response was strong and abrupt. "This was not the work of Thomas Randall. Avalon fell to the deceiver that heads yer Order now. He sent his men to Avalon and ordered them to crumble her. The island has put up quite the fight as of yet, but she still needs yer help." His voice filled with passion as he continued, filling me with the impression that he truly believed everything he was saying. "Tristan is the only one who can answer her call because he is of my blood. He is young and strong, a quick thinker, and capable of following in my footsteps. He will become the liaison of the Isle and her people to the souls of yer realm. Avalon was never meant to be guarded by anyone other than an O'Rourke. His family duty is calling him home and demanding he take up the mantle."

Tristan snorted, shaking his head. "How can ye expect me to do all of that when I have never even set foot on Érie's shore? My kinsmen fled Ireland in fear, having lost everything their ancestors worked to build for them." Tristan dropped my hand, stepping away some and stared at the man with wide eyes. "And now ye ask me to return, to take up a calling I know nothing about? I do not even know where Avalon is, let alone how to enter and save her. Do ye intend to tell me all now and hope that I will recall when the time comes? I am not a man that can decide his own fate. I am not a man that can abandon my duty to fulfill the desires of an old spirit."

"Ye are the only one who can answer the call," Cathal said again, not bothered in the slightest by Tristan's refusal. "When ye have left this place and the path ye are on now ends, ye will remember yer family duty. Ye will go to the Isle of Apples. If not out of duty to yer blood, then out of duty to The Order. Black Knights cannot exist and our treasures remain safe. Ye will protect what is The Order's with yer life, like any good Knight would."

Glancing at the sky, he sighed. "My time with ye is at its end. I know I have given ye much to consider and feel conflicted over. It was not my intention to rush it all upon ye, but I had no other choice. I hope ye will forgive me one day for my abrupt and callous nature."

He grabbed Tristan's shoulder, and smiled once more. "Our family feels much honor because of ye and yer feats of bravery. Ye have done our name and legacy well, lad. We will be with ye always. For now, I must leave ye with the shamans, for they have more to share with ye."

He dipped his head in respect, releasing him, and then turned toward the stairs. "Take good care of him, lass."

Striding away from us, he disappeared into the night, the glint of his armor fading in the dim light. Silence spread between Tristan and I as we watched him go, a strange sense of confusion and fear in the air.

While Rachel's visit had healed my heart in so many ways, Cathal's had only made me scared for the future.

"He has always been a straightforward type of man," a voice said from behind us. "But interesting, to say the least."

Turning around, I laid eyes on a man I'd never seen before. His height alone made him intimidating, but there was so much more to him that made me feel he wasn't someone I wanted to mess with. Bright eyes peered at me, his black as night skin covered with a myriad of scars and tattoos, the patterns raised up and webbing across him like some type of disease—but having a strange beauty about them, too. Many of the markings were intricate symbols and pictures, converting him into a walking piece of art. He wore an open robe, a sort of loincloth wrapped around his waist and Roman style sandals on his feet. In his hand, a large staff rested, the top of it reaching above his bald head. An aura shone brightly around him, like stars in the night sky. If I'd not known better, I would have said he was a giant, so great was his presence.

"I am Pathos," he continued, the deep, rich timber of his voice seeming to vibrate in my chest. "Guardian of this great city and leader of her people." Bowing his head, he touched his fingers to his forehead.

I'd seen the action several times while passing through the city and recognized it as a showing of respect. Hastily, I repeated the action, Tristan following suit beside me.

"It is an honor to meet ye," he mumbled, glancing back toward the stairs.

"The honor is mine." Pathos cleared his throat, gaining our attention once more. "I know you have met many spirits this night and have learned much. It is my finding that many of the souls who visit this place become somewhat taken aback by the things they learn here. I must apologize, for what you have heard already is enough to cause you to pause, but there is still more you have to discover."

"What else could there be?" I asked, half chuckling. "I feel as if everything I could've been told has already been said, and yet we're to meet at the fountain to hear more."

"This is true." Pathos laughed, a sympathetic expression on his handsome face. "There is a spirit who wishes to address your crewmates and you at the fountain. I will take you there now; however, you should know, I have one last message for you, Samantha. A word of warning, if you will."

His features darkened, and the expression made me feel cold, like ice water was trickling down my spine, causing a feeling of trepidation.

"Warning?" I said softly.

"I sense a blackened cloud in you. I felt it the moment you and your husband entered this realm. Tell me, how long have you been dreaming of Thomas Randall?"

Tristan stiffened beside me, his hand finding my own. "She's had the nightmares for some time now," he replied for me, hesitant in his answer. "I thought it was only normal, given what she'd been through."

Pathos waved, motioning for us to follow, and

started down the pathway, moving slowly so we could catch up.

"It is normal, yes. But what Sam has been experiencing as of late is not. Being kidnapped and beaten is traumatic. Reliving those memories in your sleep is an unfortunate addition to that suffering. You've been experiencing things that never happened to you though, isn't that right, Samantha?"

Swallowing hard, I nodded.

"When Thomas Randall lost his hand, he absorbed the blood of the Apache gods and saved himself, is this not correct?"

"Yes." Suddenly I wondered how the shamans knew so much about everything we'd been through. Had the spirits told them? Were they all knowing? Before I could ask him, though, he continued speaking, recapturing my attention.

"Do you know what he did with the blood of the Norse gods and the ichor he stole from Oak Isle?"

Stopping cold, I stared at him, blinking. He seemed to take this as an admittance of my unknowing, and frowned.

"He drank them. Both of them. In the months since you've seen Randall, he has taken the blood of three gods into his system. Do you have any idea what consequences he has been facing because of it?"

"I thought he had to have the Holy Grail to drink any of the blood," Tristan interrupted, his grip tightening more on my hand.

"He needs the Grail to drink the blood of Christ," Pathos corrected. "It is the only vessel that ever held the essence of the Christian god."

"He's as powerful as a god, then?" I asked

fearfully, not wanting to hear the answer. It didn't matter to me if Randall had needed the Grail or not. All that mattered was what state he was in now and how difficult it would be to confront him.

Pathos regarded me evenly. "No, he is not."

A breath of relief came from both Tristan and me, the beating of my heart slowing considerably.

"Come. We are not far from the head of the Fountain. All will be revealed there." Continuing on, Pathos led us through a small garden and another set of stairs. He spoke softly with several shamans and spirits as we passed by, leaving Tristan and me in the dark as to what else he had to say about Thomas. After a few moments, we found ourselves at the top of the city, staring at the magnificent Fountain of Youth.

It was more like a large lake, the waters of the fountain spilling over in several places, creating the waterfalls that cascaded through the city. In the middle of the pool, a steady fountain sprayed spectacularly into the air before crashing into the pond, constantly moving like a living thing, swirling as it kept the area filled. Several stone walls had been erected to keep any flooding mishaps at bay. It was like an image from a storybook, with sparkles hanging in the air and the final beams of light from the sun disappearing in the distance.

"It's beautiful," I said in awe, my nerves temporarily forgotten.

"It is," Pathos agreed. "Then again, I suppose all gods are probably as beautiful as this."

"Gods?" Tristan asked, taken aback. "This is your god?"

Laughing, Pathos shook his head. "It is the

essence of our god. I suppose you would say this is as close to blood as they ever came to having. Drinking from this Fountain will heal all wounds and restore life to those who are dying. Our god is one of mercy and forgiveness. She is one with the earth. Anyone who comes to this place, seeking her help, will receive gifts beyond what they can comprehend."

"That's why you hid it here," I added. "To protect her."

His face darkened some and he nodded. "Yes. Our foe—I suppose you would call him a leviathan. He was the only enemy we were never able to defeat. After several years of his attacks, I made the decision to ask the Goddess to take us away."

"And she swallowed you into the sea," Tristan said quietly.

"She transcended us," Pathos corrected. "If one was to search in the right spot, they would probably find the sunken remains of our city. There would be no trace of the people who lived there, though, as we all continue to live here. In her great mercy, the Goddess bade us drink from her waters, so we would survive the occasion. We were transported to this realm, much as you were when you first arrived. We have been here ever since, in the service of the power that saved us."

"Do you miss the living world?" Curious, I watched as the corners of his mouth turned heavenward, clear eyes meeting my own.

"Would you miss a world full of hatred and death? No. I find myself very content here, where life never ends and I never want for anything."

Motioning to the pool, he silently urged us forward, until we were standing at the edge of the water. "Thomas Randall," he said again, the happy tone of his voice diminishing.

Peering into the depths, I sucked in a breath as a picture slowly appeared. It was dark at first, and blurry, but the longer I watched the clearer the image became, until there was no doubt in my mind what I was seeing.

The room was dark and messy, the windows covered with heavy furs and the door barred with a chair. Broken items littered the dirt floor, the bed being one of them. On the stone walls, I could barely make out fingernail marks, the hearth holding only a few coal remnants of whatever previous fire had been there. In the center of the room, a figure bent over another, moaning and crying, rocking as it considered the unmoving body beneath it.

The point of the vision changed then, and we suddenly beheld the face of Thomas Randall as he wept, his hands and face covered in blood, shaking as he watched the body of the woman beside him.

Flinching away, I saw the mess he was covered in was hers. Her body had been ripped apart, possibly by some type of animal, based off how brutal the cuts and gouges appeared.

"No, no, no, no!" Thomas beat his hand against the side of his head, growling the words, swaying back and forth. The stump of a hand he now had was cradled against his chest, small and red looking. Then, suddenly, he reached inside the woman, pulling out a hunk of flesh with his claw like fingers, and shoved it in his mouth.

Screaming, I stumbled, grabbing onto Tristan, horror filling me. In the time I'd known Randall and the monster he was, I'd never thought he was a cannibal, or would even lower himself to such an action. The man I observed now, though, didn't seem like Randall. He was a beast, a monster—not real.

The sound of my scream seemed to somehow reach him, and he jerked up, his eyes meeting mine as if I were standing right next to him. The crazy, bloodlust in them seemed to dim slightly, and a tear slid down his face.

"Sam," he said, his voice breaking. "You came." Weeping, he reached out, his gory fingernails coming for me. "I knew you would come," he rasped. "Help me!"

Wrapping his arms around me, Tristan dragged me away from the water's edge, hissing in anger and disbelief. At the same moment, Pathos jabbed the end of his staff into the pool, disrupting the picture and banishing the vision in a matter of seconds.

"He could see us?" Tristan demanded. "What the hell was that?"

"That was worse than I thought it would be," the shaman replied, frowning. "It would appear that the gods who now inhabit Randall have given him the power to see through realms, as well."

"What do ye mean 'as well?'" Tristan demanded.

"Randall has been visiting your wife in her dreams," Pathos replied, his voice somewhat ruffled. "That is why she has been seeing things that never happened. He has been coming to her, learning what you are doing, making plans for the future. Unfortunately for the both of you, it also seems that he thinks Samantha is the one who can save him from the pain he is in now."

I couldn't even think of any words. All I could see

was the blood and carnage, reaching out for me, begging for help. It was much like the last dream I'd had of him, when he lay helpless on the floor, asking for my help.

"That's not possible," Tristan sputtered.

"Thomas Randall has the essence of three gods in his system now. It is more than possible."

"He was eating that woman." My voice barely made any sound, fear ripping through me. Randall had been terrifying enough to begin with. Seeing him like that, though, had only compounded the terror I had for him now.

Holding me close, Tristan nodded, his own hands shaking. "He was . . . crazy. Insane. I've never seen a man like that before."

"He was . . . frightened," I added, carefully examining the picture in my mind. "Did you see? He beat himself beforehand, as if he didn't want to do such a thing, but he was forced to."

"The blood he ingested came from gods who required sacrifices from their people," Pathos offered, stepping toward us. "They will require the same from him, if he intends to use their power for himself."

"I don't understand." Staring at the shaman with wide eyes, I waited for him to explain further.

Sighing, he moved and sat on the wall, rubbing his face. "Thomas Randall has, unfortunately, gotten exactly what he wanted. The power of three gods flows through him, but he did not realize the voices of the gods would also inhabit him. They demand he follow through with their rituals and do their bidding. The noise and the power of it all has caused him to lose his mind somewhat."

"Somewhat?" Tristan raised an eyebrow, anger rolling off him. "And how do ye know all of this?"

"I have been watching him. Like it or not, the two of you have sent many spirits here. James Abby was the first to warn me of Randall and his exploits. When a line of souls comes to me and says there is someone dangerous threatening the living, I tend to listen to them." Pathos sighed again, a tinge of annoyance in the sound.

"Randall is no longer a threat to just your world. If left unchecked, he could master the powers he has stolen. You would find yourselves battling against a god then, and there would be no hope for you defeating him. Now, though, he is weak and scared. It is painful, absorbing that much energy and strength. The gods have driven him to actions he does not want to do. If you are going to defeat him, now is the time to take action. Find him. Destroy him."

"You make it sound like it will be some simple thing," I countered, my shock wearing away to anger. "We were never able to defeat him when he was simply a man. How are we supposed to win against him now?"

"It will not be easy. I don't have the answers you seek. All I know is that the spirits have warned me and I would not be a good man if I did not warn you in turn. The path ahead of you is perilous and full of darkness. Your souls are bright, though. The gods have chosen you for this fight—but you already knew you had been chosen. You do not need me to tell you that."

Pathos stood, gesturing to the sky. "The sun has set. Your crew comes to meet you now."

Turning, I saw Captain MacDonald slowly approaching us, filled with awe.

411

"You aren't going to tell us more?" Regarding Pathos evenly, I knew I was right. He'd issued his warning and his time with us was now finished, just as our time with the spirits before had ended before I was finished speaking with them.

"You have one last thing to learn," he replied simply. "I have shared all I know of Thomas Randall with you. I do have one last thing to give you, though."

Reaching into his robe, he pulled out a necklace. It was a plain, leather chord, with a white crystal tied into the middle of it.

"This will protect you from any more visitations from Randall. I may not have all the answers you seek, or even know what the outcome of your battle with him will be, but I can give you this. I hope you will accept it?"

Surprised and touched, I nodded, taking it from him. Sliding the strap over my neck, I held the stone in my hand, examining it. "Thank you," I replied genuinely. "This means a lot to me."

He nodded, smiling. "I wish you both well in your travels. I will leave you with your crew now."

My head was spinning. So much information had been presented to me and it seemed I had felt all the emotions that were in my realm of capabilities. All I wanted to do was lie down and take a nap, to relax and let everything absorb into me, but the spirit realm was not done with me yet.

Grasping Tristan's hand in my own, I squeezed his fingers tightly, giving him a weak grin as he stared at me. The expression on his face matched much of what I was feeling and I giggled slightly, aware we were both incredibly overwhelmed.

"What are we going to do?" I asked softly.

He sighed, glancing to the members of the crew that had been slowly arriving. About half of them were here, milling about in groups, talking with each other or silently contemplating whatever it was they had found in the city.

"What we've always done, aye?" His response was quiet and strained, but the words brought an instant comfort to my soul. Whatever would happen, we would be together, like always. I knew this already, of course, but it was nice to hear him reaffirm that decision every now and then.

"Randall will be almost impossible to beat now," I muttered, coming closer to him and resting my head on his chest.

He wrapped his arms around me in response, kissing the top of my head, cuddling me with all the gentleness and love he'd shown me in times past. He remained quiet as he spoke, our conversation meant only for the two of us. "But not completely. Pathos is right; ye were chosen for this battle, Sam. In my ignorance, I'd hoped ye were sent here because ye were meant for me. I see now that there was always a bigger design to yer coming here."

"Maybe." Closing my eyes, I inhaled the scent of him, savoring the memories of the sea and sailing that the action brought to me. He could be right. I could have come to this time because I was meant to be part of whatever mess Thomas Randall was creating. In my heart, I was sure that wasn't the case, though. "I was always meant for you, Tristan. I have no doubt in my mind that if I hadn't fallen back in time to you, you would have risen through it to me."

"Ye think so?" He sounded amused, his fingers playing with my hair as he held me. "I don't know about that, lass."

I grinned. "Why not?"

"I'd have seen one of those airplanes in the sky and keeled over dead right then and there."

Chuckling, I pulled away, examining his face. "I guess going forward would have been more of a shock than traveling in reverse, what with all the advances my time has made from yours."

"To say the least."

Smirking, he kissed my forehead, another sigh

414

breaking from him.

"What is it?"

He paused, hesitating in his answer, and then shrugged. "We've been told all these things we must do—stopping Randall and saving Avalon—but all I can think is that I met my Rachel."

His voice caught with a strange emotion I'd never heard from him before. It took me a moment to realize that he was proud—a proud father. I'd never seen him interact with his own child until today, studied the way he spoke with her and the way he treated her, or noticed how there was a part of him that was reserved just for her.

"She was beautiful," he said softly. "No?"

"The most beautiful thing I've ever seen." Tears gathered in my eyes again, but they were happy this time. It was so different from when I'd thought of our baby before. I didn't feel sad over losing her, not as much as I had anyway. Meeting her in spirit had healed many of the gashes in my heart.

"And she has sisters." There was wonder in his tone now, excitement even, and he chuckled. "Sisters! We are going to have daughters!"

"I know." Hugging him tightly, I let all of my worries and fears be pushed to the rear of my mind, deciding instead to focus on the happy things we had discovered here.

"I love ye," Tristan whispered fiercely. "I know for certain now that we can face anything, so long as we have each other to lean on."

"I love you too." Releasing my hold on him, I took his face in my hands and kissed him gently, all of my pleasant emotions flowing through that contact.

"Eh-hem."

Breaking apart, I saw a blushing Mark, who hastily glanced away, rubbing his neck. Beside him, Abella beamed, a couple of flowers in her hands.

"You had a good time in the city, *oui*?" She beamed, tucking a strand of her long, curled hair away from her face.

"I suppose you could say that." Releasing my husband, I took his hand once more, scanning the crowd of sailors around us. It looked like everyone was here, finally. There was no spirit that I could see, though, and so I turned to our small group. "What did the two of you do? We lost you when we went into the maze."

"We stayed at the street fair for a while," Mark said. "And then we sat on the edge of the wall, watching the sun set above the jungle." His face reddened as he glanced at my friend and he bit his bottom lip, turning away quickly.

"It took much longer than expected." Abella blushed, clearing her throat in an embarrassed manner.

"I see." Amused, I watched the two of them, happy to see that they were patching things up, even if it was at such a slow pace. Perhaps it was good for them, to be thrown together like this and forced to spend time with one another.

Tristan, on the other hand, seemed to be more content with outing the pair.

"Who kissed who?"

Grinning, he watched as they floundered, partial denials and deepening blushes covering them. The longer they went on, the funnier it became to him.

"No, they didn't kiss, did they, Sam? Mark isn't

as straightforward as that, not unless pushed."

"Leave them alone." Playfully slapping him on the shoulder, I smiled at them, sensing he was right. Something had happened, whether it was romantic or not. Once again, I found that the thought of Mark with someone else didn't bother me. It had never been an amorous annoyance to begin with, but I was happy to find I wanted him to be happy with someone else.

"Praise be to God and long live The Knights Templar!"

The call drew the attention of everyone in the area, our heads turning toward the fountain, a collective gasp rippling through the group.

Grand Master Bevard stood on one of the walls, his aura-less presence sticking out like a sore thumb in our group of the living. He wore the clothes I had always seen him in, his appearance marking him as a member of the upper French society. Instead of the old man I'd known him as, though, he was much younger and brighter, a smile covering his face as he stared at the group.

"My friends," he said happily. "It is so good to see you. After my time among you was cut short, I feared I would not lay eyes on you until you had joined me in this life. It is a great comfort to see you now and know that you are all right."

"Bevard," Captain MacDonald said, his eyes wide. "Of course it's ye. I shoulda kent it."

"Yes, old friend, you should have," the spirit agreed. "But, many of you have been quite overwhelmed by this evening. I will not blame you for not guessing sooner." He grinned, clapping his hands together. "Shall we to work?"

"It was Davies who murdered ye, then?" MacDonald spoke over the group, cutting right to the question that I was sure had been at the front of everyone's mind.

"Alas," Bevard replied, frowning. "It was not."

Another shocked ripple moved through the group.

"Who, then?" Someone yelled from across the way.

"Why is Davies tryin' to have us killed?" Another man shouted from behind us.

Bevard held his hands up for silence, frowning slightly. "I know this is a trying time and full of surprises. If you will but hold your tongues, I will tell all."

This appeased the group and they fell silent, all of us watching him with hawk-like vigilance.

"Francois murdered me."

Gasps and shouts of disbelief echoed off the stones. The men watched him wide eyed, some even angry.

"Which one is Francois again?" I whispered to Tristan, whose hands had curled into fists as his face reddened with ire.

"One of the Masters of our Order—second only to The Grand Master. The lyin', conniving bastard!" His breath quickened, the sting of the betrayal this information had brought to light evident on every part of him.

Bevard, holding his hands up once more, spoke over the outrage he had caused. "Francois waited until the last moment, disappearing behind the curtains, and did the deed in a matter of seconds. I was not even aware that a threat existed from him."

Mutters filled the air, but the men slowly fell silent, waiting for him to continue. I felt a strange gripping of my chest, my heart aching to hear of the old man speak of his death so easily. It couldn't have been easy and he surely suffered with the knowledge of what had happened to him, but he spoke of it with ease and elegance, as if it were only another moment in time that held no significance to him.

"Davies has been Francois's puppet, from the very beginning. He was put in command through nefarious methods. However, I do think you all should be aware that it was against his will." Bevard paused, clearing his throat as he let the words sink in. "Francois has been blackmailing him from the start. Many of the actions you perceive to be malicious were actually attempts to save you from the fate Francois had planned to gift you."

Bevard turned to us, smiling lightly. "His attempt to rehome the four of you was from his desire to save you from the fire he knew would find you in your beds that night."

Turning toward Captain MacDonald, he chuckled shortly, shaking his head. "And he assigned new men to your crew, in the hopes that you would find your trust in him lacking and leave early, escaping whatever misdeeds he was sure Francois had planned to enact on you."

The late Grand Master sighed. "I know Davies had many enemies on this crew before he ever took my office, but all he has done has been in the pursuit of your continued lives and happiness. Even as he ordered you to tell him where your portion of the treasure was hid, he was only trying to keep the information from

Francois."

"Is Francois working with Thomas Randall?" Mark's voice hovered above the group, his face calm and passive when I turned to him.

Bevard hesitated, pursing his lips, and then shook his head. "No. This is a different group of Black Knights that have risen up."

A second ripple of dismay surged through the group, the horror of the revelation felt by myself, as well. As far as I knew, there had never been more than one faction of Black Knights at a time. What consequences could we possibly face with such a large divide in our group? How would we gather together enough to fight off two opposing forces?

The outrage and fear grew around me, the men shouting and arguing with one another. Several of them were demanding we go straight to Paris and fight. Others called for proof, something we could use to bring Francois down peacefully, without losing too many men. As they fought about what was to be done, Bevard continued to try and call them to silence once more, but no matter how hard he tried, he couldn't seem to gain the quiet he'd controlled only a moment before.

"Why would Francois try to kill us?" I asked Tristan. "Specifically, I mean? I didn't even know who he was. Why did he think I was such a threat?"

He shook his head, fuming. "I don't know, Samantha. Perhaps he thought we were Randall's greatest blockade and he didn't want us to become his as well."

"We need proof that he did it," Mark said behind us.

Tristan and I formed a small circle with him and Abella, ignoring the others beside us for a moment.

"Aye, I agree." Tristan sounded angry as he spoke. "The crew of the *Isobel* has been labeled traitors. If we show up at the Temple without proof, they will think we're only trying to seize power for ourselves."

"Surely, if you three are with them, The Order will see reason and know that they aren't Black Knights?" There was fear in Abella's eyes, and an uncertainness that might have been causing the shaking of her hands.

As if he weren't even thinking about it, Mark wrapped his fingers around hers, making a comforting noise.

"I was thinking the same thing," I confessed. "They know how adamantly we have fought against Thomas Randall. I can't see any man accusing Tristan of being a Black Knight."

"But this is a different group of heathens," Tristan replied sourly. "Aye, we have battled Randall time and time again, but he is not part of this group. They could say we only wanted the power for ourselves."

"*C'est impossible!*" Abella shook her head decidedly. "I do not think any man who knew you would accuse you of such a misdeed."

"He's right, though." Mark frowned. "I already wear the brand of the Black Knights. I am an outsider, and yet the two of you have welcomed me with open arms. That alone is enough to cause anyone to distrust you." Anger flashed across his features and he peered at the night sky, frustration exuding from him. "I've compromised your standing. Again. Why is it always me that screws everything up?"

"Lomas will vouch for you," I instantly offered.

"Abella, too. Everyone you fought with in Arizona knows where your loyalties lie."

"Yes, when it comes to Thomas Randall." His eyes darkened and he glanced at Tristan. "But not when it comes to loyalty to Francois."

"We haven't a barrel to stand on without proof." Tristan growled, seeming like he would very much like to punch something.

Bevard's voice sailed through our tiny group then, shouting over the racket. "My brothers, *calmer vous*."

Staring at the spirit, I felt an uncomfortable turn of the stomach at the expression he now wore.

"There's more," I whispered, poking Tristan's shoulder and motioning for him to pay attention.

After a moment, the men seemed to calm, their attention returned to the man on the wall.

"There will be a time for accusations and explanations, but there is a more pressing matter to be dealt with. In the time that you have been gone from Paris, Francois has broken the code on the Grand Master's map. He knows where the treasures are and how to reach them. At this very moment, he is sailing to the Gate of Atlantis, with a fleet so powerful, it would make an entire country quake. The fabrication of your traitorous status has allowed him to convince the rest of The Order that you are here to rob them and they come to protect the sacred items stored here. The majority of them have no idea they are actually part of a raid against the city, to steal the objects kept here."

"How?" Captain MacDonald demanded. "How has he convinced them to do such a thing? How have they fallen for his trickery so easy?"

"Fear is a powerful thing, my friend." Bevard

smiled sadly. "And you have taken the brunt of the hit, I'm afraid. It is your name that has been smeared with the title of murderer and traitor. The Order comes for you, to deliver the justice they wrongfully assume you deserve."

"They mean to cut the head from the snake." Captain MacDonald snorted once, humorlessly, and then turned to his crew. "I must apologize then, for the lot of ye have been besmirched because of me."

"It wasn't your fault," Dagger said, calling everyone's attention. "You can't help that someone lied about you."

MacDonald smiled. "Still. I canna ask ye to fight my battles. I will go out and meet the fleet myself. Let them take whatever justice they may, while my men—" He looked at Abella and I then, a slight laugh in his gaze. "And my women escape."

"I think not." Dagger raised an eyebrow, staring at him with a cool sense of disobedience about him.

"They'll kill you without a second thought!" Disbelief covered my features as I watched him.

Captain MacDonald nodded. "I ken that. But it's the head they're after, no? So, I will give them the head. It matters not if I live or die, only that my crew makes it out to live another day."

Dagger snorted, rolling his eyes. "You and your rule. You really mean to not let any of us die before you have?"

"I am an old man, Dagger. My life is not as important as the ones I lead. A good captain is nothing without his crew, and a good man is nothing without his sense of honor. Aye, there will be no dying among ye, not unless I've gone first." The captain matched his

423

look, not backing down in the slightest.

Dagger sighed, stepping away some. Then, scanning the group, he raised his voice. "Will we allow our captain to meet his death without putting up a fight?"

"No!" The response was immediate and resounding, causing Captain MacDonald to pause in surprise.

It was no wonder to me that my own voice had responded. In that moment, I think we all knew what we had to do—what our own honor and courage demanded we do for a man who was willing to lay down his life for all of us.

"Will we allow him to send us on our way like yellow bellied cowards while he claims all the glory in battle?" Dagger smirked as he said this one, watching his captain as if he were playing some game with him.

"No!"

"Will we mutiny if he tries to make us?"

"Yes!"

Patting the captain on the shoulder, Dagger shrugged. "Well, there you have it, Captain. You're stuck with us, whether you like it or not." He smiled then, the kind of look you would give an old friend. "You won't be dying today, William MacDonald. Not unless we go first."

The wind ruffled my hair, blowing a few strands into my face as I stood at the helm, watching the open waters. There was no sign of Francois and his fleet yet. Their impending arrival hung heavy in the air, though, like a black cloud of death and fear. The rest of the crew waited patiently on the deck, armed and ready to fight, watching the horizon with steady eyes.

It was strange, knowing that the spirit realm was right here, the entrance shielded away. It was like my whole experience there had been some fantastic dream. The proof of the visit was all around me, though. Magic still clouded the air. In the water beneath us, the shamans waited, sworn to protect their land. The force that was headed for us right now was sure to be shocked when they discovered we had mermaids gifted with such powers on our side.

"Stay close," Tristan whispered, standing behind me. "This won't be a fight like any of the others we've participated in."

"I know," I muttered. "I'll do my best."

His hand found mine and squeezed my fingers. "I know ye will. Ye're an exceptional fighter, Sam. Mind yer footwork, though, and don't charge ahead of me. I want eyes on ye at all times. For my own peace."

Glancing over my shoulder, I smiled, tightening my hold on him. "If we die, we die together."

The statement caused a shiver of fear and I looked away, swallowing hard. We'd faced impossible battles before, even going against mystical items and armies, but this felt different. We'd be facing a force so much larger and stronger, and there was almost no chance of survival. I hoped we would be fine, after hearing from Rachel that more children were waiting to come to us, and being told by Cathal we had a duty that needed to be fulfilled in Ireland. Still, there was that voice in my head that said this could be it—one or both of us could die today. Acknowledging that possibility made me grip the hilt of my sword a bit tighter and stare harder at the horizon. Any moment now, ships would appear there, and our fight for survival would be underway.

Peering around the deck once more, I let my attention settle on Captain MacDonald and Zaka, both of whom were standing on the steps leading to the helm only a few feet away.

"You will have us behind you," she was saying softly, her gaze trained on the horizon as well. "Once we have made the first move, you should advance. With any luck, we will catch the majority of them."

"Aye, I think ye will." He cleared his throat, his knuckles white as they gripped around Sheila, his expression grim. "I thank ye. It is not my choice that my crew faces this obstacle with me."

"It is their choice, though, and that matters more. I think you know that, or you wouldn't have allowed them to come."

He didn't answer, closing his eyes for a moment

and breathing deeply. I sensed some hesitation in him, as well as anger and worry. It wasn't worry for himself, however. It was clear that his only thoughts were with the people around him.

Finally, he opened his eyes, his voice so quiet I almost didn't hear what he said to her. "The last time I allowed someone to make their own choice and follow me into battle, they were killed. I have spent my entire life since then trying to keep the same from happening to others, always putting my own wants and desires to the back of my mind in favor of those around me. I dinna ken for certain that I am doing the right thing by possibly allowing them to forfeit their lives for me, as Isobel did before."

"I have spoken with your Irishwoman. What she has to say on the matter is not for me to tell you, but it would do you good to speak with her, I think. It is time you stopped avoiding her, friend. You can only run from the spirits for so long."

"Perhaps fate means to send me to her now, as a spirit myself." He smiled weakly, his eyes meeting mine as he gazed past the gatekeeper.

Embarrassed to have been caught eavesdropping, I turned away, blushing.

"Sails, on the horizon!"

The timing couldn't have been more perfect. Everyone rushed to the edge, squinting and trying to catch sight of what the man in the crow's nest had seen with his scope.

"How many do ye see?" Captain MacDonald yelled.

"At least ten ships, Captain! Moving toward us in formation."

"They'll have spotted us, then." The Captain turned, looking at the crew, his features grim. "Now is the time to flee, if ye wish to do so. I will not blame ye, and neither will any other person with any kind of sense."

We all stared at him in silence. He knew where we stood, even if he didn't like it—at his side, ready to fight.

Nodding, he took a deep breath, shouldering Shelia. "Right then. Today, we fight for our honor and for our lives. Some of ye have been with me from the start, and some only for this voyage, but ye have all shown me what it is to stand by someone in their hour of need. It has been my great honor to serve ye, as a man and as yer captain."

He bowed his head, touching two fingers to his brow, reverencing us in the same manner the Atlantians had. When he rose, he was smiling, a sparkle in his eyes. "May we continue to live well, long after this day. If not, may we die well and with so much strength that we inspire many a tale and song."

"Hear, hear!" Unsheathing his sword, Dagger raised the blade high in the air, grinning wickedly as he saluted his captain. "To living, dying, and everything between!"

All around him, the men followed suit, raising their blades and shouting. An energy took hold of the group, spreading like wildfire, the war cries growing louder. Before I knew what was happening, we were moving, setting the sails, securing the anchor, and turning the ship, heading toward the massive force.

Beneath us, the shamans swam, their colorful tails and tentacles flashing through the water. Their hands moved as one, creating a large sweeping motion that caused the water to ripple from us. As the air caught our sails, yanking us forward, they began to chant, continuing with their ritual.

Dashing up the steps to the helm, where Captain MacDonald stood, the steering mechanism in his hands, I called above the sound of the wind as it picked up. "What are they doing?"

"They're creating a bit of a distraction, in the hope of breaking apart the fleet," he replied loudly. "To the ropes now, though, lass! We need yer help bringing the sails in before the gale takes them!"

Turning quickly, I jumped the steps, running to the main mast and joined the line of men handling a long, thick rope that lead to the sails. The riggers were furiously trying to raise the billowing canvases, pulling the ropes tight and holding on for dear life. The action would basically stop us completely, but we couldn't risk losing a sail or breaking a mast.

Behind me, Tristan also handled the ropes, heaving the heavy line with ease and far more ability than I had. He did his duty like it was a dance, the movements flowing from him effortlessly, his attention trained on the task at hand.

Clumsily, I put one hand in front of the other, trying not to take a peek at the approaching convoy. I did my best to keep the rope pulled tight, frantically hoping the sails wouldn't rip and blow away before we could get them in, the wind all but howling around us. The boat shuddered beneath us, and I gasped, gazing at the water.

The shamans were still chanting and waving their arms, the water rippling from them, but there was something more out there now. I could see it slowly raising up, like ghosts from the deep, shattered, breaking the surface of the water, joining us in our approach on the Templars.

Each sunken ship appeared to have been through hell and back, holes and scorch marks painting many. Tattered sails blew in the wind, unmanned helms spun out of control, yet they somehow stayed afloat, turning their faces toward The Order and plowing forward through the waves. As I watched the abandoned vessels rise from their watery graves, I realized the shamans were trying to give us more boats to fight with, as well as terrify our enemies before we even began to face them. By the time all the ships had been lifted from the ocean floor, we had an armada surrounding us, some of the phantom boats even pushing ahead.

"Steady!" Captain MacDonald yelled from the helm.

"Sam!" Tristan's voice caught my attention and I ducked, noticing the sail above whip dangerously in the wind. Digging in my feet, I focused back on keeping the line pulled tight, my heart pounding in my chest.

Slowly, the ghost ships passed us, gaining speed as they moved forward in a straight line, their hulls so close some of them even scraped together.

"Batten the hatches and hold on, mates!" Captain MacDonald actually laughed as he called the order. "Rain's a comin' and we're about to get wet!"

Confused, I glanced at the sunny sky, my hair stinging my face as it whipped about, coming free from its bun.

"Rain?"

Tristan wasn't listening, though, his figure already crouching to the deck, the end of the rope wrapped around his waist. Following suit, I got on my knees, watching the action around us.

Zaka had taken a spot just beside us, her arms raised high, words I didn't understand streaming from her mouth. The sky overhead began to darken, clouds billowing from nowhere, heavy and black. The air turned cold, and there was a flash of lightning, bright and hot, that struck the middle of the ghost ships, accompanied by a sudden clap of thunder so loud that I screamed in terror.

The wood, despite having been long submerged, lit like a candle, the red flame jumping from one ship to the next, creating a wall of fire.

Eyes wide, I watched the phenomenon, almost unable to believe what I was seeing. "It's a blockade!" Speaking mostly to myself, I laughed in surprise, watching as the barricade crashed into the first of The Order's ships.

All around me, the men cheered, watching as those who would see us dead scrambled to miss the mess in their paths. Several other vessels were unsuccessful and plowed straight into the fire, finding themselves entangled with the broken and burning ships. Sails caught the flame and the sailor's attention was drawn from fighting to saving their own skin. Three of the ten ships came to a full halt, crashing into the wall and moving no further.

Then, as if by some cruel twist of fate, one of the ships missed the wall, then another, and another, until the seven remaining ships were headed right for us, moving quickly, sailing around, as the clouds broke and rain began to pelt down.

A flash crossed the water and I gasped, watching as the shamans darted forward with incredible speed. It was if the water weren't even there, their forms flying through the liquid speedily, weapons in hand. When they reached the vessels, they passed by the flagship, letting it continue on. The next two weren't so lucky, though.

It took the incoming boats a moment to realize what was happening. One second they were home free, moving straight for us. The next they were stopped dead in churning waters, lightning flashing as men were suddenly being picked off the sides, as if by magic. Even from this distance and with the storm, I could still hear their screams of terror as the mermaids and other creatures attacked.

As I watched, shocked and also somewhat grateful for the help, I suddenly realized that the men were being left in the water, alive.

"They aren't killing them," I said in surprise, looking back at Tristan.

"No," Zaka responded, drawing everyone's attention to herself once more. "Captain MacDonald doesn't want any deaths that could be avoided. He believes it will help The Order to believe that you are not their enemy."

"Merciful," Tristan muttered, shaking his head. "It might work, if they don't kill us all first."

"Riggers, get to yer stations and tie those sails down!" The captain's voice roared past us once more and the men were on the move.

Tristan jumped to his feet, untwisting himself

432

from the rope and tying it down properly. Without another word, he grabbed the rigging and pulled himself up, scurrying to the arms of the mast and securing the gathered sails. As I watched, I noticed that Mark was also there, working on the front mast.

Sweeping across the deck, I searched for Abella, breathing a sigh of relief when I caught sight of her by the bow, sword in hand, her attention turned upward as well. She must have been with Mark, as I was with Tristan. The knowledge gave me comfort and I knew I wouldn't have to worry about the two of them, as long as they were together.

After a few moments, Tristan joined me on the deck again, soaked to his skin and watching the shamans attack the two vessels. Their brothers in arms hadn't stopped to help them, the five remaining ships still heading our way.

"Do you think Francois realizes they aren't dead and will remember how he didn't help them?"

Tristan shook his head. "No. If what Bevard said about the man is true, he only has eyes for the treasure he thinks he's about to conquer."

"Battle stations!"

It was Dagger who shouted the order this time, his voice roaring over the noise, calling us to arms.

"Time to show these knaves how well ye handle a blade, love." Tristan smiled lightly, grabbing me around the waist with his free arm as he drew his sword once more. Kissing me firmly, he lingered for a moment, as if he were really trying to memorize what it was like to be with me like this. He then rested his forehead against mine, breathing deeply. "Stay where I can see ye?"

"Always," I responded, staring into his sparkling green eyes. "You as well."

"Ye have my word, Sam."

Breaking apart, we took our spots along the railing, watching with stony faces as the ships approached us. The rain pelted my skin, dripping into my eyes, and I shivered, wishing we could get the whole affair just done and over with. Glancing to the helm, I watched the captain once more.

"Francois is at the head." He had the spyglass held to his eye, his lips curling into a slight snarl as he watched the ship come toward us. "Good. I can take the wee bugger down myself."

A cannon fired from the deck of the flagship, narrowly missing the bow of our own. Suddenly, I felt the realization of the fight we were about to partake in become reality. If we didn't prove we were innocent right away, we would be in the fight for the long haul. If any other ship had reached us first, we might have been able to reason with her captain and fellowship them to our cause. With Francois at the helm, though, we would be fighting the very man who besmirched us, the man who wanted us dead for his own designs. There would be no negotiating, no pleading our cause. The man knew we were innocent.

He would do everything in his power to keep the others from discovering this.

More cannons shot toward us, one of them clipping the front of the boat, spraying wood chips in every direction.

Flinching, I glanced toward the captain, waiting for him to order a return fire. The order never came, though, even when the secondary ships began firing on us as well.

"Captain?" Dagger asked, uncertain.

Captain MacDonald shook his head, frowning. "They're tryin' to sink us instead of boarding. Easier on them—no casualties, and they can use the whole crew to claim the treasure. Remember, though, we dinna fight to kill." Captain MacDonald spoke as he came down the steps from the helm. "Only to survive. Innocent blood need not be spilled this day, not at our hands."

"What do you order then?"

"We fight." MacDonald growled slightly, unsheathing his sword and raising Sheila from the ground. "Leave Francois to me. I'll get a confession out of the rat, if it's the last thing I do." He paused for a moment, staring at the men opposite us, the men who should have been our friends and defenders. A strain of emotion covered his face for a moment, and then it was gone. "Hooks!" He roared. "Bring them in, lads. Let us show them what it means to face men of honor!"

The men scurried about, grabbing the grappling hooks and ropes, waiting for the opportune moment to snag the ship and draw her toward ourselves.

"Won't that just make it easier for them to sink us with the cannons?" I asked Tristan, bewildered.

"No." He took the hook and rope that was handed to him by another and smiled. "If she's anchored to us, she can't fire without risking sinking herself. The other ships won't fire either, for fear of taking out their leader."

I eyed the flagship as it came up alongside us, cannons sticking from their windows, ready to fire once more.

"Now!"

Hooks were flying through the air, catching on the railings and masts of the flagship, drawing her in with a surprising amount of ease. Peering over the edge of the boat, I saw several shamans who were also using their powers to pull the ship close.

For the first time since I'd seen the fleet on the horizon, I thought we might have more than half a chance of winning this fight.

A battle cry caught my attention and I looked up, seeing a man from the flagship swinging toward me on a rope. Others were scrambling to follow him, including several of the men on our side, each party boarding the other's ship.

The real fight had finally begun.

Brandishing my blade, I shouted, turning to face those who had come over to meet us. Without a second thought, I charged one of them, swinging and spinning, engaging him in a fight he seemed eager to partake in.

The man was larger than I was, by about one hundred pounds, but the added weight didn't seem to affect his speed at all. He darted around the deck like a rabbit, meeting my every blow. For a split second, I thought I might not be able to beat him, but then he slipped, falling flat on his back.

Remembering the captain's orders to not kill any of the men, I slid down as well, pinching one of the sailor's pressure points as hard as I could. He struggled, hitting me in the side with the hilt of his sword, and then finally slipped into unconsciousness.

Grabbing him under the arms, I heaved him from the middle of the deck, laying him against the side railing. I saw Tristan doing the same to someone he was fighting. There was no time to speak or congratulate one another, though, as more men were flooding over the railing and attacking.

Darting forward, I growled, meeting my next opponent. He fell much quicker than the previous one, as did the next man I faced. After a few moments, it occurred to me that we were still battling just the flagship. Glancing over the water, I saw the other four ships standing by, waiting.

"They'll only come if they think their ship needs help," Tristan called to me, spinning and smashing his pommel against one man's head. The enemy crumpled like a rock, his eyes rolling back. He would have a killer headache when he woke, but he was still alive.

We were handling ourselves well. As far as I could see, none of our crew had fallen, though a few had bad injuries. I caught sight of Abella dragging one such man into a corner with her good arm, her free hand protectively covering the cut on his chest.

At that exact moment, one of the other ships seemed to notice how well we were doing, suddenly moving forward.

"Brace yourselves!" Dagger yelled a few men over, punching a Templar in the face. "More are coming!"

The second ship pulled next to us, throwing her own hooks and drawing close. A flood of men jumped over the railings, beating us back. Some of them were plucked away by mermaids waiting in the deep, but there were so many sailors that it was impossible to keep them all from boarding.

Feeling somewhat frantic, I slashed every which way, trying to keep anyone from getting too close to me. The fight was spread over all three ships now, but there were so many of them and so little of us by comparison, I felt any hope I'd had slipping away with the tide.

The sound of a cannon firing made everyone

glance toward the other three ships, watching in horror as the ball smashed into one of our masts. The wood shattered into a million pieces, the large pole falling in slow motion, it seemed. The ropes strained and pulled as it swung low, crashing to the deck and falling over the bridge of space between our ship and the flagship. It tangled with the ropes there, smashing through the railing of the other boat and securely latching us together.

War cries came from the water, the shamans launching another attack on the ship that had fired on us. Men were plucked from her rigging and pulled through cannon windows, deposited into the water. The other two ships were left alone, though, giving a clear message—they wouldn't be bothered, if they left us alone.

My examination of the event was cut short as yet another Templar rose to greet me, a wicked smile on his face and a sword in his hand.

Tossing my blade between hands, I smiled as well, ignoring the fact that I was out of breath and tired from my other battles. We stared at each other for a moment, and then, not wanting to give him the upper hand, I stepped forward, engaging him in the fight.

The rain had made the deck slick and we both slipped as we moved around, thrusting and jabbing at each other. My desire to not kill him had me at a disadvantage, but I refused to give in and finish him. Captain MacDonald was right. These were our brother's in arms, even if they didn't see it that way. We were not the enemy and we did not need to act like we were for Francois's benefit.

Sidestepping the stab he'd aimed for my thigh, I

brought the hilt of my sword down hard against his back, shoving him against the railing.

He cried, arching the wounded area, and then rounded on me, pulling a small dagger from his belt. The blade flashed in the lightning, coming toward me with speed I hadn't expected from him.

Stepping away, I leaned back, hissing as the blade nicked my chest, cutting a small space just below my breast. The Templar was even quicker after that, slicing across the back of my hand as he pulled the blade toward himself. The cut was deeper than the first, stinging badly as blood welled from the wound and slipped over the edge of my hand onto the deck.

Growling, I brought my foot up, kicking him between the legs. He immediately dropped both of his blades, grabbing himself, and fell to the floor.

I may have been a bit too rough with him when I kicked him in the head, knocking him out cold.

"Sam!"

Turning to Tristan, I saw him watching me with wide eyes. Confused, I glanced at my hand, realizing that it was now almost completely covered in gore and still dripping on the deck.

"I'm fine!" I yelled, wiping the filth on my pants. All it did was make me seem like more of a mess, though, and I sighed, turning to find my next opponent.

"Francois!"

Captain MacDonald's voice shouted across everyone, drawing their attention to his form as he crossed the fallen mast, Sheila in one hand and a somewhat bloody sword in the other. Someone had cut him on the arm, the filth soaking through the sleeve of his shirt, but he was otherwise whole. Everyone paused for a second as he advanced to the flagship, yelling at the top of his lungs.

"I'm the one ye want, ye rat! Come and face me yerself, ye coward! Stop hiding in yer cabin like a wee babe! If ye're goin' to lie to all these good men and condemn us all to death, ye could at least be a man about it!"

Some of the Templar's hedged at that, seemingly surprised that the Scotsman would insist he had been lied about.

"That's right," he said to them, stopping before he reached the broken railing of the flagship. "Francois has lied to all of ye. I'm no murderer or Black Knight. He is!"

"Enough!"

An old man appeared from the captain's quarters, his body clothed in light armor and a sword in his hand. Rain spattered against his bald head, his wrinkled skin pale in the light, but there was a fierceness about him that made my breath catch. There seemed to be a dark shadow in his eyes, his lips turned into a frown as he stared at MacDonald.

"How dare you stand there and accuse me of betraying our most holy Order!" Francois snarled, his French accent thick and strong. "You, who murdered Bevard! You, who planned to steal the treasures of Atlantis!"

"If I'm the murderer and thief ye say I am, why do the Atlantians come to my aid?" Captain MacDonald shot back. "I have spoken with Bevard in the spirit realm and he has revealed to me that ye are his killer. It was he who warned us of yer approaching fleet and intent to take the treasures for yerself."

441

Francois froze, fury covering his face. When he finally did speak, he sputtered, so angry he could barely get the words to leave his mouth. "H-h-how dare y-you! B-blackening the g-g-good name of our d-departed Grand Master to f-further your own designs!"

There was a flash of movement, and Francois raised his arm, firing the pistol he'd been concealing at his side. The shot missed the captain, but it had its intended effect; chaos erupted on the decks again.

Something was different now, though. Many of the Templars were hesitating, looking around as if lost. Captain MacDonald's speech had caused them to falter in their convictions and they no longer knew who to fight. Several of them stared at the water, watching the mermaids below, a slow acceptance appearing on their faces.

And then it happened. The first of the Templars threw down his sword, shouting to his comrades. "He's right! Why are the Atlantians helping them? Something isn't adding up."

They were all hesitating now, turning to their leader, watching as he took on Captain MacDonald by himself.

The two men dueled close together, swords flashing and clanging. Captain MacDonald was as impressive as ever, dual wielding his weapons, but Francois was absolutely stunning. I had never seen anyone, let alone a man of his age, fight as gracefully and expertly as he was. It was like watching a dance, their feet crossing and beating across the deck to music no one else could hear, eyes locked on one another.

Swinging the hammer, MacDonald smashed its head into Francois's shoulder, the old man crumpling like a piece of paper as he cried in pain. The armor he was wearing had saved him from being hurt too badly, though, and he rose again in an instant, slicing across the captain's leg.

Captain MacDonald bellowed in pain, falling to one knee, his form disappeared from my view for a moment, Francois circling around him triumphantly. Then, he got back on his feet, shoving the Frenchman to the side, growling viciously, and their battle began anew.

"Do ye not see yer men hesitating around ye?" MacDonald spoke loud enough for all to hear, a smile on his face as he limped slightly, the two of them pacing together. "They dinna ken who to trust. Makes one think they kent their trust in ye was flawed from the beginning, no?"

Shouting, Francois rushed him, shoving the Scotsman against the wall of the captain's cabin. "You are a murderer and a traitor. Confess! All you have done here is make yourself look like a fool. These men will never believe you. Why should they, when their Grand Master has told them the truth of your deeds?"

Captain MacDonald laughed, a breathy, pained sound, and shoved him away. "The Grand Master you cheated into power, ye mean? The one ye're blackmailin'?"

Francois recoiled some at that, surprise crossing his features for a second before he covered it up with cool indifference. "Lie all you want, MacDonald. God will take his revenge on Bevard's murderer this day, no matter what you say."

"He's telling the truth!"

The shout came from the other Templar ship, a

hooded man standing on the railing, looking across at all the Knights ahead of him. Slowly, he removed his hood, revealing his face. Shocked gasps and cries came from the men, all of them instantly turning to stare at him.

"Davies!" Tristan sounded as surprised as the rest of them, staring at the man with an open mouth.

"That's the Grand Master?" Shocked at the full weight of this turn of events, my own mouth popped open.

"You are supposed to be in Paris!" Francois voice cut through the air like a knife, hissing from him like a snake. When I looked at him, I could practically see the hate seething from him, murder in his eyes. "You stupid, stupid boy!"

"It is you who are the stupid one, Francois!" Davies tone was like a whip cracking in the space. "Did you honestly think that I would stand idly by and let you steal the treasures of The Knights Templar? That I would let you condemn an innocent man and his crew to death, just to cover your own tracks? You may have gotten me this seat in our Order, but I am still the Grand Master. I will do what is best for my men, no matter the cost to myself!"

Dropping all appearances of being an honest and faithful member of The Order, Francois snarled. "You will never see your wife and child again."

Davies flinched, nodding. "I know. Truth be told, I have long suspected that you have already killed them. If that is not the case, I will be happy simply knowing that they are alive. There is time yet for me to look for them. You, on the other hand, will not live to see another day." Motioning to Captain MacDonald,

Davies sighed. "Take him."

Lurching to the side, Francois grabbed a gun from one of the men standing closest to him. Taking aim, he fired just before Captain MacDonald tackled him to the ground. The shot rang out like a gong and the Grand Master flinched, grabbing his chest in surprise. Then, slowly, he crumpled, falling off the railing and disappearing to the deck of the ship he'd been hiding on.

An outraged roar filled the air, all of the Templars rushing to his aid. A few remained with Captain MacDonald, holding Francois down as he writhed beneath them, shouting curses and all other sorts of profanities at them.

Still somewhat shocked, I remained where I was, jostled to the side by those trying to check on Davies. Right before my eyes, the deck of the flagship emptied, as if there had been no fight happening there moments before.

"We . . . did it." Staring at Tristan beside me, I blinked, caught off guard by how suddenly everything had changed.

"Aye, we did." He appeared somewhat dazed, but he also craned his neck, trying to see what was happening on the other ship with the Grand Master. Slowly, a mournful cry began to drift over to us and his face went pale.

"What's happened?" He called, to no one in particular, still trying to see what was happening.

The word traveled quickly through the group, the men hanging their heads and uttering prayers. Dagger, who had been standing just in front of us, turned around and frowned.

"Davies is dead," he said softly. "Bled out before anyone could stop it."

Francois laughed, as if he knew, his eyes crazy when I peered at him. Captain MacDonald was holding his arms behind him, a blade held against his throat.

"No one betrays me," Francois said vehemently.

Glowering, I went to ask Tristan what we would do now, with no Grand Master and a Master who had been sentenced to death.

A low, deep rumble vibrated through the ships, the water going suddenly still as the ripple of sound shot through it.

"What was that?"

The shamans were darting through the water once more, picking up men and literally throwing them onto the decks of nearby ships. They seemed frantic, shouting at each other as they moved, gathering together into a large group.

"What are they doing?" Confused, I watched as the continued to clump together, seeming to argue as they waved at each other.

Another rumble shook the ship, stronger this time, knocking everyone to the deck.

"Francois!"

Stumbling to my feet, I viewed the captain, seeing that the shaking had caused him to lose his hold on the traitor.

"Look out!" I shouted, watching as the Frenchman grabbed a blade and rounded on his captor.

Captain MacDonald scooted away just in time, the tip of Francois's blade barely missing him as it dug into the deck.

Another rumble shook us, and we were suddenly

riding a large wave, all three ships tugging at one another. The ties that held them together stayed strong, though, causing them to bump together and throw us around even more.

Screaming, I held on to the rail, completely caught off guard, my eyes squeezed shut.

"Holy shit!" Mark's voice pulled me from my panic and I opened my eyes, feeling my stomach turn with sea sickness. All of my worries and fears were forgotten in an instant, though, as I stared at where we had been sitting.

The only way to describe it was to say it was a monster. The creature raised out of the water at least one hundred feet, its dark, scaly skin glistening in the light of the sun as the storm faded away. It had two arms, beefy and bulky, currently lifting from the water. Long claws rested at the end of its fingers, matching the ferocious teeth in its mouth. The eyes were what scared me the most, though. They were dark, like the skin, but there was an intelligence to them that made my own skin tingle. As the beast examined the scene before it, I knew it was actually seeing all of us, thinking, and making plans.

For a moment, nothing moved, everyone simply staring at the thing while it scrutinized us. Even the shamans were still in the water, watching the creature with hesitation.

Then, it let out a terrible roar, swinging at the two ships that hadn't joined the battle. With a deafening crack, they exploded into tiny bits, the monster causing giant waves as it moved through the water.

I didn't need anyone to tell me that the creature was the Leviathan, the thing that had caused the

Atlantians to sink their city in terror. Just staring at it now, I knew that it was the beast. We must've caused such a scene in the water it had drawn him here and revealed the shamans to him. The only question I had now was how in the hell were we going to get out of this situation alive?

The shamans attacked then, darting through the water, battling the beast with little effectiveness. He easily threw them aside, obviously the superior being in the fight.

"Break the ships apart!"

Captain MacDonald's voice shattered the bubble I was in, bringing my attention to the ships and the danger we were in. He was still fighting with Francois, incredibly, trying to gain the upper hand. Like always, though, his first thought was for his crew.

"Break them apart and sail away, as fast as ye can!"

The well-oiled machine he had trained and commanded for years jumped into action, cutting lines free and separating the *Isobel* from the secondary ship that had attacked it. The majority of the Templars were on that ship, and they wasted no time in setting a course away from the Leviathan and his battle with the shamans.

Dashing over to the broken mast that connected the flagship to ours, I desperately tried to shove it to the side, or even lift it enough to drop it in the ocean.

"No!" Captain MacDonald slapped Francois across the face, catching him off guard and dazing him for a moment, and shouted at me. "All of ye onto this one! Ye willna be able to sail fast enough with the broken mast. We must leave the *Isobel* behind."

He was right, of course. Mentally kicking myself for not thinking of that, I turned to the rest of the crew. "Everyone on the flagship! Now!"

A flood of crew was crossing the broken mast then, cutting the lines from the other side, working to desperately free themselves from the captivity of the *Isobel* and the imminent danger of the Leviathan.

Finally, we were free, except the mast. It had become stuck under the rubble of the broken rail and stairs it had fallen into, the ropes of the Isobel tangled in a large knot with those of the flagship, the mast refusing to budge until they had been cut.

"Out of the way!" Francois snarled as he pushed through the group, sword in hand. "I will not die today, by your hands or this monster's!" He sliced through the knot and began hacking at the wood, little chips of wood flying out around him.

"Ye'll never get it that way, ye old loon." Captain MacDonald appeared beside him, shoving him aside. Raising Shelia high, he peered across the space to Dagger, smiling slightly.

There must have been something in that look that no one else caught, because Dagger was suddenly shouting, shoving people, trying to get to the mast and his captain, but it was too late.

Captain MacDonald smashed the hammer against the mast, freeing it from its stuck position. Leaving the mallet where it landed, he grabbed one of the rapidly retreating ropes, and was suddenly flying through the air, back to the *Isobel* as we broke free from her.

Screaming, Francois hit the deck, his feet caught in the remains of the knot he'd undone. Before anyone could grab him, he was also flying through the air, smacking into the side of the *Isobel*.

Flinching, I tried to tell if he was simply unconscious, or if the collision had killed him. He hung there, limp, giving no sign of what had happened. Captain MacDonald hurried to the side, pulling on the rope that held the old man in place, until the body was in his arms.

"Go!" He yelled, waving at us. "I'll do my best to hold the creature off!" Laying Francois on the deck, he ran to the helm, taking control of the steering once more. After a moment, it became clear that he was aiming the bow right at the Leviathan's midsection. The first cannon that had hit us had left a jagged piece of wood sticking out, like a giant spear.

In that moment, it seemed to dawn on all of us what he was planning to do. There was a collective gasp from the crew, horror covering their faces.

"Are you mad?" Dagger screamed at him. "You'll die if you ram it with that!"

The captain only smiled. Turning to face us, he saluted, and then turned to the helm, the air of a man who was ready to meet his fate surrounding him.

Staring at the creature, I saw the shamans still trying to fight it, the other Knights screaming for help as they tried to swim and sail away. Any time they would get any distance between them and the Leviathan, though, it would reach out and pull them back, like it was playing a game with them.

"Turn us around!" Dagger ordered. "We have to go after him!"

I knew we wouldn't make it, though. Captain MacDonald was already plowing through the waves, coming behind the creature fast, despite the loss of one of the sails. He would hit it before we could ever catch him, and he probably knew that.

Covering my mouth in horror, I watched as he squared his shoulders, standing steady. Tears filled my eyes, but I couldn't look away. I'd never seen someone so brave or selfless before. He had truly meant it when he said no one would die unless he went first. Here was a man who had treated me with kindness and respect, even when he didn't have to, who cared for the health and wellness of his crew above all else. I knew that for all of time, The Order would speak of William MacDonald and the sacrifice he was making right now, in front of my very eyes.

The makeshift spear of the Isobel slammed into the Leviathan, causing it to scream in pain as the wood dug deep into its spine. Twisting around, the creature slapped at the boat, crushing it into the water as blood poured from him like a faucet. In a matter of seconds, the water around him was red and thick, the remains of the boat sinking to the bottom of the ocean.

You could have heard a pin drop on the deck of the flagship. Without even checking, I knew I wasn't the only one crying. We were all frozen, staring at the beast as it crumbled into the water, the shamans continuing to attack it as it faltered, its eyes rolling into its head. Not far away, I caught sight of the ship that had managed to break away, her crew also watching in horror as Captain MacDonald went down with his ship.

Finally, with one last groan, the Leviathan slipped beneath the waves and did not resurface. The churning of the water slowed, until all we were left with was a bright sky and a red sea to stare at.

"He saved us," I said softly. Staring at the gory water, I wiped a tear from my face, still not able to believe what I had just seen. "Without even thinking about it. He jumped right in and took the fall."

"Captain was like that," Dagger responded roughly. "I should have expected it, to be honest."

"Ye couldn't have stopped him," Tristan said gently. "Even if ye tried."

"Look!"

Everyone turned to Abella, who was pointing at something in the water. At first, I thought it was an odd piece of wood, but then I realized what she had already seen.

"She's bringing him back!" Trying my best to not be blinded by the tears in my eyes, I searched for anything we could throw out into the water and tow the pair in with, desperately. "Someone get a ladder or something!"

It was odd, seeing Isobel outside the spirit realm, but I had no doubt that it was her. She appeared somewhat ghostly and tired, as she struggled to keep Captain MacDonald's head above water. There was blood on his face, and one of his arms was bent the wrong direction, but he was obviously alive, thanks to the spirit that had rescued him from the deep.

Finally, they were beside the boat and we were lifting them, having thrown down a rope for her to tie around him. When they reached the deck, she laid him carefully down, brushing her hand across his cheek.

Slowly, his eyes fluttered open, his stare landing on her face. He sucked in a hard breath, wincing as he tried to touch her with his broken arm.

"Isobel." His voice caught, and his lips trembled as he took her appearance in. "Will ye accept my death as penance for yer own?" he asked her softly, a tear escaping him and rolling down his skin to the deck.

She laughed, her own tears bright in her eyes. "Ye're not dead yet, ye fool. Not if I have anything to say about it." Leaning forward, she kissed him gently on the lips, her other hand resting on his chest.

The action caused him to cry even more, much to my surprise.

"Ye're not mad at me?" He was barely whispering, unaware of all of us around them. The stare he gave her made me think that perhaps he had only ever seen her and was living life with her memory always at the front of his mind.

Her expression fell and she shook her head, kissing him again before answering. "Mad at ye? No, love. I hurt for ye. All this time and ye still blame yerself for my death. It was never yer fault, Will. Never. And if I could go back to that day and do it all over again, I would do it a million times." She took on a stern look, frowning as she took his good hand in hers. "But I am mad at ye for avoiding me. Damn it, Will. All I wanted to tell ye was to forgive yerself and move on. I couldn't hardly stand watching ye be so miserable."

He laughed, wincing as his arm moved, tears still falling from his eyes. "I kent ye were mad about something. I could see it in yer eyes."

"There hasn't hardly been a day since I met ye that ye didn't make me mad, William MacDonald. Ye know that just fine." She smiled widely, wiping away one of his tears.

He paused for a moment, grasping her hand in his own, and then sighed, blinking away his tears. "I dinna ken how to live without ye, lass. I dinna ken how I did it before and I dinna ken how I will do it now, knowing that ye hold no malice for me and are here, waiting."

Her expression softened and she ran her fingers through his beard, smiling through her own tears again. "Ye'll do it the same way ye always have. One day at a time. That's how I do it."

"Ye couldna have just let me die now and come to ye?"

He was joking, but I could see the pain in his eyes as well. There was a part of him that would have preferred he died today, just so he could be with her. The realization made my heart hurt for the both of them. I knew I would have felt the same, if it were Tristan and I that were in their places.

As if he were thinking the same thing, Tristan took my hand, squeezing it tightly.

"No, Will," Isobel said softly. "Ye are going to die an old man, in yer bed. And I will come and get ye when it happens. Ye have my word."

"I'm old now," he joked.

"And ye have much still to do." She smiled, and it

suddenly seemed that everyone knew she had to go now.

"I love ye, Isobel," Captain MacDonald said roughly.

Kissing him in response, she rose, turning toward the railing and the waiting spirit realm. "I'll see ye when it's time."

Sitting in the overstuffed chair beside the window, I sipped my tea, watching Abella as she hemmed one of her skirts on the other side of the room. The street lamps of Paris were the only light I could see outside, no sign of Mark or Tristan having returned from their midnight meeting at the Temple.

The new house was nice—nicer than our previous one, actually. I'd been surprised when The Order offered it to us, not expecting such grand accommodations. Still, I'd been glad to return to the city for once, feeling like I'd finally healed from my wounds. Tristan and I had even been talking about having another baby, depending on what the new Grand Master would assign him to.

"Who do you think they'll vote in?" I asked Abella, not able to keep my thoughts to myself any longer.

"Captain MacDonald, certainly," she replied with a smile. "Mark said he'd not heard one man say otherwise on the return crossing. The news of his sacrifice spread like fire once we returned to Paris."

"I was with him when someone suggested he be

455

the new leader." Laughing, I thought back on the memory with fondness. "He was absolutely mortified. I agree, though. He has proven himself as a leader. If anyone deserves to be Grand Master, it's him."

Silence fell between us, and I debated asking her about Mark. She had brought him up, after all, but I didn't know if there was much to tell. As far as I knew, they hadn't spent much time together since our return.

I was saved having to ask by the door opening, my husband appearing in the entryway with a large smile.

"Was it the captain?" I asked excitedly, putting my cup down.

"It was." He laughed, sweeping into the room and taking me in his arms. "MacDonald will be so good for The Order! I can't say I've ever been more pleased with our choice of leader, really."

My reply was cut off by a yawn, causing him to chuckle even more.

"It is quite late. I didn't expect you to actually stay up and wait to hear."

"I wanted to," I replied happily. "We were all hoping William MacDonald would come out on top of the vote. I didn't want to wait until morning to know what the verdict was."

"Aye. Shall we to bed, then?" He glanced past me to Abella. "Assuming ye have nothing else ye'd like to do at this godforsaken hour of the night?"

Abella giggled shaking her head. "No. I'm quite ready for sleep myself."

"Very well."

Taking my hand, Tristan led me from the sitting room and along the hall, stopping in front of our bedroom door. "I forgot to tell the cook that Mark is coming by for dinner tomorrow. I'll run down and leave him a note, aye?"

"That's fine."

Kissing me on the cheek, he dashed off, disappearing around the corner.

Snickering to myself happily, I went in to our room, sitting at the desk. A large mirror hung on the wall behind it, the dark hall reflecting in the glass.

Opening one of the drawers, I carefully removed the necklace that Pathos had given me in Atlantis. I wore it to bed every night, wanting to make sure I stayed nightmare free. Pulling the chord over my neck, I took the stone in my hands, examining it as I so often did when I put it on.

Footsteps sounded in the hall and I smiled, dropping the stone back against my skin. "You know, every time I put this on, I can't help but admire how beautiful it is," I said casually, looking up at the mirror.

My breath caught in my chest and I froze, gripping the desk with both hands. Closing my eyes for a second, I tried to convince myself that I was dreaming, that what I was seeing wasn't real, but I knew it was.

Staring at his reflection again, I tried not to growl.

"Hello, Sammy," Thomas Randall said breathlessly.

Continue reading for a teaser from
Taken Away, the origins story of
Captain William MacDonald.

*William MacDonald feels his life is missing
something. With an arranged marriage soon
approaching, and the knowledge that he's expected to
someday take his father's place in society, he pushes
forward, holding himself to the high standard of
honor he always has. However, when a strange
woman arrives on the clan lands, William's world is
turned upside down. While everyone whispers the
stranger is a witch, and a rival family threatens to
destroy the peace everyone has become accustomed
to, William finds himself contemplating one thing:
what is more important--honor, or love?*

The silverware clinked around the table as everyone happily ate their dinner, a general air of contentment resting on all of them. Besides the deer steaks, there was bread, cheese, and cabbage soup, as well as whiskey and milk. A warm fire burned in the hearth beside them, adding even more to the candlelight that kept the cold dark away. The fresh scent of lavender spread under the aroma of the food, wafting from the bowl of dried petals left over from last summer's harvest.

"I take it ye took care of the rest of the meat, Willy?" Da stared at him evenly, wiping his mouth with his fingertips.

"I buried some of it so it would freeze, but aye. It's all taken care of." Popping a piece of bread in his mouth he grinned at Rowan, who was discretely trying to feed some of his cabbage to the dogs under the wooden table.

"Good. I was hoping ye'd be finished with it. There was some talk amongst the families that live out beside the Stewart lands that I wanted ye to check on." Pausing to clear his throat, the elder William grimaced some, as if this weren't good news.

Worried by the expression, Will raised his eyebrows in surprise. "It's not the Campbells again, is it? I thought we were finally getting to a good enough place with them that we wouldna have to deal with them any longer."

The question caused everyone in the room to pause and look to the head of the family, apprehension filling the space. MacDonalds and Campbells famously did not get along, no matter where they lived. However, living right on the boarders of the two clans' lands had made life particularly difficult at points. Things seemed to be relatively peaceful at the moment, due to extreme effort on the MacDonalds part, but there was never any telling when the rival family would decide to end the peace.

Shaking his head, Da picked up his cup and took a long drink. "Dinna fash yerself about the Campbell family now. It's not anything like that."

Everyone relaxed at that, a breath of relief seeming to sweep the room. Eating resumed with ease, the earlier happiness of the evening quickly warming them once more.

"What's botherin' them, then?" Laoghaire questioned, helping herself to another biscuit.

"It seems someone has moved into the old shack just up the mountain. They think it's a young lass, but none of them are willin' to get close enough to find out for sure. It's right close to the border for one thing, and as for the other reason—"

"They think she's a witch," Alastair piped up, grimacing as his father frowned at him. "Sorry, Da. I dinna mean to interrupt ye. Little Jamie from across the way passed through the pasture this morning and told me about it. He was taking bets on how long it would take someone from the church to send a witch hunter to question her."

"Hush yer mouth!" Laoghaire scolded him, rising from her seat. "We know nothing about the lass! There's no sense in spreading such a vicious rumor without knowin' the truth of it." All the same, she glanced out the window, toward the direction of the old, abandoned hut up the mountain, and flicked her fingers, making the sign to banish evil.

"I thought only witches lived by themselves, though." Rowan spoke confidently, smiling as he looked around the room. "Spell casters and old maids."

"Well, she's no old maid, from what I've been told," Da muttered, raising his glass for another drink.

"And just what do ye want me to do about it?" Will asked incredulously. "March right up there and ask her if she's the Devil's bedmate? If she were, she'd curse me right on the spot!"

"And if not, she'd likely slap him across his face," Laoghaire added, nodding in agreement. "He can't walk up to a stranger and accuse them of something like that."

"I dinna want him to do any such thing," Da replied easily. "It will put everyone's mind at ease to know that someone went up and spoke with her, though. The lass is new to the area; perhaps it wouldn't be such a bad idea to invite her down."

"And I suppose ye want me to find out why she's alone and what business she has moving into a house that's barely standing anymore." Pursing his lips, Will watched as his father confirmed his suspicions with another nod.

"If there's going to be one more mouth to feed this winter, she needs to help with the work. I dinna care if she's here, so long as it doesn't rile everything up, ye ken?"

"Aye, I understand ye well enough." Taking a drink of his own milk, Will thought it over for a moment before answering. "I'll go up and see what I can find tomorrow. What shall I take with me, though? I can't be showing up with nothing but a basket of questions."

"Take some of the honey," Laoghaire replied, thinking quickly. "We can easily get more and it will be a fine, welcoming gift."

"It's settled then. We've been making due without ye in the fields for a few days now. One more will be fine." Da smiled, leaning back in his chair.

"Soon ye'll have yer own family to take care of and work for in the fields." Laoghaire smiled warmly, settling back into her chair. "Fiona will make ye a fine wife. Yer little ones will be a sight to see, too."

"Maw." Will groaned slightly, trying not to roll his eyes.

"What? I'm excited for grandkids. Yer twenty-three years old. I thought I'd have them well before now."

"I sincerely apologize for not engaging in acts of fornication and giving ye grandchildren earlier, but I had it in my mind to wait for the right lass. Since she hasn't shown up yet, I assume ye'll just have to wait." He did roll his eyes then, looking to his father for backup, but was met with a knowing stare instead.

"I know ye wanted to marry for love, Willy," Da said softly, leaning forward and resting his elbows on the table. "Yer mother is right, though; Fiona is a fine young woman and will be the best of wives. I'm sure, in time, ye'll learn to love her."

"I understand," Will replied roughly, looking down at his plate. "We are a good match. There isn't much anyone else for her to marry, unless her mother wants to send her away. She needs someone to take care of her and their family has been missing its head since her father died. I wouldn't have agreed to the arrangement if I didn't think it would be good for everyone involved.

"I'll be close to home, where I can help still if needed. We can combine our livestock and gain a higher profit when we take them to market. I . . . I enjoy Fiona's company as well."

Truth be told, he found her boring. She had no apparent interest in anything he did and was often found pouting beside the fire over something insignificant. The life he imagined with her was a frustrating one, with little joy. But, as he'd so often seen, love did come in time to such matches. Perhaps, as the years went on, he would find her personality endearing and feel a love for her grow in his heart.

His speech didn't really seem to convince his father, but Laoghaire's face shone with happiness as she looked at him.

"Fiona MacDonald is one of the finest women I've ever met," Alastair added, blushing slightly. Rather than follow the statement up, he grabbed his cup and gulped down a swallow of whiskey, clearing his throat awkwardly.

"I think she's stupid."

Hastily converting his laugh into a cough, Will watched as their mother launched into scolding Ro for being rude, lecturing him on everything from honor and manhood to respect for the trials a woman faced. The sermon was lost on the young boy, though. His eyes glazed over, his attention clearly diverted along another path.

Slowly, dinner finished, Da retiring to his study while Maw cleaned up. Rowan was put to bed with much protesting and Alastair excused himself to go check on the newborn calf and its mother. Left alone,

Will found himself on the front step, the dogs resting their heads in his lap as he stared up at the night sky.

What do I do? He asked the stars silently. The prospect of a marriage to Fiona did not excite him at all, nor did any marriage, really. He had truly wished to wait until he fell in love, but there was no way for that to happen. He would have to leave home, abandon his family, and hope that he would find his woman somewhere out there. What if she simply didn't exist? No, there was no way he could betray his family's trust in him like that, or disregard his honor so easily. When Da died, he'd become the head of the family. If he was off gallivanting across the country, they would have nothing. Fiona's family would have nothing. The whole community would suffer under the burden of having to take care of what should have been his.

"Ye look like a man staring at the gallows, son."

Looking over his shoulder, Will smiled tightly at his father, watching as the man came and sat beside him.

"What's bothering ye? Fiona?" Concern covered his features, his hand resting lightly on Will's shoulder as he looked at him. "Is marrying her really that bad of a prospect for ye?"

Shaking his head, Will looked back up at the sky, not sure what to say. The heavens sparkled with such beauty and size, he was suddenly struck with a feeling of insignificance. "It feels like life is getting the better of me, ye ken? Like I'm missing something important, but I don't ken what it is."

"What can I do to help?" Da squeezed his shoulder, shaking him slightly. "Maybe ye need some time away, to find yerself?"

465

"What do ye mean?"

"I've been hearing that some young men are going to France for a year or two, to work for the military. We would miss ye here at home, but if it helped ye at all, it would be worth it."

Shocked, Will pulled away from him, gaping as he absorbed what he'd been offered. "But, I canna do that! We can't afford it, Da. Traveling to France would take lots of money and I wouldn't be able to help with the farming or selling the livestock. Besides, what about Fiona? I canna just leave her without a single care when she's expecting to marry me in a few months' time."

"If it helped ye, it would be worth it to me. We would get by without ye, truly. Alastair already does more than his fair share. He'd learn the things I've been teaching ye about running the house and such easily, if anything were to happen to me."

The look on his father's face was so sincere and kind, it made Will want to hug him tightly and thank him for everything he'd ever done. Instead, he sighed heavily, shaking his head.

"I canna. I only want to do the right thing and choosing myself over the needs of others . . . it isn't honorable. My own issues aside, I'm needed here. I will deal with my decisions and their impending consequences with grace, Lord willing. Thank ye, Da. Truly. It means a lot to me that ye would offer, but my family comes first. *Per mere per terras.*"

"By sea and by land," Da repeated, the MacDonald clan motto giving the discussion an air of finality. "Yer a good man, Willy. I dinna know why the Lord in His goodness decided to grace me with such a child, but I'm glad he did."

"There's no one else I'd want as a father." The chilly air suddenly felt too emotional for him and Will laughed, embarrassed, looking back up at the stars. Thinking back to their earlier dinner conversation, he quickly changed the subject. "Do ye have any advice for how to greet a lass who may be a witch?"

"I'd start with a nice hello, if it were me." Patting him on the shoulder again, Da rose, quietly letting himself back inside and leaving Will with his plethora of thoughts.

Taken Away is now available wherever ebooks are sold, or as a FREE gift for joining the Kamery Solomon Books Mailing List!

Acknowledgments

Every time I somehow manage to write another book, I'm reminded of the literal village that helps me get it done!

As always, thank you to my husband, Jake, for putting up with me and my endless prattling about story lines, alternate history theories, and gushing over my heroes. I could not do any of this without you and your support. You are every hero I've ever written and loved. Thank you for being awesome and being mine <3

I would never get anything published if not for my mother, Lacey Weatherford, who does her fair share of listening, as well as helping me with edits. I also have to thank my sister, Kysee, for letting me bounce story ideas off her and helping me with edits as well. I love you both!

Jessi Gibson, my author coach, can't slide by without getting mentioned in the acknowledgments, either. She pushed me to do my best and get my work done. If not for her, I probably would have been so far behind, I wouldn't have known what to do with myself. Thank you for all of your help and guidance, Jessi!

Hidden Away would not have been what it is without the Arizona Renaissance Festival and their new mermaid exhibit, haha! I worked on the stage crew there when the "sea fairies" show opened and it was something I so needed in my life then. The characters of William MacDonald, Dagger, Valentine, and Smithy are all based off of people who worked on that crew with me and I had to let the mermaids make an appearance when we got to Atlantis. Thank you all for being such wonderful coworkers and friends. I can't imagine where my life would be right now if I hadn't decided to just go for it and join you all for some fun in the desert. I love you all!

~Kamery~

About The Author

Kamery is not the person who grew up dreaming of the day that she would clutch her very own novel to her chest, tears brimming over the rims of her eyes as she thought about how she'd written it herself, finally! In fact, anything remotely like that didn't even happen until she was actually holding her first book in her hand, amazed that she'd written it and wondering how on Earth she'd managed to do it when it hadn't ever occurred to her to write one until months before. Surprisingly, though, it was just what she never realized she loved doing.

When starting out in life, Kamery had (and still has) big dreams to perform on Broadway. She loves music and acting very much, while she and dance have a love/hate relationship; she would love to do it and every form of dance decides it hates that about her, haha! The one constant she always had between the performing world and the book world were the stories, tales that transported her to other worlds and made her feel like she really could do anything. Finally, she decided she wanted to do that for someone else and sat down to write.

It's been a few years since she held that first book, realizing that she really liked writing and wanted to do more, but the love that blossomed in that moment has only grown. Currently, Kamery works from home in Arizona, while taking care of her two adorable kids, a girl and a boy, and talking her sweet husband Jake's ear off about the insane amount of characters in her head who are ready to fight to the death for a chance at their own novels.. It truly is a wonderful life!

www.kamerysolomonbooks.com

Made in United States
North Haven, CT
26 May 2022

19544723R00261